DE
OF
DUBLIN

WALL STREET JOURNAL BESTSELLING AUTHOR
BB EASTON

Copyright © 2022 by BB Easton
Published by Art by Easton
All rights reserved.

ISBN: 979-8-9850730-4-1
e-book ISBN: 979-8-9850730-3-4

Cover Design by Damonza
Cover Photography by Regina Wamba
Cover Model: Jered Sternaman
Content Editing by Traci Finlay and Adele Halpin
Copyediting and Formatting by Jovana Shirley,
Unforeseen Editing, www.unforeseenediting.com

No part of this book may be reproduced or transmitted in any form or by any means, electronic or mechanical, including photocopying, recording, or by any information storage and retrieval system without the written permission of the author, except for the use of brief quotations in a book review.

This is a work of fiction. While many of the locations mentioned in this novel are real and several situations were inspired by actual events, all of the characters and scenes depicted in this book are fictionalized products of the author's imagination. Any resemblance to specific persons, living or dead, is entirely coincidental.

The publisher acknowledges the trademark status and trademark ownership of all trademarks, service marks, and word marks mentioned in this book.

The excerpt at the beginning of chapter twenty-two is from the poem "Leda and the Swan" by W. B. Yeats, originally published in 1924. It is within the public domain.

"Whiskey in the Jar" and "Finnegan's Wake" are traditional Irish folk songs dating as far back as the seventeenth century. They are within the public domain.

The proverbs at the beginning of chapters eleven and thirteen (one of which is also the tagline on this book's cover) are traditional Irish sayings. They are not the intellectual property of the author.

For Grandpa Pat and Aunt Kate

AUTHOR'S NOTE

Dear reader,

I'm so happy you're here. Together, you and I are going to frolic through the sheep-dotted meadows and mystical forests of County Kerry, Ireland. We're going to fall in love with someone forbidden. Mysterious. Dangerous. And we're going to follow our hearts instead of our minds, all the way to the cutthroat, urban underbelly of Dublin. It'll be the journey of a lifetime, a romance for the ages, but it will not be safe for everyone.

If you are a sensitive reader or find certain topics to be emotionally triggering, please exercise self-care and select a different book. While this story is deeply romantic and exaltingly beautiful, those intoxicating highs are only made possible by first exploring some of the darkest aspects of humanity, including secrets that were kept buried by my family, as well as the Catholic Church, for decades.

To avoid spoilers, I've placed a comprehensive content warning on my website. Please consult it if you are unsure whether or not to proceed: https://www.artbyeaston.com/devil-of-dublin-content-warning

Devil of Dublin is intended for mature audiences who enjoy dark subject matter, tortured anti-heroes, explicit sexual content, graphic violence, heart-pounding suspense, fairy-tale worthy love, and gorgeous Irish scenery. If that sounds like you, then welcome to Glenshire!

XO,

BB

CHAPTER 1

DARBY

I sank my fingers knuckle deep into the spongy wool, trying not to squeal as I closed my fists around two satisfying handfuls of fluff.

"Darby," Mom snapped in that *stop it right now* tone. "Be sweet."

"But, Mama, he can't even feel it." I beamed. "Look!" I squeezed the sheep's wool again.

The animal continued to ignore me, finding the grass in my grandfather's pasture much more interesting than the annoying American girl who'd come to visit.

I'd never been to Ireland before. I'd never even been on a plane before, so the entire trip to attend my grandmother's funeral was full of new sights and sounds, but the one that delighted me the most wasn't the view from the clouds or the rainbow-colored shops and houses we'd passed on the bus to Glenshire. It wasn't the musical accents or old-timey clothing of the people we'd met along the way. It was the big, colorful dots spray-painted on every fluffy white sheep in my grandfather's village.

"Grandpa, why do all your sheep have blue spots on their butts? Is it so they'll match your blue house? Is blue your favorite color? My favorite color's green. I like it here. Everything's green, green, green. Mama says that's why they call it the emerald eyeball."

"Emerald *Isle*," my mom corrected. "Isle means island."

Her eyes were red and puffy that day, and her mouth was frownier than usual. It made me anxious whenever she was upset about something. Or when she got sick. Or when she was too tired to play with me.

My mom was all I had.

While she stood there and scowled, my grandfather snickered at my *emerald eyeball* comment. He was sad about my grandmother, too, but that didn't keep him from smiling when he spoke to me. I hadn't seen him since I was a baby, so I didn't remember him or my grandmother at all, but as soon as I'd gotten there, he'd acted like we were already best friends.

Grandpa bent forward and sank one knee into the grass, making himself as short as I was. He did that a lot. It made me feel special, like he was on *my* team instead of the grown-ups'.

"I do paint their wool to match my house. Yer very smart," he said. "Sheep are wily creatures. Even though they look fat and none too nimble, they're skinny under all that wool, and they can jump like a billy goat. I seen a sheep squeeze through a gap in the fence no bigger than yer arm. But spray paint is a lot cheaper than a good fence, so the other farmers and I paint our sheep to match our houses. That way, when one gets out, everybody knows who the little bugger belongs to."

I giggled and squeezed the sheep's wool again, right on that bright blue spot.

"Darby, gentle," Mama hissed.

Grandpa looked up at her like he was about to do something naughty. Then, he gave me a little smirk.

"Lass"—his green eyes sparkled—"ya ever been on an adventure?"

My mom glared at him in warning.

DEVIL OF DUBLIN

"No." I shook my head. "I have been on an airplane though."

He laughed, and I thought he looked just like a leprechaun. His once-bright orange hair had faded to a golden blond by then, and he had so many freckles that his face looked like a wrinkly, old, speckled egg, but the twinkle in his eye was just as sharp and mischievous as a child's.

"Da, where ya goin' with this?" My mom's Irish accent had gotten stronger since we'd arrived.

Grandpa ignored her warning and kept talking to me as if we were the only two people on earth.

Pointing across the street from his house, he said, "Down the hill, ya got more farms, if ya wanna see what colors the other sheep's butts are."

I turned my head and gazed into a valley as soft and green as a velvet pillow. And adorning the hills—like a scattering of rhinestones and pearls—were the other jewel-toned farmhouses and fluffy white sheep of Glenshire.

"But up the hill ..." Grandpa continued, pointing behind us at the woods that began just beyond his property.

The trees were shorter than the tall pines I was used to back home in Georgia. Cuter. I could still see the shape of the landscape. The rise and fall of the hills behind Grandpa's house that changed from green to blue to gray until they rose up into a tall purple mountain off in the distance.

"*That's* where the fairies live."

"Fairies?!" I squealed. My eyes darted from the woods to Grandpa, then over to my mom, hoping she would verify this miraculous news, but her expression was more annoyed than excited.

"Aye." Grandpa leaned toward me, lowering his voice. "But ya have to be quiet if ya want to see one. Quiet as a mouse. Fairies have excellent hearin'. If they sense a human nearby, they'll use their magic to disappear like *that*." He suddenly snapped his fingers, making me jump.

Beaming, I looked up at my mom and gave her my best Disney princess eyes. "Can we go see the fairies, Mama? Please, please, pleeease?"

She was going to say no. I could tell from her scowl, but when she opened her mouth, Grandpa spoke instead.

"Yer mam's gonna stay here and keep the oul fella company. It's been six years since last I seen her. I'd better enjoy it. The next time might be at *my* funeral."

"Da."

"G'wan now," Grandpa said, continuing to ignore his daughter. "Have a bit o' the craic."

I didn't know what *the crack* was, but I knew that my mom was less than enthusiastic about it.

"Da, she's eight. Ya really think it's a good idea for her to go play in the woods by herself?"

Grandpa stood up and brushed the dirt off his knee. "If memory serves, I believe you found a whole village of fairies back there when you were her age. Or was it a kingdom?"

"A kingdom!" I yelled, bouncing up and down.

"Yeah, but—"

"Ah, ya been livin' in the States too long. There's nothin' to fear in these woods 'cept for Tommy Lafferty's old sheep dog that keeps wanderin' off." He looked down at me with a serious face. "If ya see him, he's likely to lick ya to death, so be on the lookout."

"I'm more concerned about her gettin' lost," Mom protested, crossing her arms over her chest.

"Aye, that's easy." Grandpa held up two hands, one high and one low, cupped like domes. "Ya go up the hill," he said, giving the lower hand a little shake, "ya go down the hill. Ya see a lough at the bottom."

"Ooh. Do I need a key?"

"Lough means lake," my mom corrected.

"And legend has it, this lough has a spirit in it. A moody oul thing. Can be mean as a snake if ya cross her, but I hear she likes presents."

DEVIL OF DUBLIN

My eyes went wide, but Grandpa just kept talking like it was perfectly normal to have a haunted lake behind your house.

"On the other side of the lough"—he gave the hand up high a shake—"ya see the mountain. Don't go to that side of the lough. A witch lives over there, and if the rumors are true, she likes to eat little children. The cuter, the better. So, stay on this side of the lough, and when you get to missin' me handsome face, just go back to the top o' the hill, look for the blue house, and you'll find himself."

Grandpa liked to refer to himself as *himself*. He even had a coffee mug with the word on it.

I was astonished by all this new information, but my mom just rolled her eyes. "A witch, Da? Really?"

"Aye, don't ya remember?" he said with a little wink. "Nobody goes to the witch's side of the lough, lest they wanna be turned into a toad."

"I thought you said she eats children," I clarified, trying to sound super brave.

"Aye." Grandpa tapped me on the head with a smile. Like he knew I was smart.

I was a bright kid—my mother was a teacher and insisted that I always be above grade level in all subject areas—but it made me feel good to know that Grandpa thought I was smart too.

"It's the grown-ups she turns into toads," he added. "We're not as tasty."

"Da, stop it. Yer gonna scare her." Turning toward me, my mom sighed and reached into her pocket. "I s'pose you can go, but"—taking out her phone, she tapped the screen a few times before tucking it into my back pocket and covering it with my T-shirt—"don't you dare go near that lough. I mean it. And when that alarm goes off"—she pointed at my pocket—"you come straight home. Ya hear me?"

I hugged her so hard that she made a groaning noise before I took off running straight for the woods.

"Stop in and grab ya a biscuit 'fore ya go," Grandpa yelled behind me. "If ya find a fairy ring, put it in the middle and see if ya can lure one out. The good people *love* biscuits."

"Heeeere, fairy, fairy, fairy," I whispered as I tiptoed into the woods, holding that sugary treat out in front of me like a homing device. It took all my willpower not to eat it myself.

Biscuits, I'd discovered, were just delicious sandwich cookies with vanilla custard cream in the middle that you were allowed to eat if you pretended to like tea.

In the shade, the air was damp and cool. Much too cool for summertime. I shivered as goose bumps spread across my arms and legs. It felt tingly, like there were soda bubbles bursting all over my skin.

Must be the fairy magic, I thought.

Not only was it darker in the woods than I'd expected, and colder, but it was greener too. Even the tree trunks were green and fuzzy.

Maybe that's so the fairies can climb the trees without getting splinters.

The thought made me smile, but then it made me think about my father. He'd been the official splinter-puller-outer at our house. He had this technique with a safety pin and a pair of tweezers that was unrivaled. He'd say something silly to distract me, and before I knew it, no more splinter. But that had been before he got mean. Before my mother made him leave. Before he lost custody completely.

I tried extra hard not to get splinters after that.

I bet Daddy could find a fairy if he were here.

He could prob'ly find that witch too. And beat her up for eatin' all those kids.

My dad was the drummer for a one-hit-wonder rock band. He was covered in tattoos and had big, muscular arms that he liked to show off by wearing sleeveless T-shirts all year long. When I was a kid, I thought he could beat anybody up.

DEVIL OF DUBLIN

The only thing my mom had told me when he lost all visitation rights was that he needed to go "work on himself," but that hadn't made any sense to me. If somebody needed to get their car fixed or their house worked on, it only took a couple of days. Weeks at the most.

Meanwhile, I hadn't seen my dad in three years.

"Heeeere, fairy, fairy, fairy," I whispered again, bending down so I could look under a fat, little mushroom; a big, tickly fern; and in between the rows of wavy fungus growing up the side of a decomposing log.

Nothin'.

I knew I should have asked Grandpa what a fairy ring was before I left, but I'd been so afraid my mother was going to change her mind that I didn't want to wait around for details. But now, I had no idea what I was looking for.

When I finally made it to the top of the hill, I had to cover my mouth with my hand to keep from gasping out loud and scaring off all the fairies. There, on the other side, was a sea of flowers, their blossoms pointing down instead of up, like tiny, purple church bells.

This must be where the fairies grow their hats!

I proceeded with extreme caution, careful not to step on a single flower. I didn't want some poor fairy to have to wear a smooshed hat because of me.

I bet they use the stems as slides. I would if I were a fairy. Ooh! I should make them a swing to go with all these slides!

As I searched the forest floor for something to make a swing with, I stumbled upon an adorably chubby red mushroom with white polka dots. It reminded me of a Smurf house. Then, I saw another one and another one. So, I gently moved the bluebells out of the way and noticed that the mushrooms formed a circle. Or a …

Ring! Oh my gosh, oh my gosh, oh my gosh …

My heart raced as I slowly extended my tea biscuit toward the center of the formation. My hand shook, which I naturally attributed to the strength of the fairy magic.

Maybe they're home! Maybe I'll get to see one!

But before I could set the biscuit down, I heard something that made me go "still as a statue." That was what my teacher had called it whenever she wanted us to shut up and freeze.

It sounded like the fairies were *laughing*. I bit my lip to keep from laughing, too, and put on my best "listening ears." Then, I heard it again. Maybe it wasn't laughing, but something out there was definitely making noise. Sniffling? Snorting? But it did *not* seem to be coming from the mushroom circle.

I headed down the hill in the direction of the sniffle-snorts, scanning the ground for new mushroom villages to investigate. As the noise got louder and the mushrooms got scarcer, I finally lifted my head and found myself standing right in front of a crumbling stone wall. It was a few inches taller than me, but I could tell it used to be way taller than that. The rocks were all jagged at the top. And it didn't have sides. The wall was curved. Like a ...

Like a circle!

The sounds were loud now, and they were definitely coming from inside. I decided that walking around the outside to look for a door would probably make too much noise and scare whatever it was away, so I climbed onto a nearby boulder. It was hard to scale with a biscuit in my hand and slippery moss covering the flat places, but I did it. And once I felt stable enough, I found two good places to put my feet and slowly pushed myself to stand.

From that vantage point, I saw that I was right—the wall was one big circle—and it had an opening on the right, where a door used to be. It had probably been a cute little cottage once upon a time, but now, it was just a ruin. An *empty* ruin, I thought at first, but when I scanned the parts that I could see again, I noticed a dark spot, down low on the wall to my left. Pushing up onto my tiptoes, I craned my neck and raised my eyebrows—as if that would make my eyeballs higher—until the spot turned into a headful of glossy black hair. Black hair that belonged to ...

A *boy*.

A real boy, curled up against the wall with his arms around his knees, crying into the crook of his elbow.

At least, I thought it was a real boy. He didn't have wings. Or pointy ears. But the way his hair flipped and curled at the ends seemed pretty fairylike to—

"Ahh!" I squealed as my foot slipped off the rock.

The second I hit the soft leaves below, I scrambled over to the doorway in a panic, hoping to block the exit before the fairy could run away.

I succeeded, only because, instead of running, the commotion caused the boy to hide against the wall next to the doorway, probably hoping to slip out unseen if someone were to enter. It would have worked if I hadn't been looking for him. He blended into the shadows like he belonged there.

"Why were you crying?" I asked, using my softest, sweetest voice. "Did your grandma go to heaven too?"

The boy only growled in response, baring his teeth and squinting his eyes like a dog.

My mother had taught me to always put my hand out whenever I met a strange dog. She'd said it was like they could tell by smelling you whether or not you were a good person. So, with a deep breath, I extended my hand and watched the boy's face change from vicious to ... something else.

At first, I thought he must like the way I smelled, but then I realized that it was what was *in* my hand that had caught his attention. His pale eyes widened as he stared at the sugary treat.

"You want it?" I nudged the cookie in his direction. "You can have it."

The boy made that snarling face again, but then he snatched the biscuit out of my hand so fast that it made me jump.

He shoved the whole thing into his mouth and chewed wildly with his eyes narrowed and fixed on me.

I stood with my back pressed against one side of the doorway. He scared me, but the idea of letting him get away scared me more.

"Why were you crying?" I asked again.

Chew, chew, chew.

"Where's your mom?"

Another glare. More chewing.

"What's your name? My name is Darby Collins. D-A-R-B-Y C-O-L-L-I-N-S."

No response.

"I'm eight. I just finished second grade, and I already know my times tables. How old are you?"

The boy swallowed and crouched down slightly, as if he were about to bolt.

Or attack.

"Are you eight too?"

He shook his head, letting his wild, dark hair fall into his face.

"Nine?"

No.

"Ten?"

He nodded.

"Do you want to play with me?"

The boy squinted his eyes at me again—which I could barely see peeking through his curtain of hair—but at least he wasn't growling anymore.

"Ooh! I know! We should play Harry Potter! This place looks just like the Forbidden Forest! And this could be Hagrid's house! It looks just like this! You should be Harry 'cause you got all that black hair, and I could be Ginny Weasley 'cause I got red hair. They get married at the end, you know? Spoiler alert."

The boy just stared at me as if I were speaking Greek.

"You do know what Harry Potter is, right?"

His head swiveled left and right so slightly that I almost missed it.

"You don't? Oh my gosh, it's so good! It's a story about kids who are wizards and witches, but not mean witches, like the one that lives down by the lake—I mean, *lough*."

He cocked his shaggy black head to one side, just an inch or so.

"You don't know about the witch *either*?"

Another head shake.

"Oh my gosh! Come on." I beamed, reaching out my hand. "Let's go see!"

The boy looked at my outstretched palm. Then, he glanced up at my face. I could see one of his eyes through a part in his hair, and it was such a strange, pale gray color that for a moment—just one moment—I thought maybe he was the witch in disguise. That it was all a trick, like in *Hansel and Gretel*. Only instead of luring me into her cottage with candy, this witch pretended to be a crying, frightened child. I was one second away from running straight back to my grandfather's house when the boy finally placed his hot, timid hand in mine, and I felt it—the same tingly, fizzy sensation I'd felt when I'd entered the woods.

He couldn't be the witch, I decided.

He had fairy magic all over him.

As we walked down the hill toward the lake, I stopped to pick up two nice, straight sticks.

"Here," I said, handing one to the boy. "This is your magic wand. Maybe if the witch sees us and thinks we're witches, too, she'll leave us alone."

I waved my stick around, but he just stared at his.

"Hey ... don't worry," I said. "She won't get us. Grandpa says we're safe on this side of the ... *lough*, and Grandpa knows everything."

I put my hand on his shoulder to reassure him, but he jerked away from me immediately.

Jeez.

We started walking again, but this time, I didn't offer him my hand.

Eventually, the bluebells gave way to blackberry bushes that grabbed at my shoelaces and scratched at my legs. But I could see the lake sparkling on the other side of them, so I forged ahead, wiggling through every gap in the brambles that I could find.

For a minute, I didn't think the boy would follow me, but when I made it to my final hiding place—a massive oak tree on the edge of the lake—I heard the bushes rustle beside me and saw a head of messy black hair appear out of the corner of my eye.

I had to turn away to hide my smile. "Do you see her?" I asked, pretending that I was looking for the witch.

He didn't answer, of course.

Clutching my wand tighter, I scanned the edge of the water, looking for signs of anything ... *witchy*. There was nothing on my side of the tree, so I turned to look at the bank on his side, which meant that I also had to look at *him*.

The boy was staring out over the water, lost in thought. Even though he was as still and drab as a black and white picture, something about him reminded me of fire—his dark, unruly, chin-length hair that twisted and waved like flames, his smoke-colored eyes, his ashen skin. He didn't even have a single freckle. That made me sad. Grandpa had told me that everywhere you have a freckle is where an angel kissed you. I must have been kissed a million times, but this boy hadn't been kissed even once.

Maybe that's why he was crying, I thought.

Or maybe it was because of the cut on his bottom lip. The small red gash was the only colorful thing about him.

Suddenly, the boy darted behind the tree. His shoulder smashed against mine as he clutched his wand to his heaving chest.

"Did you see her?" I whispered. My heart began to pound, and I didn't know if it was because of the witch or the fact that this boy was touching me again.

He shook his head and pointed at the lake with his wand. Taking a deep breath, I peeked around my side of the tree. I didn't even know what I was looking for. The water looked normal, kind of a murky brownish, greenish, blue. There were blackberry bushes on the other side of the lake and more trees that went on forever. I squinted as I peered into them, searching for a bear or a wolf or something equally terrifying, and that's when I saw it. Stony and round and missing a roof.

The witch's house.

I pulled my head back behind the tree and stood shoulder to shoulder with the boy, squeezing my wand, still as a statue again. But statues don't breathe, and I'm pretty sure I was breathing loud enough for the witch to hear me all the way across the lake. She would find us and eat us for sure.

"Let's get out of here," I whispered. "Run!"

The boy and I scrambled back through the thorny bushes and up the hill as fast as we could, not caring how many fairy hat flowers we stepped on along the way. We didn't stop running until we were safely back at Hagrid's house with our backs against the cool stone wall.

"We need to make a potion to protect us against the dark arts," I panted. "That's what Professor Snape would do. I'll get the ingredients. You find a cauldron."

I crept through the doorway, which was thankfully on the side of the cottage that the witch couldn't see, and started foraging for enchanted objects. It didn't take me long to find two mushrooms, three sparkly rocks, a variety of pretty leaves, and the most magical ingredient of all, a real snail shell. That would *definitely* keep a witch away.

With my hands full, I tiptoed back into the stone circle, but when I looked up, the boy was gone.

Jumping up so that I could see over the wall, I scanned the woods for any sign of him, but it was like he'd just … vanished.

"… they'll use their magic to disappear like that."

The sound of my grandfather's snapping fingers rang in my ears.

I sat down in the middle of the leaf-covered floor and crossed my arms with a *humph*.

Maybe he needs to go work on himself too.

I crumbled up one of the big, crunchy leaves I'd found until it was nothing but confetti. Then, I threw it as hard as I could. Of course, the pieces just fluttered in the air and landed gracefully on the ground in front of me, which only pissed me off more.

"Humph."

I didn't feel like making a potion anymore.

I started to crumble up another leaf, but the sound of leaves crunching *outside* of the cottage caught my attention. I sat perfectly still.

Crunch, crunch, crunch.

The hairs on the back of my neck stood up.

The noises were definitely footsteps. And they were *definitely* coming from the direction of the lake.

As the crunching got louder, I swore that in between every few steps, I heard a soft splashing sound too.

It's the witch! She swam across the lake to get me, and now, she's all drippy and wet, and she's gonna eat meeee!

I clutched my wand and squeezed my eyes shut and tried to remember the spell that Harry had used to blast all those Dementors when he was at that spooky lake all by himself.

Expelli something. No, expecto. Expecto something. Expecto what? Expectoooo …

The *crunch-splash-crunch-splash* got louder and louder until I could finally see the top of the witch's head on the other side of the wall.

With a big, deep breath, I jumped to my feet, pointed my wand at the doorway, and yelled, "*Expecto blasto!*"

But instead of a beam of white light slicing through a lake witch, all I saw was a boy, looking at me like I was crazy, holding his wand stick in one hand and a scuffed black leather shoe in the other.

I immediately burst out laughing. I laughed, and I smiled, and I lowered my not-so-deadly weapon with a sigh of relief.

"I thought you left."

The boy walked in very slowly, very carefully, and set the shoe down on the ground as if it were a bomb that needed defusing. But instead of exploding on contact, a little water sloshed out of it.

My eyes lit up.

"Wait … is that … our cauldron?"

The boy nodded, his face expressionless.

"And it even has water in it?"

He didn't respond, but something in the tilt of his mouth told me that there was more to the story. And that was when it hit me.

DEVIL OF DUBLIN

"You got this from the lake, didn't you? You went back down there all by yourself?!"

His silvery eyes sparkled with pride.

"This is gonna be the best potion ever!" Sitting cross-legged on the ground next to our makeshift cauldron, I gathered my ingredients and handed the leaves over to my new friend. "Crumble these up real small. They'll go in last."

While he was doing that, I broke the mushrooms into little pieces and dropped them into the dark water. They floated on top like marshmallows. Next, I dropped in the rocks, followed by a piece of my hair.

As I stirred the mixture with my magic wand, the boy sprinkled his leaf pieces on top. Then, he reached up and plucked a strand of his own hair as well. I didn't know if witch repellant called for red *and* black hair, but I figured it couldn't hurt. I watched the dark, wavy strand sink into the potion before remembering the most important ingredient.

"And finally," I said, handing the treasure to my assistant, "the shell of a mystical Emerald *Isle* snail."

As I placed the pearly spiral in his outstretched hand, my fingers grazed his skin, causing a lightning bolt to zap up my arm. It sizzled, and it scared me, but it didn't hurt—kind of like holding a sparkler on the Fourth of July.

Fairy magic, I almost whispered out loud.

He dropped the swirly shell into the murky water, but instead of hearing a plop, all I heard was an annoyingly loud beeping sound. I had no idea what it was until it registered a moment later that my butt was vibrating.

"Shoot." I pulled the phone out of my pocket and tapped the screen until the noise stopped. "I gotta go."

In Harry Potter, they drank the potions they made, but there was no way I was going to drink that shoe water, so I did what the priest had done at Grandpa's church and dipped my thumb into it instead.

The boy sat perfectly still as I lifted my thumb to his forehead and drew a wet plus sign right in the middle. He held his breath and squeezed his eyes shut when I touched him, but he let me do it.

"You are now protected against the dark arts," I whispered.

When he opened his eyes again, they were all red and watery, like I must have hurt him, but I couldn't figure out what I'd done.

Maybe a drop of water ran into his eye, I thought. That had to be it.

The boy stared at me, and even though I knew it was rude, I stared back. It was like he had some kind of power over me. I couldn't breathe. Couldn't blink. And something in my chest felt like it was burning.

"Darrrr-byyyy!" My mom's voice came charging up and over the hill.

Shoot.

"Coming!" I shouted back with my hands cupped around my mouth.

The boy frowned, causing me to notice the cut on his lip again. I wanted to kiss it and make it better, like my mom used to do for me, but he was a stranger. And a boy. My mom said that kissing was only for boyfriends and girlfriends and not until I was at least twenty-five.

Then, I got an idea.

I kissed the end of my magic wand and placed it as gently as I could on his hurt lip. The boy squeezed his eyes shut again, but this time, he didn't reopen them. Instead, his face crumpled in on itself, and I sat there, watching with a knot in my throat and another one in my belly.

I couldn't tear my eyes away until my mom finally yelled, "Darrrr-byyyy!" in her angriest teacher voice yet.

I jumped to my feet and turned toward the top of the hill just as my mom's long red hair came swishing through the trees. I registered the *crunch-splash-crunch-splash* noises again, but this time, they were moving away from me. And they were going much, much faster than before.

I glanced back over at the place where the boy had just been sitting, but he was already gone.

DEVIL OF DUBLIN

And he had taken our cauldron with him.

"Darby Elaine Collins! What did I tell you? I said that when that timer goes off, yer supposed to—" She stopped marching halfway down the hill and covered her mouth with both hands. "Oh my God."

Walking the rest of the way with wide, shimmering eyes, my mom did a full lap inside the cottage while I scanned the woods for any sign of the boy.

"I completely forgot about this place," she said, running a finger along the jagged seam between two stones. "I used to play back here all the time ... with your auntie Shannon and uncle Eamonn."

Gesturing to the left, she said, "We had a pretend kitchen right here, where we made mud pies with Mam's pots and pans. Shannon would dig up the dirt, Eamonn would get water from the lake, and I'd mix it together ..."

For the first time since we had arrived in Ireland, my mom smiled. Then, she looked back over at me. "Did ya have fun?"

I couldn't help my answering grin as I nodded vigorously in response.

"Good," she said, her sad eyes shining. "That's good."

Taking my hand, she led me away from my new favorite place and back up the hill. "So, did ya find anything magical back here?"

I glanced around to make sure he wasn't within earshot. Then, I cupped my hands around my grinning mouth and whispered, as quietly as my giddiness would allow, "I think I found a real-life fairy."

CHAPTER 2

DARBY
ONE YEAR LATER

I tried to walk as quietly as possible through the woods so that I wouldn't scare off the fairies, but that was kind of impossible with my grandmother's porcelain tea set rattling in my nervous hands.

After my grandmother passed, my mother felt so bad about how long she'd been away from Glenshire that she'd promised my grandfather we'd come back and visit every summer. We'd had to cut back on things like eating out and buying new clothes in order to afford the plane tickets, but I didn't care. I would have eaten rice and beans for every meal if it meant that I could play with my new friend again.

My suitcase had barely crossed the threshold before I gave Grandpa a quick hug and made a mad dash for the back door. My mom called my name and told me to wait, but instead of shoving a phone into my pocket and giving me a lecture about safety, she shoved a silver tray containing a blue-and-white floral teapot, four matching teacups and saucers, a sugar bowl, and a creamer into my hands with a wistful smile. She said that she and her sister used to have tea parties in the "playhouse" all the time.

I thought a tea party sounded like fun until I got halfway up the hill and realized that there wasn't going to be a party with all the clinking and clanking I was doing.

I walked more slowly to see if that would help.

I was glad that my mom had let me go play, not only because I was dying to see if I could find the fairy again, but also because her brother and sister—Uncle Eamonn and Aunt Shannon—were at my grandfather's house, too. All they wanted to do was sit around and talk about grown-up stuff. And because my uncle never had kids and my aunt's kids were already adults, they didn't even bring any cousins for me to play with.

Grandpa would play with me sometimes, but not when Uncle Eamonn and Aunt Shannon were there. They'd both moved away to bigger cities once they finished school, so he didn't get to see them very often either. The year before, he'd taught me how to play poker. My mom had said that game wasn't "appropriate," but she was too tired to play with me herself, so she'd let it go.

She was always too tired to play with me.

I made it to the top of the hill and almost burst out laughing when I saw all the bluebells on the other side.

Fairy hats. I shook my head at my naive younger self as I tiptoed between the flowers, holding the tray even tighter to keep it from being jostled. I passed a ring of red-and-white polka-dotted mushrooms and trees carpeted with fuzzy green moss, but when I spotted a fallen trunk with wavy plate-like things growing up the side, I lifted my eyes with a hopeful gasp.

And there it was.

About fifty paces down the hill.

The ruins of a gray stone cottage, and sticking up over the back wall was a headful of glossy black curls.

I wanted to jump up and down and squeal in delight, but I had to stay calm to keep from scaring him away. Plus, it looked like he was concentrating really hard on whatever he was doing, and my teacher always said that it was rude to distract your friends when they were trying to concentrate.

As I got closer, I realized that the boy's head was bent sideways, looking down the length of a stick that he was holding on top of the wall as if it were a gun. Then, his body jerked rapidly—*ra-ta-ta-ta-tat*—like he was firing a machine gun.

The boy then ducked and covered his head with both hands, disappearing beneath the wall before popping back up to throw a rock. He stuck his fingers in his ears and turned around, facing me with his eyes squeezed shut as his imaginary hand grenade exploded somewhere behind him.

I stood in the doorway, making sure to block the exit before I spoke, in case he tried to run.

"Can I play?" I asked, teacups quivering against their saucers. I'd never played Army before, but I did remember a scene from *Toy Story* where Woody told the green plastic Army men to go on a mission.

Setting the tray down on the ground next to the door, I stood at attention and put my hand up to my forehead in a salute. "Sergeant, establish a recon point. Code red. I repeat, code red."

The boy took his fingers out of his ears and slowly looked up at me. His eyes widened from slits to saucers as his lips parted. When they closed again, I swore, he was almost smiling.

I was *definitely* smiling. So big that I was sure he could see every missing tooth in my nine-year-old mouth.

His eyes moved from me to the tea set on the floor, and he dove for it, sniffing it like a dog.

"The good people love biscuits."

I lifted the lid on the little blue-and-white sugar bowl, revealing three or four biscuits—however many I could fit inside before I'd left—and offered one to him. "Is this what you—"

Just like the time before, the boy snatched the vanilla treat out of my hand and shoved it into his mouth, chewing and grunting with his eyes closed, as if it was the best thing he'd ever tasted. Then, he picked up the teapot and shook it, but it was empty. His face fell.

"Are you thirsty?"

He shoved his dirty hand down into the cookie jar and pulled out the rest of the biscuits.

"I can get you some water. My grandpa lives just over the hill, in the blue house."

The boy lifted his head and stared at me with his cheeks full of sugar and his eyes full of hope.

"Do you wanna … come over?"

He glanced up at the hill behind me, chewing more slowly as he mulled it over.

"Come on." I grinned, picking up the little porcelain teapot. "I'll get some water, and you can see Grandpa's sheep too. They're really nice, and they have blue spots on their butts!"

I took a step backward out of the doorway. Then, another and another, never breaking eye contact with the wide-eyed boy in the cottage. I was beginning to think that he wasn't going to come when he finally stood, clutching the now-empty sugar bowl in both hands.

"We can get more of those too." I grinned. "My grandpa has a whole bunch of 'em!"

The boy emerged from the cottage, and I noticed that his jeans were at least two inches too short and had holes in the knees. I decided that those must have been his playclothes.

Whenever I got a stain on my pants or wore holes in the knees, my mother would always say, "Well, I guess those are playclothes now."

My school clothes had to look nice because my mom was a teacher at my school, and *how I looked was a reflection on her*—or something like that.

I also noticed that the boy was careful not to step on the bluebells, which I thought was silly because they were obviously too big for him to wear as a hat, but then I realized that maybe he just didn't want to hurt them.

Most of the boys I went to school with loved hurting living things. They pulled the wings off of butterflies and stomped on ant hills and chopped worms in half with sticks and ripped the leaves off of trees. But those were human boys.

Maybe fairy boys were different.

When we got to the edge of the woods, I pointed at the blue house in the middle of the pasture. "That's it." I smiled.

Some of the sheep lifted their heads when they heard my voice and began walking toward the fence.

"You wanna pet one?" I asked, unlatching the gate. "They don't bite."

I opened the gate, and Sir Timothy McFluffles—that's what I called the one with the wonky ear—stuck his nose in my hand, sniffing for treats.

"See?" I turned my head and found the boy standing at the edge of the forest, mostly hidden behind a fat oak tree.

I wondered if the fairy magic kept him from leaving the woods. I hadn't thought of that before. Now, I felt bad. He probably really wanted to pet a sheep, but he couldn't.

"Here." I set the teapot down and yanked a long piece of grass out of the ground.

Sir Timothy McFluffles was unimpressed with my offering, but he followed me through the gate anyway and over to the tree where the boy was hiding.

"Pet him, quick!" I said, holding the blade of grass with both hands as Sir Timothy bit the end of it right off.

That almost smile returned as the boy leaned over to touch his wool, but the moment he took a step forward, a twig snapped under his foot and Sir Timothy took off running.

"Dang it!"

I chased after him, but the boy was way faster. He caught up to Sir Timothy in seconds, bending over and scooping him up in his arms like he weighed nothing. My mouth fell open as he walked back toward me, carrying Sir Timothy like he was just a giant, disgruntled stuffed animal.

I knew that Grandpa had said that fairies were fast, but ... *wow*. This one was fast and strong.

I followed him through the gate, locking it behind us to make sure that none of the other sheep got out, and watched as the boy set Sir Timothy McFluffles back on his feet. When he stood back up, I realized that he was a lot taller than I remembered. And ... prettier.

"Thanks," I said, feeling a blush creep into my cheeks. "I woulda been in so much trouble."

His eyes darted around the pasture, as if he were nervous. Like he'd just realized that he wasn't in the woods anymore.

Oh man, now he's the one who's gonna be in trouble.

"Do you need to go back?" I asked. "It's okay if you do. I can get some water and bring it—"

"Oi!" a voice bellowed from the direction of the house. "Shove off, lad, 'fore I loose the hound on ya!"

I turned to find my grandfather marching through the grass, waving his hands in the air as if he were trying to shoo away a bird.

"Grandpa!" I spread my arms and stood in front of the boy, mortified by my grandfather's behavior. "This is my friend. He was just helping me—"

"Get in the house, lass. Go on."

"But—" I felt a rustle of wind at my back and turned toward the boy, but all I saw was the back of his head as he hopped the fence and disappeared into the woods.

My grandfather's arms wrapped around me then, pulling me so tightly against his chest that I could hear his heart beating inside.

"Jaysus, Mary, and Joseph," he said, squeezing me even tighter. "Ya scared me half to my grave, lass."

Then, he released me and tapped his forehead, chest, and both shoulders with two fingers, drawing an invisible cross.

"Why?" I asked. "Is he a fairy, Grandpa? Are fairies dangerous?"

I wanted to tell him that I'd touched him before and felt a zap of magic, but I didn't think Grandpa would be too happy about that.

Steering me by the shoulders, Grandpa turned and marched me back toward the house. "That boy is no fairy," he grumbled. "He's somethin' else entirely. Rumor has it, his mother was an *unsavory* character. A devil worshipper. She brought Kellen to

DEVIL OF DUBLIN

Father Henry a few years ago when he was just a wee lad. Said he was the product of a *relationship* she'd had with the Devil himself. She couldn't take care of him anymore, so Father Henry took him in. Thought he could save his soul. But the lad doesn't speak. Doesn't smile. Got kicked out of school for bitin' and growlin' all the time. He's pure evil, that one. Ya best to stay away."

"He's not evil, Grandpa. He's a fairy, I swear! He has these pretty, silver eyes and lives in a fairy ring and eats sweets. Just like you said! And he's nice. He doesn't even step on flowers, and he brought Sir Timothy back when I accidentally let him out of the gate."

I slapped a hand over my mouth. Grandpa wasn't supposed to know about that last part.

"Don't be fooled, lass." He glanced down at me, lifting a bushy reddish-blond eyebrow in warning. "Ya know what they say about the Devil. Once upon a time, he was God's most beautiful angel."

I glanced over my shoulder at the tree, where the boy—*Kellen*—had been hiding just minutes earlier. I hoped to find him standing there, watching me.

But he was gone.

And so was Grandma's teapot.

CHAPTER 3

KELLEN
ONE YEAR LATER

I placed two good, straight sticks on the ground in the shape of an X and pulled one of the nails I'd stolen from Father Henry's workbench out of my pocket. I wasn't stupid enough to risk taking his hammer too, so I drove the nail through with a rock.

Wham!

Three days. Darby had been back for three days, and she hadn't come looking for me once.

Wham! Wham! Wham!

I knew because I'd been watching her granda's house every day since school holidays had started. I'd even put his damn sheep back a time or two, hoping he'd see me being helpful and change his mind about letting Darby play with me, but ...

I smashed the nail again—my gangly twelve-year-old arm mustering the force of someone twice my size and every bit as pissed off—and split the top stick right down the middle, rendering it useless.

"Fuck!"

I threw the mangled twig over the wall of the cottage and heard something I hadn't in three hundred and sixty-eight days. The prettiest sound in the whole goddamn world.

"Kellen?"

My guts twisted into violent knots as I jumped up, facing the hill. I saw her instantly, a riot of color in a sea of green. Coppery-orange hair. A rainbow-striped hoodie. And a pair of wellies as yellow as Mr. Lafferty's farmhouse.

I held my breath as she bounced down the hill, careful not to step on a bluebell or trip on a tree root. She was carrying a brown paper sack, and when her eyes finally lifted, they landed right on me.

With a smile.

That gap-toothed grin destroyed me. Ran me through with medieval brutality. It wasn't clean. Or quick. It was slow and jagged and splintered as it pierced my heart, twisting on the way in, dragging on the way out. It left a million brittle shards behind, ensuring that I would never *ever* forget who that organ belonged to.

Darby Collins.

The only person who ever smiled when they saw me.

"Hi." The word just ... came out of me. It was just a breath with a sound really. A whisper. But when Darby heard it, her mouth went from grinning to gaping.

"You *can* talk!" Her big, round eyes got even bigger and rounder as she came bounding the rest of the way down the hill. "I thought I heard you say something when you threw that stick, but then I was like, *Nah, Kellen can't talk*, but then ... oh my gosh, Kellen! You can talk!"

And just like that, the iron door in my throat slammed shut again. I could practically hear the chains and bolts and locks sliding into place, trapping all the words I wanted to say inside of me, holding my thoughts prisoner along with my ability to at least pretend to be a normal fucking person.

"Freak."

"Demon."

"Satan's bastard."

DEVIL OF DUBLIN

"I heard he can't talk because his tongue is forked like a snake."
"I heard he has a tail with a pitchfork on the end."
"I heard he killed his own mam."
"You know his da is the Devil, right?"
"He's pure evil, that one. Just look at those eyes."

I couldn't breathe. The fire and frustration in my belly grew into an inferno that scorched my skin and made me sweat. I spun around and untucked my hair from behind my ears, pulling it forward to hide the redness in my infuriated cheeks.

Darby's heavy footfalls grew louder as she clomped over to the cottage.

"I've been tryin' to come play ever since I got here, but it's been raining for days! Mama won't let me play outside in the rain 'cause I'll get my clothes all dirty, but I thought that was the whole point of havin' playclothes. I told her that, but then she got on me for back-talkin' and said I needed to spend time with my aunt and uncle and Grandpa. But they're so borrrring. And Grandpa doesn't have any kid stuff at his house. I've been making designs on the floor with his poker chips and playing cards for three whole—oh my gosh!"

Darby stood in the doorway, her shadow spilling across my work, and gasped.

"Kellen! You got furniture!"

She walked into the center of the cottage, turning slowly as she clutched that paper bag to her chest, and the look of wonder on her face felt like a cool breeze against my blazing skin.

While she studied every branch chair, stump table, and straw bed in the cottage, I studied her. She was a little taller. Her hair a little longer. But it was as if the moment she'd stepped into those woods, the past year of my life—every shitty second of it—had just disappeared.

"Wait." Her head swiveled toward me. "Did you *make* all this stuff?"

I nodded.

I'd been working out there every day since she'd left. Making things was the only way I knew to take my mind off the waiting. And maybe, I thought, if I fixed the cottage up properly,

I could live out there one day. Just … run away and never come back.

"Oh my gosh! Grandma's tea set! I totally forgot about that!" Darby picked a tiny teacup off the tray I'd set on a stump table in the designated kitchen area. "And look … there's even tea inside!"

She pursed her lips and pretended to sip the rainwater spilling over the top. Then, she set it back down on its flooded saucer with a giggle.

Turning around, Darby's smile faded the longer she stared at me.

Everyone was always staring at me.

I lowered my head, letting my hair fall forward and cover more of my face. Father Henry had been wanting to cut it for years, but every time he brought it up, I would just point to a picture of Jesus on the wall—there was one in every room of the house—and he'd shut up about it.

I didn't actually want to look like Jesus—God and his son were both as dead to me as I was to them. I just needed a buffer between me and the staring eyeballs of every arsehole in Glenshire.

The kids at school were the worst. They dared each other to trip me, punch me, spit on me, cut pieces of my hair off. They called me Hellboy, said I was the son of Satan.

And I was. Father Henry had told me so. He'd told the whole fucking village.

But he hadn't told Darby.

"Wow." She beamed. "Your hair is getting so long."

All I could see were those bleedin' yellow boots as she walked up and stood right in front of me.

"I brought you something."

She shoved the paper bag into my stomach. A grunt punched out of me as I reached up to grab it. It was heavier than I'd expected.

I peeked down at her through my hair and had to bite the inside of my cheek to keep from smiling. She was bouncing up and down, grinning like a fool.

"Open it! Open it!"

I set the bag on the ground next to me with a *thunk*. Reaching in, I pulled out a glass gherkin jar. Only instead of pickled cucumbers, it was full of—

"Water!" Darby squealed. "Grandpa only has glasses and stuff to drink out of, so I had to put it in an old pickle jar, but I washed it real good first!"

I unscrewed the lid and sniffed the contents. It still smelled like brine, but I didn't give a shite. I hadn't had a drop to drink since breakfast. I didn't want to go home in case Darby showed up.

Honestly, I didn't want to go home ever.

I chugged the vinegary water until I had to stop to take a breath. Then, I chugged some more. I felt it trickle down the sides of my mouth and into my collar as Darby giggled.

"You *were* thirsty!"

When I couldn't stomach another drop, I screwed the lid back on and wiped my mouth with my shirt, feeling my cheeks heat again. Darby must have thought I was disgusting, but if she did, she was polite enough to not show it.

"There's more!" she said, pointing into the bag. "Look! Look!"

I set the jar down and took a deep breath. Then, I reached into the bag again. My fingers brushed over something rough and crumby. A lot of somethings.

"They're your favorite!" Darby clapped as I pulled out a handful of crushed biscuits.

My mouth watered at the sight of them, but my throat locked up completely as heavy, rusty chains of emotion tightened around my neck. Breathing was difficult. Swallowing? Impossible.

I put the biscuits back in the bag, and Darby frowned. I wanted to tell her I was sorry. I wanted to tell her I'd missed her every fucking second since she'd left. I wanted to tell her that I couldn't eat because something was wrong with me, with my throat, and it wouldn't let anything through. Not even the words *thank you*. But I couldn't, and it made her sad.

Darby stared at her rubber boots with her bottom lip poking out, and an icy panic washed over me.

She was going to leave.

If I didn't do something, she was going to leave.

I couldn't speak. I couldn't eat. So, in a moment of desperation, I did something I hadn't done to another human being since I was five years old.

I stepped forward, and I gave her a hug.

Darby's head barely came up to my shoulder, but she wrapped her arms round my waist and squeezed me so hard that I almost laughed.

With her face pressed against my chest, she said, "Grandpa says I should stay away from you 'cause your daddy is the Devil, but I don't care about that. He says my daddy is a *son of a bitch*, but you'll still play with me, right?"

I didn't feel like laughing anymore.

She knew. She knew, and she'd come back anyway.

I squeezed my eyes shut and nodded through the pain, letting my chin tap the top of her head so that she would feel my answer.

"Good!" Darby chirped, letting go of my waist and taking a step back. "Let's play barber shop!"

Grabbing one of the chairs I'd made, she set it down in front of me with her tongue poking out of her mouth and her eyebrows pulled together.

"Will this hold you?"

I nodded, almost completely paralyzed by the rush of emotions I'd been flooded with during our hug.

"It will? Wow. You should make furniture when you grow up."

Darby took a few things off the tea tray, poured the rainwater out of them, and set them on the wall behind me. Then, she picked up two small sticks and made a V with them, snapping them open and closed with both hands, like scissors. Once she was satisfied with her setup, Darby gestured for me to sit.

"Hello, sir, and welcome to the Little Cottage Barber Shop. What brings you in today?"

The chair creaked as I sat and stared at the ground.

Darby stood right in front of me, her delicate fingertips grazing my forehead as she swept the hair out of my face.

"A ball at the castle? My goodness! Well, don't worry, sir. We'll get you cleaned up in no time."

I closed my eyes and concentrated on my breathing as her fingers slid through my hair again and again. Touching me. Removing the only thing I had to hide behind, a few strands at a time.

Dropping her fake barber shop voice, Darby said, "This is fun. Maybe I should do hair when I grow up. I used to think I'd be a teacher, like my mom, but she's so tired and grumpy all the time. She says teaching is the hardest job ever. She also says they don't pay her enough because '*society devalues traditionally female occupations.*'" Darby said that last part in a deep, grown-up voice.

After pulling my shoulder-length hair back behind my ears, Darby began running a stick over it, like a comb, and I didn't know if I wanted her to stop or keep doing it forever. It hurt so much. Not the knots or the tangles, but the tenderness. It felt like she was sawing my heart in half with that fucking stick.

"I want to be a YouTuber when I grow up too. I already have my own YouTube channel. It's called Adventures in Teddy Bear Land. I make videos of my stuffed animals. They all live in Teddy Bear Land, and there's a king and a queen and a castle. In my last video, it was the queen's birthday, so all the stuffed animals got dressed up and got in their cars and drove to the castle for a party. I used my mom's shoeboxes for cars. She'd said I could."

Suddenly, a memory flashed in my mind. An image of my own mother, kneeling over the side of a bathtub, washing my hair when I was little. It felt like I wasn't even in my body anymore. I was standing behind her in that dimly lit bathroom, watching over her shoulder as she massaged the bubbles into my scalp.

I could smell the shampoo. The sweat under her arms. I could even smell the glass of wine she knocked off the edge of the tub with her elbow. I watched as it fell into the water with a splash, as four-year-old me scrambled toward the back corner of the tub in horror, the red liquid spreading toward me like a pool of blood.

My eyes flew open with a gasp.

"Sorry," Darby said, stilling her hands. "I'll try to be gentler. You got a lot of tangles back here."

Darby dropped the stick and began pulling sections of hair up to the crown of my head. Her fingertips felt like razor blades as they dragged across my scalp. It was too intense. Too fucking painful. No one had touched me like that since …

Since *her*.

"So, at the queen's birthday party," Darby continued, "all the stuffed animals brought presents and danced, and they even had a food fight! I have a bunch of plastic food from my play kitchen that I made them throw at each other. It was so funny. The king and queen did it too."

I closed my eyes and immediately saw my mam again, but this time, I wasn't in the tub. I was in the passenger seat of her car in front of Father Henry's house. Her eyes didn't look right. The white parts were too red. And she had sores on her lips. She licked her fingers and raked them through my hair, telling me to be good for Father Henry. Telling me that she had to go away.

A different set of fingers slid through my hair, tugging and twisting sections at the back, and I had to remind myself that it wasn't her. It was Darby. Not *her*.

She was gone. And she was never coming back.

"Then, the dragons flew in and delivered the cake!" Darby cheered as her fingers slid across the back of my neck, gathering up the rest of my hair. "They also delivered a present from Sir Whiskers McLongtail. He was home sick and couldn't make it."

I couldn't breathe. I couldn't fucking breathe.

"But the king and queen of Teddy Bear Land were so nice that when the party was over, they asked the dragons to fly them straight to Sir Whiskers's house so that they could give him a piece of birthday cake and some chicken soup. Theeee … end!"

Darby rested her hands on my shoulders, and my burning hot eyes filled with tears.

"That video has almost a hundred likes now! Can you believe it?"

Panicking, I swiped at my eyes with the heels of both hands. I couldn't cry in front of her again. I wouldn't.

But I was. My fists and cheeks were smeared with tears as Darby walked around to the front of the chair.

"Okay, sir. You're all done. That'll be—"

I stood up so fast that I knocked the chair over as I bolted for the doorway.

Everything hurt. My eyes, my throat, my lungs, that worthless fucking muscle in the center of my chest, my arms as the branches and brambles ripped and tore at them. I couldn't think about *her*. I *never* thought about *her*. But Darby's tenderness, her touch, it had shattered the locks that kept her memories away. It had shattered *me*.

I couldn't stop the tears from falling, just like I couldn't stop the pictures from flashing behind my eyes. A birthday cake. Her singing. A present with dinosaur paper and a bow on top.

As Father Henry's house came into view through the trees, the church's steeple looming behind it, I felt as though I were being burned alive. His house was small—provided by the church for the priest to live in alone—and it sat at the back of the graveyard, on the edge of the woods.

Racing past the cemetery, I burst through the front door and ran through the living room, where Father Henry was sitting in his armchair, watching TV.

"Oi!" he yelled, sloshing whiskey over the side of his glass. "What'd I tell ya 'bout slammin' doors?!"

I couldn't let him see me cry either.

My feet were loud on the wooden stairs that led up to the attic.

Father Henry's were louder. "Get back here!"

I threw myself onto the bed and buried my face in the pillow just as the flip of a switch bathed the room in nicotine-colored light.

"What the fuck did ya do to yer head, boy?" Father Henry roared. "Ya look like a fuckin' lass!"

I'd never heard him say the word *fuck* before, but whatever he was mad about, it was bad enough to make him say it twice.

I reached up and felt the back of my head. My hair was woven into a braid that went from the crown of my head all the way down to the nape of my neck. The same way the girls wore their hair at church.

Shite.

I curled into a ball and covered my head with my pillow, but Father Henry ripped it out of my hands and yanked me up by the bottom of the braid.

"I always knew ya were an abomination, but this? Under me own roof?" He spat on the floor as he dragged me off the bed.

I struggled to stay on my feet as he pulled me across the room and over to the stairs by my hair.

"Leviticus 18:22. *Do not practice homosexuality, having sex with another man as with a woman. It is a detestable sin.*"

I didn't know what that meant. I never knew what any of the Bible verses that he shouted at me meant—except that something bad was about to happen.

"Leviticus 20:13. *If a man practices homosexuality, having sex with another man as with a woman, both men have committed a detestable act. They must both be put to death, for they are guilty of a capital offense.*"

I didn't want to go back downstairs. That's where he did his rituals. Where he punished me. There was nothing in the attic for him to hit me with, other than his own belt.

I grabbed the railing at the top of the stairs with both hands and tried not to scream as Father Henry yanked on my hair even harder.

"Boy! You let go this instant!"

His palm crashed against the side of my head, and my entire body swung sideways. My ribs cracked against the railing as a ringing sound exploded in my right ear. Stunned, I lost my grip on the railing, but I quickly grabbed one of the wooden spindles to keep him from dragging me down the stairs.

Father Henry immediately grabbed my hands and began prying my fingers off the splintery rod one by one.

I gritted my teeth and gripped the piece of wood tighter, but Father Henry was stronger. With another blasphemous curse, he bent two of my fingers backward until I cried out in pain.

"This is a test," he grunted, his breath hot and reeking of liquor as he wrapped his sweaty body around mine. As I felt his excitement pressed against my lower back. "The Lord knew it would take a man of the cloth to save yer wicked soul."

He pried another finger back and I screamed again, but I wouldn't let go. I refused to let go.

"I will not fail, my Lord! Do ya hear me? I ... will ... not ... faiiiiil!"

With an ear-splitting roar, Father Henry yanked the entire spindle free from the stair railing, sending us both crashing to the floor. I let go of it as soon as I began falling, cradling my mangled fingers to my chest.

Father Henry did not.

As he pushed himself to stand, hovering over me with that damn length of wood in his hand, all I could think was, *Grand. Now there's something up here for him to hit me with.*

And he did.

I didn't open my eyes. Not at first anyway. I wasn't ready to face reality all at once.

First, I felt the wooden floor under my cheek, and I remembered where I was. Then, I felt the pain—shooting up my fingers, throbbing in my head—and I remembered how I'd gotten there.

Stifling a sob, I sat up and brushed the hair away from my face. Only instead of sliding behind my ears, it came away on my hands like a spiderweb.

My eyes flew open, but I couldn't register what I was seeing. What was stuck to my fingers. What was lying in heaps all over the floor.

Reaching up, I touched the spot just above my ear, the place where my head felt like it was going to explode. And sure enough, my fingers found a trickle of warm, sticky blood … and nothing else.

No.

I ran my hands over the top of my head. The back. The other side.

No, no, no.

Again and again, I raked my scalp, but it was gone. It was all. Fucking. Gone.

NO!

Boiling hot tears blurred my vision as I looked around at the sea of black waves and chunks of braid surrounding me. Loose curls rolled off my chest and pooled in my lap. At least the ones that weren't stuck to the dried blood on my shirt.

I swept the strands into a pile on the floor and held them in my mangled hands.

It was mine. *Mine.* And he'd fucking taken it.

"No."

I heard the word that time, not just in my head, but with my ears. I'd said it out loud, and I wanted to do it again.

"No."

I pictured a fire blazing in my belly, turning my tears into steam before they could even fall.

"No."

My blood became rivers of molten lava, melting away my sadness, my weakness, my shame, my self-hatred. Distilling it down into pure, undiluted rage.

"No."

The iron door that had kept me silent for so many years melted and slid down my throat as my voice echoed off the unfinished walls, loud and clear and strong.

"No!"

DEVIL OF DUBLIN

My hands balled into fists, squeezing the hair, squeezing as hard as they could despite the pain radiating through my fingers. Then, I ripped and tore and shredded the strands until they were in a million little pieces, but it wasn't enough.

I wanted to kill something.

The fire roared through me as my eyes darted around the attic, looking for something else to destroy, but everything there belonged to Father Henry. He would punish me if I so much as knocked over a glass of water. There was only one thing in that house that he didn't care about … and that was me.

I looked down at my arm, took a breath, and pinched it as hard as I could. My eyes squeezed shut as I twisted the skin as far as it would go, as a cooling wave of pain rushed over my shoulder, up my neck, and into my face.

I did it again and again—my arms, my legs, my chest, my stomach—pinching, hitting, clawing, biting until the pain on the outside blanketed me, snuffing out the fire on the inside.

But when I'd finally extinguished that bloodthirsty rage, the pain remained. The side of my head pounded. My fingers throbbed and swelled. My arms and legs screamed in a thousand different places. And my throat felt like it had been stitched shut with razor wire.

But I was also left with a terrifying realization.

There was something inside of me that hadn't been put there by God. It was dark and violent and evil and cruel. It had a power all its own. And it wanted to kill.

I knew I could never let it out again. I knew I could never let them see …

That all along, they'd been right about me.

CHAPTER 4

DARBY

"Darby, keep up. We're gonna be late." My mom tugged on my hand, and I hustled to keep up despite the blisters that were forming under my hard white church shoes with every step.

Grandpa was already fifty feet ahead of us. The church was just down the road from his house, and he always insisted on walking because driving on Sunday supposedly went against the Bible. But that didn't make any sense to me. If Sunday was a day of rest, why was I breaking a sweat in my polyester thrift-store dress?

Oh, right. Because of Father Henry.

He'd really put the fear of God into his congregation. My grandfather had told us before we left that the last time someone had been late to one of his sermons, Father Henry had made them stand up in front of everyone and recite a prayer to ask "our heavenly Father" for forgiveness. Grandpa acted like it was the worst fate in the world, but to a ten-year-old who only went to church once a year, asking for forgiveness sounded a hell of a lot better than losing all the skin on my feet to those cruel shoes.

"I can't go any faster, Mom. My feet hurt!"

"D'ya have any idea how mortified I'm gonna be if we have to stand up and say the Our Father in front of the entire village, and *you* don't even know the words? Yer grandfather will find out I haven't been taking ya to church."

She glanced down at her watch as she quickened her pace.

"Shite. Repeat after me. *Our Father, who art in heaven, hallowed be thy name …*"

My mom dragged my protesting body around a curve in the road, and the chapel rose up in the distance. Gray stone. Stained glass. One tall steeple and two big, medieval-looking red doors with heavy black hardware. When I'd first come to Glenshire, I'd felt like the church wanted to eat me.

The fact that my grandmother was buried in the cemetery out back probably hadn't helped.

"Okay, now, you say it."

"What?" I blinked up at my mom as she turned and glared at me over her shoulder.

"Ya weren't even listenin'! Darby! In a few minutes, Father Henry's gonna make us stand up in front of everyone and—"

"Can I just stay outside?"

My mom stopped walking and turned to face me, her exhausted hazel eyes suddenly glimmering with hope. "Darby, you're a bleedin' genius."

Kissing me on the head, she pointed to the grass area next to the parking lot. "If I run inside, can I trust ya to stay right here until the service is over?"

I hadn't even finished nodding before my mom hitched up her dress and took off in a jog across the gravel parking lot, reciting the Our Father under her breath the entire way.

Grandpa held the heavy front door open for her as she darted inside, a look of confusion on his face about why I wasn't coming too. She must have told him it was okay because he gave me a wave just as the bells in the steeple began to chime. I counted each deep clang before it disappeared into the morning mist.

Ten of them, to be exact.

DEVIL OF DUBLIN

I stood there in my itchy white church dress and my lacy white church socks and my stupid white church shoes for I don't even know how long. Organ music began to play inside the chapel. It sounded scary, like the music you'd expect to hear coming out of a haunted house.

Everything about that place was scary, especially the cemetery behind it, but the patch of grass I was standing on was perfectly ghost-free. And it had yellow dandelions growing on it—the same color as the rain boots my mom had bought to keep me from ruining another pair of shoes in Grandpa's muddy pasture. I liked those boots. They were super comfortable, and Kellen seemed to like them, too. He'd stared at them a lot the day before. Or maybe he was just staring at the ground. With all that hair in his face, it was hard to tell.

He'd looked so handsome with it pulled back in a French braid. Like one of those soldiers from the Revolutionary War.

The thought of him made my chest hurt. I sat in the grass and picked a dandelion, twirling it between my fingers as I remembered the way he'd looked just before he ran away from me.

He was always running away from me.

I pulled my dumb shoes and frilly socks off and planted my bare feet on the grass. I knew my mom would be livid if she saw me sitting in the grass in my church clothes, but she was always mad about something. Whenever I asked her why she was so grumpy, she'd say it was because she was exhausted from having to be the mom and the dad all the time. But that didn't make any sense to me. Dads didn't do anything.

They didn't even remember to call on your birthday.

I tucked the yellow flower behind my ear and decided to pick another one for Grandma. I knew how it felt to be forgotten. I wasn't going to let her feel that way, too, just because she was stuck in a scary, old graveyard.

Standing up, I brushed the grass off my butt, grabbed my shoes, and walked over to the metal gate that led into the cemetery. It creaked loud enough to wake the dead when I pushed it open, but inside, it wasn't scary at all. What *was* scary was the creepy little house *behind* the cemetery. I hadn't noticed it before, but there it was, on the edge of the woods—a dirty white stucco shack that looked like it was being slowly swallowed by the forest. I felt like it was staring at me. Or maybe it was the ghosts inside that were staring at me through the windows. That was probably why the cemetery didn't feel so scary, I decided. Because all the ghosts were in *there*.

I was careful to walk in between the graves, just in case their spirits really were watching me, until I got to Grandma's. Her tombstone was cleaner and shinier than all the rest.

Mary Catherine O'Toole
1942 ~ 2008
Devoted wife, beloved mother, terrible cook.
She will be missed dearly.

I remembered my mom being so mad when she saw what Grandpa had put on her tombstone.

She'd said it was "in bad taste," but Grandpa had just laughed and slapped his knee and said, "Bad taste. Aye, that's a good one."

I put the flower on the ground, right around where I thought her ear might be. "Here, Grandma. Now, we can be twinsies."

Something caught my attention over by the woods, but when I lifted my head, the only thing I saw was that awful little house.

Maybe Grandma's in there with the other ghosts, waving to me.

I squinted my eyes to try and see in the windows better. The window to the left of the door had its curtains closed, but the one on the other side of the door …

I gasped and covered my mouth as a pair of sunken, shadowy eyes stared back at me through the glass. Then, with a blink, they were gone. The curtain snapped back into place, as if it had never happened.

But it had.

I dropped my shoes next to Grandma's grave and took off running toward the house. The back gate of the cemetery was wide open, but the ground was muddy between it and the house. I tried to stay on the clumps of grass as I covered the distance, hopping like a frog until I made it to the front door.

"Kellen!" I yelled between panting breaths, knocking on the door as hard as I could. "Kellen, it's me! Darby!"

When he didn't answer, I really began to worry.

What if he's in there with the ghosts? What if they grabbed him yesterday when he ran off, and now, they won't let him out? What if he's trapped in there?

"Kellen?"

Knock, knock, knock.

I pressed my ear to the door and didn't hear a sound, so I ran back into the grass and grabbed two short sticks. Holding one in each hand, I knocked one more time, my heart pounding in my chest as I grasped the doorknob.

The door was the same deep shade of red as the church's. It creaked and groaned as it swung open, coughing stale cigarette smoke into my face. I took one last breath of fresh air before I stepped inside, holding my sticks out in front of me in the shape of a cross.

It was dead silent in the house and *definitely* haunted. I looked all around for Kellen, but the only eyes staring back at me belonged to the Jesus paintings on the walls. The furniture was old-timey. Most of the curtains were drawn shut. And the ashtrays were overflowing as well as the dishes in the kitchen sink, which I could see through a narrow doorway across the room.

"Kellen? Are you—"

The sound of hardwood creaking under someone's weight paralyzed me with fear. I froze, holding my breath as I listened. When I heard it again, it sounded like it was coming from the kitchen.

With my heart pounding in my ears and my hands sweating around those two damp sticks, I tiptoed over to the doorway, took a deep breath, and peeked inside.

Motion exploded to my right the second my face crossed the threshold. Turning, I caught a fleeting glimpse of a skinny boy sprinting up a narrow flight of stairs. Based on the groans of the wooden steps under his feet, it sounded like he was taking them two at a time.

"Kellen, wait!"

I dropped my sticks and took off after him. The air smelled less like cigarettes and more like mildew the farther up the staircase I traveled. It turned in the middle and deposited me into a pitch-black attic, lit only by the light that made it past the bend in the stairs.

"Kellen?" My heart was racing. "Can you turn a light on? It's so dark up here." I slowed down as I climbed the last few stairs.

"Is this where you live?"

Step.

"Why do you keep running away from me?"

Step, step.

I slid my hand along the wall until my fingertips grazed a switch. When I flipped it on, the space was instantly illuminated by a single dim bulb in the center of the room. No, not a room. An attic. Drafty. Dusty. Dank. Unfinished. The ceiling was pitched with exposed wooden beams. The walls were bare. The floor was covered in rough, uneven wood planks. And pacing across it, with both hands on his head and a scowl on his face, was the boy I couldn't stop thinking about.

The second the light turned on, Kellen snatched a yellowy-brown pillow off the cot next to him and held it up in front of his face with both hands. He was wearing the same clothes he'd worn the day before, but his T-shirt now had a reddish-brown stain on it.

The same color as the one on the floor by the stairs.

That must have been why he'd run off so suddenly the day before.

DEVIL OF DUBLIN

I smiled. "It's okay," I said, taking a step closer. "You don't have to be embarrassed. I get nosebleeds sometimes too. I know it can be scary, but—"

My words trailed off as Kellen's chest began to rise and fall, faster and faster. He squeezed the pillow until his knuckles turned white. Then, he buried his face in it and growled. I'd never heard anything like it. It wasn't human. It was deep and guttural and horrible and hurt. His knees buckled, and his bony back arched forward as he unleashed that sound into the pillow, but instead of a headful of loose black curls tumbling forward, all I saw was ... nothing.

I gasped, and Kellen's entire body went rigid.

Standing back up, he lowered his hands slowly—the dingy, flattened pillow shaking in his grip—until I could see his entire face. I didn't even recognize him at first. His soft gray eyes were narrowed to slits. His teeth were bared, and his nostrils flared with every breath he sucked in.

He didn't look like a fairy anymore. He looked like a demon.

I'd seen Kellen like that once before—when I'd found him crying in the cottage. He'd been so mad; it was as if he'd turned into a wild animal. As if he wanted to hurt me.

I told my legs to run—my heart was pounding as if I were running already—but my feet refused to move. Because I knew why Kellen was so upset. And it wasn't a stupid nosebleed.

Tears filled my eyes as I took in the rest of him. Kellen's beautiful hair was gone, buzzed off in uneven chunks with a few straggly, long pieces on one side.

And it was all my fault.

"Kellen, I ..."

I took a step closer, but he immediately growled and showed his teeth again. God, he was so mad. Hot, remorseful tears spilled down my cheeks as I stared into his hate-filled eyes.

"I'm sorry. I'm so, so sorry."

The last time I'd braided my mom's hair, I'd knotted it up so badly that she yelled at me, saying she thought she was going to have to "cut the damn thing out." I wasn't allowed to braid her hair anymore after that. And now I'd gone and done it to Kellen.

A sob broke loose as I realized that he was probably never going to play with me again. He acted like he could hardly tolerate me as it was—never smiling, always running away—and now, this?

I took another step forward. "Can I at least fix it for you?"

His eyebrows slammed together as his nostrils flared with every dragon-like breath he sucked in.

I lifted a shaky finger and pointed to the side of his head. "You missed a spot, but I can fix it. I won't mess it up this time, I promise. Do you have some scissors?"

Kellen ran a hand over the side of his head, still clutching the pillow with the other. As soon as he found the long section I'd pointed at, his entire face turned bright red. Tossing the pillow onto the cot behind him, Kellen bolted past me and ran down the stairs.

"Kellen, wait!"

I chased after him, but by the time I got to the kitchen …

Snip!

Kellen was standing in front of an open drawer with a pair of scissors in one hand and a lock of shiny black hair in the other.

He was staring at it like it disgusted him, his eyebrows furrowed and his mouth in a scowl, but I thought it was the prettiest hair in the entire world.

Or it had been, before I'd ruined it.

"Can I have it?" I asked, taking a few more steps into the kitchen.

Kellen's forehead wrinkled, and he looked up at me like I was just as stupid and ugly as the hair in his fist.

I smiled even though I wanted to cry and held out my hand.

When Kellen didn't budge, I glanced down at the floor and felt my cheeks get hot. "I want to take it home with me, so I can remember you."

Something silky and smooth tickled my palm, and for some reason, that made my heart hurt even more.

Closing my fingers around the wavy ribbon of hair, I swallowed the lump in my throat and glanced back up at Kellen, who was standing directly in front of me now.

With our height difference, he seemed to loom over me, but his face had softened significantly. He wasn't breathing all hard anymore either. That was good. It was easier to look at him when he wasn't so angry. In fact, I couldn't stop looking at him. With his hair gone, I could see his entire face. Maybe for the first time ever. It was breathtaking.

"You're, like, really handsome," I blurted out.

I reached up to touch his new short hair—it looked so soft, like teddy bear fur—but he jerked his head away with a growl.

Snatching my hand back, I watched with shocked tears in my eyes as Kellen stomped past me, through the kitchen and into the living room. Grabbing the front door, which I'd left partially open in case I needed to run from a ghost, Kellen yanked it the rest of the way open and turned to glare at me.

"I said I was sorry!" I yelled, feeling that lump in my throat return, but Kellen just stood there, waiting for me to leave.

"Fine!" I pouted, jutting my chin in the air. "I don't want to play with you anymore anyway. You're mean!"

Then, I threw the hair on the floor and ran past him, making it all the way to the cemetery gate before the tears began to fall.

"Darby!" Kellen called out behind me.

It was only the second word he'd ever said to me, but I acted like I didn't care. I was too proud to let him see how much he'd hurt my feelings. Too concerned that he'd think I was being a baby. I wasn't a baby—I was brave. Brave enough to go into a haunted house to see if he was okay. And I was brave enough to run across that cemetery to get the hell away from him too.

"Darby!"

I tried so hard not to step on the graves, but I couldn't help it. I could hear Kellen right behind me, and he sounded so angry.

Grandpa was right, I thought, pushing my legs to go faster. Feeling the mud and grass squish beneath my bare feet.

"He's pure evil, that one. Ya best to stay away."

I ran straight toward the parking lot, promising God that I would learn every prayer in the Bible if he'd just let me get inside the building before Kellen caught me. But God must have been mad at me too—probably for skipping church—because instead of helping me, he made me trip over my own stupid shoes that I'd left lying on the ground.

I got grass burns on both hands and knees as I tumbled to the ground and slid to a stop, but I didn't have time to check and see if I was bleeding or worry about my mom killing me over the state of my dress. I tried to scramble to my feet, but I wasn't fast enough. The moment I pushed up onto all fours, I was being pushed back down into the dirt.

Grabbing me by my shoulders, Kellen rolled me onto my back and held me down on the ground. I tried to push him away, to kick him, hit him, but he was kneeling next to me, and I couldn't reach him. Not with my legs and not with my arms, which he'd pinned to my sides. The only thing I could do was turn my face away from him as I grunted and struggled and tried not to cry.

Then, two brittle, broken words stole the fight from my body and the breath from my lungs. Two words that landed on my heart like a branding iron, marking me forever.

"Remember me."

He pushed a finger into the hollow of my fist, shoving something silky and soft down inside. Then, he clamped his hand over the opening and squeezed.

"Please. Please come back."

Releasing me, Kellen sat back on his heels and pressed his palms against his eyes. In the sunlight, I could see that there was a scab on the side of his head, almost as big as a nickel. A trail of dried blood ran from the wound, down behind his ear, and along the side of his neck, and when I looked again at his T-shirt, I realized that the bloodstains were mostly below that spot.

Kellen hadn't had a nosebleed.

And he wasn't just upset about the haircut.

Something had happened to him.

Something really, really bad.

DEVIL OF DUBLIN

"Hey." I reached up and tugged on his forearms until he lowered his hands.

He wouldn't look at me though. Instead, he turned his head, wiping his wet cheek on his bloodstained shoulder.

"It's okay."

It was *not* okay—*he* was *not* okay—but Kellen nodded like my words made him feel better anyway. Then, he lay down on the grass next to me. He threw one arm over his face, hiding it in the crook of his elbow, but the other one landed in the grass. Next to mine.

The sides of our pinkie fingers barely touched, but the magic shot up my arm like a bolt of lightning anyway. It forked across my ribs, causing my lungs to stop breathing. My heart to stop beating. I squeezed my eyes shut and reminded myself that it wasn't fairy magic. That it was the Devil's magic. That Grandpa was right about him and I should stay away.

But when I turned my head and stared at the side of his face, I knew it was already too late.

Long black eyelashes spread out over high, smooth cheekbones. A perfectly straight line connected the tip of his elfish nose to a pair of dark, worried eyebrows. And when I looked at his full, frowning lips, all I wanted to do was make them curve the other way.

"Once upon a time, he was God's most beautiful angel."

"I promise," I whispered, hoping God wouldn't hear me. "I promise I won't forget."

Kellen's little finger locked around mine, and another sizzle of lightning seized my chest.

I watched in a breathless state of paralysis as he turned his head and looked at me. With the clear summer sky reflected in them, Kellen's pale gray eyes looked the tiniest bit blue, and for some reason, that put me at ease. It made him seem almost ... human.

Kellen opened his mouth, as if he was about to speak, but then he slammed it shut again and turned to face the cloudless sky.

The lump in his throat slid up and down, as if he were swallowing something, but it must have just been his words.

CHAPTER 5

DARBY
TWO YEARS LATER

I loved a good rainy day back at home. Seeing it get all dark and spooky outside always gave me a little thrill. But in Ireland, where I only had seven days to see Kellen and two of those were travel days, every second I spent staring out of a rain-streaked window felt like an eternity.

I'd done it all night on the plane. I'd done it all day on the bus. And now that we were finally at my grandfather's house, I was doing it in the living room while my relatives sat around, talking about other relatives and drinking something called "Irish lemonade" that they wouldn't even let me try.

At least on the bus, Mom had let me play Angry Birds on her phone.

She said I couldn't be on technology while Aunt Shannon and Uncle Eamonn were over, so instead, I was sitting on the floor, making designs on the rug with Grandpa's poker chips.

Like that was *sooo* much better than Angry Birds.

My mom and Aunt Shannon were sitting on the couch in front of the window. I hadn't been listening to their conversation, but when their voices got low, like they were gossiping, my ears perked up.

"How's Jason doing?" Aunt Shannon whispered, referring to my dad.

My mom sighed. "Same old shite. Drunk. High. Livin' in a bachelor pad downtown with his disgusting bandmates. I won't even let him do his supervised visitation there now that …" I peeked up just in time to see my mom tip her head in my direction.

Aunt Shannon looked at me. Then, she cupped her hands in front of her boobs, and my mom nodded.

Oh my God! I screamed internally. *I'm literally sitting right here!*

"I can only imagine what all goes on inside that house." My mom shook her head. "How was I ever that stupid?"

"Tattoos." Aunt Shannon laughed. "Dimples and tattoos."

God, this is so awkward!

"Oh, speakin' of making babies …" My aunt grinned, pushing her frizzy, bright red hair out of her face. It had been naturally red when she was younger, like my mom's and mine, but ever since I'd known her, she'd been dying it the color of the church's front doors. "Don't tell her I told ya, but …" Aunt Shannon leaned in closer to my mom and placed a hand on her knee. Her fingernails matched her hair. "Maggie and Rob have been tryin' to get pregnant for almost two years now."

Maggie was my cousin. She'd married a British guy and moved to England, which Grandpa had said was a "proper penance for eight hundred years of oppression." I didn't know what that meant, but Aunt Shannon had smacked him on the arm for it.

"I'm sorry to hear that," Mom said, taking a sip of her adult lemonade.

She looked so skinny, sitting there, hunched over her drink, on the couch next to her sister. Where Shannon was plump, my mom was concave. Where she was rosy, my mom was paler than usual.

Maybe she didn't sleep well on the flight either, I thought.

"Do the doctors know what the problem is?" my mom asked.

"Not yet, but I'm startin' to wonder if it's related to what Mam had."

"Ovarian cancer? At her age?"

"No, but maybe she carries the same gene." Aunt Shannon looked toward the kitchen, where Grandpa was, and lowered her voice even more. "Think about it. A good Catholic woman like that … married over forty years and only three children? I think she had problems conceivin' too." My aunt crossed her arms with a scowl. "I'm startin' to think I'm never gonna have grandbabies."

"There it tis." My mom's Irish accent always got stronger when we were in Glenshire. Especially when she was drinking. "I was waitin' to see if you'd find a way to make this about you."

"So, Darby, how's school goin'? Ya have a boyfriend yet?"

I turned my head toward Grandpa's old recliner, where Uncle Eamonn was sitting in his full Garda uniform—that's what they call the police in Ireland. I wondered if he hadn't had a chance to change clothes or if he was just trying to impress his new girlfriend, Sherry. Poor thing was half-sitting, half-standing on the armrest with Eamonn's arm around her waist. It looked super uncomfortable.

Mom and Aunt Shannon had hardly even acknowledged her. I'd heard Aunt Shannon call her a "home-wrecker" before they arrived. But I didn't think she looked like a home-wrecker. A car-wrecker maybe. She was so young; she probably didn't even have a driver's license.

"No, *sir*." I tried not to smirk.

In Georgia, people are so polite that their way of being rude is to call you *sir* or *ma'am* with a subtle, smartass tone.

I made sure to call Uncle Eamonn *sir* every time I saw him.

"Hogwash." He rocked back in Grandpa's recliner, and poor Sherry almost fell off the armrest. "A pretty girl like you? Betcha got two or three lads nippin' at yer heels."

Sherry smiled with her big, glossy lips. "Especially with that hair," she added. "Fellas love redheads."

"Till they marry one!" Uncle Eamonn cough-laughed, slapping his own knee. He made the chair rock so hard that Sherry had to stand up to keep from falling off.

I rolled my eyes while he wasn't looking.

When his laughter finally died down, Eamonn asked, "What're ya, thirteen, fourteen now? You've shot up like a weed since last I saw ya."

"I'm twelve, *sir*."

"Twelve! With a set of knockers like that? Bollocks."

"That'll be quite enough," Grandpa said, frowning at Uncle Eamonn as he shuffled out of the kitchen with a glass of something too brown to be lemonade. The slight tremor in his hand made the ice clink.

"Apologies, lass. Ya best go out and play 'fore ya pick up any more foul language from my eejit son." Grandpa lifted his eyes from me to the window above my head. "Looks like the rain's finally pushed off to England, where it belongs."

Poker chips scattered across the rug as I bolted through the kitchen and out the back door before Mom could tell me that it was too wet to go outside.

Unfortunately, I didn't remember that I was barefoot until I felt the mud squish between my toes.

"Shoot!"

I tiptoed through the mushy yard around the house to the front steps, where my mom had made me leave my new yellow rain boots. Of course, now they were full of water—*thanks, Mom*—which I dumped onto my feet to wash the mud off before yanking them on over my skinny jeans. I would never have worn those boots at home—they were so babyish—but as soon as I'd found out that we were coming to Glenshire, I'd bought a pair with my own allowance.

With my boots on and my mom occupied, I hustled across the backyard toward the gate. I wanted to run so bad, but I'd learned the last time I was there that when you ran through mud, you kicked it up behind you, and I really didn't want to have brown splatter marks on my butt when I finally saw Kellen.

I didn't want to smell like a wet farm animal either, which was why I dodged Sir Timothy McFluffles when I saw him trotting toward me, his wool all soggy and saggy from the rain.

"Sorry, buddy." I grimaced apologetically as I opened the back gate. "I'll give you a pat when I get back, okay?"

I felt bad, rejecting him like that. Not only because he looked so sad when I latched the gate shut behind me, but also because my hair probably didn't look much better than his. I could already see it frizzing up in my peripheral vision.

I pictured Aunt Shannon and shuddered.

Thankfully, my hair was way longer than hers. I pulled it over one shoulder and wove it into a quick braid as I entered the woods and trudged up the hill, but when I went to pull an elastic band off my wrist, I discovered that I didn't have one.

Dang it!

Looking around, I decided to improvise. I tried tying the end of my braid with a fern stem, but it broke on the first knot. Next, I pulled a much stronger-looking vine off a tree, but it was so strong that I couldn't even get it to detach from the ground. I chomped down on it with my teeth and was in the process of trying to saw it free with my molars when someone nearby cleared his throat.

Spinning in the direction of the sound, I glanced up the hill with an expectant grin on my face.

And then I froze.

I'd remembered Kellen as being this willowy, delicate, beautiful thing, like a black butterfly. Rare and exotic. Easy to scare away.

Now, Kellen was the one doing the scaring. His hair was buzzed short, like an Army man. His dark eyebrows were pulled together in an angry V. His once-soft, rosy cheeks were gaunt and sharp. And his scowling mouth looked like it hadn't smiled since the last time I'd worn yellow rain boots. And maybe not even then. I couldn't remember.

But I grinned at him all the same.

"Kellen!" I tossed the vine to the ground, hoping he hadn't seen me trying to gnaw it in half. "I was just coming to find you! Oh my gosh, you're so tall now!"

Two narrowed, steely eyes stared down at me from inside a face that seemed to have been carved out of stone. Where it had once been soft and rounded at the edges it was now angular. Cold. Hard.

I held the bottom of my braid in my hand, feeling like an idiot.

"I just got here a little while ago. We had the worst flight ever. The turbulence was so bad that the lady next to me threw up ..." I heard myself rambling to fill the silence as I walked the rest of the way up the hill.

When we were kids, I would just come up with something to play that didn't require Kellen to talk, but he was a teenager now. What the heck did teenagers like to play?

"So, you're, like, in high school, huh?" I kept my eyes glued to the forest floor to avoid tripping over a tree root *or* Kellen's angry stare. "That must be so cool. I can't wait to be in high school. Middle school is sooo—"

The words dried up in my mouth the second Kellen's dirty combat boots entered my field of vision. I had almost walked right into him. Tipping my head back, I looked up the length of his body and realized that I'd been wrong about him. He wasn't cold. He was blazing hot. I could feel the steam coming off of him like a screaming teakettle.

He was breathing fast too. It reminded me of the last time I'd seen him. At Father Henry's house. God, he'd been so angry ...

"Hey ..." I took an instinctive step backward. "You, uh ... you okay?"

I tried to find that hint of blue behind his icy stare, to remind myself that he was still flesh and blood. But it was gone along with the rest of the boy I remembered.

Kellen shook his head and turned his back on me, stomping over the hill and deeper into the woods.

"Kellen, wait!" I chased after him, careful not to step on the bluebells.

He trudged right through them.

"At least slow down!" I glanced past him to try to see where he was going, and my mouth immediately fell open.

The cottage had become a full-blown house. Bricks and boulders and chunks of old fence post had been cemented together to rebuild the top half of the walls. A ratty blue tarp, held down with rocks, made a watertight roof, and a blue-and-white striped shower curtain hung in the doorway, finishing it off.

Kellen shoved the hanging sheet of plastic to one side as he marched in and jerked it shut behind him. It was the shower curtain equivalent of slamming a door.

Undaunted, I followed him in. "Will you please tell me—"

As soon as the makeshift door closed behind me, we were plunged into darkness. A strip of shady forest light cut across the floor where the shower curtain didn't quite reach the ground, but it was only enough to highlight the edges of a sleeping bag, the legs of a chair, and the black soles of Kellen's boots as they paced back and forth between them.

"Wow." I looked around at the furnishings as my eyes slowly adjusted to the darkness. "It's like a real house now. How did you—"

Something crashed against the wall across from me, causing me to yelp and cover my head.

"Kellen, what is wrong?" I shouted into the darkness. "Just talk to me!"

His answer was a roar so deep and so loud that it shook the plastic door behind me. "You promised!"

I couldn't see his face, but I could see his boots as they came to a stop right in front of me. I could feel the heat radiating off his body. And I could hear his breathing, heavy and fast.

Squeezing my eyes shut, I turned my head to the side with a whimper.

Kellen immediately took a step back. When he cleared his throat, I got the sense that he wanted to say something else, but instead, he turned and began pacing again. Back and forth. From the chair to the sleeping bag.

He'd been sleeping out here.

"Remember me."

"Please come back."

That's what he was so upset about. I hadn't come back the year before.

I pictured Kellen waiting there for me, day after day, all by himself, and my eyes began to water. "I'm so sorry," I whispered. "I wanted to come. I wanted to come so bad, but my mom said she couldn't afford it last year." My voice shook as I watched his adult-sized boots wear a path into the freshly swept dirt floor. "My dad hasn't been paying his child support, and she had a lot of medical expenses come up, so it took her an extra year to save up for our plane tickets."

Kellen's feet stopped moving.

"I wanted to tell you."

Reaching out my hand, I took a step toward him. Into the darkness.

"I tried to find you online, but I don't know your last name."

Step.

"I tried to find the church online too—I thought maybe I could mail you a letter there or find an email address for someone who might know you—but it doesn't have a website."

Step.

"And I couldn't ask my grandpa to give you a message because he doesn't want me hanging out with you."

With one final step, my hand landed on Kellen's hot, heaving back. His T-shirt was damp with sweat, and his shoulder blades rose and fell with every fierce, feral breath he took. I dropped my eyes to the sleeping bag on the floor and wondered how often he'd slept out there by himself. I wondered what had happened to him the day we met, when I found him crying in that same spot with a busted lip. I wondered what had happened the last time I saw him, when he was covered in blood with his hair chopped off. I wondered where his mother was and if she had any idea that she'd left her son in the care of such a horrible person. But mostly, I wondered why I'd never wondered those things before.

Being near him when he was that upset was terrifying—he was like a wild, caged beast, all jerky movements and darting eyes, bared teeth and fiery breath—but I didn't have a choice. A prickly, tingly cord of magic had coiled itself around my heart and was slowly reeling me in.

The inches between us disappeared one by one as I moved to stand in front of him. Without taking my hand off his heaving back, I wrapped my other arm around Kellen's hot, damp, fire-breathing body and closed the distance completely. Pushing up onto my tiptoes, I rested my chin on his shoulder, and as soon as our pounding hearts were lined up, I felt the invisible gears that had been pulling me closer grind to a halt. I could almost hear the *click* of it, like a key fitting into a lock.

"I didn't forget about you," I whispered, squeezing him tighter. "I'll never forget about you."

Kellen didn't move at first, and he quit breathing altogether, but eventually, he raised his fisted hands from his sides and wrapped his arms around my waist. He dipped his chin, pulling me tighter, and when he finally exhaled, his shuddering breath spread over my skin like a warm blanket.

It was the best feeling in the entire world.

We stood there like that for a long time, the side of his neck throbbing against my cheek with every beat of his racing heart. I wanted to turn my head and press my lips to that exact spot.

So … I did.

The moment my mouth met his warm, summer-scented skin, Kellen's breathing stopped again. His entire body went rigid in my arms as I stood there on my tiptoes, kissing his neck.

Slowly pulling away, I felt my cheeks blaze with the fire of a thousand mortified suns.

But then I felt Kellen's head move, and I was the one holding my breath as a pair of soft, hesitant lips pressed against my temple.

That blaze moved into my belly as a grin took over my face. Squeezing Kellen tighter, I planted five more kisses on the side of his neck with a giggle.

I hadn't been lying when I'd told Uncle Eamonn that I didn't have a boyfriend.

But if he asked me again, I might have to.

"Come on," I said, grabbing his hand and leading him out of the cottage before I did something really crazy, like kiss him on the lips.

Before I could push through the door tarp, Kellen's long arm reached out and swept it to the side, holding it open for me. I smiled so big and blushed so hard as I walked through that I couldn't even look at him. Kellen was in high school! I had to be cool. *Cool, cool, cool.*

"So, what do you do around here for fun besides build stuff?" I asked, hoping to sound mature or bored or something.

When Kellen didn't answer me, I turned so I could read his face and immediately wished that I hadn't.

His eyes, which had been so hard and hateful moments ago, were shut tight. His dark eyebrows furrowed in frustration as his neck strained and swallowed, hard enough for me to hear it.

I'd asked him a question, and he was trying to answer me.

My soaring heart plummeted back down to earth, landing in a puddle of mud with a *splat*.

It suddenly made perfect sense why he'd retreated to the darkness of the cottage before speaking to me earlier. He hadn't wanted me to see *this*. The few words Kellen had spoken to me in the past seemed almost accidental. Like he'd been relaxed or upset enough to lose control, but watching him struggle to speak on purpose was heartbreaking. As much as I wanted to hear his voice again, I wanted to put him out of his misery more.

Reaching out, I took his hand. His fingers didn't feel right. They were knobby in places, and one of them didn't bend correctly. But he squeezed my hand anyway.

"It's okay," I said, sliding my thumb across his rough knuckles. "You can just show me."

DEVIL OF DUBLIN

Kellen nodded, his shoulders sagging in both relief and defeat.

That made me feel even worse.

Without letting go of my hand, Kellen led me down the hill along a path that he must have traveled a thousand times since I'd been there last. It was only wide enough for one person, so I walked behind him, acorns crunching beneath our boots like gravel.

Even though the rain had stopped, a canopy of gray clouds still hung heavy above the trees. There was no sunlight dancing on the water when we approached the lake that time. Just thick fog and drifting, swirling leaves that must have been blown off their branches in the storm.

Just before we got to the thorny blackberry bushes that grew along the edge of the lake, Kellen stopped and turned toward me with a look on his face that filled my stomach with fluttery black butterflies. His lips were slanted in an almost smile, and his eyes sparkled with mischief as they darted from me to the giant tree next to us.

I followed his gaze to where an old wooden ladder was leaning against the trunk. Above it, hanging from a branch so high that I didn't know how any human could have possibly tied it, was a long, thick piece of rope, knotted at the end.

Kellen arched a single eyebrow, and that was all it took to seal my fate.

That look would have convinced me to jump off a cliff. Into an active volcano.

But not until he did it first.

Sensing my willingness, Kellen smiled—really smiled—and it made all the trouble I was going to be in when I came home soaking wet totally worth it.

I put my hands on my hips in defiance even though I couldn't help but beam back at him. "I didn't say I was going to do it."

But Kellen just sat on the ground with that smile on his face and began unlacing his boots. Then, he glanced up at me before intentionally dropping his gaze to my feet.

"Ugh, fine," I huffed. Leaning against the tree, I yanked off one wet rubber rain boot, followed by the other. "But if I die—"

Kellen's black T-shirt landed on the ground in front of me, and I suddenly became *very* aware that he was now shirtless, just a few feet to my left.

Don't look. Don't look. Don't—

Ziiiiiiip.

Out of the corner of my eye, I saw Kellen's body bend at the waist. Then, a few seconds later, a pair of worn-out, ripped jeans landed on top of his shirt.

Oh my God.

A flash of pale skin and plaid boxers passed in front of me, but my eyes were still focused completely on the pile of clothes lying at my feet.

The ladder beside me creaked and groaned as Kellen swiftly climbed to the top.

I was paralyzed by indecision. I needed to watch him do it, so I could learn how to do it too, but staring at Kellen in his underwear just felt so ... *wrong*.

The creaking stopped, and Kellen cleared his throat.

Oh my God, I have to look.

With a gulp, I turned and squinted up at the nearly naked boy on the ladder, and ... it wasn't so bad. It was like he was wearing a bathing suit. I saw boys in their bathing suits all the time at the pool in my apartment complex. This was no. Big. Deal.

Kellen held up the rope, showing me that it had a big knot in the bottom and another one about five feet above that. Grabbing the higher knot with both hands, he jumped away from the ladder, landing with both feet on the bottom knot as the rope swung out over the lake. As soon as he was out as far as the rope would go, Kellen let go of the rope, arching backward and doing a perfect backflip before landing feetfirst in the water.

A hole appeared in the fog where he'd landed, getting bigger and bigger until he finally broke through that spot again, this time from underneath. The water rippled away from him as he shook his head from side to side. It was the same move the boys at my apartment pool did to get the wet hair out of their faces, but Kellen didn't have long hair anymore. All he had left was the habit.

That made me sad.

But when he glanced over at me and grinned in triumph, that feeling went away pretty quickly.

I tried not to stare as he climbed out of the lake on the other side of the tree where the blackberry bushes didn't grow, but I couldn't help it. Kellen had ab muscles now. Ab muscles!

Maybe it's just 'cause he's skinny. I'd probably have ab muscles too if I were that skinny.

Oh God, he's going to see how not *skinny I am.*

And those ugly purple stretch marks on my hips.

And the ugly cotton sports bra I wore on the plane so that I wouldn't have to sleep in a real bra. Oh my God!

I should just keep my clothes on.

But then they'll get wet, and Mom will know I went in the lake, and I'm not supposed to go near the lake.

Screw it.

"Stay over there," I called out, standing on the opposite side of the tree. "And turn around!"

I could have sworn I heard a tiny snicker as I peeled off my own T-shirt and jeans, dropping them on top of Kellen's pile. I didn't want to get them dirty and give my mom one more thing to be mad about when I got home.

"Don't look, okay?"

I stared down at my body before hoisting it up onto the ladder and sighed. I missed my old body so much. My new one bled and ached and swelled and stunk if I forgot to wear deodorant, but what I hated most about it was how much people stared at it. The boys at the pool. The girls at the pool. The teachers at my school, who scolded me for wearing tank tops and measured the length of my shorts with a ruler. Grown men, like Uncle Eamonn. In my old body, I was just Darby. In my new body, I was just a body.

At least my ugly cotton bra and panties matched. I didn't know why, but that made me feel better.

The ladder wobbled and swayed against the tree trunk as I began to climb. I made it up to the third rung from the top before I realized that, as much as the thought of Kellen watching me climb a ladder in my underwear made me want to die, the thought of falling off and actually doing it seemed *slightly* worse.

So, I sucked it up and asked for help.

Or at least, I tried to ask for help, but by the time I stammered, "Uh, Kellen, do you think maybe you could—" he'd already read my mind, sprinted over, and braced the ladder against the tree with both hands.

I glanced down at him, mortified by the proximity of his face to my ass, but Kellen wasn't looking up at me at all. His eyes were fixed on the ground in front of him.

"Thanks." I smiled.

I was shorter than him, so for me to reach the top knot on the rope, I was going to have to climb all the way to the top. But the ladder felt a million times more stable, so with a deep breath, I wrapped my arms around the tree trunk—there wasn't enough ladder left to grab with my hands—and stepped onto the second-highest rung. The ladder shifted an inch to the right under my weight, but Kellen steadied it immediately.

Then, I exhaled and did it again.

As soon as I made it to the top, I realized three things in rapid succession: one, there was no way I was climbing back down; two, there was no way I could reach the rope without first letting go of the tree; and three, there was no way I could fall from that height and not break at least one bone.

"Kellen?" I squeezed my eyes shut and gripped the tree tighter. "I ... I think I'm stuck."

I felt the ladder move underneath me, just a bit, before I heard the unmistakable sound of Kellen's feet crunching on the leaves and acorns at the bottom of the tree.

I opened my mouth to scream at him to come back, but I shut it again when I felt the ladder sink an inch deeper into the ground. It shuddered and shook with every step Kellen climbed, and when it stopped, I felt something damp and rough slap against the side of my body.

Glancing down, I found Kellen standing halfway up the ladder, holding a long, mossy stick above his head. His face was inches away from the backs of my thighs, but he wasn't looking at me at all. Instead, his eyes were trained on the rope he'd hooked and pulled over to me with the end of his stick.

The top knot of the rope was now only a few inches away from my shoulder. All I had to do was reach out and grab it.

I can do this, I thought, staring at that twisted hunk of twine. Actually, *I have to do this. It's literally my only way down.*

I swallowed hard as I stared out over the sea of blackberry bushes between me and the lake.

Letting go of the tree trunk with my left hand, I reached up and grabbed the rope, just above the top knot.

So far, so good.

Then, I blew out a breath and grabbed the rope with my other hand.

And everything after that happened in slow motion.

As soon as I let go of the tree, the rope started to pull me away from it. In a panic, I jumped off the ladder and managed to get both feet onto the bottom knot, but I only had half a second to celebrate that accomplishment before I realized that I hadn't pushed off hard enough. I'd barely swung out past the blackberry bushes before I was careening back in the other direction.

Only now, I was spinning.

Just before I hit the tree, I caught a glimpse of Kellen, standing at the top of the ladder with his arm stretched out. I was so relieved to see him, so confident that he was going to save me—and so disoriented and dizzy in general—that I completely forgot to brace for impact.

I slammed into the unyielding oak hard enough to knock the air out of my lungs.

And the knot out of my hands.

By the time I realized I was falling, I was already halfway to the ground.

The last thing I saw before a million tiny thorns ripped into my flesh was Kellen's horrified face as he looked down at me from the top of the ladder.

Holding an empty rope.

CHAPTER 6

KELLEN

One second. That was all it took for Darby to go from being just within my reach to being ripped out of it completely.

Watching her slip through my fingers was a nightmare, but it was nothing compared to the sounds of her fall. A shocked scream, branches breaking, hair tearing, skin shredding. But the worst was what I heard after the final *thump*.

Silence.

Her name burst through the iron door in my throat as I leaped off the ladder and scrambled to the place where her body lay motionless between two blackberry bushes. Her head had hit the ground, but her long red hair hung suspended around her face like a lion's mane, tangled in the thorny branches that had broken her fall. Her arms were caught in the bushes as well, weeping from a thousand crimson slashes. And her eyes, always so bright and full of life, were now shuddered by two pale, purple-tinged lids.

"Darby!" I shouted again, reaching into the brambles to extract her limbs from the thorns that were now ripping my own hands and arms to shreds.

With a grunt, I lifted her limp body off the ground, cradling the back of her head in my hand. Her face emerged through the tangled web of hair caught in the bushes on either side of her, but the bushes didn't want to let go. It was as if they were trying to keep her for themselves.

I felt the fire inside of me roar to life. Felt it burn through the iron, felt it turn my tears into steam and flood my veins with power and rage and the urge to kill.

"Let … gooooo!" I growled, pulling with all my might until the branches bowed to my fucking will. Until they gave me back my girl.

Even after I stumbled backward, clutching her limp body to my chest, the fire inside of me grew. It wanted to destroy something. It wanted to burn the fucking woods to the ground. It wanted to scorch the earth to make it pay for what it had done to her. For what *I* had done to her.

I was breathing too fast. The ground shifted beneath my feet, and the trees began to spin. I needed to calm down. I wouldn't be any help to her if I blacked out. I needed to *think*.

Think, fucker! Think!

The answer came to me as a wordless knowing. A deep blue beckoning that mobilized my body with a single destination in mind.

The lough.

The lough would put out the fire.

Cradling Darby in my arms, I stumbled around to the other side of the tree where the bushes didn't grow and waded out into the water. I could hardly see the surface through the fog, which was thicker than it had ever been. The mist summoned me with slow, curling fingers, and I followed, letting it draw me in deeper.

By the time the water was up to my waist, I could no longer see the shore in any direction. It was as if a cloud had fallen out of the sky and swallowed us up, leaving my rage and panic behind.

"Darby," I whispered, shocked to find that even my throat had relaxed. The word had blown through the open iron door as effortlessly as a summer breeze. So, I tried it again. "Darby, look."

When she didn't wake up, I waded in deeper, sinking below the surface until the water rose up past her shoulders. When it grazed her chin, Darby's lips parted on a startled gasp. Her eyes locked on to mine—wide and green and surrounded by freckles—and the relief I saw in them lit a new fire within me. A flickering glow, like the flame of a candle, deep in my godforsaken soul.

Darby's head turned from left to right, sending ripples out in every direction as her long, tangled hair swept across the surface of the water.

"Where are we?" She marveled, reaching out to touch the fog as if it were whipped cream that she could dip a finger into.

"The lough," I said, liking the sound of my own voice. But I liked the look on Darby's face when she heard it even more.

Cradling her nearly weightless body with one arm, I reached up to brush a strand of wet hair away from her face, but Darby grabbed my wrist before I could touch her.

"Kellen, your arm."

I glanced down and watched as every nick, scratch, and cut on both of our arms revealed itself, filling with blood that, just a moment ago, the water had been washing away.

"Does it hurt?" I asked, hoping she would answer for the both of us. I was too busy staring at her delicate fingers wrapped around my wrist to feel anything even close to pain.

Darby shook her head and turned my hand over, staring at a particularly deep thorn scratch on my palm.

Lifting her own hand, she found a cut in the same spot. Hers was shorter but just as deep.

Her eyes lifted to mine, round and sweet, and without a word, without a plan, without a clue as to why we would do such a thing, Darby and I pressed our bloody palms together.

And kissed.

The moment her lips touched mine, the same still blue presence that had beckoned me into the water returned. It wrapped around my mind like the tail of a cat, warm and soft and cautiously curious.

Then, it spoke.

"*Is fíor bhur ngrá*," it purred. "*Tugaim mobheannacht daoibh.*"

I didn't know what it meant, but it filled me with joy. I'd never felt such euphoria in my entire miserable waste of a life. It overwhelmed me, bringing tears to my eyes as I held Darby closer, threading my bloody fingers through hers. I held my breath as we kissed, hoping I could stretch that moment out forever. I would have died that way quite happily had it not been for Darby's startled gasp.

"Kellen, look."

Reluctantly, I opened my eyes. Then, I blinked and opened them wider.

The fog was gone. The clouds had parted. And everything from the sky to the water to the surface of Darby's eyes was streaked with oranges, pinks, yellows, and purples. She smiled, and that same rosy pink flooded her cheeks as well.

Then something flashed across her face, a realization, and that smile disappeared just as quickly. "I have to be home before dark," she said, dropping her chin. "I wish I didn't have to go."

Pressing my lips to her forehead, I soaked up the last few seconds of the best moment of my life. Then, with a full, heavy heart, I set Darby back on her feet.

I hated the way my arms felt when she wasn't in them.

Without letting go of her hand, I led Darby through the sunset-stained water toward the edge of the lough. And when I glanced back at her, she was still blushing.

I wanted so badly to say something, to tell her how much she meant to me, but I couldn't find the words. Only, for once, it wasn't because they were trapped inside of me. It was because they simply didn't exist.

At least, not in this language.

CHAPTER 7

DARBY
EIGHT YEARS LATER

"Thank you for comin', everyone. As you all know, we are gathered here today to celebrate the life and mourn the loss of a beloved member of our congregation, Mr. Patrick O'Toole."

The priest behind the podium was a stranger to me. I knew he would be. I'd read the article about Father Henry enough times to recite it from memory. But seeing someone else standing in his place, talking about my grandfather like he knew him, just felt wrong.

Glenshire felt wrong.

But then again, so did the rest of my life.

I tried not to look at the closed casket in front of the podium—polished and gleaming, even under that gray February sky—as I lowered my gaze to the scaly red rash spreading up the ring finger of my left hand. The cause of that rash had been polished and gleaming too, when John slipped it on my finger and asked me to marry him a few days before. But by the time we'd arrived in Glenshire, the gold had already started to tarnish.

My skin seemed to be eating it, or it was eating my skin. I couldn't tell which. All I knew was that the itch had gotten ten times worse since we'd landed in Ireland, and I was grateful for it. The pain served as a distraction. One I desperately needed.

The second I swiveled that embarrassingly large diamond around backward and began rubbing the enflamed skin with my thumb, John noticed and swatted at my hand.

"You're making it worse," he whispered without taking his eyes off of Father Doherty.

I glanced over at him, and it struck me how out of place he looked there. Normally, John owned any room he entered—that was part of his allure—but there in the grass, surrounded by sheep farmers in woolen sweaters and paperboy hats, John's perfectly tailored BOSS suit and three-hundred-dollar silk tie looked almost alien.

If he could feel me staring, he didn't show it. He didn't show much of anything. Ever. They'd probably taught him that in law school.

"It was my humble honor to be there, by Pat's side, when he passed," Father Doherty continued, reclaiming my attention. "The nurses at the hospital had called to inform me that his time was near, so I went to his bedside. There, I blessed him and read him a few passages from the good book. He was in and out of consciousness, but he did manage to say a few words there at the end. With his eyes closed and his breathing shallow, Pat whispered to me, 'Father, tell the folks back home ... that I pissed in all their wells, so they won't be too broken up about my passing.'"

Everyone laughed, except for John.

"Aye." Father Doherty smiled, wiping a bittersweet tear from his eye. "That was our Pat. Quick-witted and always thinkin' of others, up until his very last breath. I imagine his wife, Mary Catherine, and daughter, Elizabeth—who preceded him in death—are gathered round him, laughin' over one of his knee-slappers right now."

DEVIL OF DUBLIN

Father Doherty glanced over at me with soft, sympathetic eyes as I clutched the cardboard box in my arms a little tighter. I'd forgotten I was even holding it. I'd been clinging to my mother's ashes for so long that I didn't even notice the weight of her anymore.

She'd passed away less than a year after my last visit. Ovarian cancer, same as my grandmother. I remembered her being tired all the time, and she'd seemed to be getting skinnier by the day, but she just dismissed it as stress. By the time I finally convinced her to go to the doctor, it was too late. Six months later, she was gone, and I was being dropped off at my deadbeat dad's apartment by a social worker, carrying a garbage bag full of my belongings.

Instead of asking her thirteen-year-old to host a funeral, my mother had left instructions for me to hold on to her ashes until I was old enough to bring them back here, to Glenshire.

I was twenty now, but I still didn't feel old enough.

I leaned against John's side, needing his comfort more than ever, and blinked back tears of relief when his strong arm wrapped around my shoulders.

For so long after Mom had died, I'd felt alone, adrift ... afraid of my own shadow. But then John came along and changed everything.

When we first met, I was a struggling eighteen-year-old waitress at a trendy steakhouse downtown, and he was the handsome thirty-year-old corporate attorney who came in for happy hour every Friday with the guys from his law firm. We had nothing in common. He came from old money. I came from an old mattress on the floor of my dad's bachelor pad. He'd graduated from Emory Law. I took the subway to Georgia State and could only afford to go there because I'd gotten a scholarship. His vocabulary included words like *mergers* and *acquisitions*. Mine included sophisticated terms, such as *bejankety* and *thirst trap*. But for some reason, John decided to take me in. My friends said, some more politely than others, that he was just looking for a "pretty little trophy wife"—someone who would kiss his ass and do as he said and look good on his arm at corporate events, until he decided to trade me in for a younger version, of course—and I couldn't say that they were wrong. John wasn't exactly Mr. Romance. But compared to the life I'd been living before, it was an offer I couldn't refuse.

"Pat was a man of many words, most of them about himself—"

The crowd laughed again, deep and hearty, bringing my thoughts back to Grandpa.

"So, to honor his gift of gab, who'd like to come up and say a few words of their own?"

A blubbering cough-snort erupted from somewhere up front. Uncle Eamonn stepped forward, lumbering past his father's casket like it was a couch or a coffee table. Chin up. Belly out. He was still on the Dublin police force, but he was a detective now, which made sense. His criminal-chasing days were definitely behind him.

Acorns crunched under Father Doherty's feet as he moved to stand beneath the oak tree behind the podium, giving Eamonn plenty of space. I couldn't tell if he was just being polite or if he disliked the man as much as I did. Eamonn had never been my favorite person, but ever since he'd found out about Grandpa's will, he'd been extra *unpleasant*.

My uncle cleared what sounded like a decade's worth of cigar tar from his throat before running a liver-spotted hand through what little hair he had left. "Ladies. Fellas. I thank ya for comin'. I just want you fine people to know that if anybody here's lookin' to procure some additional sheep, I'm sellin' the oul fella's flock for a fair price. Da's farm isn't gonna run itself, and the new *caretaker*"—his shifty eyes landed on me—"couldn't tell ya the difference between a wether and a yow."

The crowd snickered but quickly fell silent once they realized that the person he was talking about was standing a few feet away, holding her dead mother in a cardboard box.

Beside me, John cleared his throat. My cheeks heated as everyone in attendance turned to look at the "Yank" in the suit.

"With all due respect …" John said, dropping his arm from around my shoulders and standing to his full height. He was only about five foot nine, but with his aggressively perfect posture, you'd think he was eight feet tall. "The will clearly states that Darby Collins is the sole inheritor of Mr. O'Toole's property, including the flock thereon. Should anyone wish to *procure* anything, they'll need to contact her or myself directly."

"And who the feck might you be? Her babysitter?" Eamonn scoffed. "Ya look old enough to be her da."

"I'm Ms. Collins's attorney, John David Oglethorpe, *Esquire*."

Oh my God.

"Her attorney, ya say? Well, the girl ain't got two pennies to rub together, so I think we all know what she's been payin' ya with." Eamonn's eyes darted around the crowd, but this time, they were polite enough to keep their laughter to a quiet snicker.

"He's my fiancé," I blurted out, trying to come to John's defense or possibly mine, but nobody seemed to hear me.

"Well, Mr. *Esquire*, isn't there some law in yer fancy law books about *children* not bein' allowed to own property?"

"There is, but that law doesn't apply here because Ms. Collins is an adult."

"If she's an adult, I'm the bleedin' Queen of England." Eamonn grasped the belt holding up his impressive beer gut as he let out a humorless chuckle.

Then, his slimy gaze slithered back over to me.

"Tell me somethin'," he said, nodding in John's direction. "This arsehole ask ya to marry him before *or after* he found out about yer little inheritance?"

"Stop it, Eamonn! Honestly!" my aunt Shannon snapped from the front row. Her frizzy red hair bounced with every syllable as her husband, my uncle Fred, wrapped a protective arm around her shoulders.

My two cousins, now in their thirties, stood on either side of them, clutching their own children.

"Da gave that house to Darby for a reason." She dropped her voice on that last part. "The poor child was left with nothin'."

"I'm his only son!" Eamonn shoved a hand in the direction of Grandpa's farm. "That property's my birthright, goddamn it."

Father Doherty stepped up to the podium and placed his hand over the microphone, but it did little to muffle his stern warning. "Eamonn, if ya can't behave yourself, I'll be askin' ya to leave."

"Bollocks!" Eamonn threw his arms up and stomped off toward the parking lot, giving John and me a murderous glare the entire way.

John lifted his chin defiantly.

With a heavy sigh, Father Doherty shook his head in a silent apology. "Would anyone *else* like to say a few words?" He gave my aunt a gentle smile. "Shannon?"

Her red frizz swished from side to side.

"Very well then." He nodded. "I think we could all use a stiff drink after that, so without further ado, let us clasp hands and bow our heads in prayer."

Casting a sad smile over her shoulder, Shannon extended her hand to me. I took it and squeezed gently, watching in devastation as her puffy pink eyes drifted from my face down to the cardboard box I was clutching like a teddy bear.

"Into your hands, O Lord, we humbly entrust Patrick Murphy O'Toole. Please welcome him into your kingdom as we have all welcomed him into our hearts. Please help us find comfort in our sadness, certainty in our doubt, and the courage to go on …"

With one last squeeze, Shannon dropped my hand and turned to face Father Doherty. She then wrapped an arm around her daughter, Maggie, who curled into her side and let out a quiet sob.

It was as if there were a spotlight shining on the two of them, highlighting everything I was missing. Unconditional love. Comfort. Kindness. It had been years since anyone had held me like that. I would have killed to have someone do it again.

Even if they didn't mean it.

With my head bowed in prayer, I glanced over at John. He looked as handsome and intense as ever with his hands clasped in front of him and his dark brown eyebrows furrowed in concentration. It looked as if he were hanging on Father Doherty's every word—until I noticed the glowing screen discreetly hidden between his cupped palms. John's scowl deepened as his thumbs began tapping out what was most likely a strongly worded reply to a work email.

Father Doherty said a few more beautiful things, but I didn't hear them. In fact, the entire funeral seemed to disappear as my gaze drifted to the far-right corner of the cemetery.

I'd been trying not to look. I'd read about the fire. I knew what I would find. But in that moment, my need for someone to hold me was stronger than my need to stay in denial.

On the edge of the woods, where a squat little house had once sat like an old stump, stood a new, modern cottage, all clean lines and square angles. The stucco was bright white. The door was Popsicle red. And the spotless windows sparkled like eyes in a smiling face.

It wasn't the same house, but I searched the windows anyway, desperate, hoping beyond all reason that I'd find the face of a black-haired boy peering out from between a pair of nicotine-stained curtains. But all traces of him—and the horrors that had happened there—were just ... gone.

There were only three people who'd ever really cared about me. Whose touches had made me feel better instead of worse.

And I felt like I was burying all three of them on the same damn day.

I glanced at the spot next to my grandmother's grave, where Kellen had chased me down all those years ago and begged me not to forget about him. But even that patch of grass was gone, gouged from the earth to make way for the rest of my loved ones. And at the foot of it, mocking my pain, was a shiny new headstone.

BB EASTON

Patrick Murphy O'Toole
1940 ~ 2021
Devoted husband, beloved father, terrible braggart.
"Early to bed, early to rise, makes a man healthy, wealthy and wise."

"Darby?"

"Hmm?" I blinked over at Father Doherty, who had come down from the podium and was now standing next to my grandfather's casket.

The rest of the crowd had thinned significantly, and the ones who were left had formed loose groups on the edges of the cemetery. I found John standing with my aunt and her family. He shook my cousin David's hand with the enthusiasm of a politician. David was a real estate agent in Killarney, so he was probably just trying to work a deal. I had a sheep farm to sell, after all.

"The ashes, love."

"Oh." I looked down at the box in my arms. At the little heart stickers I'd put on top when I was in ninth grade. At the corners I'd crudely reinforced with duct tape when it had started showing signs of wear. I tried to swallow the lump in my throat as I cast another glance at John. I couldn't do this by myself. I didn't want to.

I sent him a telepathic plea for help, but it went completely unreceived. Instead, John laughed and clapped my cousin on the shoulder as I prepared to say good-bye to the most important people in my life.

With shaky hands, I began to scratch and gouge at the brittle, yellowed seven-year-old strip of tape holding the top of the box shut, but Father Doherty stopped me before I could get very far.

"Let's do this, dear."

He reached for the box, and I froze as he gently plucked the last connection I had to my mother out of my arms. The pain I felt was so sharp and so deep that it was as if he'd reached into my body and pulled out one of my organs. Something vital. Something I didn't know how to live without. He smiled sadly as he carried my spleen, my liver, my still-beating heart over to the polished wooden casket.

I watched in silent agony as he lifted the lid. Father Doherty positioned himself so that I couldn't see Grandpa's face, but I had a perfect view of his arm and bluish, freckled hand as the priest lifted it and wrapped it around the box containing my mother.

"There now," he said, closing the lid and turning back toward me. "She's come home."

The kindness on his face was unbearable. I squeezed my eyes shut, causing the tears that had been building to spill down my cheeks as a brutal sob racked my body. I wrapped my newly empty arms around myself, needing something to hold now that my mother was gone.

Needing someone to hold *me*.

"Hey, Darb?" a polished, accent-free American voice called out from behind me.

Oh God.

I frantically tried to wipe my tears away as John's approaching footsteps grew louder. I couldn't let him see me like that.

Or maybe I couldn't bear to see the indifference on his face when he did.

"Come on. Everybody's going to the pub for the reception."

I tried desperately to regain my composure, but I was too far gone. The tears were falling faster now, and the more I tried to breathe normally, the worse I hyperventilated.

"I'm in the process of convincing your cousin to list the house for us commission-free, as a family favor, so we need to at least make an appearance." His tone was blunt. Factual. Cold.

And it was getting closer.

My eyes locked on a small gap in the trees next to the house.

"Are you even listening to me?"

The sharp edge to his voice was my only warning. I knew what would happen if I defied him after that, but I couldn't make myself turn around.

Instead, I took a step forward, away from my future and straight toward my past.

Then, I took another one.

"Darby. I'm talking to you."

I kept walking, faster and faster, every step making me crave fifteen more.

"Where the hell do you think you're going? Hey!"

I heard John's heavy footfalls quicken in the grass behind me, so I grabbed the hem of my black shift dress with both hands, hiked it up over my thighs ...

And I ran.

CHAPTER 8

DARBY

"Where do ya s'pose she's goin'?"
"I haven't a baldy notion."
"Darby! Get back here!"
"Mad as a box of frogs, that one."
"Can you blame her? Poor child."
"Darrrr-byyyy!"

The murmured voices of the villagers, mixed with John's angry American shouts, only pushed my legs to pump harder. Kicking off my heels, I broke into a sprint, relishing the cool grass beneath my bare feet. It was the only thing about Glenshire that felt the same.

Even the trail that led from Kellen's house to the cottage was gone—a realization I made as soon as I darted into the woods and found myself confronted with a dozen possible paths and none of them his. But I kept running anyway, head down, eyes on the ground immediately in front of me, until my toes caught on a tree root hidden under a bed of leaves.

I stumbled and nearly fell, landing shoulder-first against the tree whose root had just injured me. Panting, I rolled so that my back was against the trunk and lifted my foot to make sure it wasn't injured. It wasn't. My lungs, on the other hand, were screaming.

I closed my eyes and tilted my head back, waiting for my breathing to return to normal. The crisp, damp air chilled the back of my throat on the way down.

I'd never been to Glenshire in the winter before. I didn't like it. Instead of being green and lush and buzzing with nature sounds, the woods were silent. Brittle. Gray.

It was as if all of Ireland were mourning with me.

The thought was oddly comforting.

When I was finally ready to keep going, I pushed off of the tree, only to find that I had no idea which way to go. Nothing looked the same as I remembered. All I knew was which direction I had come from, and I was definitely not going back there.

Careful not to step on any more roots or rocks or pine cones, I walked slowly in what I assumed was the direction of our old playhouse. I just needed to see it again. I needed evidence that I wasn't crazy. Evidence that Kellen, and everything we'd shared, had been real.

I'd wanted to come see it the second we landed yesterday, but after renting a car, driving to the lawyer's office, signing the paperwork for the house, and grabbing dinner, it had been well after dark by the time we'd finally made it to Grandpa's house.

I couldn't stand being at the house without Grandpa. It felt haunted. Other than whatever Eamonn had taken before we arrived, his things were all right where he'd left them. His reading glasses on the kitchen table. His toothbrush by the bathroom sink. His secret stash of biscuits in a metal tin by the bed. His sheep, which I had no idea how to take care of. Luckily, his kindhearted neighbors had been coming over to tend to them since he'd passed.

Seeing them again had made me smile though. They were still so cute with those bright blue spots.

Then, I lifted my eyes and saw something that made me smile even more.

The cottage.

DEVIL OF DUBLIN

My pace quickened as I jogged toward the little stone house, marveling at how complete it was.

Kellen must have found matching stone. And figured out how to make a proper thatched roof! Oh my God, it's so adorable! I could just live here forev—

At the sound of my footsteps crashing through the otherwise silent woods, a face emerged from the doorway, but it was *not* the one I'd been hoping to see.

An old woman with eyes like spoiled milk glared at me through a parted curtain of long, scraggly gray hair.

I recognized her immediately. Not that I'd ever seen her before, but my grandfather had told me stories. Looking past the cottage, I realized now how close I was to the lake.

The *wrong* side of the lake.

Gulp.

I was staring. I'd stopped running, and now, I was just staring at that poor old woman, and there was no such thing as witches, and she was *not* going to eat me *or* turn me into a toad or any of the other awful things Grandpa had told me. He'd just been trying to keep me from venturing too deep into the woods, and now I was being rude to a very real, probably very sweet person because of it.

"Hello," I said, my voice hoarse from all the crying and running and the cold. "Sorry if I ... disturbed you. I just got lost for a minute and thought I was somewhere else."

"Aye," she said, her cloudy bluish eyes sizing me up. "Ya been lost a lot longer than that now, haven't cha? Come in, child. Let's get ya out of the cold."

She stepped out of the doorway completely and gestured for me to enter, resting her weight on a knotty, old tree branch she'd repurposed as a cane. Her frail body was shrouded in yards of tattered, dust-colored linen, and a patchwork shawl—which appeared to be made out of a dozen or so small animal pelts—rested on her stooped, rounded shoulders.

My initial fear was quickly overshadowed by a deep, slack-jawed sense of wonder.

How long had she been living out there?

How had she been living out there?

I registered the sound of leaves crunching under my feet again as curiosity got the better of me.

"I'm Darby," I said, pausing to make eye contact just before I crossed the threshold.

"I know who ya are, child," she said as I passed, her voice even raspier than mine.

Inside, the cottage looked similar to the one Kellen and I used to play in. One dark, round room full of furniture made from stumps and reclaimed wood, a pallet of blankets on the hard dirt floor, and only the most essential household objects. But one thing our cottage definitely did *not* have was yards and yards of string crisscrossed overhead with the hides of tiny woodland creatures hanging from it like some kind of macabre clothesline. I ducked to avoid walking face-first into a skinned squirrel, realizing a moment too late that coming in might have been a terrible mistake.

The only light in the room came from a few square windows, the crack beneath the door—which had just shut behind me with an ominous creak—and a small fire glowing in the corner, heating a black cauldron-like pot.

Holy shit. She really is gonna turn me into a toad.

Gesturing to a tree stump next to the fire, the old woman simply said, "Sit."

I did and decided that being a toad wouldn't be so bad as long as I got to keep sitting next to that fire. I hadn't realized just how painfully cold my feet and hands had gotten.

"Thank you for inviting me in." I smiled weakly, holding one foot and both hands up to the flames. "Obviously, I hadn't planned on getting lost in the woods today."

When she said nothing, I looked over and found her shaking her head at me in disapproval, a scornful frown tugging even harder at her already-downturned mouth. She wasn't looking at my face though. Her judgmental gaze was aimed directly at my hands.

I glanced down and noticed immediately what must have caught her attention.

DEVIL OF DUBLIN

Crap.

Folding my hands together in my lap, I covertly slid the diamond around to the inside of my finger, but the motion made me wince from the itchy, hot rash beneath the band.

The woman took two sure-footed steps toward me and pointed her cane directly at my lap. "Take it off," she demanded, her thin, wrinkled lips turning white as they formed a hard line.

"I ... I should go." I went to stand, but my host only crowded me more, preventing my exit.

"You've got some nerve, ya know that?"

"I'm ... sorry if I've offended you somehow," I sputtered, trying to figure out the path of least resistance to the door. "I'll just see myself out."

"It's not me you ought to be worried about offendin', dear. It's *her*."

That gave me pause.

I looked around just to verify that we were in fact alone. "Her *who?*"

The old woman pointed her cane at the nearest window and tapped it on the leaded glass. "Saoirse."

"Sur-sha?"

"Aye. The lady in the lough." The old woman smirked. "She is none too happy with you." There was an amused tone to her voice, like this was prime woodland gossip.

Part of me thought she was crazy, but the other part of me—the *Irish* part, the part that had been taught to believe in fairies and witches and lake spirits—forced me to stay and hear her out.

"Can you tell me more about this *Sur-sha* woman? I don't believe I've ever met her, but—"

"Ah, but ya have." Her eyes widened with excitement as she reached out and snatched my wrist.

I gasped as her cold, bony fingers seized me, holding my left hand up into the light. "She gave ya this." Shoving my ring up to the next knuckle, the woman tapped the three freckles just below it with her knobby index finger. "*This* be yer weddin' ring, child. Not that atrocious thing."

She released my hand, but I kept it raised, staring at the perfectly round, evenly spaced freckles that cut across my ring finger in a dotted line.

"You really don't know, do ya?"

My eyebrows pulled together as I shook my head from side to side.

With a huff and a lot of effort, the woman lowered herself onto a tree stump in the center of the cottage. Her long gray hair fell around her hunched shoulders, and in the firelight, I could see glimmers of the beauty she must have once been. High cheekbones, made higher with the gauntness of age. A square Irish jaw, like my mother and aunt. Long, feathery white eyelashes. And a mischievous twinkle in her cloudy eye, like my grandfather.

"A thousand years ago, Glenshire was a farmin' village, much like it tis today. Back then, the wealthiest man in the village was an awful, loathsome crook. He bought the most beautiful maiden's hand in marriage by cancelin' her parents' debts to him, but Saoirse never grew to love him. His inability to buy her affection enraged him, and over time, he became mad with jealousy. He was convinced that every other man in the village was in love with her and that she must've had a secret lover. So, after findin' himself at the bottom of a whiskey bottle one night, he dragged her to this very lough and drowned her. Said if he couldn't have her love, no one else would either."

I gasped and covered my mouth, but the old woman simply shrugged at my reaction.

"She was his property. He could do with her as he pleased. But news of her death terrified the other women of the village. They knew similar fates could befall them just as easily. A precedent had been set. So, they began bringin' gifts to the lady in the lough—trinkets, baubles, flowers—hoping to earn her favor ... and protection. Soon, they started bringin' their suitors to visit her as well. They'd pretend like it was just a wee stroll around the lough, but really, they were hopin' that Saoirse would judge their hearts and give them a sign as to whether the men were good or bad.

"Over the years, the tradition of bringin' suitors to the lough became so commonplace that the villagers began getting' married here as well. After recitin' their vows, the couple would prick their fingers with a blackberry thorn and spill their blood into the water to prove their devotion to the lady in the lough. Legend has it, if Saoirse deemed their love to be true, she would bless their union with an eternal bond, tetherin' their souls to one another for all eternity."

Blackberry thorns.
Blood.
Water.

The room was suddenly sweltering. I pushed the tight-fitting sleeves of my dress up my arms. Arms that still bore the scars from the day that Kellen and I had spilled our own blood into that water.

"And, how, um, would they know if … their union had been … blessed?"

A smile lifted the heavy corners of the woman's sagging mouth as her gaze once again fell to those three identical freckles on my ring finger.

I shook my head in disbelief. "I was just a dumb kid who fell out of a tree. That's hardly a wedding."

"Try tellin' that to her." She smirked, pointing her cane toward the lake. "Saoirse hasn't bestowed that blessin' on anyone in centuries, and now you come back here with another man's ring on your finger?" The woman's soft chuckles devolved into a laughing, coughing fit. "Her wrath will be grand!"

I shot to my feet. Needing air. Needing space. Needing to get the hell away from that woman and her creepy supernatural threats.

Turning to head for the door, I walked face-first into a hanging rabbit pelt and screamed. The woman only laughed harder.

"You know what?" I spun around and glared at her cackling, wrinkled face. "This is ridiculous. I can marry whoever I want. Because even if this lake spirit lady is real, the boy she supposedly bonded me to for eternity, Kellen, well … he's *dead*." My voice broke on that last word along with my heart as I realized what I'd really been running from. The real reason why I hadn't come back to Glenshire sooner. The truth that I'd been avoiding ever since I'd found that article when I was fifteen years old.

The woman's amused eyes blazed like two blue flames behind a pair of frosted windowpanes.

"If you really believed that"—she grinned, revealing a mouthful of teeth that looked like they'd been carved out of rotten wood—"you wouldn't be out here lookin' for him, now would ya?"

Stumbling backward, I turned and sprinted for the exit, swatting my way through her collection of hanging carcasses as her cackle-cough resumed behind me.

As soon as I pushed through the door, her laughter evaporated into the late afternoon air as quickly as the heat escaped from my bones. I tugged my sleeves back down with a full-body shiver that had nothing to do with the cold and everything to do with what I knew I would find if I looked back over my shoulder.

The only cottage on this side of the lake was a ruin. I'd seen it a dozen times.

And so was my mind, I supposed.

As I stared out over the misty water, the makings of a panic attack began to tighten around my lungs.

I was going insane. That was the only logical explanation.

It was as if I were looking at my past through the dirty, dystopian filter of a future I never wanted. The outline was the same, the basic shape of it, but what had been green was now gray. What had been right was now left.

What had been alive was now dead.

The sky darkened, and thunder rumbled, rattling the earth and putting my bare feet in motion. I watched my step but moved quickly as I fled from the cottage that Grandpa had warned me about.

Grandpa.

That serpentine dread coiled tighter around my chest as I pictured his bluish, wrinkled hand draped gently around my mother's ashes.

Mom.

My arms felt so empty without her in them. I wrapped them around myself, wishing they belonged to someone else. To *him*. I glanced at the spot where we'd kissed all those years ago—in the center of the lake, where the fog floated thick and heavy, like a fallen cloud.

Kellen.

It was as if he'd never existed at all. The woman was right; I was searching for him. I'd been searching for him since the moment I'd arrived, but everything he'd ever touched was just … gone. His house had burned and been rebuilt. Our spot in the cemetery had been gouged from the earth. The trails he'd spent years wearing into the forest floor had vanished into thin air. But when my eyes traveled over to the giant oak by the lake, the one next to the thicket of blackberry bushes, my fleeing feet and reeling mind stopped completely.

As I stared at a frayed, knotted length of rope swaying in the bitter wind.

I could tell myself that witches weren't real. That vindictive thousand-year-old lake spirits weren't real. That my grandfather had made it all up and I was just suffering from some grief-induced mental breakdown. But there was one thing he'd warned me about that *had* been real—and that rusty, old ladder lying sideways in the leaves was my proof.

Grabbing the hem of my dress, I hiked it up over my thighs again and took off running.

Hopping over the fallen ladder, I paused to give the oak tree's wide trunk a quick hug before turning and racing up the hill.

Like almost everything else Kellen had touched, the trail to the cottage was gone too, but I didn't need to see it to know it was there. I could feel it vibrating under my cold, wet feet.

CHAPTER 9

KELLEN

Drive to Cork Harbour, do a quick drop, be back in Dublin by midnight with the money. That was my only assignment for the day, the easiest one the Brotherhood had given me in years. It made no fucking sense—they had an army of new recruits for shite like that—but I didn't ask questions. I figured, if they were sending *me*, it wasn't gonna be as easy as they'd let on.

My plan had been to get to the docks early, scope the place out, make sure there wasn't a way in or a way out that I didn't know about, and generally prepare for the fucking worst.

But those plans had changed.

As an enforcer for the United Irish Brotherhood, I had to pay close attention to the news. Missing person reports, mysterious warehouse fires, *death notices*—I had to make sure my cleanup efforts had been convincing.

Which was how I'd discovered that "Patrick Murphy O'Toole of County Kerry would be laid to rest next to his beloved wife at Glenshire Catholic Church at four o'clock" that same day.

So, instead of taking the motorway straight to Cork, I was on a crumbling two-lane road over a hundred kilometers from there, headed straight toward a place that had only existed in my nightmares for the last five years.

I'd razed that house of horrors to the fucking ground when I was only seventeen. Scorched it from the earth—and what had happened there from my mind—with a can of petrol and the flick of a match. I'd watched it burn until the sun came up. Then, I'd walked to the bus station, bought a one-way ticket to Dublin, and promised myself I'd never come back.

As I rounded the bend and came face-to-face with a small stone chapel and two giant red doors, I wished I'd kept that promise. My heart pounded against my ribs as I drove past without slowing down. I couldn't risk being seen there. Not after what I'd done.

I continued around the curve and parked off on the side of the road. The car was a burner, one of many in the Brotherhood's collection—fake serial numbers, fake tax discs, fake registration. If a job went arseways, you ditched it, no questions asked.

But my jobs never went arseways.

With a deep breath, I pulled on a black beanie, zipped up my black flight jacket, and jogged across the street. I kept to the trees next to the church's car park, careful not to tread too loudly.

She's probably not even here, I told myself.

I'd just give the crowd a quick glance, satisfy my own sick, masochistic curiosity, and then I'd put Glenshire—and Darby Collins—in my rearview mirror forever.

As I crept along the fence surrounding the graveyard, I realized that I might have been too late. The service was over. Everyone was moving around, and it was hard to keep track of who I'd seen and who I hadn't.

A flow of arseholes filed into the car park through the cemetery gate—some I vaguely recognized from my time in Glenshire, some I didn't. It was amazing how much I'd managed to erase from my memory in five years. The names and faces of people who'd sneered and spat at me now danced on the edges of my mind, just out of reach. They were as insignificant to me now as the sheep dotting the hills.

All, except for one.

I crept along the fence, staying hidden behind the trees, scanning every last body in attendance until I found her. I couldn't see her face, but I'd know that hair anywhere. I saw it in my dreams. Long and wavy, coppery red. Twisting into soft ringlets at the bottom. But her posture was nothing like Darby's. Darby had marched through the woods in those yellow wellies like she was queen of the goddamn forest. This woman looked hollow, concave, like she was about to collapse in on herself. She looked like a …

Like a burning building.

I glanced past her, to the opposite side of the graveyard, as an acidic surge of bile climbed up my throat.

The place where I'd finally taken a stand, taken my life back, stood again. Shiny and new. A glimmering white monument to my misery. A taunting parody of my pain.

All I could hear was the blood rushing in my ears.

All I could see was the flames.

My breath shot out in hot bursts of steam as my mind unlocked a door that I'd sworn I'd never open again. As the sights and sounds and smells from that day all breached my carefully constructed barricades at once.

I squeezed my eyes shut and grabbed my head with both hands, as if I could physically force the memories back into their cages. I refused to lose control of my own mind. I refused to give him that kind of power over me ever again.

As my breathing slowed and returned to normal, it was the sound of shouting that finally brought me back to the present moment. When I opened my eyes, it wasn't the house that commanded my attention anymore. It was the woman sprinting past it.

Darby's hair whipped behind her like a coppery cape as she kicked one foot out in front of her, followed by the other. Two black high heels sailed into the air, spinning off in different directions as Darby grabbed the bottom of her tight black dress, yanked it up to the fullest part of her hips, and took off running into the woods.

I followed like a cannonball crashing through the trees until I came to the trail that led to the cottage. It was buried in leaves, but I could have found it blindfolded. I'd spent more time in those woods growing up than I did in my own home.

His home.

I went perfectly still and listened for her, but all I heard were voices calling her name from the cemetery.

The sky darkened, and the wind picked up. There was an electrical charge in the air, and a thrill that I hadn't felt since I was fourteen years old pumped through my veins as I raced toward the old cottage.

Once I got there, I noticed that the shower curtain door was long gone, but the tarp roof was still somewhat intact. It bowed in the middle, heavy with rainwater, and a section was flipped over where one of the boulders holding it down had fallen off. My throat tightened at the sight of it.

My old friend.

I approached and placed a hand on the stone, silently apologizing for my neglect as I readied myself to face whatever was inside.

I was familiar with fear. Fear kept me alive. Kept me sharp. But this feeling was different. It was dangerous. Not because it could get me killed, but because it had the power to make me wish I had been.

With a deep breath, I stepped through the doorway and found it almost exactly the way I'd left it five years ago. The sleeping bag had more mildew. The furniture I'd made—and smashed against the wall when I finally gave up on her ever returning—lay in splintered pieces on the floor. The tea set that I'd never been able to destroy, even during my worst rages, still sat in its place of prominence. And, as usual, Darby wasn't there.

I ripped the beanie off my head and shoved it into the pocket of my jacket as I stepped back outside, needing to feel the cool air on my skin. Needing to find her. I circled the cottage, peering through the trees in every direction, listening for the snap of a twig or the crunch of a leaf, but there was no sign of her anywhere.

There was never any fucking sign of her.

Next, I tore my jacket off and tossed it to the ground, but the winter wind did nothing to cool my skin. The flames of shame that I'd been suppressing since the day I'd left this godforsaken town tore through me like a forest fire. I'd forgotten how difficult the rage was to control, how it demanded violence, craved pain. But being back—seeing that house, seeing *her*—it felt as if I'd never left.

I was thirteen, fifteen, sixteen all over again. Waiting. And pacing. And burning alive.

Fuck this.

I was just about to grab my jacket off the ground and go find a tree trunk to put my fist through when the sound of softly approaching footsteps rooted me to the spot. My head whipped to the side, and there—marching up the hill, barefoot with the bottom of her dress in both fists—was a bleedin' apparition. A vision in black.

Darby fucking Collins.

The breath I'd been holding spilled from my lips as I drank her in. She was perfect. Absolutely fucking perfect. Although her body had filled out in all the right places, her cheeks and nose were just as flushed and freckled as I remembered. Her hair was just as golden orange. And her pouty pink lips were pursed in concentration, the way they always were when she was thinking about something.

Being invisible was how I survived. I kept my head down, moved in silence, and left no trace behind. It was why I was so good at what I did. But for the first time in a long time, I didn't want to be invisible. I felt like a kid again, watching her walk my way, hoping she'd notice me, waiting for her to lift those big green eyes and say my name with a smile.

My name. Fuck.

I hadn't heard it in years. Not once since leaving Glenshire. Kellen Donovan—the mute, motherless, powerless reject—was just as dead to me as Father Henry. So, when the Brotherhood took me in, I didn't give them a name. I told them they could call me whatever the fuck they wanted. At first, they went with Boy—I was only seventeen at the time—but after I made my first few kills, the elders began calling me *Diabhal*.

Devil.

That was when I realized that it didn't matter how far I ran from Glenshire; I'd never be able to outrun what I truly was.

So, I stopped trying. I'd found a place that celebrated the evil that lurked inside of me, paid me handsomely to unleash it, and that was good enough. It wasn't much of a life, but it was better than the one I'd been living here.

Except for the fact that Darby wasn't in it.

I wanted to clear my throat, put my hands in my pockets, do something to get her attention, but I couldn't. I'd been a ghost for so long; I didn't know any other way to be.

"Ow! God." Darby stopped walking and leaned forward, coppery hair spilling over her shoulder as she pulled something small and sharp out of the bottom of her foot.

Just then, another gust of wind blew up the hill from the lough, catching her hair and sending it flying into her face. As Darby sputtered and swiped at the strands, every ounce of elation, of *hope*, I'd allowed myself to feel was instantly engulfed by the fire raging inside of me.

Because there, on her finger, was a diamond the size of my hatred for humankind.

All I'd wanted since I was fourteen years old was to hold Darby Collins in my arms again. Feel her head on my shoulder, her smiling lips on my neck. She'd been my everything. My entire world. She was the only person on the planet who hadn't treated me like shite. The only one I could relax around enough to speak. The only one I'd trusted enough to touch.

The day I left Glenshire was the day I gave up on ever seeing her again—on ever being *seen* again. I hadn't thought anything could possibly hurt worse than that.

I was fucking wrong.

Braiding her windswept hair over one shoulder and holding the end with her left hand—the hand with that goddamn rock lashed to it—Darby finally lifted her eyes.

But I wasn't there to see them.

CHAPTER 10

DARBY

I lifted my head at the sound of rustling leaves in the woods—a smile on my lips and Kellen's name on my tongue—but it was just the wind. It howled through the skeletal trees, scattering brittle brown leaves across my path ...

And along the side of the cottage.

Our cottage.

I'd found it.

It stood in proud defiance of the forest that had been trying to reclaim it for centuries. Like the rope and the ladder, it felt like a touchstone. A portal back to another time. Another life. It looked exactly the way I remembered it but less playful somehow. More ... depressed.

Like a toy that had become a tombstone.

Tossing the chunk of pine cone I'd just pulled out of my foot to the ground, I limped closer to the last place I'd felt truly happy. But with every step I took, it became more and more apparent that my happiness had had nothing to do with a crumbling circle of stones and everything to do with the boy I'd once found inside.

"Kellen?" I called out, my voice shaky and hoarse, but the only answer I got was my own echo bouncing off the naked trees.

I'd known he wouldn't be there, but it wasn't until I turned the corner and poked my head through the doorway that my last ember of hope finally blew out.

The place was as abandoned as the aching cavity in my chest. Slivers of wintry light seeped in where the tarp had torn or folded over. Kellen's tree-branch furniture lay smashed in a pile by the wall, soft from wood rot and half-buried under several years' worth of decaying leaves. And in the back, perched on a tree stump as if it were a pedestal, was my grandmother's tea set—the only thing left unharmed. The stagnant water brimming over the edge of each tiny porcelain cup sputtered and popped from the rain that had begun to fall through an opening in the tarp above.

The sight felt like a sucker punch to my already-tapped-out soul. I stumbled backward through the doorway as if I'd been physically hit, the shock of reality forcing the air from my lungs.

He really was gone.

The magic, the joy, the color—all of it was just ... gone.

I took another step backward, letting out a startled cry as my foot nearly slipped out from under me. Looking down, I found myself standing on something surprisingly silky and soft—a black flight jacket, I realized upon closer inspection—and when I picked it up, it was still warm.

My heart soared as I clutched the material to my chest, my head swiveling wildly from left to right, scanning the woods for any sign of life.

Of *him*.

Another gust of wind peppered me with freezing rain drops and turned my braid into a bludgeon. It felt aggressive, that wind. Intentional. I glanced back down at the lake, half-expecting to see it swirling like some kind of evil whirlpool portal to hell, but what I found instead startled me even more. The surface appeared to be *boiling*.

"She is none too happy with you." The woman's amused warning echoed in my ears.

There is no lake spirit, I told myself. *It's probably just raining down there, harder than it is up here.*

It took me a minute to realize that not only was I right, but the wall of rain was also coming straight toward me.

"Shit."

I threw the discarded jacket over my shoulder and limped up the hill as fast as my recently stabbed foot would carry me, but the rain moved faster. Within seconds, freezing cold sheets of water began to crash down on me without mercy. I gasped in shock but forced myself to keep moving, the ground becoming slippery and unstable under my feet. Thunder shook the earth as I grasped at tree roots to help pull myself up the steepest part of the hill, and when I got to the top, a falling branch ricocheted off a nearby tree, narrowly missing my head. I dove to the ground in my attempt to get out of the way, tumbled over a short ledge, and slid halfway down the hill, scraping up both of my legs and losing a fingernail as I dug my hands into the rocky earth to slow my fall. The sky had gone so dark by the time I made it to the edge of Grandpa's fence that I could hardly see the house through the downpour. But I knew it was there. All I had to do was drag myself across the pasture ...

No sooner had I opened the rusty gate than golf ball–sized chunks of ice began falling from the sky as if they were being hurled from it. I lifted the jacket up over my head like a soaking wet umbrella as I limped across the muddy minefield, careful to avoid stepping on the thousands of shimmering chunks of ice that had already littered the pasture between me and my final destination.

Frozen rocks pelted my forearms through the fabric and battered my shins as they bounced off the grass. When I lifted my head and finally got a visual on the back door, I realized in horror that the keys to the house were still in my purse.

Which was tucked under the seat of our rental car.

Which we'd driven to the church.

Please be unlocked, please be unlocked, please be unlocked ...

Falling hail shattered around my ankles as I limped across the back patio, but I only had to stand there for a second before the doorknob turned mercifully in my hand, welcoming me into the dry, dark, quiet kitchen.

I slammed the door behind me and slid to the floor, gasping for breath on the decades-old doormat. Everything hurt. My punctured feet, my scraped thighs, my bruised arms and legs, my chattering teeth. But all of those pains paled in comparison to the gnawing, gnashing black hole that was eating away at me from the inside out.

Slipping my battered arms into the wet, silky sleeves of the jacket, I closed my eyes and inhaled. It smelled like a man. Not a man who wore expensive cologne and got his clothes dry-cleaned, like John. Not a man who smoked two packs of Marlboro Lights a day and sweat vodka out of his pores, like my father. But a real man. Clean. Masculine. Earthy. Intoxicating.

I knew deep down that it didn't belong to Kellen, but in that moment, I needed a friend more than I needed the truth.

Zipping the jacket up to my chin, I pulled my knees inside and buried my face in the neck opening. And for just a few minutes, the outside world disappeared. It was just me and that scent and the fantasy of who it belonged to. I allowed myself to imagine that it was *his* strong arms wrapped around me rather than my own. That *he* was holding me. Comforting me again.

That I wasn't completely alone.

But then a car door slammed outside, and the reality of just how *not* alone I was about to be came crashing down around me.

My heart began pounding in my chest moments before a fist began pounding on the side door.

"Hurry the fuck up!" John shouted. "It's pouring!"

I jumped to my feet and flipped on the overhead light, nearly slipping on the hardwood floor I'd dripped all over as I darted across the kitchen.

The second I unlocked the knob, the door flew open, and John pushed past me. "The fuck took you so long?"

John had an Ivy League education and prided himself on his impressive vocabulary, full of ten-dollar words and obscure legal

DEVIL OF DUBLIN

jargon. He rarely cursed, and whenever I slipped up and cursed around him, he never failed to remind me that my "white trash" was showing. But when he drank, all those lower-class words he'd been trying so hard to suppress came flying out like bullets.

And they were usually aimed at me.

Dropping his keys onto the table, John lifted his heavy arms and grimaced down at his drenched designer suit. His tie was completely undone along with the top button of his soaked dress shirt. His hair, perfectly coifed that morning, was now plastered to his forehead, and I was sure the water dripping from it would have tasted like overpriced pomade if he could taste anything after consuming that much alcohol.

"I can't fucking believe you ran away from me." John swayed on his feet as he struggled to remove his sopping wet suit jacket, mumbling, "Crazy bitch," under his breath.

I reached out to help him, but he swatted my hand away like a petulant toddler wanting to do something himself.

"I went to the pub—along with everybody else in this backward-ass town, except for *you*—and the bartender cut me off. Can you believe that shit? I'd only had, like, three shots. Four max. Then, when I had the *audacity* to challenge him about it, the fucking Mick kicked me out!"

Finally freeing himself from his jacket, John dropped it on the table next to his keys with a *splat*.

Crossing the kitchen, he grabbed a dish towel off the counter and ran it back and forth over his wet head. "Then, I hit a fucking sheep on my way home. Dumb fuck was standing right in the middle of the road."

"Oh my God," I gasped. "Is it okay?"

"*Is it okay?*" he echoed in a mocking tone, grabbing the counter to keep from falling over as he toed off his ruined wingtips. "I have an Amex Black Card, dummy. I could drive that piece of shit off a cliff, and it'd be covered."

"Not the car. The sheep."

For the first time since he'd gotten home, John looked at me. *Really* looked at me. And as I watched the expression on his face morph from annoyed to enraged, I knew that the worst night of my life wasn't over yet.

It was just getting started.

"What *the fuck* are you wearing?"

I looked down the length of my body and swallowed.

"Oh, this?" I shrugged, taking a step away from him. "I don't know. I found it in the woods. Hey, you want me to make you some dinner? You're probably starving."

"You little ... fucking ... whore." He seethed, steadying himself on the counter as he reclaimed the distance I'd put between us.

"Seriously"—I forced a smile, taking another step back—"it was just ... on the ground."

"Don't lie to me. That's why you ran off tonight, isn't it? To go fuck some old flame?"

John's nostrils flared, and his glassy eyes widened with excitement. I knew that look all too well. He loved to fight, to dominate, to win. It was what made him such a successful attorney, but I'd learned early on not to react to his aggression at home. I nodded and smiled, changed the subject, rolled over, went limp. He'd behave like a cat with a dead mouse for a while—batting me around, trying to get a rise out of me—but when it didn't work, he'd get bored and leave me alone.

But after everything I'd been through that day, I was having a hard time remembering how to do that. How to override my instincts and play dead. How to think when I was so full of feelings. How to go numb while I was in the worst pain of my life.

"It's been a long day," I said, walking toward the doorway that led from the kitchen into the living room. "So, if you're not hungry, I'm just gonna—"

John grabbed me by the elbow and jerked me back toward him. "Who is he?" he roared, his breath hot and reeking of whiskey as he jerked me again. I hated that smell. It smelled like my father.

"No one," I grunted, trying to pull my arm loose.

"No one?" he snarled, grabbing the shiny black material and giving my body a hard shake. "You're wearing his fucking jacket!"

"John, stop it," I cried out, again with too much feeling, and pushed against his chest with all my might. "Just let me go to bed."

He let go without warning, and I flailed as my body hurled backward. The floor around us was so wet that I couldn't find my footing. I caught the countertop behind me square in the back before crashing to the floor with enough force to blur my vision.

"You said, *let me go.*" John's humorless chuckle brought my wits back in an instant.

I didn't have time to analyze my injuries because he was suddenly in my face, wrapping his hand around my jaw and slamming my head against the cabinet I was slumped against.

"I pulled you out of the fucking gutter." His whiskey-scented spittle peppered my face. "And *this* is how you repay me? By spreading your legs for some fucking farmhand the second you get the chance?"

My mind was blank. Frantic and blank. All my logic, my hard-learned life lessons—they were just *gone*. I couldn't remember what to do. What to say.

I just shook my head and rambled mindless excuses, like, "Nothing happened, I swear. I got lost—that's all. Let's talk about this in the morning, okay? You've just had too much—"

Wham! John slammed my head back against the cabinet door again.

"Too much what, Darby? Too much *what?*"

I squeezed my eyes shut and held my breath.

"That's what I thought. You're not even old enough to drink. What the fuck do you know? *Nothing.* Other than how to spread your fucking legs."

When John didn't say anything else, I cracked one eye and watched his gaze rake over my body, like the drag of invisible claws. Then, still holding my jaw with one hand, he shoved his free hand up under my tight, wet dress. I immediately pressed my legs together, causing a predatory thrill to flash across his face.

Releasing my face, he grabbed both of my knees, and despite my resistance, my pleas, and my head shaking, he jerked them apart with a swift explosion of force.

One second. That was all it took for my body to react—for the scream to leave my lungs, for my bare foot to kick him in the chest—but I felt like I was watching it happen in slow motion, like it was a glass of milk being knocked over, just out of reach. I would have stopped it if I could. But by the time I realized what was happening, it was too late.

I had already made the biggest mistake of my life.

John caught my ankle, and his red-rimmed eyes flared with a wild, frenzied hunger.

The mouse still alive, and now, he knew it.

Hooking his elbows around my thighs, John yanked my entire body forward. My back slid down the cabinet and landed on the floor as he dragged my ass up onto his lap. Leaning forward, John pinned my thighs to my chest with his upper body as he fumbled to unbuckle his belt with his arms wrapped around my legs.

"What are you doing?" I shouted, trying to wriggle free, to shove him off, but I had no leverage from my position on the ground. "John, stop it!"

"You like to spread your legs, bitch?" he grunted, the sound of a zipper causing bile to rise in my throat.

"Get ... off!" I shoved him again. When he didn't budge, I reached up and grabbed his face, sinking my fingernails into his clean-shaven cheeks and dragging them forward.

John reared back onto his heels as his hands flew to his face with a snarl. "You fucking cunt!"

I seized the opportunity. Flipping over, I scrambled toward the back door, but before I could get there, two hands wrapped around my hips and slid me backward across the floor. In an instant, John's arm was around my waist, squeezing me so tight that I could hardly breathe, and his fully erect dick was pressed against my lower back.

I screamed and thrust my elbows backward into his ribs, but John let go of my waist and grabbed them both, twisting my arms behind my back until my spine arched and I screamed in pain.

"Fuck, I love it when you fight me," he panted against my ear as he held my tangled arms with one hand and shoved my dress up over my ass with the other. "Makes me so fucking hard."

John pushed my panties to the side and pressed his cock against me again, this time probing, seeking entrance. A panicked, strangled growl clawed its way out of my lungs. I struggled and thrashed, threw my head back, but I couldn't connect with anything vital. John chuckled at my unsuccessful attempt to headbutt him, but when I managed to plant one foot on the ground beneath me and pushed back hard enough to knock him off-balance, the laughter stopped.

The next thing I knew, a hand was on the back of my head, shoving it down toward the hardwood floor. A blinding white pain exploded behind my right eye, and for a moment, the world just … disappeared. The hands on me, the yelling, the fear, the smell of alcohol, the taste of stomach acid. The only thing that remained was my pain—a sharp, shooting throb that radiated up my cheekbone; a slash of soreness across the center of my back; and the dull, soul-deep ache of shame. I remember thinking how unfair it was that I still had to feel so much while I was unconscious, and that's when it hit me. I was awake.

The world hadn't disappeared.

John had.

My instincts told me not to move.

Dead mouse, I thought. *You're a dead mouse like this. Maybe he got bored and left.*

Or maybe he's just waiting for you to wake up.

My jugular pounded against the hardwood as I tried to keep my eyes closed and breathing even. Reaching out with my other senses, I searched for any sign that he might still be in the room. I couldn't feel him pressed against my back. Or smell his breath next to my face. And for a moment, I didn't think I could hear him either.

Until I did.

It was a soft, throaty, gurgling sound. Like nothing I'd ever heard before. I wasn't even sure it was coming from him until I felt his knee shift against the inside of my calf. Swallowing my fear, I opened my eyes, just a crack, and peeked over my shoulder at the man kneeling behind me. The first thing I noticed was that his face was the wrong color. It was a deep reddish purple, and his eyes were bulging halfway out of their sockets. His hands clawed and tore at something around his neck, and when I turned my head an extra inch to get a better look, I discovered what it was.

John's rain-soaked necktie was wrapped around his throat at least twice, and the ends were wrapped around the fists of a man standing behind him.

With a startled gasp, my gaze shot up to the face of John's attacker, and for the second time in less than a minute, I felt as though time were standing still.

No, it felt as if it had gone backward. Because staring back at me were two haunting, silvery pools of moonlight that I hadn't gazed into since I was twelve years old. I saw an entire lifetime swirling in those depths—laughter and tea parties, blackberries and magic spells, bloodstained T-shirts and tearstained cheeks, stolen glances and sweet, soft kisses. But that was where the nostalgia ended because the rest of him was unrecognizable. His features were chiseled, powerful, and covered in a shadow of dark stubble that disappeared into a full head of buzzed black hair. His hard jaw was clenched shut, his nostrils flared with every silent breath, and the veins in his neck, temple, and biceps bulged from exertion.

Exertion because he was strangling my fiancé.

A thousand words shot through my mind and bottlenecked in my throat as time galloped back to full speed, but the only one I managed to get out was, "Kellen." It tumbled from my lips like a sigh of relief rather than a plea for mercy, and the moment he heard it, Kellen's eyes slammed shut, as if he were in pain.

With a low, guttural sound, he stood up to his full height, biceps bulging as he lifted John off the ground by his own necktie until his knees no longer touched the floor.

I screamed and tried to sit up, more words—like *No! Stop! Don't! You're killing him!*—on the tip of my tongue, but as John's jerking, flailing body rose above me, all of those unspoken protests turned to acid in my throat. Because John's cock was now directly in my line of sight.

And it was still hard.

It jutted out over me like the blade of a guillotine, and all the powerlessness and panic I'd felt moments earlier came rushing back full force. I couldn't speak. Couldn't breathe. Couldn't do anything other than stare up at Kellen and silently beg him not to let go. And he didn't. He held my gaze as his muscles shook and sweat beaded on his brow, as he squeezed the life out of the man I'd promised to spend the rest of mine with.

As I watched my entire future go limp in his arms.

CHAPTER 11

DARBY

May those who love us, love us,
And those who don't love us, may God turn their hearts,
And if he doesn't turn their hearts, may he turn their ankles, so we'll
know them by their limping.

I don't know how long I sat there on the kitchen floor, staring vacantly at the framed proverb on the wall across from me before the symbols and letters finally started to make sense.

Grandpa had told me once that it was a traditional Irish blessing, but he'd lied.

It wasn't a blessing.

It was a curse.

And I had the limp to prove it.

Kellen had been in constant motion since … *what had happened* … while I just sat and stared blankly at the wall. I didn't even know what all he'd been doing, but at that particular moment, Kellen was standing across the kitchen with his back to me, taking something out of the freezer.

Alive and well.

He'd been a tall, gangly teenager the last time I saw him, but there was nothing gangly about the pillar of muscle standing before me now. He reminded me of a soldier with his shaved head, sculpted body, fitted black T-shirt and jeans, and well-worn combat boots. That, and the way he seemed to know exactly how to … do what he'd just done.

He must have joined the military after Father Henry died.

It made perfect sense. Kellen would have needed somewhere to go, something to do with all that pent-up rage. And they wouldn't have expected him to speak unless he was directly spoken to.

My heart swelled with admiration for the man that Kellen had become despite his circumstances. Then, it plummeted into a vat of stomach acid when I realized what this could mean for his future. Kellen had spent his entire childhood in a living hell. If anybody found out what he'd just done, he'd spend the rest of his adulthood there as well.

"Kellen, you have to go," I blurted out. "You have to get out of here. Right now. I'll call the cops as soon as you leave. I'll tell them I did it—that it was self-defense."

Kellen closed the freezer door and turned around. I held my breath, waiting for him to look at me again, needing to feel the grounding weight of his gaze. But instead, his eyes were cast down as he folded a handful of ice into a dish towel.

Stepping over John's body—which he'd graciously covered with his suit jacket—Kellen knelt beside me and placed the homemade ice pack on my cheekbone. I expected it to feel cold, but all I could register was a prickly heat blooming in my cheeks from his unexpectedly kind gesture. I couldn't see his face through the ice pack, so I turned my head as I reached up to take it from him. My hand covered his, and for a moment, I felt something I'd thought died along with him.

Fairy magic.

Slipping his hand out from under mine, Kellen rested his forearm on his knee and pinned me with a stare that I didn't like. This look wasn't grounding. This look was leveling.

"You don't think they'd believe me."

Kellen shook his head from side to side. Slowly. Apologetically.

Of course not. No one would believe that I'd strangled a grown man by myself.

"Fuck." The expletive was barely audible, but the moment I said it, I bristled with fear. My eyes darted around the room before I realized, with a nauseating mixture of dread and elation, that I didn't need to whisper that word under my breath anymore.

Or any other word, ever again.

"I have to do something." My gaze landed, unfocused, on a muddy footprint on the floor across the room. "I can't let you take the fall for this."

"I won't."

Two words. Soft and deep and clear. I let them vibrate all the way through me before I glanced back at the man who'd spoken them. I could probably count on my fingers and toes the number of words Kellen had said to me since we'd first met. They felt like tangible, finite things—smooth, round tokens of his trust that I could put in my pocket and take home to add to my most cherished collection.

Kellen's gaze was steady. His breathing deep and even. But a hot, simmering rage swirled around his massive body like steam.

"What can I do?" I whispered.

Without hesitation, Kellen replied, "Find rope."

Ten minutes later, I was using the flashlight feature on my cell phone to illuminate Kellen's path as he carried a one-hundred-and-sixty-pound corporate attorney over his shoulder into the forest.

I'd never experienced darkness like this. There were no streetlights in Glenshire. No strip malls or ambient lighting of any kind, so at night, especially in the woods, you couldn't see an inch in front of your own face.

But you could practically hear your own heart beating. The rain had completely stopped, and all the insects, birds, frogs that used to fill the summer air with their pleasantries had gone silent for the winter. It made it so that every leaf crunch and twig snap sounded like a cannon blasting through the silence.

I was just about to ask if we'd gone too far—it felt like we'd been walking forever—when something sharp dug into my knee. I hissed and shone the light down at my leg, which was now partially submerged in a particularly thorny blackberry bush. At least I'd had the presence of mind to throw on a pair of rain boots before we left.

As I extracted my leg from the shrub, I realized that I could see the other bushes beyond it, even without the flashlight. Their spiky, gnarled edges were outlined in the subtlest silver, and when I lifted my head to look even further, I saw a sea of it. The lake looked like liquid chrome, as still as death and lit by a full white moon so heavy and low that I felt like I could reach out and trace its craters with my finger.

How long had it been since I'd seen that same body of water being pummeled with rain, its entire surface choppy and enraged? An hour? Two? And now, it was as serene as a still life painting.

Kellen walked around our tree—the wide oak with the rope swing—stepped over the fallen ladder as if he'd known it was there, and dropped John on the muddy bank of the lake with a grunt. Then, taking his own phone out of his pocket, he turned on the flashlight and shone it into the woods until he found what he was looking for. I could hear his footsteps as he disappeared into the brush. He wasn't far away, but he was far enough that I felt the need to hide behind our tree until he came back. As if John might suddenly jump up and try to finish what he'd started in the house.

Kellen had stripped him down to his boxer briefs before we left, and his alabaster skin seemed to glow in the dark. Looking at John lying there, limbs limp, body lifeless, I felt my fear begin to subside. But the feelings I'd thought would rise up to replace it—sorrow, panic, guilt, remorse—they never came. Instead, all I felt was the cool splash of relief when Kellen finally returned, rolling a boulder the size of a Buick down the hill.

DEVIL OF DUBLIN

After removing his boots and socks and hiking his pant legs up, Kellen dragged John's body into the lake until he was submerged on his back in the shallows. Then, he spread John's legs, rolled the massive rock in between them, grabbed him by the arms, and lifted his upper half until it was slumped over the stone. It was as if he had done it a thousand times. Kellen used the rope I'd found in Grandpa's barn to tie his arms and legs around the boulder. Then, he walked back onto the shore and began removing the rest of his clothes.

All of them.

Moonlight kissed every swollen muscle that rippled down his torso as he peeled his shirt off over his head. Shadows pooled in the valley between his broad shoulder blades as he leaned over to step out of his jeans. And when his boxer briefs followed, when he stood, naked and perfect in the moonlight—not with the intention of fucking me, but of freeing me—a dam inside of me broke. A tidal wave of emotion rushed in, filling every numb corner, every carefully constructed compartment I had built to house my shame, flooding the chasm of nothingness I believed I deserved.

As I watched him carry the weight of my past into the freezing cold water, a yearning more powerful than anything I'd ever experienced compelled me to follow. Demanded it. I unzipped the jacket that had set everything into motion and tossed it to the ground, followed by the rest of my clothes. I could see my breath as I stepped out of my rain boots—the ones I'd bought years before because they reminded me of him—but the damp winter air couldn't touch me. I walked without a limp to the edge of the water, the pain of my injuries reduced to whispers by the siren song of the lake. And when I stepped into its arms ...

It grabbed me and pulled me under.

It took less than a second for the icy blackness to swallow me whole. The cold was excruciating. It felt like being burned alive. My skin screamed, and my muscles contracted, but I forced my limbs to keep moving. They thrashed in jerky, shivering spurts but did nothing to slow my descent into the lake.

I couldn't feel what was pulling me down, but I knew in my aching bones that this was my punishment. I'd been so stupid to think that I could ever be free. I had told John I would spend forever with him, and now, I would—at the bottom of Glenshire Lough.

But I wasn't ready. I wanted more time. I wanted *him*. I wanted to feel his fairy magic on my skin again. I wanted to be looked *into* instead of looked *at*. I wanted to be held instead of held down. I knew I didn't deserve those things, but for the first time in my life, I was willing to fight for them anyway.

As my lungs began to burn, the backs of my closed eyelids brightened.

No!

My eyes flew open, expecting to see a tunnel of light that I wasn't ready to enter, but instead, I found myself surrounded by an ambient blue glow. It rose up from beneath me, surging and retreating, pulsing like a heartbeat. It felt ancient, powerful, *alive*.

As my feet settled on the slick, rocky lake bottom, the blue glow brightened, illuminating a treasure trove of coins, jewelry, art, and cutlery scattered about in all directions.

"Saoirse hasn't bestowed that blessin' on anyone in centuries, and now you come back here with another man's ring on your finger?" The old woman's cackling threat echoed and warbled around me as if it were being played through an underwater speaker. Some words were louder than others. Some were muffled and barely audible.

But the message I received was loud and clear.

"Her wrath will be grand!"

I was being punished, but not for killing John.

My crime had been agreeing to marry him in the first place.

Violent, uncontrollable shivering racked my extremities as I fought in vain to push off from the bottom, but it was as if my feet had turned to lead.

I wasn't going crazy. Mental breakdowns didn't have the power to drag you to the bottom of a lake and drown you against your will. This was really happening.

I was really about to die.

My lungs screamed for air as panic gripped my mind, lying to me, begging me to take a breath. But just before I succumbed to the agonizing urge, the blue glow hummed again, this time with the sound of my grandfather's voice. It vibrated on every sweet syllable, penetrated through my panic.

"Legend has it, this lough has a spirit in it. ... Can be mean as a snake if ya cross her, but I hear she likes presents."

Presents!

I glanced down again at Saoirse's glowing collection of gifts. Baubles, trinkets. Gold and silver.

Grandpa had been right. About everything.

I only hoped it wasn't too late to start listening.

I clamped my jaw shut, battling with my body to override its most basic functions as I yanked the massive diamond off my finger and held it out in front of me with shaky hands.

Death lingered in the shadows—I could feel it hovering just beyond the blue light—as a school of bubbles swirled from my shoulder to my wrist. They tickled and taunted me, circling my hand until the desperate need to inhale became almost unbearable, but I gritted my teeth and held on. Everything I'd ever wanted was on the other side of that breath.

And when the ring vanished from my fingers and the lake went black, I knew she was going to let me have it.

CHAPTER 12

KELLEN

I knew plenty of ways to dispose of a body, but after what the fuck I'd just seen and heard, I needed the cold of the lough to calm myself down. I was so enraged, so consumed by the flames inside of me that I didn't know how much longer I'd be able to maintain control. I wanted to destroy so much more. I wanted to kill him over and over again. I wanted to shatter each and every finger that had dared to touch her, pulverize every knuckle with a hammer while he screamed. I wanted to rip the arms from his body for holding her down. And the look on her face when she saw his cock—the terror—*fuck*. He was lucky she'd been there, or I would have done some truly sick shite to finish him off.

I'd only killed out of anger twice in my life, and both times, it had been in fucking Glenshire.

With every step deeper I took into the freezing lough, the calmer I felt. The better I could think. The easier it was to convince my body that it was over. That Darby was safe.

And that the bloated rapist pig I was carrying would never fucking touch her again.

When I got to the spot in the center of the lough where the rocky ground disappeared under my feet, I took a deep breath and heaved Captain America into the void. He vanished beneath the surface without so much as a splash.

But I heard one anyway, coming from somewhere behind me.

Spinning around, I found the source. Ripples radiated out from a spot on the surface of the water just a few meters offshore. I thought maybe Darby had tossed in a rock, but she was nowhere to be seen.

I wanted to call her name, but I could already feel my throat beginning to close with fear. The woods were silent. My eyes darted all over. The rope swing wasn't swinging. There was no flashlight beam in sight …

But there was something shiny and yellow on the ground by the tree.

Her fucking boots.

"Darby!" I yelled, forcing the word out through the chains tightening around my throat. "Darrrbyyyy!"

When she didn't answer, I immediately dived beneath the surface, skimming the bottom of the lough with my hands, reaching, feeling, frantic, fucking insane.

I burst above the surface with a ragged, strangled cry, my eyes darting in all directions, trying to remember where I'd already searched.

And that was when I saw them.

Bubbles. Right in the center of the lough.

Diving back in, I pumped my arms and legs as hard as I could, pushing myself straight down into the black. Three, four, six meters deep. My ears popped, and my head felt like it was going to implode, but I sensed her. That was the only way to describe it. It was as if I could see her in the dark. I *felt* her reach for me. *Felt* her relief. And when I extended my arms and reached for her too, she was there.

She was actually fucking there.

Pushing off the bottom, I shot us to the surface in seconds. The moment our heads broke through the water, Darby's desperate gasp for air was the sweetest sound I'd ever heard. I clutched her to my body as I swam sideways toward the shore, probably squeezing her tight enough to crack a rib but I didn't care. I wasn't letting anything take her from me again. Not even God himself.

Once we were at a place where she could touch the bottom, I set her on her feet to let her catch her breath, but I wasn't fucking letting go. I held her shivering, coughing, naked body against mine, and for a second, I was fourteen again, holding my girl in the middle of Glenshire Lough. It was as if the past eight years—hell, the past eight minutes—had never happened, and I was starting over again from what had been the best day of my life. Back before I snapped. Before I became the monster Father Henry had warned everyone about. Back before I sold my soul to the Brotherhood for a roof over my head and a bite to eat.

Overcome by the need to relive that moment, I lowered my gaze to Darby's beautiful mouth. But the pale pink lips I expected to find were now a deep, dark purple. Her teeth chattered quietly behind them despite her clenched jaw, and her shivers were now full-blown body tremors.

Fuck.

Lifting her off her feet, I cradled her shaking body against my chest as I waded the rest of the way to shore.

I wanted to ask her what the hell she'd been thinking, jumping into the lake in the middle of winter, but I had my own reasons for doing the same thing, didn't I? None of which I felt like talking about.

I'd found my voice the day I let the fire inside of me take over. The day I burned Father Henry's house to the ground with his mutilated corpse inside. From that moment on, I swore I'd never fear another person as long as I lived. I spoke when necessary. Kept the flames of hatred stoked in my belly, hot enough to burn through the blockages I'd suffered from as a kid. But I'd learned pretty quickly that words were a liability in my new world. They only served to weaken you. Humanize you. Being quiet made fuckers fear me. It made me untouchable. And after my time spent with Father Henry, being untouchable was my only fucking goal in life.

Until now.

Setting Darby on the ground next to her pile of clothes, I felt a sharp pang of loss as I turned my back to give her some privacy.

"Get dressed," I said, walking over to my own pile of clothes. "We need to get you warm."

"Wh-wh-why aren't you f-f-freezing too?" Darby asked over the sound of zips and fabric rustling behind me. "There's l-l-literally s-s-steam coming off of you."

Because I got one foot in hell, I thought, zipping up my jeans. *Keeps me nice and toasty.*

I pulled my shirt back on and stepped into my unlaced boots. "You decent?"

"Y-y-yeah."

I turned and couldn't help but smile at the sight of Darby trying to zip up *my* fucking jacket. When I'd seen it on her in the kitchen, it'd only fueled my possessive rage. Seeing it on her after the fact had a very different effect.

"C'mere," I said, walking over to help.

Her hands were shaking so badly she couldn't get the zip started. I stopped directly in front of her and felt her eyes on my face as I took the metal tab from her frozen fingers and slid it all the way up to her chin.

"K-K-K-Kellen?"

The way Darby's teeth were chattering, that single word sounded like machine gunfire, which was fitting because it tore through me like a bullet.

"D-d-do you have th-th-three freckles on your l-l-left ring finger?"

Pulling my eyebrows together, I glanced down at my left hand. Then, I lifted it, revealing the answer to her question—three freckles, slashed across my finger, right above the final knuckle. I'd never given them a second thought—when your body had as many scars as mine, a few freckles didn't make much of an impression—but Darby looked at them as if they were the most magnificent thing she'd ever seen.

Her eyes filled with tears, and her trembling purple lips split into a blinding smile.

Just before they crashed into mine.

I'd kissed other girls, women, since that day in the lough, but it never ended well. I couldn't tolerate their touch for more than a few seconds before the flashbacks would start. The pounding heart. The feeling of suffocation. The flames eating me alive. I'd end up shoving the poor lass away and storming off, frustrated and goddamn furious that I couldn't just fuck like normal people. That he'd taken that away from me too.

So, when Darby's mouth sealed over mine, I held my breath, waiting for the rush of panic to come, but it didn't.

When she lifted up onto her toes and placed her ice-cold hands on my cheeks, I didn't recoil from her touch.

And when she parted her lips, my tongue slipped inside like it belonged there. Like it had missed her tongue as much as I'd missed her.

Lifting my hand—the one with the freckles that, for some unknown reason, she seemed to love—I wrapped it around the back of her head and deepened the kiss.

And it felt amazing. My chest swelled. My blood thrummed. There was no flood of fear, no overwhelming dread, just pure fucking euphoria.

Until Darby's entire body shuddered violently in my arms.

Breaking our kiss, I stared into her hooded eyes and tried to commit that look to memory. Because if I didn't get her into a warm bath soon, it might be the last time I saw it.

CHAPTER 13

KELLEN

May you be in heaven half an hour before the Devil knows you're dead.

That's what the plaque on the wall in Darby's granda's spare bedroom said, and I couldn't get the phrase out of my mind. While Darby was soaking in the tub—I'd told her not to come out until she could feel all twenty of her fingers and toes again—I went round and packed up everything that belonged to her and that rapist piece of shite. It only took about ten minutes. Five to do the packing and five to stare at that fucking plaque.

Darby was my half hour in heaven.

I'd never gotten more than a few blissful moments with her before she disappeared again, leaving me stranded in the bowels of hell for months, years. She'd only been back in Glenshire for a few hours, and I'd nearly lost her. This time forever.

Because I didn't belong in heaven and I certainly didn't belong with *her*. Darby was an angel in the flesh, and if the rumors were true, I was the spawn of Satan himself.

But I didn't give a single solitary shite.

If the Devil wanted to drag me back to hell now, he was going to need a fucking body bag.

While I cleaned the muddy footprints off the floor, put the kitchen back in order, and erased any trace of my presence, I came up with a plan.

I still had a job to do for the Brotherhood that night—a simple gun drop in Cork. We'd ditch Darby's rental car on our way out of town, take the burner to Cork Harbour, sell the guns, and use the money to disappear. Buy new identities. Leave the country. Maybe we could get out before Darby was even reported missing.

One last job—the easiest one I'd had in years—and I'd be free.

I didn't know what I'd tell Darby about my past or what I was running from, but I'd figure something out. I had to. Losing her again wasn't an option.

Unfortunately, neither was ditching the rental.

After loading Darby into her silver Ford Fiesta—along with everything she and that fucker had brought—I drove down the road to the spot where I'd parked the burner. Only, instead of seeing a black sedan with fake plates waiting for me on the side of the road, I saw a fallen tree lying across half the street, crushing the hood of my car.

Fuck.

I was already running late for the drop. I didn't have time to stash the rental *and* steal something new. Nor did I think Darby would be too excited about becoming an accessory to murder *and* car theft in the same night.

We were going to have to take the fucking Fiesta.

Branches and debris from the storm crunched under the tires as I pulled over in front of the fallen tree.

"Oh my God," Darby gasped. "Is that ... your *car*?"

Hopping out of the driver's seat, I jogged over to the hunk of steel and plastic that the Brotherhood had provided me with specifically for this job.

The windscreen was smashed in as well as the roof, but I was able to get in through one of the back doors. The car was

DEVIL OF DUBLIN

clean—no prints, no personal items, other than the one I'd left stashed in the glove box. Using my knuckle to unlatch the compartment, I reached in and grabbed a fully loaded Beretta M9.

I tucked it in the back of my waistband and went to collect the only other thing I'd left in that crushed tin can of a car.

Lifting the boot, I breathed a sigh of relief as I stared down at my ticket to freedom.

A large, unmarked black bag containing a dozen American-made, fully automatic AR-15s. They had a street value of twenty-five thousand euros, which was just enough to buy two fake identities and a couple of flights to anywhere Darby wanted to go.

The United Irish Brotherhood had been called a lot of things over the years—a political party, a militia, a terrorist organization, a revolution—and perhaps those things had been true before The Troubles. But now, they were like any other organized crime family. Corrupt. Obsessed with power. Poisoned by bloodlust. They claimed their goal was to free Northern Ireland from the tyranny of British rule and reunite the Irish people under one sovereign flag. The elders in the upper ranks even refused to speak English. They insisted that we would never truly be free from the blight of colonization until our Gaelic language and culture were restored. It was a noble cause—in theory. One that sounded good on paper—or to a homeless seventeen-year-old kid who'd just been busted picking pockets at Connolly Station.

It was Séamus himself, the UIB's quartermaster, who'd caught me that day. Instead of turning me in, he took me to the Brotherhood headquarters and introduced me to their soldiers. A team of outcasts, like me, who did their dirty work—hacked computers, tapped phones, made bombs, broke kneecaps, anything to help fund and protect the Brotherhood. Especially gun running. That was their bread and butter, and business was good. But Séamus didn't start me as a soldier. He said he wanted me for security.

I wasn't the biggest lad there. I was still growing and severely malnourished, but Séamus saw something in me. What I'd done. What I had the potential to do again.

He knew I was a killer.

And that was exactly what he trained me to be.

I spent my days eating, weight lifting, sparring, and shooting. And I spent my nights learning the Irish language. I didn't hang out with the other soldiers. I didn't speak unless I was spoken to. And when I made my first kill, protecting Séamus during a routine gun drop that went arseways, I didn't so much as flinch. Within a year, I went from security to enforcer, and by my twentieth birthday, I became the UIB's most notorious hitman.

I had traded one cell for another. Only this one fed me better and didn't fucking touch me.

But all that was about to change.

Jogging back over to Darby's rental car, I dropped the bag in the boot and returned to the driver's seat. My heart was fucking pounding.

"Change of plans," I said as calmly as possible, pulling back onto the road that would take us the fuck away from Glenshire, for good this time. "We'll have to drive this a little longer."

Sitting in the passenger seat, Darby already looked like a criminal. She was wearing my black flight jacket and the black beanie I'd made her put on before we left—her hair was still wet, and I'd be damned if she was getting hypothermia on my watch. A pair of dark sunglasses, and she'd be ready to rob a bank.

Hopefully, it wouldn't come to that.

She turned to face me, pulling her legs up under her like a child. "If we leave your car here, won't you become a suspect?"

I shook my head.

"You don't think so? A mysterious car shows up in Glenshire the same night that two Americans go missing? They'll probably run the license plate number and come looking for you."

"Car's not mine. Nothin' is. As far as the government's concerned, I don't even exist." I cast a sideways glance at Darby and watched her mouth fall open the tiniest bit.

"What do you do?" she whispered.

That question made my fucking guts churn. I focused on the tarmac disappearing at eighty kilometers per hour in front of my headlights as I tried to come up with an answer that wasn't the truth.

Needing to reassure her but not knowing what the fuck to say, I reached over and squeezed Darby's hand. The moment her fingers closed around mine, my mind screamed at me to pull away. My already-pounding heart began to race faster, but I forced myself to ignore the sirens going off inside my head and breathe through it. I looked over at her to remind myself whose fingers were clutching me. That I was fine. That I was better than fine.

Darby ran her thumb lightly over my knuckles. The tenderness had me ripping my gaze away and swallowing hard. My throat, my eyes, my fucking lungs—everything burned.

"It's okay if you're not allowed to tell me." Her voice was hushed, like she was talking to a caged animal. "I think I've figured it out anyway. Your hair. Your clothes. The way you ... knew what to do back there. Claiming you don't exist. You're some kind of ... special forces, aren't you? Like a secret agent or a spy or something. I don't know."

She thinks I'm in the bleedin' army. Jesus Christ.

"You don't have to tell me. I just ... want you to know that I'm really proud of you. And really ... grateful. If you hadn't come ..." She shook her head, not allowing herself to go down that line of thought. "I have no idea what you're risking to help me." Her voice broke on the word *help*, and it splintered something in my chest along with it.

Help.

I wasn't helping her. I was fucking kidnapping her.

Darby had seen slivers of the darkness inside of me, but instead of allowing herself to acknowledge what it truly was, she'd told herself a fairy tale about it. Made up a story in her head, just like she had when we were kids. She used to go on for hours about teddy bears who lived in castles, and witches who ate children, and magic potions that would protect us from evil. And now, she was doing it again—only in this fairy tale, I wasn't the soulless, heartless Devil of Dublin, as the Brotherhood had taken to calling me. I was a hero. A decorated soldier who had to put a top-secret mission on hold to come to her rescue. It was a lie, but if it kept her from seeing me the way the rest of the world did, if it kept her from seeing the truth about the monster I'd become, it was a lie that I would die to protect.

"Can you ... at least tell me where we're going?"

Her voice was so soft and so timid that I wanted to scream. I wanted to grab her downturned face and force her to look me in the eye. Make her tell me what the fuck had happened to cause the happy, headstrong girl I'd once known to cower beside me like a scared little girl—knees tucked inside my jacket, hand clinging to mine, hesitantly asking where I was taking her, as if she didn't have the right to know. As if she was now my property and I could do with her what I pleased.

"The docks," I bit out through my clenched teeth. "Cork Harbour."

"Oh," she said in surprise. "Are we ... getting on a boat?"

I shook my head. "Gotta drop something off. It'll be quick. Then, we'll head to Dublin."

"Dublin. Is that ... where you live?"

I nodded.

"It's not, like, a military base or anything, is it? I don't want you to get in troub—"

"No," I cut her off, unable to listen to the lie I was allowing her to believe for another second.

Darby went quiet. I was afraid I'd been too much of an arsehole to her, but when I glanced in her direction, the corner of her perfect mouth was tipped up in a way that was anything but offended.

"What?" I asked, softening my tone, acutely aware of the fact that she had begun stroking the back of my hand with her thumb again.

Even in the dark, I could see Darby's cheeks flush. She dropped her eyes and smiled down at my scarred knuckles.

"Nothing. It's just ... when we were kids, I always hated that I had to go home when it got dark. I wanted to stay out ... with you. And now, I can."

I stared straight ahead as I tried to swallow the massive, jagged lump in my throat.

"I can't believe you're really here." Darby squeezed my hand tighter as her smile disappeared. "I thought you were dead."

My head snapped in her direction.

"I Googled you," she said, locking eyes with me. "All the time. Every day. But nothing ever came up ... until I was fifteen."

Pulling my gaze away, I swallowed again.

Fuck.

" 'Beloved Glenshire Priest Dies in Tragic House Fire,' " Darby recited the headline from memory. "I don't know what upset me more—the fact that they made that monster out to be some kind of saint or the part where they said that the remains of the 'troubled boy' he had taken in were 'yet to be found.' For five years, I searched for an update, but they never bothered to follow up. Just ... *yet to be found.*"

My heart felt as though it might suffocate me, swelling against my lungs, climbing up into my throat. I'd thought she'd forgotten about me. I thought she'd moved on. After three years of waiting, I'd given up on her completely, but Darby had never given up on me.

I barely got the car onto the side of the road before I grabbed her by the back of the neck and kissed the shite out of her. She gasped as my lips crashed against hers, smiled as her tongue twisted around mine, and when I tilted my head and plunged into her deeper, her soft, answering moan swept through me like a drug, bringing me to my knees, making me its slave.

Darby pressed both hands—one hot from being held in mine and one ice cold—against my cheeks and kissed me back with relief and concern and need ... for *me*. Darby's joy pumped into my veins like pure, uncut sunshine after eight endless years of night.

But in the back of my mind, I knew it wasn't real. I knew that Darby only felt that way about the white-knight version of me that existed in her head, not the real me. The real me would send her running for the hills. But the part of me that had been dying ever since she'd left didn't give a flying fuck.

My cock strained against my jeans as Darby's lips wrapped around my tongue. As my hand closed around a fistful of damp red hair. As the sounds she made changed from delicate to desperate.

"Kellen," she panted against my mouth, the sound of my name on her wet lips nearly causing me to come in my jeans. "Let's go home."

And with those three words, reality came crashing back down around me.

Home.

I couldn't take her *home*.

Not only because I was going to have a price on my head in a few hours when I didn't show up to give Séamus his cash, but also because, from the sound of her voice and the look in her hooded eyes, Darby was going to expect me to finish what I'd started once we got there.

What would she do when she found out that I couldn't?

When she found out just how fucked up I really was?

I'd been so stupid to think this time could be any different.

I had one foot in hell.

And my half hour in heaven was almost up.

CHAPTER 14

KELLEN

The clock on the dash announced that it was *10:11* in sickly green numbers as I approached the unmarked side entrance to the docks. I was late by over an hour, and I felt absolutely fucking nauseous about it. In five years with the Brotherhood, I'd never been late for a job.

But I was feeling cagey for another reason too. I just couldn't work out what it was. I told myself it was because Darby was with me. I didn't want her anywhere near Brotherhood business. So, instead of pulling round back like Séamus had told me to, I parked in front of the main building in a spot that was fully visible from the road and next to the main entrance.

Leaving the key in the ignition, I turned toward Darby and tapped the clock on the dash. "If I'm not back in fifteen minutes, leave."

Her eyes went wide. "What?"

"Leave."

Not waiting around for more questions, I got out, adjusted the gun in my waistband, grabbed the bag out of the boot, and headed toward the back of the building. The docks were closed for the night, and the lights were off, but the side gate was open, so I knew the man I needed to see was still there.

At least, I hoped he was.

If not, my whole exit plan was fucked.

Pulling my phone out of my pocket, I tapped the screen to check the time again and found four text messages and two missed calls from Séamus.

Shite.

I walked faster as I scrolled through the texts—mostly him just asking where the fuck I was over and over again—when a pair of voices cut through the night air. I'd been told I was only meeting one guy—a German—so I pocketed my phone and reached for my gun as I approached the corner of the building.

"Zis is bullshit! You say vait, I vait. Over vone hour. No more!"

That accent wasn't German. It was fucking Russian.

"Alexi, wait! He'll fuckin' be here. The man's never been late a day in his life."

And *that* voice was one I would know in my sleep, only because he loved the sound of it so goddamn much that he never shut up.

Creeping closer to the edge of the building, I held my breath and took a quick glance round the back. I spotted them in half a second, standing between two shipping containers in a cloud of cigar smoke.

I didn't recognize the Russian, but the pot-bellied bastard standing across from him was supposed to be back in Dublin, waiting for me to drop a sack full of money off by midnight.

Suddenly, everything began to make sense.

"Ve had deal!" the Russian shouted. "You give us man who kill my uncle, zis *Devil of Dublin*"—he spat on the ground at Séamus's feet—"and ve don't declare var on UIB."

My usually overheated blood ran cold.

One of the UIB elders had ordered a hit on one of the Russian elders, Dmitry Abramov, just a few days before. He'd shown up in Ireland, unannounced, and the Brotherhood said they had intel that he was there to intercept a shipment of guns we had coming up through France. It hadn't sat well with me—taking out a high-ranking Bratva, unprovoked—but the elders had wanted to send a message.

And we all know what happens to the messenger.

"How's about we take care of him for ya?" Séamus offered—that fucking turncoat. "Once he turns up, we'll send his head to yer father, along with a coupla AR-15s as a peace offerin'."

The AR-15s that were strapped to my back at that very moment, I presumed.

"Ve don't vant his *head*." The Russian let out a gruff, humorless laugh. "Ve vant him alive. You see, zis Devil make UIB too bold. Because of *him*, you sink you can do vhatever you vant. Kill whoever you vant. You, wrong. You kill wrong Russian. Now, I take avay your toy. Devil is our toy now, and ve vill break him piece by piece. Deliver him before I go back to Moscow, or I return, and bring entire Bratva army."

I'd started walking back toward the car long before he finished his evil-villain monologue, but I had to choose between being quick or being quiet. I opted for slow and quiet, clutching the bag to my chest to keep the guns from rattling as I stepped gingerly over the sea of crumbling tarmac beneath my boots. But when I heard a car door slam shut, followed by Séamus's livid cursing and another door slam, I knew I'd chosen wrong.

I was on the side of the building with the open gate, and they'd be coming my way any second.

Taking off in a sprint, I hoped I could make it to the end of the building before I was spotted, but I didn't get even halfway there before the ground ahead of me lit up, revealing the long black shadow of an Irishman running for his life.

The car behind me revved its engine, and I knew it had to be Alexi. Or rather, his driver. There was no way he'd deal with the Brotherhood alone after what I'd done to Dmitry. *What they'd made me do.* Séamus was after me too, but he wouldn't rev his engine about it. He was losing his best enforcer after all.

My legs pushed harder, pumped faster, as the first shotgun blast rang out. The wall behind me exploded, peppering the back of my neck and arm with jagged shards of brick and mortar.

New plan.

Running back to the rental was out. I couldn't let them get anywhere near Darby. The Bratva dealt in human trafficking—sex slavery, forced labor, organ harvesting, drug mules. If it involved human bodies, it was for sale. And with a body like Darby's, she'd be their crown fucking jewel.

Pulling the gun out of my waistband, I suddenly darted to the left, running directly in front of the oncoming car. I fired a few rounds into the windscreen, and the second I saw it shatter, I sprinted straight toward the side entrance without looking back. The sound of metal crashing against brick told me all I needed to know.

One car down, one to go.

Two men shouted at each other in Russian just before another shotgun blast rang out. A chunk of the gate exploded beside me as pain ripped through my left side and shoulder blade.

But I kept running. A few more meters and I'd be through the entrance. I'd sprint along the fence, drawing them away from Darby, until I found a way to get back in. Then, I'd hide on top of a shipping container and pick the fuckers off one by one before they ever got close enough to touch me.

Or Darby.

But when I glanced over my shoulder as I disappeared through the gate, I discovered that she was already gone. The car park sat empty.

I stopped running and stared at the spot where I'd left her.

I couldn't believe she'd actually listened to me. That changed everything.

I didn't need to lure them away anymore. I could take them out right where they fucking stood. I had cover from the brick wall surrounding the shipping yard, and with Alexi and his henchman busy yanking Séamus's portly arse out of his own car,

I could take all three of them out before they even got a visual on me.

Ducking behind the bricks next to the open gate, I dropped the bag, aimed my Beretta, zeroed in on Alexi Abramov's thick, bald skull, and exhaled as my finger tightened around the trigger. But before I could pull it, the sound of an engine so weak that it wouldn't power a lawnmower wheezed and sputtered behind me.

Alexi's head snapped up at the sound, and the last thing I saw before I dived behind the wall was him raising his shotgun.

BAM!

A pile of bricks hit the tarmac, but I wasn't there to take the brunt this time. I was scrambling into the passenger seat of a silver Ford Fiesta.

"Reverse!" I shouted, palming the top of Darby's head and shoving it down below her open window.

"I can't see!" she shouted back, but her hand found the gear-stick and her foot found the accelerator.

The car made a whirring sound like a toy helicopter with low batteries as it skirted away backward. Grabbing the wheel, I yanked it to the left as soon as we reached the main road. Darby squealed and took her foot off the pedal.

"Drive!" I shouted, slamming the shifter into position.

"I can't!" The terror in her voice was the only thing keeping me from yelling at her for coming back for me.

I could have killed all three of those fuckers and been done with it, but instead, I was going to have to get her the fuck out of there while driving a glorified roller skate with even less horsepower.

Glancing back, I saw Séamus's black BMW come barreling through the gate. Because the car was so fucking small, I barely had to lean over to slam my palm down on Darby's right knee, forcing her foot to stomp on the accelerator.

She squealed as the car took off, but it wasn't going nearly fast enough to outrun Séamus's 5 Series.

"Kellen!" she gasped, white-knuckling the steering wheel as I turned round to watch for the Beemer. "I don't know how to drive on this side of the road!"

"I don't give a shite which side ya drive on," I said, staring into the empty street behind us. "Just do it as fast as ya can, and turn ... now!"

I held on to the headrest, watching behind us, as Darby jerked the wheel to the right. I thought we could disappear onto a side street before we were spotted, but no such luck. Séamus's car came flying onto the road, fishtailing as it took the turn at full speed, and it was definitely not Séamus in the driver's seat.

"Now what?" Darby asked, stomping the accelerator on her own this time.

"Now, ya do it again. Keep turning till we lose 'em."

She jerked the wheel again almost immediately. The injuries on my left side screamed as I clung to the seat, but it was nothing compared to the pain I'd be in if they caught us. The Bratva did not enjoy doling out quick deaths. Especially not when revenge was on the line.

I kept my eyes fixed on the stretch of black road behind us. The docks were in an industrial part of town. There were a few B&Bs and restaurants that catered to the exhausted cargo ship crews that came in and out of the harbor, but their lights had been off for hours. These folks were hardworking early to bed, early to rise types, so there wasn't a soul on the roads but us.

And the Russians.

Darby cut the wheel again, this time remembering to stay on the left side of the road.

"Did we lose 'em?" she asked, a tinge of excitement defying the fear in her voice as she stomped down on the accelerator.

I hadn't seen anyone behind us in three turns, so I finally allowed myself to relax and face her. Darby looked like a rebellious teen who'd stolen her parents' car, sitting on the edge of the driver's seat in order to reach the pedals, an oversize black jacket and beanie swallowing her soft features, and a mixture of exhilaration and terror on her pretty, freckled face.

DEVIL OF DUBLIN

I got an even better glimpse at that expression when it was suddenly illuminated by the distant yellow glow of oncoming headlights.

I looked round for a place to turn, but the road was one long straightaway, flanked on both sides by dense woods. Then, I recounted the number of turns Darby had taken and the half-second of relief I'd allowed myself to feel turned to arsenic in my guts.

A right and three lefts.

We were no longer being chased by Alexi. We were barreling straight toward him.

"Kellen?" Darby asked, the thrill in her voice completely gone.

"Get down."

"What?"

"Keep yer foot on the pedal," I said, never taking my eyes off the headlights flying toward us like the wrath of Satan, "and get the fuck down. Now!"

Darby did as I'd said, and I grabbed the wheel with my left hand the moment she let go. Leaning my body over hers, I braced my wrist on her open window and took aim at the black-and-chrome nightmare screaming toward us.

I locked eyes with Alexi, who was leaning out the passenger window, staring me down over the barrel of a shotgun. His meaty face contorted into a sneer, but when I exhaled and squeezed the trigger, it wasn't his skull that I sank a bullet into.

It was his driver's. The bear-sized security guard that I'd snuck past the night I killed Dmitry.

As soon as the windscreen shattered, I knew I'd hit my mark. The BMW began to spin out, but not before Alexi fired off one last shot.

Covering Darby's whimpering body with mine, I heard the metallic pings of buckshot peppering the door beside our heads and ripping through the back of her seat. I braced for impact, but it never came. All I felt was the violent shuddering of rocks under our tires as they drifted off the road.

I righted the wheel and lifted my head, just enough to watch in the side mirror as Séamus's pride and joy took a swan dive into the woods. The trees seemed to open up and swallow the vehicle whole. I held my breath and stared at the now-empty road behind us as I found myself doing something that I'd sworn I'd never do again.

Something I couldn't seem to *stop* doing ever since I'd come across Patrick O'Toole's obituary that morning.

I hoped.

I hoped Alexi was dead.

I hoped Darby was okay.

I hoped she wouldn't run screaming from me the second she got the chance.

I hoped I could get us the fuck out of Ireland before it was too late.

But when the silhouette of a large, four-legged creature crawled out of the forest—when it climbed the embankment, stood on two legs, tipped its bald head back, and roared into the night—I remembered why I'd sworn off that useless fucking emotion in the first place.

Hope was a killer.

Just like me.

CHAPTER 15

DARBY

I didn't know how much farther Kellen had driven with his body draped over mine, but I did know that when he finally pulled over, I missed the weight of him.

In a matter of seconds, we had gone from careening out of control through a hurricane of bullets to sitting in a state of eerie, silent stillness. It was so disorienting that I began to wonder if I was dead. But then Kellen's fingertips were brushing the hair away from my face and his voice was asking if I was hurt, and I clung to both as proof of life.

I tried to focus on my body. I didn't feel any pain other than a dull throbbing in my cheekbone, but then I remembered where I'd gotten that injury—I remembered *everything*—and I felt like I was going to be sick.

Opening my eyes, I half-expected to find myself in bed, waking from some twisted nightmare, but instead, I was curled up in the driver's seat of a tiny car with the steering wheel in the wrong place.

As I blinked away the brain fog, I turned to find Kellen's silhouette looming over me. His features were shrouded in darkness—backlit by the soft, warm glow of lights outside.

Tears stung my eyes at the sight of him, and I didn't know if it was because I was relieved that he was okay or because I was realizing just how not okay things really were.

Taking my arm, Kellen helped me sit up. His wild eyes and rough hands skimmed my body, my head, looking for signs of injury, while my gaze drifted past him to the building we were parked next to. It was a row of small stucco townhomes, maybe six, each painted the color of an Easter egg. Pastel blue, purple, peach, yellow. The ones on the end didn't have any lights on, so I couldn't tell what color they were. It was as if the night were trying to swallow the building whole, and it had started with that side.

"Where are we?" I asked, my voice sounding like I hadn't used it in days.

"A B&B off the main roads," he said, tilting his head toward the building. "Stay here."

"No." My eyes darted back to his shadowy face. "Please don't leave me in the car again. I want to come with you."

Kellen sighed and ran a hand over his head. As he did, a few shards of broken glass tumbled out of his buzzed hair, sparkling like crystal raindrops as they fell onto the seat. "Fine." He nodded. "But ya gotta be quiet."

Walking down to the dark end of the building—Kellen carrying a heavy black duffel bag as well as my suitcase—I noticed that the street we were on felt more like an alley. It was hardly wider than one lane, dotted with dumpsters and standing puddles of water, and the power lines sagged overhead, ancient and depressed. But across from the townhomes, in a gap between the backs of two other dilapidated buildings, I could see the harbor.

I expected Kellen to knock on one of the doors or call someone to let us in, but instead, he headed around to the back of the last townhome. After listening through the door and trying the knob, he grasped the wrought iron handrails on either side of the stairs, leaned back, and kicked the door open.

I flinched, but it wasn't nearly as loud as I'd thought it would be. Kellen disappeared inside, and for a few seconds, I watched the light from his cell phone dart around in the house. Then, he reappeared in the doorway, gesturing for me to come in.

The moment the door closed behind me, Kellen grabbed a wooden chair from the kitchen table and propped it up under the doorknob. Then, he took me by the arm, and using his cell phone again, he shone a light on the floor to guide me up the stairs.

I had so many questions but was terrified to speak. Kellen had told me to be quiet, and after everything that had happened that day, I was beginning to realize that when Kellen told me to do something, not listening could get one of us killed.

Taking me into an upstairs room, he closed the door behind us and turned on a lamp. The room was tiny—just big enough for a full-size bed and a dresser—and had a single blackout curtain covering its only window. I didn't have time to take in much more than that because the second the space was illuminated, I noticed that the back of Kellen's black T-shirt was shredded on one side.

And soaked in blood.

I gasped, immediately covering my mouth to muffle the sound.

Kellen just stood there with his back to me, muscles bunched, head hung, one hand gripping the edge of the dresser, the other gripping the back of his neck. Suddenly, he slammed his fist into the wooden surface, over and over and over.

I pressed myself against the back of the door as he stormed past me, but he had nowhere to go. Once he reached the end of the room, Kellen turned and headed back, rubbing his head with both hands as he paced the length of the narrow room.

"Kellen?" I whispered, figuring that if he could make that much noise, then I could make a little too.

No response.

"Kellen."

He blew past me again, the scent of blood reminding me with every pass just how badly injured he was.

"Talk to me. Please."

It was as if it physically pained him to stop pacing. On the opposite side of the room, Kellen took an enormous breath before turning to face me, agony marring his usually stoic features. He laced his fingers together on top of his head, and it reminded me of the way criminals stood when they surrendered to the police. He was giving up. I just didn't know what he thought he was losing.

Finally, with a soul-deep sigh, he said, "There's a Garda station down the way. Take the car, tell 'em ya got lost near the docks and accidentally witnessed some kind of ... transaction. The criminals shot at yer car, and when ya veered off the road, they tried to kidnap you and yer fiancé. You escaped, but they hauled John into a black BMW and drove away."

"What?" I sputtered, feeling like the floor itself had dropped out from under me.

"They'll take care of ya." Kellen's voice cracked as his hands fell to his sides. "Get ya back home."

He wanted me to leave.

He was telling me to leave.

Panic, hot and frenzied, slithered under my skin.

"Kellen, I ... I'm sorry. I'm so sorry."

"For what?" he snapped, his anger causing the tears that had been welling up to finally spill down my cheeks.

"I ... I took too many turns," I said, shaking my head. I closed my eyes and covered them with my hands, searching for words to explain something I didn't fully understand. "I don't know. I don't know what's happening, but you needed me to get you out of there, and I didn't. I took too many left turns or something, and now you're hurt, and you're mad at me, and—"

My eyes flew open as Kellen's hand wrapped around my face. I hadn't even heard him move. His gunmetal gray eyes were brimming with madness as they shifted between mine. But I wasn't afraid.

I knew fear. I'd been living with it since I was thirteen years old. In fact, the only time I hadn't felt it was every second since Kellen had come storming back into my life. Even though danger chased him like a shadow, even though I might never know what he was involved in or when the next threat would appear, I couldn't deny that I'd felt safer with him in a hail of gunfire than I had in my own home.

"You did nothin' wrong," he growled, his gruff voice vibrating through my skin. "*Nothin'.* Ya understand? But yer not safe here anymore. Not with me. Go home, Darby. *Please.*"

Something in the way he said *please* felt like he'd just reached inside of my chest and returned my heart.

Pressing a hand to his cheek, I watched through watery eyes as Kellen's face crumpled under my touch. As his strong eyebrows pulled together in pain and his throat worked to swallow the emotion I could feel radiating off of him.

I wanted so badly to tell him that I *was* home—that *he* was the only thing in my life that felt safe and familiar and warm and comforting, not a house, not a place—but how could I? We'd only been reunited for a few hours, and during those hours, Kellen had proven that he was anything *but* safe. It made no sense, but the fact remained—I couldn't make myself say goodbye to him if my life depended on it.

And it probably did.

Maybe it was because when I stroked his rough, chiseled cheekbone, I pictured it the way it used to look—soft, like a cherub's, and hidden behind a curtain of shiny black curls. Maybe it was because I remembered the way it used to turn pink whenever he spoke to me. *Only me.* Or maybe it was because I knew that cheek had probably been punched more times than it had ever been kissed.

Pushing up onto my tiptoes, I closed my eyes and pressed my lips to the hard, stubbled ridge of Kellen's cheekbone. And just like always, an avalanche of tingles washed over me the second we touched, leaving my entire body covered in goose bumps.

Fairy magic.

"I want to stay here. With *you*," I whispered, sliding back down to my flat feet.

"You don't know what yer sayin'," Kellen rasped without opening his eyes. His grip on my jaw softening. "You don't know what I am."

Tilting his face down with both hands, I waited for him to open those crystalline eyes so that he would see the sincerity shining out of mine before I finally said, "Yes, I do."

Kellen held his breath as I reached for the hem of his T-shirt.

"Now, let me see how bad it is."

I don't know what I'd been expecting, but half a dozen gaping holes in Kellen's side and shoulder blade—each about a third of an inch wide and dripping blood—wasn't it.

Jesus Christ.

Kellen insisted that I couldn't take him to a hospital, so I rummaged through my suitcase until I found a pair of tweezers and some hand sanitizer to sterilize them with.

I had him lie facedown on the bed and knelt beside him with a few wet washcloths arranged on a towel, like some kind of Civil War–era medic. I should have been freaked out, and I was, but I'd be lying if I said I wasn't a little excited too. It was the first time I hadn't felt completely useless in a long, long time.

"I feel like I should give you some whiskey or something first," I said, cleaning the first wound with a washcloth.

Kellen winced. "I don't drink."

"Really? And they haven't kicked you off the island yet?"

A tiny smile tugged at his lips, but it was quickly replaced with a grunt and a grimace as I dug a small, blood-smeared silver pellet out of the wound with a pair of eyebrow tweezers.

He sighed in relief as soon as it was over. "If they did, I wouldn't be able to go farther than Great Britain."

"Why not?" I dropped the buckshot onto the towel.

"No passport." Kellen winced again.

"Sorry." I dabbed his next wound a little more gently.

"Like I said before, I don't exist. Not on paper anyway. I tried to find me birth certificate years ago, so I could get a driving license, but there's no record of a Kellen Donovan being born anywhere in the country within a year of when I think I was born."

"What do you mean, when you *think* you were born? You don't know?"

Kellen gritted his teeth as I dug for another pellet. Then, he shook his head.

"I remember having a birthday cake once, when I still lived with me mam. It was so dark and cold in our flat that I didn't want to blow the candles out, so I know it was winter—maybe January or February? And I must have been turnin' five because she left me at Father Henry's not long after that, and I started school."

Oh my God.

I forced a smile to mask my heartbreak as I leaned down to look him in the eye. "I think that's the most you've ever said to me."

A bashful smile brightened his dark features ... and sealed my fate along with it. I couldn't walk away after seeing *that*. I was doomed to spend the rest of my life trying to make him do that again. As often as possible.

"You know, today might be your birthday," I mused, committing the image of his smiling, stubbled face to memory. "But then again, I hope it's not. This would be a pretty shitty way to spend your birthday." A nervous laugh percolated in the back of my throat when I realized that, once again, no one was going to yell at me for cursing.

"I disagree." Kellen's gaze held me captive as that sweet, shy smile morphed into something a little more ... heated.

My face flushed immediately, and I sat back up, trying desperately to remember what the hell I'd been doing before Kellen's smile happened to me.

"So ..." I cleared my throat, dabbing another wound. "If you don't have a birth certificate, I guess you couldn't get your license."

"No license. No passport. No credit cards. Nothin'."

"So, how did you join the military if there's no record of you?"

Kellen's back muscles tensed at the question, causing fresh blood to seep from a few of his wounds.

Good God.

"You really can't talk about it, can you?"

He shook his head. All traces of that boyish smile from moments ago were long gone.

"Can you at least tell me if the guys who shot at us are"—*dead*—"still out there?"

Kellen squeezed his eyes shut with a grunt as I yanked another pellet from his back. Then, he was quiet for a long time.

My stomach soured as I realized that he wasn't going to answer that question either.

"Is this just ... normal for you?"

Is this what my life is going to be like if I stay with you?

Kellen shook his head. "Sometimes I go weeks without an assignment."

"Really?" The hopefulness in my voice was almost embarrassing. "What do you do?"

He shrugged. "Work out, read, target prac—ah!"

"Sorry!" I dropped another pellet onto the towel. "I think that was the last one. I'm gonna wipe you off, okay?"

Kellen seemed to relax as I used the wet washcloth to clean the blood off his back. The entire surface was a patchwork of scars, both old and new. It made my stomach turn to think about how much he'd already endured in such a short amount of time. He was only twenty-two.

Maybe twenty-three.

I patted his skin dry and placed six small, round bandages on his wounds. I'd tossed them into my suitcase just in case my high heels gave me blisters at the funeral. I had no idea I'd be using almost the entire box to patch Kellen Donovan's buckshot holes.

When I was done, Kellen rolled onto his good side so that he could look at me.

I tried not to gawk at his bare chest or the way his ab muscles flexed as he propped his head up on his hand.

"Thanks," he said, that single word strangled with emotion.

I dropped my eyes and busied myself with the items on the bed, the intensity of his stare making me restless. "Don't thank me yet. It could still get infected."

"With the number of plasters you put on there? Not likely."

I glanced up just in time to see another small smile brighten Kellen's exhausted face. He must have been in so much pain, but he didn't let on.

"It's after dark," he said, his smile fading.

I nodded, my heart suddenly pounding as I tried to keep my eyes on his face instead of the deep, muscular Adonis belt disappearing into his black jeans. "Mmhmm."

"So ... what happens now?"

"What ..." I swallowed the drool in my mouth as I tried to shrug nonchalantly. "What do you mean?"

"Earlier"—he paused to wet his lips—"you said, when we were kids, you wanted to stay out with me ... after dark."

I nodded, feeling my cheeks heat.

"I never"—Kellen's voice trailed off along with his gaze—"did that."

Was he saying that he'd never had a sleepover or that he'd never ...

No. Kellen was a living, breathing temple of masculinity. I'd only been in his shirtless presence for five seconds, and most of my brain cells had already died and diverted all of their resources to my ovaries. Obviously, he'd had sex.

"You never went to a sleepover?" I asked, just to clarify.

Kellen shook his head, just a fraction of an inch, and in that moment, those dove gray eyes were the same exact ones I'd stolen glances of in the woods all those years ago. That sweet, honest face, shunned by an entire village. My blood boiled as I thought about what life must have been like for him. What it could have been like if he'd been raised by literally anyone else.

"Come on," I said, extending a hand to help him up.

"Where are we goin'?"

"Camping." I beamed.

CHAPTER 16

KELLEN

While Darby busied herself, making a "campsite," I paced in the kitchen, planning possible escape routes.

Not from the Russians or the UIB, but from the American bird in the next room who was rambling on about Girl Scout badges and fire-building techniques.

I wanted to bolt with every fiber of my being. I wanted to run until my lungs burned and my legs gave out. I wanted to get as far away from Darby and the train wreck that was about to happen as I possibly could.

But another part of me—the part that kept me there, pacing like an eejit—wanted Darby even more.

I flexed my back until the wounds peppering my left side sang in pain. It was the only thing that helped release the pressure building inside of me. I was about to be humiliated in front of the only girl I'd ever cared about—and I was powerless to stop it.

"Did you find any food?"

I spun around to find Darby standing wide-eyed in the doorway, illuminated by the harbor lights shining in through the kitchen window. She was wearing a Georgia State University jumper and a pair of black leggings. It was probably what she'd changed into before we left Glenshire, but she'd been wearing my jacket the entire time. An irrational wave of anger washed over me at the sight of her without it on.

God, I was fucked.

I shook my head.

"That's okay." She beamed, reaching over to take my clammy hand. "We'll have a giant birthday breakfast in the morning."

She had to practically drag me into the living room, where the sound of a crackling fire and scent of cedar logs swirled in the air. She'd laid the comforter from the upstairs bed on the floor in front of the woodstove and thrown the curtains back so that the night sky was on full display.

Here we fucking go.

Tugging me down to the blanket along with her, Darby lay on her left side, and with my heart sprinting and my stomach in knots, I mirrored her. My bullet wounds protested at the movement, but the wave of pain helped calm me down. I closed my eyes and held on to it as long as possible.

With my eyes screwed shut, the sounds and smells of the fire helped calm me as well. Fire used to scare me when I was younger. It reminded me too much of hell, of the evil that everyone said burned inside of me. But after I finally let it consume me, let it unleash its fury on Father Henry, let the flames burn his body and everything he'd ever loved to the ground, I didn't fear it anymore.

The flames had set me free.

Opening my eyes, I found Darby staring at me, her orange hair shining like strands of forged copper in the firelight.

"What were you thinking about?" she asked.

"The fire," I answered truthfully.

"This one or ... the one back in Glenshire?" Her face fell.

"Both."

"Oh God. Kellen, I'm so sorry." Darby sat up, as if she were about to douse the thing with a bucket of water. "I wasn't thinking. I can put it out if—"

DEVIL OF DUBLIN

I grabbed her forearm and smiled when she glanced over her shoulder at me in mortification. "It's fine." I shook my head, more than a little amused over her concern. "It's ... nice."

Darby beamed with pride, her shoulders relaxing as she sat with her legs crossed, facing me. "It is, isn't it? I haven't lived anywhere with a fireplace since my mom ..." Her smile faded as her gaze drifted to the floor.

"I'm sorry ... about yer mam."

Darby's eyes shot up in surprise.

"Yer not the only one who has access to the internet, ya know." I smirked. "I mighta looked ya up once or twice."

The smile that comment earned me made me want to pound my chest with pride. Instead, I did something even stupider.

I lifted my arm and said, "C'mere."

Darby dropped her eyes and bit her lip as she crawled toward me, and I immediately knew that my relationship with fire was about to change. Because I was playing with it, and I, of all people, knew how badly that could end.

By the time Darby's head rested on my bicep, I was already hard as a fucking rock. I wanted to pull her body flush against mine. Hell, I wanted to roll her onto her back and fuck her until the sun came up, until she screamed my name and clawed my arms and wept from exhaustion. I'd been fantasizing about doing unspeakable things to Darby Collins for half my life. But fantasy and reality were two very different things.

In reality, I was paralyzed the moment her breath hit my neck. My pulse skyrocketed. My chest rose and fell like a piston, and my muscles tensed, preparing me to fight or flee.

"Kellen?" Darby's voice was featherlight. Gentle. Concerned.

It's not him, I told myself, trying to regain control of the one thing that he'd never relinquished power over. Not even in death. *It's over. It's done.*

But my body wouldn't listen. My breaths came harder, faster, as I struggled to hold on. To fight my urge to bolt.

"Can I ... tell you a ghost story?" Darby asked, her voice intentionally soothing as she watched me with wide eyes. "It's a very important part of the sleepover experience." She smiled weakly.

I knew what she was doing, and I was eternally grateful for it.

As soon as I nodded, Darby rolled onto her back and stared out the window. Her head was still propped up on my arm, but having the extra breathing room helped.

"Once upon a time," she said, drumming her slender fingers on her stomach, "there was a little girl who met a fairy prince in an enchanted forest. Only she didn't realize that he was a fairy because fairies are excellent shapeshifters, as you probably know."

I hadn't heard one of Darby's stories since I was a kid. Even though her voice was huskier now, more mature, the rhythm of it hadn't changed a bit. I relaxed as the cadence of her American accent took me back to a time when I felt no pressure to speak or ... *perform*. When I could just be Kellen. When listening was enough.

"It turned out," she continued, "that the fairy prince had been stolen from his kingdom and was being held prisoner in the woods by an evil sorcerer. He had no other fairies to play with, so the girl quickly became his only secret friend.

"They played every summer until, one year, the girl stopped coming. The fairy thought she didn't want to play with him anymore when, really, she had been captured by a different sorcerer—her own father—and was being held prisoner on the other side of the sea."

Darby wouldn't look at me. She kept her eyes locked on the moon, as if the story were written on the side of it. As if it hadn't actually happened to her.

"There were other sorcerers in her father's kingdom." Darby laced her fingers together, needing something to hold on to. "Bad ones. They would creep into her dungeon at night while her father was passed out from all the ... *potions* they liked to share, and they would ... touch her."

I couldn't believe what I was fucking hearing. My heart was pumping so hard that my entire body shook with every surge of blood. I knew Darby had to feel it, throbbing through my bicep beneath her head, but she didn't react to it. She just stared out the window. Lifeless. Vacant.

"She fought back at first," Darby said, her voice hardly louder than a whisper, "but … they liked that. They liked it when they had to hold her down, muffle her screams. And she hated being held down. She hated it so much that, eventually … she learned how to die."

Darby's eyes flicked to mine, just for a second, but the emotion I saw in her tortured stare was one I'd felt more times than I could even admit to myself. Desperation. Fear. Shame.

Pure, undiluted hatred flooded my body, demanding vengeance. Seeking a release. But I forced myself to breathe through it. To reach over and squeeze her knotted hands and listen even though it was torture.

"Whenever a sorcerer came in, reeking of potions, the girl's ghost would leave her body and fly up to the moon. There, she would look down on the enchanted forest over the sea and dream about the fairy prince until it was safe for her to come back to life."

Darby squeezed my hand back, and it almost fucking killed me. All those years, I'd thought she'd forgotten about me, moved on to some less complicated fella, one who could actually speak, give her a normal life, and all the while, she'd been …

Christ.

"Then, one day," she continued, "a handsome prince came and took her away from the dungeon. He promised to take care of her, to make her a princess, but … he was just another sorcerer in disguise."

Captain America. That rapist piece of shite.

"She had to become a ghost so often she almost forgot what it felt like to be alive. But, when the girl's grandfather died, she and the evil prince took a trip across the sea, back to the enchanted forest. And when she got there, she realized that she couldn't die anymore. Her ghost was trapped inside her body. So, that night, when the evil prince came for her, tried to hurt her, she fought back, like she used to. She kicked and screamed and fought so hard that the fairy prince heard her cries and came to her rescue."

She looked at me with tears in her eyes and a grateful smile on her perfect, freckled face. "He saved her, just like he had already saved himself."

Without thinking, without a shred of fear, I pulled her body flush against mine.

Darby released a shuddering breath as her face nuzzled into the space between my shoulder and neck. Her body molded to mine like it had been carved from it. But the moment her hip came to rest against the bulge in my jeans, I tensed and tightened my grip. The vein in my neck began to throb against her cheek, but Darby didn't pull away this time.

And I didn't want her to.

Pressing a kiss to the side of my neck, just like she'd done when I was fourteen years old, Darby murmured, "It's okay. We can just stay like this. I won't touch you, I promise."

And with that handful of whispered words, I felt as if a ten-ton weight had been lifted off my chest. I could breathe again, think again. My muscles relaxed as I buried my face in her hair, as a silent sob lodged itself in my throat.

Soft, lingering kisses peppered my collarbone, my neck, the hard line of my jaw, but somehow, they didn't trigger my panic. In fact, they had quite the opposite effect.

Tilting my head down, I met Darby's deep green gaze and felt nothing but need. The need to protect her, the need to please her, the need to possess her, body and soul. Longing—a lifetime in the making—surged through my veins, hot enough to burn away all the hatred that had come before it.

I dropped my hooded gaze to her lips and watched as her glistening tongue slid along the seam, wetting them in response to my silent question. The next thing I knew, my tongue was sliding along that same cleft, tasting her, seeking entrance. And Darby granted it. Tilting her head, she opened up for me, welcomed me in. And I felt something inside my chest do the same for her.

DEVIL OF DUBLIN

It was unlike anything I'd ever experienced. Up to that point, kissing Darby had been the highlight of my short, pathetic life, but even in those moments, I hadn't been able to fully enjoy it. I was always so afraid that I'd freak out, like I always did. That one wrong move would cause me to shove her away—or worse, hurt her. But with Darby's promise that she wouldn't touch me, I felt free. The panic disappeared, leaving only pleasure.

I thought Darby felt freer as well. Her thigh slipped between my legs as her hand slid up the back of my head, clutching me tight. It was as if she couldn't get close enough. She moaned softly against my mouth as I took my time, savoring her, tracing the swell of her lips with my tongue, finding a rhythm, and once I did, Darby matched it with her rolling hips. Our pace was slow and torturous, the most exquisite agony I'd ever felt.

And through it, Darby kept her word. With one hand tucked between our chests and the other raking its nails over my buzzed scalp, I felt completely safe. Not from her, but from *myself*.

Soon, our tongues, our breaths, and our bodies began to collide faster and faster. I could practically see sparks behind my eyelids when Darby eventually tore her mouth away from mine.

"I'm on fire," she panted, pulling her jumper off over her head.

I gazed down the length of us and watched, mesmerized, as a pair of firm, round tits threatened to spill over the top of a black lace bra. As Darby's hips rolled against my rigid cock—the tip of which was now visible above the waistband of my jeans, swollen and glistening. As she arched her back and whimpered softly.

Fuuuck.

I had the skills necessary to take a life with my bare hands or from thirty meters away, but *nothing* had ever made me feel more powerful than discovering that I had the ability to make Darby Collins make *that* fucking sound.

As her mouth crashed into mine again, I shifted my body so that she was no longer grinding against my hip. She was grinding against *me*. The thin fabric of her leggings was slick and hot against my sensitive, exposed flesh, her need obvious and maddening. I wrapped my hand around the back of her head, clutching her to me as her whimpers evolved into a chanted plea. And when she finally came, her fingertips curling against my scalp, I devoured her cries, swallowed them, drank them in like a desperate, starving man. Darby clung to me as she writhed in pleasure, my cock straining painfully against my jeans until one needy, whispered word sent me over the edge.

"Kellen."

Squeezing her even tighter, I buried my face in her hair as a tidal wave of ecstasy and emotion crashed over me, racking my body, laying waste to everything I was or ever had been before that moment.

I was no longer human or demon or even fucking breathing. I was simply *hers*—mind, body, and cursed black soul.

CHAPTER 17

DARBY

I knew he was gone before I opened my eyes. I didn't know what city I was in, what room I was in, or even what day it was, but I knew that wherever I was, Kellen wasn't there. I could feel it in my bones.

I rolled over and looked around, waiting for my groggy brain to wake up and start working again. The last thing I remembered was falling asleep in Kellen's arms on the living room floor, and after that ... sweet nothing. I'd never slept so deeply in my life. My muscles tingled as I stretched and groaned, the remnants of some delicious dream just beyond my reach.

I could tell that I was in a bed, and the slivers of light sneaking in through the sides of the blackout curtains illuminated just enough of the room for me to recognize where I was. At some point during the night, Kellen must have carried me upstairs and tucked me in.

Sitting up, I shook off my sleepy stupor and listened for him. I ran my hand over the side of the mattress where he would have slept. It was cold.

Dread gripped me like a fist, pulling me out of bed and dragging me over to the window.

Sliding the edge of the curtain back just an inch or two, I peeked outside. The wintry gray sky blotted out the rising sun and dulled the already-faded colors of the rusty shipping containers stacked in the port below. But the water in the harbor sparkled in spite of it. Just like the metallic silver paint on the Ford Fiesta parked down the street.

I exhaled in relief.

Leaving the curtain cracked for light, I dug a clean sweatshirt and a pair of jeans out of my suitcase, but I was definitely going to need to shower before I put them on. Memories from the night before came rushing back—of our sweat-slicked bodies crushed together; of the desperate clinging, writhing need; of the warmth that splashed across my stomach and chest when Kellen finally let himself go.

The same tingly heat I'd felt the night before spread across my skin again, until another memory chased it away: The terrified look on Kellen's face when he'd first come to lay by the fire. The paralysis. The hyperventilating. It had felt like I was looking into a mirror. I knew Kellen had been abused by Father Henry—I'd seen it with my own eyes—but until that moment, I'd had no idea just how bad it had been.

The image of Kellen's shiny black curls scattered all over a bloody attic floor flashed behind my eyes, and my stomach lurched. What other horrors had taken place in that windowless room? What else had Kellen endured in silence?

I was thirteen years old the first time one of my father's drug buddies crept into my bedroom in the middle of the night. The ink hadn't even dried on my mom's death certificate when I had my innocence ripped away from me. I knew how threatening it felt when someone so much as looked at your body after that, let alone reached for it. I at least had thirteen years' worth of memories to remind me what real affection felt like. I knew, on some level, that not all touches hurt.

I doubted that Kellen did.

I drifted down the hallway, so lost in my own thoughts that I didn't hear the water running until I opened the bathroom door and walked face-first into a wall of steam.

"Oh! God! Sorry!" My eyes darted over to the shower in the corner of the room, and I can't deny that I was more than a little disappointed to discover that the glass door was already fogged up.

I should have let him have his privacy, but after waking up alone, my need to be near him wouldn't let me leave.

"Actually, do you mind if I brush my teeth real quick?" I didn't wait for an answer.

Crossing the small bathroom, I picked up my toothbrush, which was already wet.

"You used my toothbrush?" I grinned, watching Kellen's blurry silhouette turn to face me behind the glass.

"After last night, I didn't think you'd mind."

I glanced in the mirror to see if I was blushing as hard as I thought I was, but the mirror was fogged up too. It was for the best. I didn't want to see the bruise I could feel blooming across my cheekbone. I wanted to pretend like everything that had happened since the last time I'd seen Kellen never really happened at all. Like I'd hopped in a time machine and traveled from one of his kisses to another, bypassing all of the darkness in between.

I took my vitamins and birth control and brushed my teeth on autopilot as I watched Kellen slowly turn in the spray, his hands skimming over his chest. His arms. His thighs.

"How's your back?" I mumbled around the plastic handle in my mouth, hoping that he would tell me it was fine. That he could stay in the shower all day.

With me.

"Oh, it's grand."

I spat and rinsed my mouth out. "I doubt that."

Silence stretched between us as I felt that same pull, low and deep in my belly, that I'd felt the night before, watching Kellen wade into the lake. The one that commanded me to follow. The one that took control of my body, stripped me naked, and sent me into uncharted waters, freezing and alone.

I couldn't have stopped myself if I'd tried. All I could do was hold my breath and count my thundering heartbeats as I shed my clothes, crossed the room, opened the glass door, and stepped inside.

Kellen stood, facing me, his broad shoulders blocking the spray, and the sight of him took my breath away. He was a mountain, covered in hard expanses of muscle with deep, sweeping valleys in between. Veins climbed up his chiseled arms like vines, and two thick ridges led from the top of his hips down to a long, thick cock that made my mouth water.

I had never understood desire before. I didn't *want* men; I wanted to avoid men. I wanted to become invisible to men. But Kellen wasn't a man. He was a god. Powerful and divine and impossibly perfect. From the moment I'd first laid eyes on him, I'd been captivated by his supernatural beauty. His singular attention. His silent, calculating intelligence. But seeing his virility in the flesh made me want to drop to my knees and worship.

Kellen's chest began to rise and fall faster, his nostrils flaring with every inhalation, as I tried to figure out what to do next.

Closing the door behind me, I stepped toward him, stopping just before his cock grazed my belly. Kellen's heated stare raked over my body, like the drag of a match just before it caught flame.

I held my breath as he dropped his eyes and lifted his hand to my breast, but he didn't touch it. His palm hovered next to it, so close I could feel the heat radiating off his skin just before he raised his hand higher and clasped my jaw instead.

When he lifted his gaze to mine again, Kellen's pupils were fully dilated. It was as if I could see the black hole of darkness swirling inside of him, growing by the second.

"How can you stand it?" he asked, his voice like sandpaper. "How can you stand to be touched after what they did?"

The breath I was holding burned in my lungs before I finally whispered, "Not all touches hurt."

Sliding his hand from my jaw to the back of my neck, Kellen pressed his forehead against mine. He was breathing like a dragon, and I could practically see the war going on behind his closed eyelids. Tilting my chin up, I pressed a soft kiss to his frowning mouth and was rewarded with one in return.

I was learning that Kellen could kiss me without hesitation even when the rest of his body was coiled like a cobra, ready to strike. And sadly, I knew why. Kissing was easier for me too, because *they* never kissed me. Father Henry had probably been the same way.

Which gave me an idea.

"Kellen?" I whispered. "Can I kiss you … somewhere else?"

His entire body went deathly still as I glanced up into his shuddered stare.

"I won't touch you," I said, turning and looking at him over my shoulder so that he could watch me lace my fingers together behind my back.

Kellen's throat bobbed as his hard gaze slid down to my bare ass and the hands that were now clasped there.

Turning back around, I searched his guarded face for consent. Kellen wore a mask of granite, but it did little to hide the heat in his eyes. The longing. The captive desire and all-consuming fear sparring inside of him.

"You can tell me to stop anytime." I gave him a small smile, hoping to put him at ease. Then, with a silent prayer, I leaned forward and pressed my lips to the center of his chest.

Water cascaded down the hard planes of muscle. They rose sharply with his sudden intake of breath and fell shakily as he exhaled through his mouth.

When Kellen seemed ready, I did it again, a few inches lower, and smiled to myself when his answering breath was a little more controlled.

I'd never been this forward with anyone. Sex had always been something that I'd endured, not enjoyed. But Kellen was different. He didn't want to take anything from me. And knowing that made me want to give him the world.

As I worked my way down his stomach, I added my tongue, sucking from the stream of water that ran down the crease between his sculpted abs.

And he stood perfectly still. He was hardly even breathing. There was no pressure. No impatient hand on my head. No demeaning dirty talk. Only trust and fear and raw vulnerability. He was giving me complete control, and the freedom I felt was intoxicating.

I held Kellen's gaze as I sank to my knees, giving him time to prepare before I slowly extended my tongue and licked him from root to tip.

The sudden groan of pleasure that left his body made me feel more triumphant than anything I had ever done in my entire pointless life. I didn't know exactly what had happened to Kellen, how much Father Henry had taken from him, but I hoped that with every pass of my lips over his tender flesh, I could help him get some of it back.

I looked up as I dragged my tongue along his rigid length again. Kellen's head was tilted up, so I had to gauge his reaction from the tightness in his jaw, the way his Adam's apple bobbed in his throat, how quickly his chest rose and fell. His muscles were tense, hands fisted at his sides, but his breathing was slowing. And when I made it to the tip…

Mmm.

That sound again. God, it turned me on.

Kellen was so tall and long that I had to stand back up and bend at the waist to take him in my mouth. But I took my time, circling his swollen crown with my tongue, enjoying the freedom he'd given me to explore, before I finally closed my lips around him and sucked.

Kellen's knees buckled slightly, and I smiled around his length.

This time, when I looked up at him, I found two endless pools of molten platinum staring back at me, deep and hot and hypnotizing. I held his stare as I found my rhythm, swirling my tongue over his sensitive head with each pass, but it wasn't long before Kellen tore his gaze away, his eyes rolling skyward as his hands found their way into my hair.

I twisted my fingers together behind my back as I sucked him faster, and Kellen twisted his fingers in my hair just as tightly, clinging to me as he fought for control. A fight that he was quickly losing.

"Fuck," Kellen hissed, but as his hips began to jerk, as his grasp on my hair became tighter, a different voice cursed at me from the recesses of my mind.

"That's why you ran off tonight, isn't it? To go fuck some old flame?"

Guilt slithered into my stomach, making it roil with sudden disgust.

"I pulled you out of the fucking gutter, and this is how you repay me? By spreading your legs for some fucking farmhand the second you get the chance?"

Kellen's length skimmed the back of my throat, and I gagged violently. I felt like I might puke. I couldn't breathe. *I couldn't breathe.*

"*You little … fucking … whore.*"

Then, just as I began to panic, the world around me fell away. I could no longer feel the spray of the shower, or the flesh on my tongue. I couldn't hear John's voice anymore, or the ugly truth in his words. All I could feel, as I floated up to the moon, was sadness because I'd wanted to do something nice for Kellen and I'd failed.

Just like I always did.

CHAPTER 18

KELLEN

Darkness lurked at the edges of my vision as I struggled to keep my demons at bay. But it wasn't the regular monsters I was fighting—the ones that threatened to grab me and drag me back into that dank, dark attic, the ones that told me to fight or flee. Instead, it was the black, bottomless pit of shame festering inside of me that wouldn't let me out of my own head.

I tried to ignore it, to focus solely on Darby. I shoved my hands into her thick, wet hair. I watched her fingers twist and coil around one another where they rested on her arched, round arse. And I concentrated on the sheer fucking bliss of having her sweet pink mouth wrapped around my cock. But not even that could distract me from the fact that I was a piece of shite for letting her do it.

I deserved to rot in hell for the things I'd done, not have God's most perfect angel on her knees before me. It was wrong, letting her suck me off like I was some Prince Charming, when the truth about me would send her running in the opposite direction. Darby was just trading one demon for another, and she didn't even know it.

My fists tightened in her hair as I considered pulling her off of me. Telling her to leave again. Forcing her to do it this time. But my body wasn't listening. As Darby sucked me faster and faster, my hips met her rhythm, thrusting with every soft pull of her mouth as the immaculate pleasure seized me in its grip.

"Fuck," I hissed, hating myself for losing the battle between my conscience and my cock.

My balls tightened. My shaft stiffened and jerked in her mouth. But just before I surrendered to the darkness and the self-loathing I knew would follow, I heard something that brought me crashing back to earth.

A sound I'd heard dozens of times before.

A sound I'd *caused* dozens of times before.

The wet, muffled gag of someone being choked.

I jerked away immediately, and with my hands still in her hair, I tilted Darby's head back so that I could see her face. But she was gone. A string of saliva hung from her panting, parted lips as she stared, unfocused, off to the side of the shower. Her hands were loose where they rested on her arse, and when I guided her to stand, twin tears rolled down her vacant, freckled face.

"Fuck. Darby, look at me."

But she wouldn't. Instead, she closed her faraway eyes completely as her face contorted into a silent sob.

A roar tore from my lungs as I smashed the side of my fist into the tiled wall.

Darby recoiled from me with her entire body, making me feel like even more of a monster than I already did.

I reached for her but pulled my hands back at the last second. I didn't know if I could touch her like this. I didn't know if I could touch her at all. But when Darby wrapped her own arms around her beautiful body and squeezed, I wanted those arms to be mine more than I'd ever wanted anything.

I expected her to fight me. I expected her to scream. But when I picked her up and carried her into the bedroom, Darby clung to me instead. She wrapped her arms around my shoulders and her legs around my waist, and when she buried her face in my neck, I wanted to fucking die.

Sitting on the edge of the bed, I clutched her wet, shuddering body to my chest and kissed her face and whispered a thousand inaudible apologies as she sobbed. Every tear was like a dagger through my fucking heart. I'd known this was going to happen. The moment Darby kissed me by the lough, I knew I'd let this go too far. I knew I'd end up hurting her. And I'd done it anyway.

Darby began rubbing her face back and forth where it was pressed against the curve of my neck, as if she were replying no to a question I hadn't asked yet. I felt her whispered words buzz against my collarbone before I was able to figure out what she was saying.

"I heard him, Kellen. I heard his voice. It's like he was right there."

My heart pounded against hers as I realized what was happening.

Darby wasn't upset about the shower.

She was finally processing what had happened the night before. Maybe countless nights before.

"Shh …" I said, holding her closer, wrapping her long, wet hair around my fist. "Yer hearin' my voice now, and I swear, as long as I'm breathin', no one's ever gonna hurt ya like that again. Understand?"

Darby sucked in a shuddering breath but said nothing.

I pulled her head up by the hair in my fist, gently but firmly, until we were face-to-face. Darby's sad emerald eyes gleamed as they gazed upon the wrath living just below the surface of mine.

"Understand?"

Swallowing, she nodded, only breaking our stare long enough to press a soft, lingering kiss to my lips. We stayed like that for several heartbeats, and in the stillness, I realized that her slick, warm flesh was pressed against my cock as well.

"I'm sorry," she finally whispered before returning her face to the crook of my neck. "I'm sorry I'm so fucked up."

Pulling her head back again, I released a humorless laugh as I gazed into her wide, worried eyes. "Trust me," I said, giving her a smirk, "yer the least fucked up person in this room."

Darby's swollen lips spread into a breathtaking smile, and at that very second, I made a vow to myself. I didn't deserve to breathe the same air as her, but I was going to. From that moment on, I was going to be every bit the white knight she saw when she looked at me. Darby deserved a hero, and I'd be goddamned if I was going to let it be anyone else.

Her smile faded, and her eyes dropped as a pink flush flooded her cheeks. Then, Darby's hips began to move.

Sliding her fingertips up the back of my head, she repeated her promise from the night before. "We can just stay like this."

And I nodded before claiming her mouth like a fucking heathen.

Darby whimpered against my lips as she slid up and down my shaft—always keeping her hands above my waist, always so careful not to touch—and the magnitude of that gift nearly broke me. I hadn't thought it was possible to be that close to another person without panic or guilt or flashbacks. But Darby had found a way. And when her body moved up to my swollen crown, when she bit her lip and held her breath and looked at me with a silent question in her eyes, I answered with a single flex of my hips.

A silky, warm bliss enveloped me, spreading over my skin like sunshine, as Darby stilled, allowing the significance of the moment to settle in. I'd never experienced anything so pure. So perfect. I sealed my lips over hers as she began to rise and fall, adjusting to my size before we were fully joined. And once I was as deep inside of her as I could get, wrapped in a dream that I'd never thought would come true, something inside of me shattered.

Darby gasped into my mouth as I rolled my hips beneath her, thrusting even deeper, needing to fill her, claim her, be consumed by her.

With her wet hair still wrapped around my fist, I pulled her head back gently so that I could look at her.

DEVIL OF DUBLIN

Darby's eyes were hooded but focused.

"Stay with me," I begged. "Please."

Fresh tears sprang to her eyes as she nodded, and her sweet, answering smile stole the breath from my lungs ... just before I kissed it off of her.

With her tongue in my mouth and her warm body wrapped around mine, I was a fucking goner. Darby ground against me, making slow circles with her hips as I rocked into her, and with every thrust, I felt the pressure build. I held on as long as I could, never wanting the moment to end, but when I felt her muscles begin to contract, felt her teeth capture my bottom lip and her nails rake down the back of my head as she whimpered through her orgasm, I exploded.

A flood of molten hot pleasure and more than two decades' worth of pain surged through me as I clutched Darby's body to mine and let it all go. And she drank it down hungrily, her body sucking from me like she couldn't get enough. Like my darkness fed her, fulfilled her. Like she'd been starving for *me* and only me.

The need to fill her overwhelmed me. And it didn't stop with my body. I wanted to give her everything I had. My fucking life. My splintered heart. My hateful, hell bound soul. She could do with it what she pleased. I didn't care. None of it belonged to me anymore, and it hadn't since I was ten years old.

"I'm in love with you, Darby," I said, pressing my lips to her shoulder. "Always have been. And if I had a fucking birth certificate, I'd ask you to marry me right now."

My heart thundered in my chest as Darby sat up and looked at me. Her green eyes glimmered with wonder as a broad smile transformed her tear-streaked face into something I hadn't seen since we were kids. Something joyful. Something light. The heaviness of our lives lifted, and for a moment, Darby was *Darby* again—the freckle-faced girl in yellow wellies who could find magic in a rock or a broken stick ... or a motherless mute from Glenshire.

Then, she lifted her left hand and wiggled her ring finger. "You already did."

I glanced at the spot where a diamond the size of a fist used to be and found three small freckles there instead, identical to mine.

My eyebrows furrowed in confusion as her smile widened.

"This is gonna sound crazy, but … yesterday, I met a woman in the woods who said that you and I were bonded for life by a … by a lake spirit." She laughed. "That day that I fell into the blackberry bushes and we kissed in the water. She saw the freckles on my finger and said they were the mark of the spirit's blessing." Darby laced her fingers through mine so that our matching bands of freckles lined up. "I didn't believe her at first, but you have them too."

I shook my head in disbelief as I stared down at our joined hands. As the events of that day replayed in my mind. I'd memorized every second of our time together, but that moment in the lake was tattooed on my soul.

"*Is fíor bhur ngrá. Tugaim mobheannacht daoibh,*" I recited, shaking my head again as I glanced back up at her. "I heard those words, in a woman's voice, right after we kissed in the lough. I didn't even speak Irish at the time, but I never forgot them."

"What does it mean?"

I smirked. "Yer love is true. You have my blessing."

"Shut up." Darby laughed, a tear spilling over one flushed pink cheek. "Are you serious?"

I nodded. "I thought I was goin' mad."

The warmth in Darby's eyes was nothing short of breathtaking as she leaned forward and pressed a smiling kiss to my lips.

"I'm in love with you too, Kellen Donovan," she whispered, rolling her hips as I swelled inside of her. "*Always will be.*"

CHAPTER 19

DARBY

It was still early when we left. Kellen had said that all of the townhouses on that block were B&B rentals—including the one we'd crashed in—and we needed to go before they started delivering breakfasts and cleaning empty units.

It was surreal, walking with Kellen in broad daylight. The harbor was already bustling with boats, the sun had fought its way through the clouds, and every townhouse we passed was painted a different cheerful color. After the tornado of darkness and violence we'd narrowly survived the night before, it felt a lot like waking up in Oz.

Until I saw the car.

Or what was left of it.

Three of the windows were broken out, and the driver's door was peppered with buckshot holes, but somehow, the windshield was still intact.

After dropping our bags in the trunk, Kellen went around and knocked the remaining glass out of the broken windows using the side of his cell phone. The sound brought back memories from the night before, but instead of terror, all I felt was a prickly heat climb up my neck as I remembered the deliciously warm, blanketing bulletproof heaviness of Kellen's body covering mine.

I opened the passenger door and brushed the broken glass off both seats before sitting down, as if it were the most normal thing in the world, but when Kellen opened the driver's door, *that's* when my heart began to race.

It was the first time I had really seen him, the adult him, in the daylight. He was breathtaking. Fascinating. A riot of contradictions. He had the elegant features, sculpted body, and smooth skin of an angel carved from marble, but his black buzz cut, black stubble, and all-black wardrobe subverted his beauty. Cloaked it in darkness. Much like the flight jacket he was wearing to cover the buckshot holes and bloodstains on his T-shirt.

The bitterness I felt over seeing it on his body instead of mine was swift and sharp.

Kellen slid the driver's seat back a few inches before getting in, and when he did, it felt like the temperature in the car plummeted at least ten degrees. He stared straight ahead, gripping the steering wheel with both hands for what felt like minutes before he finally turned to face me.

I knew what was coming. Or at least, I thought I did.

"Kellen," I said, putting my hands up, "I know you want me to go to the police, but I told you last night—"

"I want you to leave the country with me."

I sat in stunned silence, captivated by the intensity of his stare.

"I know a way," he continued, "but if we do this, we can never come back. We'll have to cut ties with everyone, get new identities. It's not fair, what I'm askin', but—"

"You're going AWOL." My mouth fell open.

I knew Kellen had a dangerous job—some kind of secretive special forces thing—but I had no idea that he was considering defecting from the military because of it.

Or ... because of me.

When Kellen didn't respond, I leaned across the small space and planted a kiss on both his abrasive man cheek and the soft, boyish one hidden beneath. Then, I leaned back just enough to look him in the eye and asked with a smile, "So, where are we going?"

Tension rolled off Kellen's shoulders as he gripped me by the back of the head and sealed his mouth over mine. The moment our lips met, a rush of tingles washed over me, covering my skin in goose bumps and flooding every empty place with need. I knew Kellen felt it too. When he finally broke our kiss, it was with hooded eyes and panting, parted lips.

"You sure?" he asked, his pitch-black pupils locked onto mine as he started the ignition.

"Depends on where we're going." I shrugged, hoping to come across as sultry and cool, but the ear-to-ear grin on my face gave me away.

I would've followed Kellen through the gates of hell.

"New York," he said, running his thumb over my bottom lip before shifting into drive and giving his attention to the pavement ahead.

I missed his hands and eyes immediately.

He pulled off the alley and onto a road. "It's the perfect place to start over. Tons of people, English-speaking, cheap flights from Dublin, and most importantly, it's an ocean away from here."

Kellen glanced at me just in time to see me wrinkle my nose. "What?"

"Nothing," I pulled my hair over my shoulder and began weaving it into a quick braid. The wind in the car was out of control, thanks to three missing windows. "It's fine. New York is fine."

"Where do *you* want to go?" he asked, raising his voice slightly to compete with the rushing air.

"I don't know." I shrugged, a wistful smile tugging on my lips. "Somewhere magical. Romantic. Somewhere like ... Transylvania."

Kellen snorted. It was the cutest sound I'd ever heard. "Transylvania?"

"I've heard it's beautiful there. Castles, mountains, forests ..."

"You do know that Count Dracula was based on Vlad the Impaler, right? A man who decorated his yard with the impaled bodies of his enemies."

"Well, maybe they deserved it." I shrugged.

Kellen stilled, his eyes never leaving the road.

"What?" I asked.

His Adam's apple slid up and down his throat. "Could you ... love a man like that?"

"Like Vlad the Impaler?" I laughed. "I don't know. Maybe? If he did it for the right reasons."

Kellen's grip tightened around the steering wheel. I watched his knuckles go white as he glared straight ahead.

"What if he did it for no reason at all?" he finally asked. "What if it was just his job and he was the only one hateful enough to do it?"

Something in his tone, in the flex of his jaw, told me that Kellen wasn't talking about Vlad anymore. After I'd seen what he did to John—the eerie, calm expertise he demonstrated—there wasn't a doubt in my mind that Kellen had done it before. Had been trained to do it. Whatever agency he worked for, they'd taken a lost teenager with nowhere to go and turned him into a killer. And now, he had no way out.

My heart broke for him.

"Vlad had two wives," I said, desperately wanting to touch him. "His first wife killed herself to avoid being captured by his brother, and it destroyed him. It was his love for her that inspired *Bram Stoker's Dracula*. And his second wife fell in love with him while he was in prison. She married him in order to set him free. They had two children together before he was killed in battle."

Kellen glanced at me out of the corner of his eye. "How do you know all that?"

"I wrote a paper about it last semester." I beamed. "I'm an English lit major."

"Course ya are," Kellen said, his voice thick with regret as he nodded slowly.

"I mean, I *was* an English lit major," I corrected, refusing to let my smile fade. "And I will be again. I'm sure they have excellent universities in Transylvania."

Kellen exhaled a silent laugh, and I took a mental picture of him just like that. Eyes creased at the corners, full lips, long lashes, a rainbow of colorful shops and pubs blurring behind him as we passed. But no sooner had I captured the image than it was gone. Chased away by the sudden, blaring wail of a police siren.

I turned to look out the back windshield, but before I could, Kellen threw his hand out, pinning me to the seat. "Don't let 'em see yer face."

Slumping down in my seat, I glanced at the side mirror and saw a white car with blue flashing lights and the word *GARDA* emblazoned across the hood gaining on us at a rapid pace.

"Maybe they're not after us," I said, turning my head toward Kellen. "You didn't do anything wrong. Maybe if you pull over, they'll go right past us."

"Oh, no. They were waitin' for us. Fuckers."

My heart began to pound. "Do you think I've been reported missing already?"

"No," Kellen said flatly, his eyes darting between the rearview mirror and the road. "Once yer people back home realize you and yer fella aren't answerin' texts or emails, they'll still have to wait twenty-four hours before they file a report."

"So, they're not looking for me, and you weren't speeding or anything, so maybe they'll just give you a ticket for not having your ID, and we can—"

My body suddenly jerked forward, the seat belt catching me across the neck.

"Did they just ram us?" I coughed, glancing into the side mirror just in time to see them surge forward again.

"Kellen!" I shrieked, my body sliding sideways into the door as he jerked the wheel to the right.

But it wasn't fast enough. The police car clipped the corner of our back bumper as we turned onto a side street, causing us to spin until we were facing the street we'd just turned off of.

Slamming it into reverse, Kellen punched the gas, and my head was thrown forward again. He cut the wheel and spun us back around, taking off just as the siren returned and blue lights splashed across the interior of the car.

"The organization I work for has the guards in their pocket," Kellen shouted over the wind howling in through the open windows. "I shoulda known they'd be lookin' for a silver Fiesta today. Fuck!" He slammed his hand against the steering wheel.

"Uh, Kellen?" I lifted a finger, pointing at the factories and squat stone buildings passing by on our right.

Behind them, off in the distance, I could see a green-and-yellow train barreling across a field, heading toward the exact same point as us.

"Take the wheel," Kellen barked, letting go before I even processed his request.

Darting for the steering wheel, I grabbed it just as Kellen reached behind him and pulled the same black handgun from his waistband that he'd brandished the night before.

Shit, shit, shit.

"Now, slide over here and put yer foot on the pedal."

I tried to keep my eyes on the road and not the train screaming toward us as I shimmied into the driver's seat with him. The car was so small and Kellen was so big that I had to sit in on his thigh in order to fit. I gripped the steering wheel with both hands as I pushed his foot off the accelerator and replaced it with my own.

"Good. Now, whatever ya do, don't slow down. Not for a second."

The cruiser rammed us again, only this time I wasn't wearing a seat belt. My body flew forward unrestrained, slamming into the steering wheel. The air left my lungs in a sudden, violent burst as Kellen grabbed the wheel to keep us from veering into oncoming traffic.

"Breathe," he said, pressing a kiss to my temple. "Breathe and look straight ahead. Nowhere else."

Then, flicking the safety off on his gun, he turned and fired.

DEVIL OF DUBLIN

The blast sounded like a cannon in my ear and was followed by a teeth-rattling crash only seconds later. I winced and pressed the gas pedal as hard as I could, icy-cold dread seeping into my veins as I considered what Kellen might have just done.

He'd told me not to look, but I had to. I had to know. Glancing in the rearview mirror, I almost laughed in relief when I saw both officers alive and well, their car smashed into a telephone pole and their front tire mangled beyond all recognition. But my relief quickly turned to horror when the one in the passenger seat lifted a handgun of his own, leaned out the window, and aimed it directly at us.

"Get down!" Kellen shouted, curling over me as the back windshield exploded behind us.

His foot stomped down on mine as the deafening blast of a train horn filled the car. Then, for a split second, we were weightless. Kellen's weight lifted off of me as we landed on the other side of the tracks, a passenger train whooshing behind us and a river of blood rushing through my ears.

I slowly released the wheel as Kellen steered us into the Kent Station parking lot. He found a spot as far away from the road as possible, and when he turned the engine off, I realized that I was shaking.

Pulling me to his chest, Kellen kissed the top of my head. I could feel his heart pounding, almost as rapidly as mine. Opening his jacket, he wrapped both sides around me, and the warmth of his body instantly soothed my shivering muscles.

A million unspoken sentiments passed between us as we clutched one another and caught our breath.

Relief.
    Rage.
Shock.
    Fear.
Confusion.
    Concern.
Gratitude.
    Guilt.

But when Kellen took a deep, shuddering breath and finally spoke, his words were clear and determined, devoid of all emotion. "We need to keep moving."

He burst from the car, pulling me out with him, before I was even done nodding.

I followed him in a trance, my heart still racing, my mind utterly blank, as he threw open the trunk and unzipped John's designer suitcase.

"Leave yer phone and credit cards here," he said, dumping all of my ex's belongings into the trunk. "They'll be tracin' 'em as soon as yer reported missing."

Thousands of dollars' worth of clothes and shoes and watches and toiletries landed in a heap—with my phone and purse being the cherry on top—before Kellen lifted his massive black duffel bag and shoved the entire thing into John's now-empty suitcase. It sounded like it was full of lead pipes and looked just as heavy, but I didn't ask what was in it. He wouldn't have told me, and honestly, I didn't really care. There was only one thing I wanted in that moment—one simple, stupid, shiny black thing.

Pulling one of John's shirts out of the pile, I held it in both hands, my thumbs sliding across the crisp cotton as I lifted it to my nose. It didn't smell like him.

Good.

I unfolded it and held it up, right at the height that it would have been if John had been wearing it. Then, I turned toward Kellen and held it a few inches higher.

Kellen shoved his bloody, bullet-shredded T-shirt into a trash can outside Kent Station as we strolled in arm in arm—him wearing a white Armani button-up and me wearing a deliciously warm, Kellen-scented flight jacket. John's shirt was a little too small, so Kellen had rolled the sleeves up to his elbows and left the top button undone. The sight was absolutely indecent.

Unlike the train stations in Atlanta, there were no metal detectors, no ticket booths, no cops with drug- or bomb-sniffing dogs. Kellen simply purchased two one-way tickets from a machine, and five minutes later, we were boarding a green-and-yellow train to Dublin with one of everything from the café next to the platform. Our table on the train was a buffet of hot coffee and tea and biscuits and pastries and fruit and sandwiches—a breakfast fit for a fake birthday—but as we pulled away from the station and Kellen put his arm around me, I couldn't bring myself to eat a thing.

I was already bursting.

CHAPTER 20

DARBY

While I'd dozed on the train—lulled to sleep by Kellen's warmth, the endless Irish countryside rolling past my window, and the fact that no one would be chasing or shooting at us for the next few hours—Kellen had been busy. He'd searched every short-term rental site for places near the Dublin Heuston train station with availability that night, and he'd settled on a cottage that was secluded, had out-of-town owners, and looked "dodgy" enough to not have a security system.

Which was important because we were going to have to break in again.

Kellen said that his apartment wasn't safe anymore, and with him having no ID and no credit cards and me not being able to use mine, checking into a hotel or hostel was out of the question. I felt bad about squatting, but Kellen had left enough money on the kitchen table of the last place we stayed in to cover the rent for a week, so I suppose it worked out for everyone.

The cottage he'd found was on the other side of Phoenix Park from the train station, so we strolled through the green space hand in hand, pointing at wild deer and rolling our suitcases behind us like a couple of tourists. But Kellen was tense. I thought it was all the open space. He was constantly scanning, only half-listening to what I was saying. He didn't seem to relax again until we left the park and headed down a shady side street and then another and then another.

The house was the last one on a dead-end road, secluded and set back from the street. It looked like it had been drawn by a child—a little white square with a triangular roof, a bright blue door, and a single blue-trimmed window. The grass in the yard was mostly brown, and the window box spilled over with dead flowers, but the ivy was thriving—it had grown halfway up the bottom of the house.

It was perfect.

We tiptoed around to the back door, but Kellen didn't even have to kick it in. The weather-beaten thing was so old and drafty that he was able to pop the lock open with a knife—which, evidently, had been stashed in his boot the entire time.

The inside looked like a time capsule from the 1800s. Plaster walls, a whitewashed brick fireplace, creaky wooden furniture, and even creakier wooden floors. There were electrical outlets and lamps, but something didn't feel right about turning them on. Modern technology and that cottage just didn't go together.

Kellen watched me with quiet amusement as I wandered through the space. The bathroom had a claw-foot tub that had been converted into a shower, and the antiquated bedroom had a wooden ladder that led up to a square cutout in the ceiling.

Kellen leaned against the doorframe, smirking as I glanced back and forth between him and the hole above me.

"Go on," he said, lifting his chin. "Someone has to make sure there aren't any ghosts up there."

Something in his eyes told me he knew exactly what was up there, and suddenly, I couldn't climb fast enough.

The moment my head emerged through the trap door in the floor, a gasp burst from my lungs. Sunlight streamed in through a large dormer window, revealing a reading nook fit for a sultan. Where the rest of the house was simple and quaint, this tiny space was dripping with color and texture. Layers of exotic rugs, velvet cushions, and tasseled pillows covered the floor. Rows of earthy leather-bound books lined the walls. And crisscrossing above it all, like the loosened laces of a corset, were yards and yards of delicate fairy lights. Following the end of the strand to an outlet on the wall, I reached over and flipped the switch above it, marveling as the entire space glowed and flickered like firelight.

"It's not Transylvania, but it is the most magical place I could find within walking distance of Heuston Station."

I looked down to find Kellen standing at the bottom of the ladder, hands in his pockets, eyebrows pulled together in a devastating smolder.

"Oh my God, you have to see it!" I waved him up and stood to one side of the ladder as his big, warm body filled the space next to me.

Kellen gave the nook a fleeting obligatory glance before turning his attention back to me. His steely gray gaze softened as he brushed a lock of hair—still tangled and windswept from our earlier chase—away from my face and whispered, "Beautiful."

My skin tingled at that single word, that simple touch. That and the realization that we were alone. Again.

"I must confess"—his eyes dropped to my lips as his thumb traced their shape—"when I saw this room, the activities that came to mind were not exactly *literary*, but they'll have to wait. We have somewhere to be."

"Just one kiss?" I breathed, looking up at him through my lowered lashes.

Kellen's thumb rolled my bottom lip down to exaggerate my pout. He stared at my mouth for what felt like ages, then pressed his lips to my forehead.

"When we get back," he whispered, "I'll kiss you anywhere ya want."

Evidently, wherever we were going, punctuality was important.

As we walked back to Phoenix Park, Kellen explained that we were going to be picked up and taken to an undisclosed location to meet with someone called The Butcher, who could help us get new identities. He said that I was supposed to pretend to be there against my will because this dude thought Kellen was a bad guy and he had to keep up appearances.

Once our ride showed up, it wasn't hard to pretend like I was less than excited to climb inside. It was a large white box truck. The kind your mother warned you to stay away from as a kid.

No markings.

No windows.

A short, stocky man with a bushy black beard climbed out of the driver's seat. He nodded at Kellen in greeting and gave me a curious, cursory glance before opening the back doors. An arctic blast slapped me in the face along with the subtle smell of raw, refrigerated meat.

When I looked inside, I discovered the red-and-white marbleized carcasses of at least a dozen unidentifiable animals hanging from hooks in the ceiling. My stomach turned as Kellen hauled me into the vehicle by my upper arm. We sat on a wooden bench bolted to the side of the van, and once the doors slammed shut, we were plunged into darkness.

I wanted to curl up against Kellen's side, ask him where we were going, who the hell this Butcher guy was, but his body language was even colder than the slabs of meat swaying in front of us. Not that I could see them. The only thing I could see was a tiny red light in the corner of the ceiling. Pointed directly at us.

"Is that a camera?" I whispered, rubbing my nose to hide my mouth as I spoke.

"Mmhmm." The tone of Kellen's voice was light, almost playful.

He wasn't afraid, so I decided I wouldn't be either.

The ride was short, maybe twenty minutes or so, but it was long enough for the light outside to blind me once the door opened again. I shielded my eyes as Kellen dragged me out. When they finally adjusted, I found myself standing in front of the loading bay of a nondescript white warehouse. It reminded me of the docks from the night before. Industrial. Set far apart from any other buildings. Surrounded by tall chain-link fencing and equally nondescript work vehicles. Eerily quiet.

"Sorry about the ride," the driver said in an Eastern European accent as he hustled up ahead of us to open the door. His head swiveled back to glance at Kellen every half-second, as if my escort were actually an uncaged tiger. With rabies.

"It is just security precaution." He placed his thumb on a scanner to unlock the door and held it open as Kellen steered me through by the back of my neck.

I smiled at the driver as I passed. "You wouldn't happen to be from Romania, would—"

Kellen snapped his fingers at the same moment that he gave my neck a sudden jerk.

A shocked shriek lodged in my throat as my eyes slammed closed.

"Shut up!"
"Shut the fuck up!"
"Shut your fucking mouth!"

Tears burned behind my tightly closed lids as John's voice taunted me from the recesses of my mind. My muscles tensed, and my breathing ceased as I braced myself for the slap, the shove, the physical escalation that sometimes followed that particular warning.

But all I felt was Kellen's fingertips as they slid up into my hair and massaged the nape of my neck. It was a silent apology. A secret reassurance. The slap wasn't coming.

And it never would again.

When I opened my eyes, we were back in the meat truck, only bigger. Much, much bigger. Kellen and I followed the driver—who, despite being a two-hundred-pound bodybuilder, looked like *he* might cry if Kellen snapped at him too—down an aisle of horrors. More hooks. More meat. More flesh and bones and entrails than I could stomach. I tried staring at the floor, but it was covered in pink streaks slithering toward drainage holes, so I took a deep breath and stared straight ahead.

At the shiny silver doors of an elevator.

Once we were standing right in front of them, the driver picked up an industrial metal tray from a nearby table and extended it to Kellen, his eyes cast down. "If you don't mind, sir."

With an annoyed huff, Kellen reached behind his back and pulled out his gun. He set it on the tray, and before the driver turned to put it away, he glanced at me with pity in his dark brown eyes.

The elevator ride down only took a few seconds, but when the doors opened, it felt like we had teleported from the inside of a fridge to the inside of a wind tunnel.

The room we stepped into was the same cavernous size as the one above us—only instead of being filled with slabs of meat, this one was filled with rows and rows of blinking, humming, whirring computer servers. Half a dozen industrial-sized ceiling fans spun above them like saw blades, forcing the cooler air from the refrigerated main floor down into the giant electronic pressure cooker we were now standing in.

The farther we were led into the room, the warmer it got. I went to unzip my jacket—*Kellen's* jacket—but a quick squeeze on the back of my neck let me know that Kellen wanted me to stay covered up.

After a series of twists and turns, we were deposited in the doorway of a glass-walled office. Inside, a scrawny man with a wiry strawberry-blond beard was illuminated by the glow of three television-sized computer monitors.

He stood with a grin as soon as he saw us approach. His vintage Star Wars T-shirt had what looked like a ketchup stain on it, and his thin hair was pulled back in a low ponytail.

"Come in! Come in!" the man, who I assume was the one Kellen had referred to as The Butcher, said warmly as he gestured to the seats across from his cluttered desk. He turned his central monitor sideways and scooted it over so that when he sat back down, we'd be able to see him.

Guess he didn't get many visitors.

DEVIL OF DUBLIN

"To what do I, em, owe the pleasure?" he asked, nervously tidying his desk and glancing over at the driver, who stood guard in the doorway.

"I need papers." Kellen's posture was open and casual, but his voice was sharp. Commanding.

"Papers?" The Butcher relaxed instantly, flopping back in his seat with a hearty laugh. "Papers he says!"

With that, the driver started laughing too. I don't know what they'd assumed Kellen was there to do, but it was clear from everyone's sudden shift in mood that a surprise visit from him was *not* a good thing.

The Butcher wiped an errant tear from the corner of his eye as his laughter finally died down. "Jaysus Christ. Ya know, I 'bout pissed myself when I heard—"

"Enough." Kellen didn't yell, but the men behaved as if he had, their mouths snapping shut and their eyes going wide. "We need birth certificates, passports, driving licenses, a fuckin' marriage certificate, whatever ya got."

I had to bite the insides of my cheek to keep from smiling at that last part.

The Butcher let out a low whistle, his mood much less jovial than before.

"Is there a problem?" Kellen asked.

"Not unless yer broke. Two full sets of papers ... clean identities ... new numbers ... that'll run ya about twenty thousand. Cash."

Kellen nodded slowly. "Don't suppose you'd take a dozen AR-15 converted to full auto, would ya?"

My eyes widened.

So, that's what's in his bag. Jesus Christ.

The Butcher gestured behind us to his collection of servers. "Unfortunately, I only deal in data—and if anyone asks, delicious farm-raised ham"—he gave me a wink—"but I might know a fella who'd be willin' to take 'em off yer hands if ya need help gettin' the cash. He's a Brit though. I know the Brotherhood don't take too kindly—"

"Grand," Kellen snapped. "Have him meet me at The Brazen Head tomorrow. Eight p.m. And get our papers ready. I'll be back the next mornin' with your money."

The Butcher sat straight up. "For what yer askin', it's gonna take at least five days, *sir*. The data sourcin', the technology involved … we're talkin' holograms, microchips—"

"Three days." Kellen stood, lifting me to my feet by my upper arm. "And if you speak a word of this to anyone—"

"Understood," the hacker interrupted with a quick nod and wide eyes.

Whatever had been at the end of Kellen's threat hung in the air between them, unspoken—or possibly unspeakable.

Kellen turned and ushered me toward the door, but before we could leave, our host leaped to his feet and yelled, "Wait!"

I held my breath as Kellen turned with the slow, silent grace of a pit viper.

The scrawny strawberry-blond smiled tightly, holding up a webcam with shaky fingers. "I just, em … need to take some pictures, *sir*. Fer yer new IDs."

CHAPTER 21

KELLEN

It took all the patience I fucking possessed to wait until the meat truck drove away before pulling Darby into my arms. It wasn't safe for us to be out in the open, especially not in Dublin, where the Brotherhood had so many eyes, but I needed her to know that the charade was over.

I hated being such an arse to her, but The Butcher knew me as the UIB's top enforcer, the Devil of Dublin, so I had to keep up appearances. It was his fear of me that would keep him from talking. That, and the fact that he hated the Brotherhood as much as I did. They'd been trying to recruit him for years, but their polite invitations had quickly turned into violent threats and business sabotage—hence all the paranoia. The Brotherhood did *not* appreciate being told no. But I'd respected the fella for not giving in, so I'd made him a deal. I'd tip him off anytime the UIB was headed his way if he provided me with an untraceable phone and hacked whatever I needed him to hack.

"You okay?" I asked, stroking a hand down Darby's wavy copper hair.

The sun had already set, but the evening chill was still warmer than the inside of that goddamn truck.

"Yes, but you could have prepared me." Her tone wasn't angry, but she smacked me on the chest anyway.

I smiled in relief and tucked her under my arm as we crossed the street. "I promise, you were safe the entire time. The Butcher's harmless. The only reason I didn't tell ya more is because—"

"You needed me to act scared."

I nodded, the guilt gnawing at my insides, making it hard to speak. I hated that I'd made her feel that way. Darby should never have to be afraid of me. Ever.

"I don't think I was half as scared as they were." Darby laughed. "Did you see their faces? They must think you're, like, a gun runner or a hitman for the Mafia or something, huh?"

I tensed, Darby's dead-on accurate assessment freezing my thoughts, my muscles, the very air in my lungs.

When I didn't respond, she began to backpedal. "You don't actually have to answer that. Sorry."

I exhaled and gave her arm a reassuring squeeze as we turned down the next side street. "It doesn't matter what they think I am. In three days, we can both be whatever we want."

Darby gazed up at me, her wide green eyes shining in the moonlight. "What do *you* want to be?"

The question struck me like a sucker punch. No one had ever asked me that before. Not even myself.

I had only ever done what I *had* to do, not what I wanted to do. Wanting was excruciating. Wanting was emotional suicide. But ever since Darby had come back into my life, it was all I fucking did.

Want.

And it terrified me.

"You know what *I* always thought you'd be when you grew up?" Darby asked, lacing her fingers through mine as the cottage came into view at the end of the street. She looked straight ahead as she spoke, and I was grateful.

"A carpenter."

A carpenter. The words echoed in my ears, feeling foreign yet somehow familiar, like it had meant something to me in a past life.

"You were always making stuff for the playhouse out of, like, branches and stumps. Remember? And all of it was amazing. Some of that furniture lasted for years. I always imagined that, one day, you'd have your own workshop, and you'd make the most incredible things."

A flood of sights and sounds and smells filled my mind all at once—the crunch of leaves underfoot as I rolled the perfect log through the woods; my first stool with its wobbly pine legs and sap-covered seat; the sweet, mind-numbing exhaustion that only came after a few hours of chopping or sawing or sanding; and the look of wonder on Darby's face every summer when she finally got to see what I'd been working on.

She was the only one who ever saw my work.

She was the only one who ever saw *me*.

As we cut across the front yard of the cottage, emotion tightened my throat to the point that I couldn't speak. I couldn't tell her what she'd meant to me back then. That the promise of seeing her again, of showing her the things I'd made, of trying to say a few more words to her than I had the year before was the only thing that kept me from killing myself most days. That I'd lost my humanity when I lost her. That she made me want to get it back.

As we walked around the far side of the house, Darby began to pick at her lower lip. Her shoulders rose and fell faster and faster under my arm, and her eyes seemed to be looking everywhere other than at me. At first, I thought maybe she'd heard something in the woods that had scared her, but when she opened her mouth and began to apologize, I realized it was me. Darby had interpreted my silence as anger, and now, she was afraid. Of *me*.

"Sorry," she said softly. "I shouldn't have brought it up. We don't have to talk about—"

I moved like a flash of lightning, pushing her up against the side of the house and sealing my mouth over her stunned, parted lips. Darby's startled gasp was silenced along with the rest of that goddamn apology as I clutched the sides of her face and poured every word I couldn't bring myself to say right down her fucking throat.

I didn't know any other way to express to her that I wasn't mad about what she'd said. I was … I was fucking drowning in it. My heart felt like it had been run through with a dagger, and I couldn't stop the bleeding.

It was a brutal, begging kind of a kiss. I was begging her to understand me. Begging her to feel what I felt. Begging her to let me fill her with everything I couldn't hold on to anymore. Darby's hands clung to my shirt as I sucked and tasted, licked and scraped. I'd pressed my lips to hers out of the need to *give* her a part of myself, but as soon as I got a taste of her again, all I could do was *take*. The want she had awakened in me was ravenous, insatiable … *ancient*. It felt as if it had a power all its own.

A power that was greater than mine.

Grabbing her wrists, I pinned Darby's hands against the wall on either side of her head. There was so much inside of me that needed to be released—I couldn't risk letting her touch me somewhere that might trigger my panic.

My tongue swirled around hers even more deeply until Darby broke our kiss, turning her head to the side with a sudden gasp.

As I sucked the soft skin just below her jaw, my cock throbbed in time with the racing pulse I felt beating against my lips. I needed to be inside of her again. I wanted to feel her entire body pulsing around me like that, begging me to let go, to fill her with this overflow of emotion.

I was about to release her wrists so that I could unbutton her jeans and find that bliss again when I realized that Darby had gone completely stiff. Her hips weren't rolling against mine. Her head was still turned away. And the ragged breaths she was taking didn't sound lustful. They sounded …

Fuck.

DEVIL OF DUBLIN

Lifting my head, I gazed down at Darby, and what I saw was the definition of heartbreaking.

Her face was pressed against the stucco and contorted into a tight wince. Her eyes were squeezed shut. And every breath she took was jerky and shuddering, as if she was trying not to cry, but the silver streak of moonlight sliding down her cheek told me that her efforts had been in vain.

I released her wrists immediately and took a step back, watching in what felt like slow motion as Darby wrapped her arms around her waist and curled against the wall.

"No, no, no. Darby. What happened? Tell me."

But she just shook her head, letting her hair fall forward until it completely covered her face.

I wanted to scream. I wanted to put my fist through the house, but it would only scare her again. I wanted to touch her, but I didn't have the right. So, I just stood there, like a fucking eejit, staring at the side of her head.

"What did I do? Tell me. Please."

"Nothing." She sniffled. "It's not your fault. I just …" She paused for a long time, shaking her head and rubbing her arm before the words finally came out on a muffled sob. "I don't like being restrained."

I took a step back as my mouth fell open in horror.

Restrained.

How had I found her just the night before? How had I fucking found her? Pinned down on the kitchen floor, her face contorted just like that, tears in her eyes, while some arsehole tried to fuck her.

I'd killed a man for doing what I was about to do.

I took another step back. And another.

I felt like I was going to be sick.

"Kellen?" Darby's shaky voice could barely reach me as I paced across the lawn.

I raked my hands over my head, trying to reconcile what the fuck had just happened. What had come over me.

"It's okay. I can push through it. You just … caught me off guard. That's all."

"Push through it? Are you fuckin' serious?" I snapped.

Darby tensed like she thought I was going to hit her, and a growl tore from the festering black bowels of my soul.

Darby Collins used to be fucking fearless. She'd been tiny and covered in freckles and always missing at least one tooth, and she wasn't scared of shite. Not even the freak mute who lurked in the woods. She was the *only* person who wasn't afraid of me. The only person I felt like I could express myself around. Even if it came out wrong or I got upset or I lost control, Darby had never treated me any differently.

Now, if I went silent or raised my voice or so much as looked at her wrong, she cowered like a kicked dog.

The flames inside me roared to life, bitter and bloodthirsty over what those fuckers had taken from her.

But also, what they'd taken from *me*.

"I'm so sorry. I didn't mean to—"

Sorry.

My body responded to that single word like a can of petrol responds to a lit match.

I curled my hands into fists and exhaled through my nose like a fucking demon, trying to keep a grip on my anger. I could feel the fire taking over. Demanding to be fed. It was only satisfied by pain—mine or someone else's—and I refused to let Darby see that side of me again.

Taking a step away from her, I pointed toward the back of the house. "Go inside."

"What?" She blinked.

I kept walking backward to make sure she didn't try to follow me, my hands raking over my head as I tried to get my breathing under control.

I had to clench my jaw to keep from screaming at her. "Go."

As soon as my feet landed on tarmac instead of grass, I turned and stormed off down the street.

I didn't drink. I didn't smoke. I could hardly talk to anyone but Darby. And up until that morning, I didn't—couldn't—even fuck. That left me with very few options when the flames threatened to burn me alive.

Luckily, I was within walking distance of Phoenix Park … and so were half the drunks in Dublin.

CHAPTER 22

DARBY

A sudden blow: the great wings beating still
Above the staggering girl, her thighs caressed
By the dark webs, her nape caught in his bill,
He holds her helpless breast upon his breast.

I couldn't even read without thinking of Kellen.

After he'd left, I'd paced the floor for an hour or so, replaying everything that had happened on a loop in my mind. My reaction to his touch. My rejection. The way I'd recoiled from him. The gutted, horrified look on his face.

I'd never hurt someone that badly in my life. And the fact that it had been Kellen made me feel sick.

I knew how sensitive he was. How difficult touching or even talking to another person could be for him. But despite everything he'd been through, Kellen trusted *me*. He talked to *me*. He'd made love to *me*. He'd pried open his chest and handed me his tender, bleeding heart, and what had I done with it?

I'd thrown it back in his face within a matter of hours.

My own tender heart throbbed with the ache of a deep blue bruise, every beat pushing the pain through my veins until my entire body felt battered and exhausted.

When I hadn't been able to pace another step, I'd dragged myself up the ladder and into the reading nook, hoping I would find a distraction among the books lining the walls. But nothing held my attention for very long, not even Yeats. My eyes skirted over the faded letters, but all I could see was every possible worst-case scenario playing out in high definition as my thoughts spiraled out of control.

My head was screaming that something terrible was going to happen.

My heart was screaming that something terrible had already happened.

But somewhere beyond all the noise—in the quiet, still place I went to when I needed to escape my body for a while—there was a knowing. A soft blue glow, like the one I'd seen at the bottom of the lake. It didn't communicate with words or thoughts, visions or sounds, but with energy. A graceful, ageless serenity seeped into my bones and hummed through me like a lullaby, promising me that everything would be okay.

I didn't know if it was Saoirse or my mother or my grandfather or my own imagination, but for the first time in eight years, I felt as though I were being held in the arms of a loving parent. Silent tears streamed down my face as I basked in that glow. In the comfort that had come to me when I needed it most. The knowing stayed with me, calm and still and sweetly humming, until I heard the back door open and close.

"Darby?" Kellen's concerned voice was the final nail in the coffin of my composure.

Between the overwhelming presence I'd just experienced and the burst of relief I felt over knowing that he was finally home safe, my silent tears turned into a not-so-silent sob.

"Up here," I croaked, swiping at my eyes and nose with the sleeves of my sweatshirt.

Seconds later, Kellen's face appeared at the top of the ladder, and both of our mouths fell open.

"Fuck. Darby."

"Oh my God! Kellen!"

In an instant, he was on his knees, wiping my tears as I gingerly patted the swelling skin next to his cut eyebrow.

"I'm so sorry." He kissed my eyelids, my red nose, my wet cheeks, my puffy lips, all while I tried to gauge how badly he was hurt. "I'm so fuckin' sorry."

"What happened?!" I turned his face with gentle fingers until I could see the other side.

"What? This?" He pointed at his eyebrow, and I noticed that the knuckles on his right hand were bleeding too.

"Kellen!"

He shrugged. "Had to let 'em get a coupla shots in. Just to be polite."

"Who?"

"The skangers in the park. They usually get kicked out of the pubs early for fightin' and go lookin' for trouble." The corner of his mouth curled up. "They found it tonight."

"Are you serious right now? You could have gotten hurt. Or arrested. We're supposed to be laying low."

"I know." His smirk disappeared as he lifted my knuckles to his lips. "I just ... needed to clear me head. You were so scared, and I was only makin' it worse."

"I wasn't scared. I was just—"

"Yes ... you were." Kellen lowered my hand, but not his eyes. "Trust me, I know fear when I see it." His tone was haunting.

I dropped my eyes as remorse twisted like a knife in my stomach, but Kellen lifted my chin with a single bloody knuckle, forcing me to look at him again.

"That's why we're gonna start over ..."

I took a deep breath as Kellen held me captive in his stare.

"And we're gonna go slow ..." His eyes dropped to my lips.

"And this time, yer gonna tell me exactly"—he pressed a soft kiss to the corner of my mouth.—"what ya want me to do."

I held my breath as his bottom lip dragged across mine. Then, he kissed the opposite corner.

"I want to hear you"—his mouth roamed lower, kissing my jaw, the side of my neck—"the entire time."

My eyes fluttered closed as his lips blazed a trail down the front of my throat.

"So I know yer still with me."

I nodded as my fingers found their way to his warm, fuzzy head.

"I don't want yer empty body, Darby. I want what's in here."

Stretching the neck of my sweatshirt down, Kellen pressed his lips to the center of my chest, and the heart beneath them skipped a beat.

"I want yer fuckin' ghost."

Fresh tears sprang to my eyes as Kellen grasped the bottom of my sweatshirt and looked at me, waiting for permission.

I nodded with a grateful smile, but he only frowned in response.

"Ya gotta talk to me, angel. Tell me what ya want. Tell me what ya like."

I shook my head as the humiliation machine inside my brain whirred to life, reminding me that, before Kellen, the only sex I'd ever had felt shameful at best and violent at worst. That I'd never really cared for it because no one had ever really cared about me.

"I don't know," I whispered, smiling to mask my pain. "I don't know what I like."

A glimmer of sadness flashed across Kellen's steely gray eyes, but it was quickly chased away by the most panty-melting smirk I'd ever seen.

"*I* know something ya like," he said, his eyes dropping to my lips as he slowly leaned in.

A burst of excitement, followed by a sweet swell of relief, rushed through my veins as I wrapped my hands around the back of his neck and kissed him first.

Kellen thrust a hand into my hair as he smiled around the intrusion of my tongue.

It was nothing like any of our previous kisses. There was no uncertainty, no desperation or fear. It was playful and teasing. Kellen backed away and made me chase him. I captured his tongue with my teeth. But soon, those tender licks and nips morphed into deep, needful strokes. The way Kellen sucked and swirled his tongue around mine made me want to feel it *everywhere*.

I reached for the top button of his shirt and felt his body stiffen immediately. I still didn't know what all of his triggers were, and honestly, I didn't think he did either. But Kellen was right; if we went slow and paid attention, we could figure it out.

With a deep breath through his nose, Kellen's shoulders relaxed. Then, taking my hands in his, he brought them back down to his chest, where, *together*, we unwrapped the only thing I'd ever wanted. An expanse of scarred flesh and hard muscle rippled before me as Kellen peeled the snug white dress shirt off and tossed it into the corner. Desire simmered in my belly, frenzied and scalding and threatening to boil over as I watched him continue to undress.

The tiny bulbs dripping from the ceiling painted his skin a warm amber, as if it had been lit by the glow of a hundred candles, and the scent of old books made it feel as though we were trespassing somewhere sacred. Somewhere magical. Somewhere even more romantic than Transylvania.

My heart swelled at the realization that Kellen had done this for me. And when we pulled the last of our clothes off and he crawled back to my side—eyes focused, muscles flexed—I realized that he was just getting started.

Our mouths collided as Kellen wrapped his hand around the nape of my neck and guided me to lie on my back among the pillows. Then, he leveled me with a villainous smirk. A day's worth of stubble and that gash below his eyebrow transformed his already-intimidating features into something even more wicked.

If the Devil had been God's most beautiful angel, then Kellen wasn't just his son.

He was the Prince of Darkness himself.

"What do you want, love?" His voice caressed my naked body like warm black velvet.

"I want you to eat me alive." The words left me on a single breath. Unfiltered and unashamed.

Kellen's smirk widened into a wolfish grin before his mouth dove for my throat.

"Tell me more." His tongue swirled around the valley at the base of my neck.

"Tell me exactly." His teeth grazed my collarbone before sinking into my shoulder.

"You go quiet, I stop." Kellen lifted his head and gazed down at me, licking his bottom lip as he waited for more instruction.

The sight of his glistening tongue caused my nipples to harden in anticipation.

"Lower, please," I managed to whisper before a rush of heat flooded my face.

"As you wish."

Kellen lowered his head again, sucking a path of wet kisses down the center of my chest, but when he got to the hollow between my breasts, he paused with his lips still pressed to my skin and waited.

God, I loved him.

As hard as it was for me to say the words out loud, I was overwhelmed with gratitude that Kellen was making me do it. For showing me that he was different. For taking away any possibility of fear. And I realized that by telling him what to do, I was giving him the same gift.

So, with a deep breath, I ran my fingers over his head and said, "Will you ... suck my nipples. Please? And touch me? Touch me anywhere you want."

"Fuck," he hissed.

Kellen's warm breath danced across my chilled skin as he palmed my breasts and squeezed them gently. I closed my eyes and arched my back, releasing a quiet whimper when his thumbs rolled over the dusky peaks.

"Keep making that sound, angel, and I'll never give you a reason to stop."

That was all the warning I got before Kellen's mouth was on me again.

I did as he'd said, giving voice to every needy, husky sound in the back of my throat as Kellen's lips pulled and tugged at my sensitive flesh.

"Lick them too. Please," I exhaled on a moan, my back arching further as Kellen lavished both nipples with swirls and flicks and torturously slow drags of his tongue.

His big, callused hands slid over my body, massaging my breasts, warming my torso, and the farther down they traveled, the needier I became.

"Kellen," I rasped.

He looked up at me as his lips slid off my nipple with a wet pop.

"Will you … kiss me lower? Please?"

His eyes were shadowed by dark eyebrows and rimmed with a thousand razor-sharp lashes, but within their depths, I saw the flash of uncertainty.

Kellen had never done what I was asking of him.

But the trepidation on his face quickly disappeared as a salacious half-smile tugged at his lips. Pressing them to my belly, Kellen held my stare as he waited. Teasing me.

"Lower …"

He slid down my body with the grace of a jungle cat, watching me with hooded eyes as he knelt between my parted legs. I held my breath as he dropped his head again, and this time, his lips landed *much* lower, sucking on the delicate skin of my inner thigh.

I moaned as a tiny bolt of lightning shot up my spine.

I felt Kellen's stubble graze my flesh as he moved to the other thigh, and the contrast of scratchy and soft drove me wild.

"Kellen, please …"

He chuckled, deep and low, the hot hum of his breath between my legs causing my entire body to tighten.

"Please lick—"

Before I could even finish asking it, my shameless request was granted. Kellen's tongue slid along the seam of my body, and my back arched on a stifled moan.

His hand splayed over my stomach, the weight of it grounding me as he explored every line, every peak and valley. I laced my fingers through his and held on, the sensation overwhelming yet not enough, all at the same time.

"Whose blood is on your knuckles?" I rasped, glancing down at our clasped hands.

His stubble grazed my thighs again, and I knew that he was smiling. "Mostly mine."

Good enough for me.

"Will you please … ah!"

My hips lifted off the ground as Kellen went back to working me over with his tongue. His pace was faster than before. His pressure harder.

"Finger me!"

Kellen pressed me back down to the ground with the hand on my belly as he fulfilled my request. The moment his thick finger pushed inside, my body tightened around it, seeking relief.

"Mmm," I whimpered, throwing my head back, and that sound must have been Kellen's undoing.

A feral growl rumbled through his chest as he devoured me like a starving beast, sucking the marrow from my bones and filling me to the final bloody knuckle, again and again.

My hips pressed against his hungry mouth as I moaned and writhed and clung to his splayed hand as if it were the only thing tethering me to reality. The pleasure was transcendent. It was as if the sensation was so big that it wouldn't fit inside of my body. Higher and higher Kellen took me. Tighter and tighter my muscles coiled.

And when I finally floated too close to the sun, Kellen was there to catch me as I crashed back down to earth.

The fall was more intense than anything I'd ever experienced. I clutched his hand and wrapped my thighs around his head and called out his name as I tumbled backward through the miles of ecstasy separating me from the ground. But he brought me down gently, and when I finally landed, there were tears in my eyes.

"Kellen," I whispered, that single word conveying both my astonishment and my unbearable need for him. After being so high, I needed to feel his body on mine. Needed to be ground into the floor by the weight of him.

With my hands on his rough cheeks, I guided him up my body until his chest was on my chest and his sex-soaked mouth was on my mouth.

Between my legs, Kellen's length slid through the mess he'd made, and I lifted my hips on a soft moan.

"Please," was all I said.

Kellen stilled at my entrance, his entire body going rigid before his head dropped between his shoulders.

"We can stop," I whispered immediately, clutching his face.

Kellen's head shook. Slowly. It was as if his muscles were so tense that he could hardly move.

"Hey …" I ran my thumb across his cheekbone, just below a curtain of black lashes. "Talk to me."

Kellen pressed his forehead to mine, and I could feel his body shaking with restraint. Restraint and … *anger*.

Kellen's head shook again, and my face moved side to side along with it. "I saw him, Darby … hoverin' over ya. He fucked you like this, didn't he?"

Oh my God.

Kellen had been trying so hard to make me forget about what had happened the day before that I hadn't stopped to think about what it must have been like for him.

What he'd seen.

How I'd reacted to him holding my wrists.

Kellen was trying so hard to prove that he was nothing like *him*.

Now, it was my turn to show him that I knew it.

"Look at me," I said, running my fingertips over his soft, fuzzy head. "Please?"

Eyes as steely as the gun he carried lifted and locked on to mine. But even the agony in Kellen's stare couldn't keep me from smiling at his breathtakingly beautiful face. He was a masterpiece in black and white. Strong and tender. Familiar and mysterious. A lover and a fighter. Focused and yet somehow completely lost.

"I'm not afraid of you." There was no question in my voice. It was a statement. A declaration.

But the way Kellen arched his cut, swollen eyebrow told me that he wasn't exactly convinced.

"Do I look like I'm afraid of you?" The grin that had hijacked my face was beyond my control.

Kellen shook his head again as the corner of his miserable mouth curled up.

"Or do I look like I'm so stupid in love with you that I can't stop smiling, even when I'm trying to be serious?"

He dropped his eyes as the opposite corner of his mouth curled up, and I swear, a hint of pink bloomed across his cheeks.

"Whatever you want, baby ... I want it too. I promise."

Lifting his eyes, Kellen took a deep breath through his nose and pinned me with a soul-baring stare. "All I want—all I've ever wanted—is for you to look at me the way you're lookin' at me now."

It felt like all the air had been punched out of my chest.

"I won't risk losing that again. I can't." Then, Kellen lowered his talented mouth to my ear and growled, "But I also want to be inside of you more than I want my next breath."

A startled yelp burst from my parted lips as he slid his arms behind my back and pulled me up into his lap. I landed in the same position we'd been in that morning—with my legs straddling his, my arms around his shoulders, and his impossibly hard cock pinned between our bodies.

Grabbing my ass with both hands, Kellen lifted my hips and slid himself along my slippery flesh until he was poised at my entrance. Now it was his turn to say, "Look at me."

I did as he'd commanded, and the moment our eyes met, I felt my cheeks flush and that uncontrollable smile return as love and lust and fairy dust danced across my skin.

"Just like that." Kellen's full lips widened and curved in return. Then, they parted on a gasp as I lowered myself onto him, inch by perfect inch.

I forced myself to hold his stare until my body, heart, and soul were so filled with him that I thought I might cry.

Burying my face in his neck, I clung to his shoulders as Kellen wrapped an arm around my back and another under my ass. He clutched me to his chest as he thrust into me from underneath, each delicious, torturous stroke eliciting a soft sound from somewhere deep in my belly.

"Yes," Kellen hissed, thrusting harder. Faster. "Let me hear you, angel."

His words were my unleashing. My chest rumbled from the depths of my moan as my fingers curled into his flesh. My hips writhed in circles as I surrendered to his punishing pace. And when I felt him swell inside of me, felt his arms tighten around my body and his teeth sink into my neck, the orgasm that ripped through me tore a scream from my lungs along with it.

This time, when I crashed back to earth, I had Kellen's strong, warm body to break my fall. I draped my boneless, sated limbs over his shoulders as I caught my breath and smiled when I felt his hand twist around the hair at the nape of my neck.

Pulling me gently upright, Kellen took in my beaming, euphoric stupor and responded with a smile of his own.

"When we get to New York, I'm building you a fuckin' library."

CHAPTER 23

KELLEN

Darby and I had spent most of that night and the next day in bed. Talking. Laughing. Touching. Fucking. We took everything slowly, learning as we went. I'd discovered that she didn't like having a man behind her, but she *loved* being on top. And while I still couldn't imagine being touched below the waist without wanting to murder something, I craved Darby's touch everywhere else. We were never not touching.

Even in the bleedin' supermarket.

Being out in public with the Bratva and the Brotherhood still searching for me made me paranoid as shite, but if I stayed holed up in the cottage with Darby like I wanted to, we'd both die of starvation, so …

Tesco it was.

I kept her tucked under my arm as we walked down the personal care aisle, my eyes scanning the other shoppers more than the items on the shelves. I grabbed a toothbrush at random and dropped it into the basket Darby was carrying.

"Purple?" she asked, arching an eyebrow at my selection.

"It was the closest they had to black."

Darby cracked a smile, and my cock fucking swelled. I could hardly look at her without getting hard. No makeup; fat pink lips; flushed, freckled cheeks; and a mane of coppery sex hair, just begging to have my hands back in it.

"I've never been to a Tesco before."

I grabbed a can of shaving cream and a razor. "They don't have 'em where ... *you're from*?"

I'd almost said where *you live*, but Darby didn't live there anymore, and she never fucking would again.

"We have Walmart, which is the American version. So, it's twice as big, sells guns, and has a McDonald's inside."

I laughed. "I thought you were gonna say Starbucks."

"No, Target has the Starbucks." She smirked.

Fuck, I love her.

I kissed her on the head as we turned into the hair care aisle, and when I looked up, the first thing I saw was a rack of electric clippers. I watched them as we passed. For some reason, I couldn't make myself stop.

I'd been shaving my head as a *fuck you* to Father Henry ever since the day I'd woken up scalped and bleeding on the attic floor. I'd never let him know how much that destroyed me. How badly I wanted that part of me back. So, I kept shaving my head to prove to him that I didn't care, even after he was dead and gone. Every time I did it, I felt like it made me stronger. Braver. It forced me to face the world instead of hiding from it.

But being with Darby made me feel brave in a completely different way.

It gave me the courage to imagine a different life. One where I could look however I wanted, be whatever I wanted, have whatever I wanted ... because for the first time ever, those wants felt like possibilities instead of liabilities.

On the next aisle, Darby dropped a few boxes of small, round plasters and some antibiotic ointment into the basket. "How are your buckshot wounds doing?"

"Considerin' the number of hours I spent lyin' on my back under a certain redhead today, I'd say they're doin' pretty well."

"Oh my God." Darby's mouth fell open as her cheeks flushed even pinker. "Kellen, I am so—"

Adrenaline burst through my bloodstream the second I realized what she was about to say. I clamped my free hand over her mouth and pulled her against my chest, forcing her to look up at me.

"Don't," I snapped. I had to take a few deep breaths through my nose before I was able to speak again calmly.

"You do things … and say things"—I forced the words out through clenched teeth—"that I've only fuckin' dreamed about, and then ya turn around and apologize for 'em. It makes me …" I had to take another deep breath to prevent myself from saying all the excruciating things I wanted to do to the men who'd hurt her out loud. "I don't ever wanna hear the word *sorry* come out of yer mouth again. Understand? You have *nothin'* to apologize to me for, and ya never will."

My hand on Darby's mouth moved up and down as she nodded, her big green eyes glistening with sudden unshed tears. And when I finally lifted my palm, I was beyond relieved to find a soft, sad smile underneath.

"Sor—" This time, it was Darby who clamped a hand over her mouth. Nervous laughter bubbled out from behind it. "Oh my God, I almost said it again!"

I pinched the bridge of my nose and shook my head in defeat. "We're gonna have to work on that."

At the end of the aisle, Darby pointed to a display of shiny boxes, each one wrapped with the picture of a different smiling woman. "Do you think I should dye my hair? Like, as a disguise?"

"Don't even think about it." I placed my hands on either side of her eyes, like horse blinders, as I steered her away from the hair color.

After a trip through the men's clothing section for socks, pants, and anything black, we grabbed just enough food to get by for the next few days and checked out.

Darby picked at her lip as she watched me pump almost all of my cash into the self-checkout machine. "I wish I'd gotten more euros at the airport. I thought I'd be using my credit card the whole time. Sor—"

My eyes cut to hers, and she pressed her lips together with an embarrassed smile.

I gave her a pointed look before grabbing our bags. "It's fine. In a few hours, we'll have enough cash to buy our freedom and all the"—I pulled the rubbish she'd chosen out of the bag and read the label—"*custard creams* you could ever want."

Darby snatched the pack out of my hand and tore it open as we headed back to the cottage. "I haven't had one of these in eight years."

She took a bite, and the soft orgasmic sound in the back of her throat had my cock swelling all over again.

"Oh my God," she murmured, eyes rolled back, mouth full. "You have to taste this."

She held the other half of her biscuit out to me, but I went straight for the crumbs on her lips. The second that sugary vanilla flavor hit my tongue, a kaleidoscope of memories exploded behind my eyes. Darby in those yellow wellies. Darby's tiny hand holding a biscuit out to me like I was a rabid dog. Darby's fearless, gap-toothed grin as she watched me devour them.

They were the best things I'd ever tasted at the time because they tasted like *her*.

They still did.

Dropping the bags in the middle of the path, I grabbed the back of Darby's head and slipped my tongue into her sugarcoated mouth, chasing the high of those memories. Licking the sweet innocence from her lips. Tasting my first crush all over again.

If love had a flavor, it would be vanilla custard cream.

"Kellen," Darby breathed, licking her own lips with an appreciative hum. "Let's go home."

CHAPTER 24

KELLEN

Two hours, three orgasms, and an entire pack of biscuits later, we walked up to The Brazen Head pub, practically vibrating from all the sex and sugar.

I'd never felt better in my entire fucking life, which was a problem because I was about to have to play the part of a man who was incapable of feeling anything at all.

Up until two days ago, it wouldn't have been an act. I'd kept my mouth shut, gone where the Brotherhood told me to go, killed who they told me to kill, and I never gave two shites about it. They were all corrupt. They were all liars and thieves and backstabbers and wife-beaters. There was no emotion involved, other than the lava flow of hate that pumped through my veins, demanding a periodic release. And my job gave that to me. I got to kill fuckers who looked like *him* over and over and over again.

But the moment I'd gotten my girl back, that life and my memories of it had faded away so quickly it felt as if it had all been a dream. A hazy, gory five-year-long nightmare that Darby had woken me from with a single glance.

Now, I had to try to be that man again—a man I could hardly remember, a man I was desperate to forget—and I was going to have to do it with Darby in the same room.

She'd refused to stay at the cottage. With no phone, money, identification, or means of self-defense, she was terrified of being separated from me, and I couldn't blame her. As much as I hated the idea of letting her get this close to my old life, I hated the thought of not being there to protect her even more. Besides, it was a simple transaction in a public place. Darby wouldn't hear any of our conversation, and when it was over, we'd be one giant step closer to a whole new life.

As soon as she realized where we were, Darby grabbed my arm with a gasp. My jacket was so big on her that her hands were completely covered by the sleeves. "Oh my God, this place is so cuuuute!"

I gazed at the medieval brick building and smiled. It was shaped like a tiny castle, dripping with flowers and lit with lanterns. "I thought you'd like it. It's the oldest pub in Ireland."

Darby turned to me as a wry smile unfurled across her face. "Kellen Donovan, are you taking me on a date?"

"That depends." I shifted the eighty-pound bag on my shoulder. "Do ya like it?"

"I love it!" Darby's smile widened just before she pressed up onto her tiptoes and smashed it against my mouth.

She still tasted like vanilla.

Fuck. This was going to be harder than I'd thought.

Forcing myself to pull away, I held her at arm's length and pinned her with a serious stare. "You remember what I told ya?"

"Stay at the bar. Don't talk to anyone. Don't look at you directly."

"And if I give ya a signal, a look, fuckin' anything …" I gave her a scowl that would have most grown men pissing themselves in fear, but Darby only rolled her eyes.

"Go straight to the bathroom and stay there until you come get me."

"Good girl." I tapped her on the nose. Then, I stuck the last of my cash in her jacket pocket. "Try not to get too wasted."

DEVIL OF DUBLIN

I knew exactly which table I wanted and had called ahead to be sure I got it. It was an L-shaped corner booth in the back room that faced the door as well as the bar. I regretted that decision the second I sat down and realized how bleedin' hard it was going to be to keep my eyes off of Darby. Instead of sitting down, she wandered around the pub, taking in every newspaper clipping and photo that had been plastered to the walls in the nearly nine hundred years since that place had been built. She'd pulled her hair up into a knot before we left, thrown on my jacket—which swallowed her whole—and slid into a pair of ripped jeans and Converse. If I didn't know her, I would have assumed that she was the prettiest girl at Trinity College, and I would have been insanely jealous of the bloke whose jacket she was wearing.

How the fuck that bloke had turned out to be me, I still didn't know.

A hostess walked past her, escorting a posh Black man in a crisp blue suit toward my table, and I knew it had to be the Brit. Nobody in Dublin dressed like that. The fucker was wearing a pocket square, for Christ's sake.

I had to hand it to the bastards—they knew how to dress.

I didn't stand, and I didn't offer to shake his hand. I simply gestured to the seat diagonal from me in the corner booth, and with a haughty show of unbuttoning his suit jacket, the Brit sat down.

"Liam," he stated, eyeing the bag next to me, and with that single word, my hopes for an easy sale withered up and died.

Liam Cole was a high-ranking member of the Townley Firm. Those fuckers were some real *Peaky Blinders*–style gangsters. Unlike the UIB, which at least pretended like it had some righteous social/political cause, the Townley Firm fucked with people simply because they could. They terrorized South London, running protection rackets on the small businesses, committing fraud and extortion at the larger businesses, robbing the citizens at gunpoint and beating the shite out of them in the streets. Even if the Brotherhood had been willing to work with the English, they would have stayed the fuck away from the

Townley Firm. Everybody knew those arseholes were not to be trusted.

I gave the man a stiff nod. There was no point in introducing myself. He knew who I was.

Not that I had a name to give him anyway.

Over Liam's shoulder, I noticed Darby take a seat at the bar, reminding me just how quickly I wanted to put that life behind me so that I could start a new one—a *real* one—as far away from my past as possible.

"I can't believe I had to come to fuckin' Dublin for this." The Brit adjusted his tie and glanced around the room with a scowl, as if I'd asked him to meet me in the jacks.

I didn't respond.

You can tell a lot about a person by the way they behave when you go quiet.

As a kid, Darby would fill my silence with her imagination. Now, she filled it with fearful apologies.

Most normal people filled it with stammering awkwardness, but lads in the business were quick to anger. They all wanted to look tough. Any show of disrespect would be met with swift, irrational outrage. Which I always responded to by … not responding. It was too easy. I could establish dominance within sixty seconds of meeting someone by proving that I had the power to make them lose control over their emotions without saying a single word.

But Liam wasn't taking the bait. He rolled his eyes, looking mildly annoyed, but he stayed cool as ice. Fucking Townleys. Those bastards weren't in it for the pride. They were in it for the power.

I did notice, however, that he was constantly adjusting something—his watch, his pinkie ring, his tie, his vest.

He was nervous after all.

"Good God, do you eva shut up?" Glancing at the gash above my eyebrow, he added with a smirk, "Prob'ly got that from runnin' ya mouf, huh?"

I simply arched that eyebrow in a silent warning.

DEVIL OF DUBLIN

Liam grinned. "Relax, mate. It's just jokes. Everybody knows the Devil of Dublin ain't much of a talka. But I will say"—he tipped his head to the side as he gave me a once-over—"I fought you'd be ugliah."

I had to admit, the fucker was growing on me. Plus, he'd come all the way from London to help me out, so maybe it wouldn't kill me to be a little less of an arsehole. "I'm ugly where it counts," I mused, dropping the silent treatment as I placed the duffel bag between us on the corner of the L-shaped bench.

Liam snapped his fingers and pointed them at me. "Ya dangly bits, yeah? Mine are ugly as fuck, but they get the job done."

I felt a laugh rumble in my chest, but I forced my face to remain neutral. Like he'd said, I was the Devil of Dublin. The one they called Diabhal. And Diabhal didn't laugh. He didn't smile. He didn't fuck, drink, or smoke. He spoke only when necessary. And nobody outside of the UIB knew what he looked like because everyone who'd seen his face was dead.

When I finally felt my mask slide back into place, I unzipped the bag. "Twelve AR-15s, converted to full auto. No serial numbers. Twenty-five, cash."

Liam glanced at the guns just long enough to confirm what I'd said. Then, he adjusted his cuff links and smoothed his vest. "I'll give ya twenty to make up for the pain in the arse it's been, comin' all the way to Dublin."

"Twenty thousand pounds …" I rubbed my chin as if I were mulling it over, but really, I was waiting to see if he'd argue with my choice of currency.

When he didn't, I gave him a solemn nod and zipped the bag closed.

"All right then." He nodded back. "I'll go make the call." As he stood and buttoned his suit jacket, Liam added, "And 'ere I fought the UIB was just a bunch of unreasonable, terroristic cunts. Who knew?"

Unreasonable, terroristic cunts who know maths.

Twenty thousand pounds was worth almost the same as twenty-five thousand euros. We'd still have more than enough money to get our papers and get the fuck out of town.

As soon as he left the room, I let my gaze drift over to the bar.

And immediately wished that I hadn't.

Darby was perched on a barstool, being eye-fucked by an overly friendly barman and at least three fellas who'd slithered up next to her. Two of them were so close that their fucking arms were grazing hers. I cracked the knuckles on my right hand as I watched Darby cower and stare down into her half-empty beer.

As if she could feel the heat from my rage, she lifted her eyes and glanced over her shoulder at me. Raising one eyebrow, Darby silently asked if my glare meant that it was time for her to head to the jacks. That's *exactly* what I wanted her to do, but only to get her the fuck away from those drunken arseholes.

I shook my head, so subtly that I doubted anyone other than her would have noticed, and returned my icy stare to the Brit in the three-piece suit, who was breezing back in with a smirk on his perfectly groomed face.

Pointing at me, he grinned. " 'Ow's about a pint, mate? On me."

He didn't wait for my response—or lack thereof—before taking a sharp left and slapping his hand on the bar top enough times to pull the barman's undivided attention away from the hot young redhead he was drooling over. As much as I appreciated him extracting that gobshite from my girl's presence, something didn't sit right with me about his sudden interest in socializing.

Maybe he was just pleased with himself because he thought he was getting such a good deal, but if he was so annoyed about coming to Dublin, why buy a round like he planned to stay a while?

And that's when it hit me.

He wasn't buying a round.

He was buying time.

Next to the bar, down on the side closest to me, two fellas pulled out a fiddle and a banjo and began singing "Whiskey in the Jar" at the top of their lungs.

I could hardly hear myself think over the sound of their warbling, but I didn't need to think. I *knew* deep in my gut that something was off.

I rehearsed every possible escape route and worst-case scenario in my mind before the bastard in the bespoke suit returned with two pints of Guinness.

"Cheers, mate." He grinned as he slid into his side of the L-shaped booth.

When I didn't acknowledge the pint he was trying to hand me, Liam set it down in front of me, undaunted.

Whack fol de daddy-o!
There's whiskey in the jar.

"You 'ave no idea 'ow long we been tryin' to buy from the Bruvvahood," he shouted over the music before taking a gulp from his glass. "But the old cunts at the top are so fucked off about some shite that happened a hundred years ago that they won't even meet wiv us. So, we've 'ad no choice but to buy from the fucking Bratva."

Every muscle in my body tensed the moment he uttered that last word.

"They charge us a fuckin' arm and a leg, too, 'cause they know they got us by the bollocks."

My fists began to relax as things slowly started making sense. The stalling. The friendliness. Liam liked the price I'd given him so much that he was trying to work a deal for more.

A crowd had started to form around the musicians, and now, half the room was singing along.

Whack fol de daddy-o!
There's whiskey in the jar.

I decided I'd let him talk over the noise for a few more minutes. Then, I'd tell him I'd put in a good word for him with the elders, collect my cash, collect my girl, and get the fuck out of there.

The Brit leaned in closer and shouted, "But they're willin' to negotiate now." The Brit took another gulp from his pint as his eyes, as hard and hateful as mine, cut over to the front door.

I looked up as two goons, built like brick walls and probably twice as thick, stepped into the pub. They nodded in Liam's direction, but they weren't dressed like him. These fuckers were wearing tracksuits and gold chains—the unofficial Bratva foot soldier uniform.

" 'Cause, *now*, we got somefin' they want."

The entire world shifted into slow motion as I realized what was happening.

Liam wasn't trying to work a deal with the Brotherhood. He'd *already* worked a deal—with the Russians. And I was his fucking bargaining chip.

Whack fol de daddy-o!
There's whiskey in the jar.

My eyes darted from the door over to the bar. I could hardly see Darby through the clapping, singing swell of bodies that had filled the open space, but as soon as our eyes locked, she got up and headed for the jacks.

"No fucking way." The Brit chuckled, snapping at one of the meatheads and then pointing at Darby as she disappeared down the hallway next to the bar. "You brought a date. 'Ow sweet."

With a single thick-necked nod, the Russian followed her.

An inferno of rage engulfed me. I felt like I was being burned alive, and in a way, I was. As the smug fuck next to me smirked behind his glass of Guinness, the humanity I'd so recently rediscovered went up in flames. *Kellen* was reduced to nothing more than a festering pile of ashes, and in the spot where he sat, the Devil took his place.

DEVIL OF DUBLIN

"And 'ere I fought you were gonna put up a fight," the Brit mused, shaking his head before polishing off the last of his beer.

He set the empty pint on the table in triumph and turned toward me. Draping his elbow over the back of the booth, the arrogant cunt smiled into the soulless eyes of Satan's spawn. "Now, you play nice, and I'll let the lit'le birdie go. But make a scene, and—"

The rest of that threat dribbled from his gaping mouth as the entire pint of Guinness he'd just drunk spilled from his gutted stomach, running down his perfectly tailored trousers.

Whack fol de daddy-o!
There's whiskey in the jar.

The singing, clapping, pint-slinging crowd now filled the pub, blocking the Russian's view as I placed a hand on Liam's shoulder, rotated him toward me, jerked my blade out of his belly, and plunged it into his heart.

Right through his paisley fucking pocket square.

I laid his head down on the table so that it would look like he'd just passed out, slung the bag over my shoulder, and slid out of the booth. I palmed my knife as I made my way round the back of the crowd, and when I passed the Russian by the door, I waited for him to notice me before I took off running toward the jacks.

The first goon was standing outside the ladies' room. He didn't have a chance to react before I grabbed a fistful of his stupid, shiny track jacket with one hand and plunged my blade into his gut with the other. He let out a roar as I shoved him through the door into the men's room, grabbing at my neck with his meaty fucking paws. Adrenaline exploded through my veins as he found his mark and squeezed, but I had to fight through the panic. I had to stay conscious as he crushed my windpipe. I had to stay alert, even as my vision went black.

I slashed at him again and again, each swipe finding flesh, but it was going to take a bullet to put that fucker down. I was just about to reach into my waistband for my gun when the door burst open and someone shouted something in Russian. Even over the din of cheers and clinking beer steins, I heard the unmistakable click of a handgun being cocked, and with the last of my fading consciousness, I threw all my weight down and to the right.

My falling body spun the fucker into place just as his buddy pulled the trigger. All at once, I heard the hiss of a bullet being fired through a silencer, the wet crunch of it slicing through flesh and bone, and the explosion of plaster across the room, where it tore a hole through the wall.

The hands around my throat immediately loosened as over a hundred kilos of dead weight collapsed on top of my unstable body. My knife clattered to the ground as I caught myself on the edge of the sink, gasping for air. The moment that oxygen hit my bloodstream, my entire body felt like it had been injected with pure, uncut *life*.

More Russian words were shouted. Another click echoed through the room. But this time, my lungs were full, and my mind was clear.

With a sudden burst of strength, I shoved myself away from the sink as hard as I could, launching the massive corpse that had fallen across my back in the opposite direction. I spun around just in time to see the gunman's eyes go wide as his mate's body careened into his. He stumbled backward into the wall, and the moment his pistol clattered to the tiled floor, we locked eyes and dived for it at the same time.

I was farther away.

But he had a dead Russian in his arms.

The fallen Bratva hit the floor as my fingers curled around the handle, but his comrade right on top of me. He grabbed the gun by the barrel before I could turn it on him and tried to yank it out of my grasp. He kneed me in the ribs as he twisted the muzzle back and forth, but when he grabbed my fingers and began prying them off, one by one, I snapped.

Planting a boot on the fucker's chest, I launched him off of me, rolled onto my back, and fired up at him until the clip was empty. Round after round tore through his chest, his gut, his disgusting fucking face. I shuddered and squeezed the trigger again and again until the chamber only clicked. Until the memory of *him* was washed away in a sea of blood and vengeance. Until the only thing I could hear was my own racing heart and a drunken chorus of "Finnegan's Wake" filtering in through the door.

My hands wouldn't stop shaking as I scrubbed them in the sink. All I could see was red. All I could *feel* was red. There was red swirling down the drain as I washed my knife and stuck it back in my boot. Red splattered across my face like Darby's freckles. There was red pouring from the bodies on the tiled floor, crisscrossing through the grout lines as it slithered in geometric patterns toward my feet. But the only red my mind could process was the puddle of it that I'd woken up in after Father Henry pried my fingers off that fucking spindle and beat me unconscious with it.

I might have picked up my bag and walked out of that room with my body intact, but my mind was locked inside a windowless attic in Glenshire.

CHAPTER 25

DARBY

I don't know how long I'd been sitting on the floor with my back against the door, but it felt like an eternity.

I'd been pacing the bathroom floor, waiting for Kellen to come get me, worried sick about what could be going on out there, when a bullet ripped through the wall above the sink and lodged itself in the ceiling. I dove to the floor and covered my head, and that's where I stayed. Waiting. Panicking. Watching the plaster dust from the bullet holes flutter to the ground like snow.

The seconds ticked by like hours. One drinking song morphed into another. And the longer I waited, the sicker I felt. I actually prayed for more bullets to tear through the wall because bullets would mean that someone was still alive to shoot them.

My heart sputtered as the door rattled against my back.

Bam! Bam! Bam!

"Darby! Time to go!"

I released a breath that turned into a manic, desperate, relieved laugh as I rose to my feet.

He was okay. Kellen was okay.

The instant I unlocked the door, a strong hand with three freckles on one finger reached in and yanked me out.

Kellen didn't so much as look at me as he dragged me through the sea of singing, clapping, stomping bodies.

One mornin' Tim was rather full
His head felt heavy, which made him shake
He fell from the ladder and he broke his skull
And they carried him home his corpse to wake

We pushed through the exit door, and the night air was as crisp and cool as the pub had been warm and stuffy. The chorus faded quickly into the background as Kellen broke into a sprint. He pulled me by the hand down the sidewalk and over the bridge to the other side of the River Liffey. He used his free hand to secure the duffel bag strap across his chest as he ran, and my racing heart sank when I realized that it was still as full and heavy as ever.

It sank further when the distant music behind us stopped abruptly.

And was replaced with the sound of screaming.

As soon as we were across the river, Kellen darted in between two buildings, dragging me through a maze of damp, dark alleyways as screaming sirens and flashing lights bounced off the walls all around us.

My lungs burned and my legs shook as I struggled to maintain Kellen's punishing pace, but he didn't slow down until the back door of the cottage was firmly shut and barricaded behind us.

Then, before I could even ask what had just happened, the duffel bag clattered to the kitchen floor, and Kellen tore through the house to the bathroom where he disappeared with the slam of a door.

After that, all I could hear was the sound of water running through the pipes and blood rushing through my ears as I doubled over at the waist and tried not to vomit.

The bullets.

The screams.
The sirens.
Someone was dead.
Someone was dead or really, really hurt.
Oh God, was it *Kellen*?

The way he was acting, the way he hadn't let me see anything other than his back since we'd left, the way he was avoiding me …

I pictured his naked body lying in the tub, bleeding out from a gunshot wound as the shower beat down on him, and my aches and exhaustion were suddenly forgotten. I raced through the kitchen, headed straight for the door that separated me from my past, present, and—if the legend was true—eternity, and without knocking, I charged inside.

I expected to plunge face-first into a wall of steam, but the air inside the small bathroom felt even colder than the rest of the drafty, old house. I didn't see any clothes on the floor—only a gun and a knife tossed into the sink—so when I swung my head toward the closed shower curtain that surrounded the claw-foot tub, I knew Kellen must have gotten in fully clothed.

"Kellen?" I unzipped his jacket and toed off my shoes. "You okay?"

He didn't respond. I couldn't see through the dark blue curtain, but from the steady beat of the water, it didn't sound like he was moving.

Shit.

I approached the shower. "I'm coming in, okay? I won't touch you. I just want to see if you're hurt."

I pulled back the curtain just enough to step into the tub, my socked feet screaming in pain as they landed in an inch of freezing cold water. But that pain paled in comparison to what I felt when I looked up at the tortured figure standing before me.

Kellen was hunched over with one arm braced against the wall as the icy spray crashed against his heaving back. Wet clothes stuck to every bulge and plane of his muscular body, but it was what he was doing to that body that had a strangled cry climbing up the inside of my throat.

Kellen's eyes were squeezed shut, his entire face twisted in agony, as his fist jerked furiously—*violently*—at his fully erect cock.

He hadn't even heard me come in.

Kellen was gone.

I understood better than anyone what it was like to leave your body, to dissociate when something horrible was happening, but I tried to go somewhere better.

Kellen had gone somewhere far, far worse.

I didn't know what to do. It was as if he were locked inside a cage of pain that I didn't have the key to. I couldn't touch him. I was afraid to turn off the water. I felt like he *needed* it somehow. Needed it to cool off. And maybe he needed the release of touching himself too, but not like that. *That* wasn't him. It was as if *that* was being done *to him*.

Suddenly, everything became clear. Why Kellen wouldn't let me put my hands anywhere below his waist. Why even reaching for him too fast could cause him to panic. Why he could tolerate sex and kissing, but not simple foreplay.

As his hand squeezed and twisted and tore at his cock, tears welled in my eyes. I pictured his beautiful, innocent, cherubic face, half-hidden behind a fall of black curls, and released a silent sob for the boy trapped inside the man. Trapped inside that house. Trapped inside his own silence.

But he'd gotten out. Unlike me, Kellen had found the strength to leave his abuser. He'd reclaimed his voice. Reclaimed his *life*. And I knew he had the strength to fight whatever had him in its clutches now.

I just had to figure out how to reach him.

"Kellen?" I whispered, lifting a hesitant hand. "It's okay, baby. It's okay. I'm here. It's just me."

I wanted so badly to stop him, to reach out and still his arm, but he wasn't Kellen anymore.

He was a coiled rattlesnake.

Instead, I placed my mouth next to his ear, gasping from the frigid spray ricocheting off his back as I whispered his name again. The icy-cold water felt like razor blades as it soaked through my clothes in wet slashes, but I gritted my teeth and breathed through it.

"Kellen ..." I whispered again, forcing myself to bear witness to his pain. "He's gone. He's gone forever, baby. It's just me."

His eyes opened, but they stared straight down as water coursed over his face and dripped from his black eyelashes.

My heart leaped in my shivering chest.

"I'm gonna stay right here, okay? You're n-n-not alone."

I clenched my teeth to keep them from chattering, but Kellen heard it. His hand stopped moving as those ghastly gray eyes shot up to mine. Then, they slid down the length of my trembling body, every curve now shrink-wrapped in cold, wet clothing. My chilled nipples tightened to the point of pain under his predatory gaze, and my sudden gasp of anticipation caused my chest to rise eagerly.

"It's okay," I whispered, heat rushing to the surface of my frigid skin as I reached for his face. "You can touch me. Touch me instead."

I thought I saw a glimmer of awareness behind his blown-out pupils, but the second my fingertips brushed his cheek, I found out how wrong I was. Kellen's hand shot forward, clamping around my throat and pinning me to the wall. A startled yelp burst from my lungs as my eyes slammed shut, but the instant Kellen heard it, he released me with a sudden gasp.

A shadow fell over me as he stood to his full height, blocking the spray with his body.

I took a deep breath and forced myself to look at him, but the face I saw staring back was even more heartbreaking than the one I'd just seen. Kellen's eyes were clear, wide, and *horrified*.

He raised his hands to touch my neck, my face, my chest, but stopped himself each time, shaking his head faster and faster.

Tears stung my eyes—not because of him, but *for* him. He hadn't hurt me. It all happened so fast that he hadn't even scared me. But I knew that wouldn't matter to him.

"Hey." I forced a smile. "It's okay. Look at me. I'm okay."

Kellen stepped away from me, head still shaking, and when he couldn't back up any farther, he tore the curtain open and barreled out of the tub.

He behaved like a panicked, caged animal—eyes darting left and right, feet planted, knees bent—ready to run.

I shut off the water and grabbed a towel as he zipped up his sopping wet pants and shoved his gun back into the waistband. Next, he slid his knife into the holster inside his boot. He should have been taking his clothes off, not suiting up like he was about to …

Oh God.

Darting across the small space, I tried to block the door with my body, but Kellen was faster.

"No, no, no, no, no." I chased after him. "Where are you going?"

Kellen stalked out of the bathroom, raking his fingers over his wet head as he headed straight toward the back door, but this time, I was faster.

I sprinted ahead of him and blocked the exit, talking as quickly as I could before he made it to the door. "Don't do this, Kellen. Don't leave like this again. Please. There are cops everywhere—you could get arrested out there. You could hurt somebody."

The agony pouring off of him as he stomped toward me was so powerful that it pushed me backward against the door.

Kellen's eyes were wild, wrathful, and red. But defying his rage were his tears. They spilled over his ashen cheeks, bracketing lips that pulled back in a snarl as he screamed, "I hurt *you!*"

With one final stride, Kellen stopped directly in front of me, bent forward, and picked me up over his shoulder.

I released a guttural grunt from the pit of my empty stomach as he turned and stomped back into the bedroom.

DEVIL OF DUBLIN

And then he was climbing.

Thank God, I thought, watching the rungs of the ladder go by in reverse from my upside-down position. *Oh, thank God he's going to stay.*

Something I'd said must have gotten through to him. Kellen had decided to hole up with me in our little love nest until he calmed down, and in the morning, we'd figure something out.

When Kellen got to the top of the ladder, he set me down on the rug-covered floor. My cold, wet clothes clung to me, restricting my range of motion as I crawled stiffly over to the pillows, but when I turned to look back at Kellen, he wasn't following me up.

He was shutting me in.

The hinged door swung down with a *slam*, plunging me into darkness.

"No!" I screamed, scrambling back toward the trap door on my hands and knees. I clawed and groped at the glowing edges of the door, searching for a handle in the dark, but by the time I found it, I was already too late.

Kellen was gone.

And so was the ladder.

CHAPTER 26

DARBY

"You are so fucking stupid."
"This is all your fault."
"Why do you have to fuck everything up?"
"Shut your fucking mouth."
"No one cares."
"Whore."
"Gold-digger."
"White-trash."
"Stupid bitch."
"God, you're so sensitive."
"You're pathetic, you know that?"
"Useless."
"Worthless."
"Helpless."
"Weak."

John was right.
I was useless.
And worthless.

And helpless.

And weak.

I couldn't do anything right. I'd wanted to comfort Kellen, to calm him down, and instead, I'd made the situation so much worse.

Now, he was out there somewhere, losing his mind, armed with *two* deadly weapons, and wanted by the police.

And it was all my fault.

If I hadn't been so helpless that night with John, none of this would have happened.

Because of me, Kellen had killed someone. A *civilian*. Because of me, he was on the run with a missing person. Because of me, he was going AWOL to smuggle me out of the country. And because of me, he might have just killed someone else trying to get the money to pay for it.

I hugged my knees and rested my chin on the wet denim, rocking back and forth. I'd found the switch to the fairy lights, but they didn't feel magical anymore. Now, they just felt stupid.

Like me.

"Pathetic."

"Worthless."

"Weak."

"Shut up!" I shouted, squeezing my eyes closed and covering my ears with both hands. "Shut up! Shut up! Shut up!"

I couldn't spend another second cooped up in that attic. I had to get out of there. I had to do something before I went completely insane.

Throwing open the hatch, I glanced down at the floor below. It was at least a ten-foot drop down to some pretty unforgiving-looking hardwoods, but I would have risked a jump twice that high to get away from the voice inside my head.

To get away from *him*.

Grasping the edges of the opening, I lowered myself toward the ground until I was dangling by only my hands. Then, I let go. My feet slammed into the floor with a force hard enough to rattle my spine, but when I stood up, I seemed to be okay. Nothing felt sore or injured.

I tore off my soggy clothes and pulled on a dry pair of jeans and a sweater. I hadn't bothered to towel off first, so the outfit clung uncomfortably to my damp skin, but I hardly noticed. I was too busy replaying everything that had just happened on a loop in my mind.

I would never forget the look on Kellen's face when he'd realized what he'd done. It was even worse than the devastation I'd seen the night before, when he'd thought I was afraid of him. He'd stormed off then too.

And that's when it hit me.

I knew where to look.

Fifteen minutes later, I stood in front of the closest entrance to Phoenix Park, wondering what the hell I'd been thinking.

I was never going to find him. Not only because the park was about as big as the entire village of Glenshire, but also because it was completely unlit.

The stone wall surrounding the massive, wooded green space loomed over me as I peered through the open gate, but I couldn't see more than a few feet in front of my face. The moon that had been so bright and full just two nights ago was now completely covered by clouds, and I didn't even have a cell phone to light my way.

I listened for footsteps, sounds of a struggle, anything that might indicate that Kellen or *anyone* was within those walls, but all I heard was the occasional passing car and the distant, despondent hoot of an owl.

Taking a few hesitant steps through the gate, I stood and waited to see if my eyes would adjust, but it was hopeless. Darkness swallowed the path, and me along with it, as John's voice reminded me what a fucking idiot I was.

But it was Kellen's voice that had me spinning around and darting back out the gate.

"Had to let 'em get a coupla shots in. Just to be polite."

"Who?"

"The skangers in the park. They usually get kicked out of the pubs early for fightin' and go lookin' for trouble. They found it tonight."

My extremities began to ache one by one as I walked north along the stone wall, looking for another entrance that was near a pub. It hadn't felt that chilly when I left, but the longer I stayed outside with my wet hair and damp skin, the deeper the cold seeped into my bones. My fingers and toes felt like they'd been smashed with frozen sledgehammers, and my ears throbbed all the way into my brain.

But I trudged on. Stopping at every park gate to listen for signs of life, looking for pubs that might have a rough clientele. I told myself that doing something was better than doing nothing. That I wasn't stupid, or useless. That I could find Kellen and bring him home. But the farther I walked, the less true those affirmations began to feel.

And *that* was before it started raining.

As I stood, shivering in the doorway of the sixth or seventh or eleventh cemetery-like entrance, it became impossible to deny that John had been right all along.

I hadn't found Kellen.

I hadn't even escaped from the voice inside my head.

All I'd accomplished by leaving the house was getting myself stuck in the freezing rain, miles away from home, with no money, phone, or ID.

Warm tears and cold rain slid down my cheeks as I curled in on myself, huddling in the covered park entrance for shelter. Once the rain let up, I would drag myself back to the house and go back to doing nothing. The only thing I couldn't fuck up.

My pity party was interrupted by the sound of a door slamming shut nearby.

Peeking around the side of the wall, I saw a cute white Tudor-style cottage—hardly bigger than the one I'd been squatting in—wedged into the narrow space between the stone wall surrounding the park and the street. It had a few picnic tables in front and a neon sign above the door that read *Hole in the Wall* in a quirky Old English font. But as skinny and quaint as the front of the building was, the back seemed to go on forever. It was as if someone had stretched it out along the wall like chewing gum until it eventually disappeared around a curve.

A small orange light appeared in the doorway, illuminating the end of a cigarette and a rugged, bearded face behind it. As if he could feel me watching him, the man looked up and coughed out a plume of smoke.

"Jaysus Christ." He coughed again, this time followed by a raspy laugh. "Ya scared the shite outta me. Thought ya were Jonathan Swift's ghost."

"Jonathan Swift, like, the famous writer?"

"Aye. He haunts the park. Among other things." The man gestured toward me with the glowing end of his cigarette and lifted an eyebrow. "Yer not goin' in there, are ya?"

I shook my head, rubbing my upper arms with my sleeve-covered hands. "Just ... trying to stay out of the rain."

The ember glowed brighter as he took another drag. His eyes watched me with interest, but unlike the rest of his bulky, scruffy appearance, they seemed kind. Gentle.

"Yer a long way from home."

I think that was his way of addressing my accent, but the sentiment hit me unexpectedly hard. I dropped my gaze to my soaking wet Converse and nodded slowly.

"I'm Conor."

I looked up in time to see him press a hand to his chest and give me a small bow.

"The best barman in Dublin ... according to me mam."

I forced a small smile. "Darby."

He exhaled a stream of smoke with a small smile of his own before tipping his head toward the double doors just behind him. A warm glow seeped through every windowpane along with the faint sounds of glasses clanking and bellies laughing.

"Ya wanna come inside, Darby? You can tell all yer friends back home that ya had a pint at Europe's longest pub. I'm sure they'll be green with envy."

"Oh, uh ... I don't ... have any money."

"Haven't ya heard?" He flicked his cigarette butt into the street and pulled the door open. Golden light spilled out, landing at my feet like a welcome mat. "Beer's free in Ireland … unless yer ugly."

Inside, the atmosphere was even cozier than I'd expected. And Conor hadn't been kidding when he said that it was the longest pub in Europe. It felt like the longest pub on earth. But because it was so narrow, each room felt intimate. Inviting. The walls, floor, and ceiling were covered with rich brown wood, making it seem like I was walking through the hollowed-out trunk of a fallen mahogany tree. The chairs and benches were wrapped in oxblood leather, the tables were made from reclaimed wood and whiskey barrels, and in the back, next to the bar Conor was supposed to be manning, was a blazing stone fireplace.

I rushed over and knelt on the floor in front of it, holding my palms up to the flames as some of the cold left my body with a violent shiver.

One beer, I told myself. *I'm just going to dry off, wait for it to stop raining, and head back.*

Conor refilled everyone's glass at the bar, apologizing for the wait as they craned their necks to shout at the soccer game on the TV above them. Then, he brought me a glass of something that was definitely not beer.

"This'll warm yer belly," he said, handing me a short glass full of liquid the same color as the logs in the fire.

I accepted it with a grateful smile. "Thank you. Seriously."

Up close, I could see that he was younger than I'd originally thought. And handsomer. Hiding behind that scruffy beard was a boyish face with high cheekbones, bright blue eyes, and permanently smirking lips.

"You won't be thankin' me after ya try it." He winked.

I took a sip and immediately hissed in pain as my entire esophagus went up in flames.

"What *is* that?" I coughed.

"McCaffrey Irish Whiskey." Conor laughed, squatting down so that he was on the same level as me. "Our own house brand. They say it's so strong it'll put hair on yer chest."

"Well, in that case ..." I took another larger sip and squeezed my eyes shut through the burn.

Conor laughed again, and I realized that something about it made the hair on the back of my neck stand up. Maybe because it sounded like a smoker's laugh. All the creeps who'd hung out at my dad's place were smokers. And they'd all had that same cruel, raspy laugh.

"Ah, the feckin' news!" someone from the bar shouted as the rest of the patrons grumbled in unison. "The game was just gettin' good too."

"An American couple—last seen in Glenshire, County Kerry—have been reported missing."

The words *American couple* and *Glenshire* had my head snapping up to the screen above the bar. There, staring back at me from inside a box next to a female newscaster, was a picture of someone who looked a hell of a lot like me and someone who looked a hell of a lot like the man who was now just a disembodied voice in the darkest recesses of my mind.

"They have been identified as John David Oglethorpe and Darby Collins. Mr. Oglethorpe's family is offering a reward for his safe return. If anyone has any information about their whereabouts, please call—"

My eyes slowly drifted back to Conor's, which were now wide with realization.

"Didn't you say yer name was—"

"It's her!" A large, middle-aged man shoved his meaty finger in my direction from his perch at the bar. "The girl from the news! Look, will ya?!"

Every head in the room fell silent and turned in my direction.

I set my glass on the floor and backed away from Conor slowly, shaking my head in a silent plea.

His eyebrows pulled together in confusion as he watched me go, but he didn't say another word.

The rest of the pub, however, did not offer me the same courtesy.

"That has to be her."

"Look at that hair."

"Didn't she say there was a reward?"

"Nah, the reward's for the bloke."

"The reward's for both of 'em, dummy!"

"If anybody's gettin' the reward, it's me!" the man from the bar announced, turning that finger away from me and pointing it back at himself. "I saw 'er first!"

Spinning around, I broke into a sprint. But I only made it about ten feet before a tall man in a police uniform stood up from his seat and blocked my path.

I slammed into his unyielding chest so hard that I would have stumbled backward if he hadn't also grabbed me by the arms. Even through Kellen's puffy jacket, I could feel his fingers digging into me.

I froze as panic shot through my bloodstream, seizing my muscles and stealing my voice.

"Don't worry, lads," the officer snarled, tightening his grip. "I'll take good care of her."

CHAPTER 27

KELLEN

I stood in the shadows of an abandoned warehouse, only partially sheltered from the rain, as I stared across the street at my apartment. I had no fucking clue how I'd gotten there. I felt like I was losing my mind. Entire chunks of time were missing from my day, and the parts that I could remember felt like distant memories. Darby and I laughing at Tesco. The taste of sugar on her lips and salty sweat on her skin. The Brazen Head. The blood. The bodies. So many bodies.

Then, nothing.

Dread seeped into the marrow of my bones.

The only times I'd blacked out before had been back in Glenshire, during the worst of Father Henry's punishments and rituals. When I'd come to, hours later, I'd be covered in dried body fluids and bleeding from some new injury sustained during my struggle. I wasn't bleeding, that I could tell, but I was soaking wet.

And I had no idea where Darby was.

The second her name passed through my mind, an image broke through the black haze separating me from the past two hours of my life. It was Darby—in the shower, fully clothed, with a hand wrapped around her fucking throat.

The flames inside of me flared immediately, reducing the image to ashes, but it was too late. The way my stomach lurched, the way bile seared the back of my throat, the way my right hand shot open, as if releasing her, I knew.

I'd done exactly what I'd been afraid of doing since the moment she walked back into my life. What happened every time someone got too close. I'd been triggered. I'd lost control. And I'd hurt her.

No.

My heart pounded against my ribs almost as hard as my fist pounded against my thick fucking skull as I tore through the murky, putrid wasteland of my mind, searching for answers.

I saw blood seeping through a silk pocket square.

Blood crisscrossing through the cracks in a tile floor.

A gun with a silencer.

My Beretta in the sink.

A trap door slamming shut.

A bag on the kitchen floor.

A bag that should have been empty but wasn't.

That was it. That was why I was standing outside of my apartment even though everything inside of me was screaming to go back, to make sure Darby was okay, to drop to my knees and apologize for whatever I'd done. Not that I deserved her forgiveness. I hoped she hated me for the rest of her life, but until I had enough money to get her the fuck out of the country, the rest of her life might be very, very short.

As the fog began to lift from my mind, I gazed at the row of crumbling brick buildings in front of me with renewed determination.

The UIB owned the entire shitty lot of them. Twelve townhouses crushed together on the south side of the park—the dodgy side, by the train station. Half of the units had had their bottom floors converted into shops at some point during the last fifty years, but they were just a front. Lawnmower repair, bike rental, launderette, barber shop. The ice cream shop was boarded up completely. No one went in, no one came out, but the Brotherhood probably reported that they pulled in seven figures a year.

The upper floors had been converted into apartments to house the soldiers they took in. Kids like me with nowhere to go, no options, no future, and some talent that was worth exploiting. Most of them moved out as soon as they saved up enough money, but I didn't have that luxury. Even though I had enough cash to buy the entire building, without any identification, I couldn't open a fucking bank account, let alone purchase property.

The other half of the townhouses made up the UIB headquarters. They'd been combined to make one big palace on the inside, fully equipped with offices, meeting rooms, common areas, pool tables, bars, a bleedin' bowling alley, and plenty of guest rooms for mistresses. It was as decadent on the inside as it was dilapidated on the outside.

But not my place. I'd been given the apartment above the launderette, and it was every bit as shitty as it looked.

It had to be after midnight. There wasn't a soul on the street, but I knew the Brotherhood had eyes on my place at all times. All I had to do was cross the street and unlock the door, and by the time I made it upstairs, I'd probably have five UIB foot soldiers on my arse with guns drawn.

Good thing I had at least ten bullets left in mine.

I pulled the Beretta out of my waistband and took a deep breath. Closing my eyes, I visualized the flames retreating to the shadowy corners of my mind. I felt the icy-cool kiss of death course through my bloodstream, numbing everything it touched. I was in control. I was the most feared man in Dublin. I was the one they called Diabhal.

And I had come for what was mine.

As soon as I stepped out onto the cracked path, the rain stopped. It was as if the clouds wanted a better view of whatever the fuck was about to go down.

I scanned every window, every parked car, but I knew I wouldn't find anyone. Why station a lookout when you could put up a camera and get a convenient little notification on your phone as soon as your target arrived?

As I crossed the street with my gun in one hand and my key in the other, I searched for anything that might house a hidden camera. And I found it. A small, rectangular black box. It was the size of a pack of cigarettes, but instead of being fastened to the wall, like a doorbell, it had been screwed into the top of the doorframe, pointing down.

I walked up to the faded blue door, and with a single blow from the butt of my gun, the device went flying. The camera ricocheted off the door and landed at my feet, where the last thing it recorded was the bottom of my boot as I smashed it to pieces on my way inside.

I climbed the stairs as quickly as possible, listening for signs of life, but all I found when I made it to the top was a shitty, ransacked apartment.

They wouldn't have found much. Living on the UIB's property never felt safe, so I didn't keep anything personal there. Clothes, exercise equipment, the furniture they'd provided—that was it. I didn't even have a computer. I did everything from my phone—which was completely clean, thanks to The Butcher.

I only hoped they hadn't found my cash.

Running through the cramped living and kitchen area to the bathroom, I yanked the lid off the toilet tank and exhaled in relief. Inside, submerged under water, was a plastic bag containing thirty thousand euros, banded in bricks of ten thousand. The Brotherhood handed me a new stack every time I took somebody out for them, and in the last five years, I'd earned enough of them that I was running out of places to hide them all.

But the rest were going to have to stay hidden. As close as headquarters was, I had a matter of seconds to get in and get out, if that.

I shoved the dripping wet bag under my already soaked shirt and tucked it into my jeans.

Then, I spun around and faced the stairway with my gun drawn.

DEVIL OF DUBLIN

I had already taken too long, but no one was coming.
There were no foot soldiers marching up my stairs.
No enforcers.
No Russian goons in tracksuits and gold chains.
I'd thought it would take an army to bring me to my knees.
Turns out, all it took was a single text.

CHAPTER 28

KELLEN

"He came unarmed," Sean, the kid who'd zip-tied my hands behind my back announced as we stepped out of the elevator and into the garage beneath the UIB buildings.

The fact that they'd stationed a new recruit at the door could only mean one of two things. Either they were so sure that I was going to kill someone that they'd offered up their newest soldier as a sacrifice or they were so sure I was going to cooperate that they hadn't bothered wasting their muscle on me. I hoped it was reason number one, but the second I saw Séamus's smug fucking face, I knew it was reason number two.

They really did have Darby.

"I see ya got my text. Please"—he extended a hand to my left—"step into my office."

The garage spanned the width of the townhouses with an entrance on one side and an exit on the other. It could hold at least sixty cars, but it was usually only about half-full. A dozen burners, like the one I'd left in Glenshire, sat clustered on one side; a fleet of shiny black luxury sedans were parked in the middle; and on the far side were the soldiers' own pieces of shit.

My blood was pumping so hard as the grunt and I followed Séamus down the center aisle that I could hear it louder than my own thoughts. I could feel it pulsing in my temples and surging against the cable ties that bound my wrists behind my back. I could practically see it turning my vision red.

And then, all I could see was Darby.

She was sitting in a rolling office chair in an empty parking spot between two black Audis. Her eyes, wide with fear and rounded in remorse, filled with tears the second they met mine, but when she went to wipe them away, her hands jerked helplessly against the cable ties holding them in place.

She was restrained.

She hated being restrained.

"We found yer little getaway driver." Séamus said, placing a hand on the back of Darby's chair. "You know, it didn't have to come to this."

The bloke who'd replaced me as Séamus's security guard, Ronan, stood on the other side of her. He was as dumb as he was big, but I'd never had a problem with the fucker.

Until now.

Séamus watched Darby's reaction as Sean guided me to stand in front of them, but her face gave nothing away. Not even to me.

"After our ... *incident* at the docks, we had all the guards on our payroll keep an eye out for a silver Ford Fiesta. Then guess what got reported missin' the next day? A pretty little ginger and her American sugar daddy ... and they'd been drivin' a silver Ford Fiesta."

Steam rose off my hate-fueled body as I stared, unblinking, into Séamus's eyes. I was going to rip them from their sockets and shove them down his throat before this was over. He was a dead man, and he knew it.

The bloated, pig-faced fuck looked away from the death in my eyes, shaking his head before shifting his attention to Darby. "One of our guards found her at the Hole in the Wall about an hour ago, soakin' wet, no sign of her fella, and too terrified to speak."

The entire world began to spin out from under me as his words fought their way through the sound of adrenaline pumping through my veins.

She'd run away.

From *me*.

The image of my hand around her throat slammed against my consciousness again as I glanced down at Darby's lifeless face. She was staring at the ground between us, unable to even look me in the eye.

What had I done?

What the fuck had I done?

"Poor girl." Séamus turned his head, now speaking to Ronan. "Can you imagine the unspeakable shite this fucker's done to her?"

My head snapped back up to his as the anger began to cloud my vision.

"I once saw him gut a man," he continued with a hint of amusement. "It was like a zip." Séamus made a noise as he dragged his fist up and over the swell of his pot belly. "Everything just ... fell out. Disgusting. Bastard was still alive too."

"Jaysus." Ronan laughed. "No man should have to see his own innards."

Darby's eyes widened and shot up to mine.

Séamus responded to her shock with a chuckle. "Oh, you didn't know? Darlin', you were kidnapped by the Devil of Dublin himself. He's a sick fuck, this one. Yer lucky to be alive. Most people who get a glimpse of that handsome mug don't live to tell the tale."

"How many kills is he up to now?" Ronan asked, as if I wasn't standing right there. As if my entire world wasn't crashing down around me as I watched Darby's face morph from shocked to horrified to ... shuddered. That was the best way I could describe it.

It was the way everyone had looked at me in the village. The way people look at a freak when they're trying not to stare. Or the son of Satan.

Or the deadliest hitman in Irish history.

"Honestly, I've lost count." Séamus shrugged. "We keep the lad busy."

Ronan and Séamus continued their bullshit banter about me fucking the bodies of my victims and drinking their blood, but I was no longer listening. My focus had narrowed to a point no bigger than the tiny angel sitting across from me.

Her expression was unreadable, but the way her chest rose and fell, the curve of her back as she shrank away from me, and the glimmer of terror in her wide green eyes told me everything I needed to know.

The flames that had been threatening to burn through my restraints went out completely as the icy, numbing certainty of death slithered through my veins. Only this time, it wasn't preparing me to take a life. It was preparing me to lose my own.

I'd always known that it would end this way.

That Darby would find out the truth about what I really was.

That God would never let me keep her.

That I'd have to pay for the crimes I'd committed.

And knowing that I was right gave me a sick sense of satisfaction. A sense that maybe there was justice in the world after all. I didn't deserve to live. I didn't deserve an angel like her. Perhaps God had simply used me as a tool to free her from her fiancé, and now, she could go on to find all the good and wonderful things that were waiting for her.

I could live with that.

Or rather, I could die with it.

I'd gotten my half hour in heaven.

And now, the Devil knew I was dead.

CHAPTER 29

DARBY

"*Oh, you didn't know?*

"*... the Devil of Dublin himself.*
"*He's a sick fuck, this one.*
"*Yer lucky to be alive.*"

I stared at Kellen's expressionless face as the men's words filtered in and out of my reeling mind.

The police officer who'd dragged me out of the pub had handcuffed and blindfolded me before sticking me in the back of his car. He'd asked me a few questions, but I'd refused to talk. I remembered what Kellen had said about some of the cops being dirty, and no normal police officer would blindfold a missing person.

My suspicions had been confirmed when he pulled me out of the car and took the blindfold off. We weren't at a police station. We were in an underground parking garage, lit by a handful of harsh fluorescent bulbs.

The two men standing next to me now—one short and stocky with a shamrock tattoo on the back of his hand, the other massive and mean with a bald head like a bowling ball—had greeted the cop with a thick manila envelope and a hearty pat on the back. They'd greeted me with a rolling desk chair and a pair of cable ties. While the big one tied me down, the little one chuckled to himself, his thick thumbs mashing out a text on his phone.

I knew there were some bad guys after Kellen.

I knew those guys were working with the police.

But it wasn't until Kellen had shown up two minutes later—so soon that he must have already been there—and I heard the way they interacted that I finally realized what had been right in front of my face the entire time.

Kellen wasn't just one of them.

He was the worst of them.

"How many kills is he up to now?"

"Honestly, I've lost count."

I was staring at someone they called the Devil of Dublin, but all I saw when I looked at him was a busted lip peeking out from behind a curtain of loose black curls.

A cauldron made from a scuffed leather shoe.

A skinny, scarred body backflipping into an enchanted lake.

My poor, sweet Kellen.

What did they do to you?

What did they make you do?

I tried my hardest to keep my expression neutral. I didn't want him to see my fear and think it was because of him. I was afraid *for* him. I was afraid of losing him. But I had never, not once, been afraid of Kellen Donovan.

I wanted him to see that. That I believed in him. That I knew he'd get us out of this, just like he always did. But when Kellen tore his eyes away from me and loosened the hard set of his jaw enough to speak, something in his posture—in the resigned slope of his broad shoulders or the deep crease between his dark brows—told me he hadn't gotten the message.

"Take her back to the guards," he said, his sudden command slicing through their laughter. "Tell 'em to clear her name in the disappearance of her fiancé and send her back to the States … and I'll surrender to the Russians."

Surrender?

"Done." The shorter man to my left clapped his hands before opening the back door of the SUV parked next to us. "Sorry about this, lad. Ya know we love ya, but we gotta do what's best for the brotherhood."

Surrender!

Kellen refused to look at me. There was no rage rising off of him anymore. No more fiery wrath or hair-trigger hypervigilance. The air around him was as smooth and cold and peaceful as a body bag.

"No!" I screamed, thrashing against my restraints as he walked toward the open door beside me, empty eyes fixed on the cracked pavement in front of him. "What are you doing? Stop! Please!"

"Looks like Diabhal's got himself a clinger." The bigger guy snorted, mocking my pain as I swiveled and strained toward him in vain.

Reaching with desperate fingertips, I felt the plastic cable tie slice into the back of my left wrist as I gained the half-inch I needed to grab Kellen's jeans as he passed.

He froze immediately, his icy gaze traveling from the ground to my now-bleeding left hand.

"Don't," I whispered, my voice trembling as my fingers curled deeper into the fabric. "Don't do this. Please. There has to be another way."

I followed his stare to the three freckles dotted across my ring finger, and the small, hollow smile he gave them shredded my soul.

"*Is fíor bhur ngrá,*" Kellen recited, his voice as soft and sad as his haunted gaze. "We have eternity, remember? Maybe I'll deserve you by then."

My eyes filled with tears, blurring the last memory I might ever have of Kellen Donovan as he disappeared into the back of a black SUV.

CHAPTER 30

DARBY

There were no words to describe my grief. It swallowed me whole. It carried me deep inside its cavernous belly, where my thoughts couldn't reach me. Where my ears couldn't hear. Where an army of individual pains—despair, guilt, frustration, rage, worthlessness, uselessness, powerlessness—swarmed me as one, eating me alive bite by never-ending bite.

I stared out the car window, but the world passing by outside was just as black as the one in my head. There were no streetlights. No oncoming traffic. Wherever we were, it was remote. Desolate. And it was definitely *not* the highway to Glenshire.

But I'd known that it wouldn't be as soon as they put me in the backseat.

They'd zip-tied my hands behind my back and lashed my feet together at the ankles.

You don't worry about someone running away if you plan on setting them free.

Kellen had sacrificed himself for nothing.

No, for something worse than nothing—for *me*.

"I gotta hand it to ya, girl. You must have some top-tier pussy to bring a bastard like that to his knees."

By the time the driver's deep, rough laugh penetrated my sorrow, it was little more than a muffled rumble.

I dragged my eyes to the rearview mirror, where the whites of his were glowing blue from the digital instrument panel. The man was a giant, the kind with big, meaty hands and rolls on the back of his bald head. And unlike Kellen, he seemed to really like his job.

His crooked grin made my stomach turn.

"I didn't even think he had a cock." The driver chuckled. "Figured that's why he's so pissed off all the time."

Then, he dug a small vial out of his pocket. I couldn't tell what was in it, but after tapping it on the back of his hand a few times, he lowered his head and snorted whatever it was up his nose.

I watched his dashboard-blue eyes roll back in his head as he rubbed the side of his nose with a guttural groan.

I pulled my knees to my chest and returned my attention to the desolation outside, but I could still see his reflection in the glass as he snorted another bump off his hand.

"Now, he's a pussy-whipped little bitch." He pocketed the coke without taking his eyes off me. "Can't say I blame him though. I'm getting' hard just from lookin' at ya."

I heard the jingle of a belt, the drag of a zipper, and somehow, my decimated heart found a way to beat again. To *pound*. The driver's hand began moving up and down in his lap, and I realized that being shot in a field wasn't the worst thing that was going to happen to me that night.

Not even close.

"Fuck, that cunt's gonna be so tight."

Adrenaline shot through my bloodstream as my eyes darted around the inside of the car, but there was nothing I could do. No weapons. No escape. Even if I managed to jump out of the moving vehicle, my hands and feet were tied together. I'd never get away.

I'd never get away.

With that realization, the blue lights on the dashboard seemed to shine brighter and brighter until I was completely surrounded by a watery cerulean glow. It ebbed and flowed with the slow, hypnotizing rhythm of a lullaby. A sense of peace washed over me, and like I'd experienced the night before, a still, certain *knowing* settled into my bones.

Only this time, the knowing didn't tell me that everything was going to be all right.

It wasn't there to comfort me.

It didn't hold my hand or stroke my hair.

It lifted my chin, squared my shoulders, and said, NO.

Not with words, but with energy. A buzzing blue hum that stopped hard, like a period at the end of a sentence.

NO.

It was a decree. A demand. A line drawn in the sand.

NO.

I would *not* let another man touch me without my permission.

NO.

I would *not* abandon my body and let it be attacked.

NO.

I was *not* powerless. Helpless. Or weak.

In fact, I was the most dangerous force on earth.

I was somebody with nothing to lose.

With my knees still pulled up to my chest, I lifted my ass off the seat and slowly slid my cable-tied hands under me, bringing them around to my front.

"Ya must be into some sick shite to fuck that psycho." His wild eyes met mine in the mirror. "You like it rough, don't ya, bitch?"

The *smack-smack-smack* sound of skin on skin was suddenly drowned out by the crunching of gravel under tires as he turned onto a single-lane dirt road.

It was now or never.

"Yeah," I replied in a breathy voice as I slid over to the seat behind him. Leaning forward, I glanced over his shoulder, pretending like I wasn't disgusted by the hunk of flesh in his hand while I reached for the seat belt next to me. Without making a sound, I pulled the slack out as far as it would go, forming a loop at the farthest point. Then, I licked my lips, turned my mouth toward his ear …

And dropped the loop over his head.

I immediately released what little slack was left and pulled as hard as I could, pressing my bound feet into the back of his seat as I yanked. I knew I wouldn't be able to hold him for long, but I didn't have to.

When he slammed on the brakes, the seat belt locked in place.

I held fast anyway, just in case he let off the brakes, digging my heels into the leather upholstery as he clawed and raked at the indestructible fabric. I closed my mind to the sound of his struggle. To the gurgles and strangled grunts and hysterical, panicked shrieks. And instead, I thought of Kellen. I pictured his focused, determined face as he did the same thing to John. I channeled his quiet, simmering rage. He'd lent me his strength when I'd needed it most. He'd killed for me. Faced his fears for me. Risked his life for me. And as my forearms burned and my biceps shook and my knuckles split open—as the victim became the executioner—the backs of my tightly closed eyelids were bathed with a blinding blue light.

And the knowing smiled.

CHAPTER 31

KELLEN

The walls felt like they were closing in on me.

I didn't do well in confined, windowless spaces.

Like the attic in Glenshire.

One way in. One way out. And when the lights were off, you couldn't see your hand in front of your face.

Or the sick fuck coming to *teach you a lesson.*

One of the boarded-up storefronts on the UIB's block used to be an ice cream shop. Now, the only part that they used was the walk-in freezer. It made the perfect holding cell/torture chamber. Windowless. Soundproof. Escape-proof. I'd heard about it, but I'd never seen it.

Until I was the one locked inside.

I had no idea how long I'd been in there. The freezer was completely empty, which was smart. Anything could be used as a weapon in the right hands. I'd backed myself into the corner, facing the door, and waited for my exhaustion to finally pull me under, but the only thing that found me there in the dark was everything I'd been running from.

The scent of whiskey on Father Henry's rancid breath.

His groping hands and grinding hips.

His belt.

His fists.

The weight of his head in my hands as I'd bashed his skull against the floor.

The sound of it crunching. Over and over.

The heat from the fire as I'd watched my entire life go up in flames.

The faces of every man I'd killed since.

My shame.

My self-hatred.

But mostly, my complete and utter stupidity.

Because when I replayed my last moments with Darby—in every gut-wrenching, soul-shredding, heart-eviscerating detail—I noticed something that I hadn't before.

Darby hadn't been blindfolded.

Séamus had let her see his face. Ronan's. The new recruit's. He'd let her see the UIB building. He'd talked about Brotherhood business in front of her.

Séamus had never intended on letting her go.

I'd told myself I was sacrificing my life for hers, but the truth always found me in the dark.

I'd run away. Just like I always did. I'd run, and I'd left her there to die.

My body contracted, curling in on itself as the room shrank to the size of a coffin.

I tore at my arms, clawed at my scalp, screamed from the depths of my festering black soul as the flames burned me alive, welcoming me back to my own personal hell.

Hot tears seared my face as I pressed my grimacing mouth to the freckles on my left hand.

"Please," I begged, my voiceless whisper ragged. Shattered. "Please help me find her again. I'll be everything she deserves next time. I'll be anything you want. Just, when they finally kill me, help me find her again. Please."

I'd never considered myself to be a man of faith. But I was. I believed in a god who'd forsaken me. I believed in a devil whose blood ran in my veins. And I believed in the only blessing I'd ever been given.

I had to. It was all I had left.

A sliver of blue light appeared in the distance, like a fissure in the fabric of the hellscape I was trapped in. Then, it widened, beckoning me to come closer. I leaned forward, crouching on all fours, as reality injected itself back into my nightmare.

A hand reached in through the sliver of light and placed two water bottles on the ground—one empty and one full.

"You can piss in the empty one, if ya need to wee."

It wasn't Saoirse.

It wasn't a sign.

It was just fucking Sean, the new recruit.

"Is she dead?" I asked, my voice raw and brittle as the dimensions of my cell slowly came back into focus.

The hand stilled.

"Darby!" I roared. "Is she fucking dead?"

"I, em ... I don't know if I can—"

I surged forward and barreled into the door, shoving it wide open and knocking Sean on his arse. He reached for his gun, but I grabbed his arm before he could pull it out of the holster, twisting it behind his back until he screamed in pain.

"You have three seconds—"

"Somebody took her!" Sean shouted. "She's gone!"

I yanked the gun out of his hand and pressed the barrel to the center of his forehead. "Talk."

Sean squeezed his eyes closed as he lifted his shaky hands in surrender. "Ronan took her to the old Wicklow mines to ... ya know ... *take care of her* ... but he never came back. Wasn't answerin' his phone either. So, Séamus sent Mikey to look for him, and he found the bastard dead on the side of the road. Fuckin' rope burn around his neck."

"Strangled?"

"That's what he said."

"Ronan?"

"Aye."

"Who the fuck is strong enough to strangle Ronan?"

"I … I don't know, but … whoever it was, they got yer girl."

Fuck.

I lowered the gun and stared, dumbfounded, at Sean's terrified face.

"Alexi," I said. "He saw her with me at the docks. It has to be him. No one else knows she exists."

That motherfucker was going to use her to break me.

"Please don't escape." Sean's voice trembled as he leveled me with a pleading, watery stare. "Please. Séamus'll kill me if I let you get away."

"Oh, I'm not goin' anywhere." I stood and extended my hand to the blubbering man on the ground. "Alexi's got my girl, and Séamus is gonna take me right to him."

Sean exhaled a shaky sigh as I pulled him to his feet.

"But," I added, tucking his pistol in the back of my jeans, "if you don't want him to find out that I took yer gun, I'm gonna need a favor."

CHAPTER 32

DARBY

"In one hundred meters, turn right."

After spending over two hours behind the wheel of the dead guy's Audi, I figured out where the turn signal was ... and that was about it. With my hands still lashed together, I flipped the blinker on *without* triggering the windshield wipers—that was a first—but when I tried to slow down, I accidentally lurched the car to a complete stop in the middle of the street. Again. Braking, I'd discovered, is kind of an all-or-nothing thing when your feet are tied together.

Thankfully, it was almost four o'clock in the morning, and no one was around to witness my struggle.

Or my inability to remember which side of the road I was supposed to drive on.

"In fifty meters, your destination will be on the right."

Another thing I was thankful for: the fact that Ronan—I'd seen his name on his driver's license—used a fingerprint to unlock his phone instead of a security code. I had no idea where we were, so I'd had to use his cold, bluish thumb to access the GPS on his device.

I'd never touched a dead body before, but I was surprised by how little it bothered me. Maybe it was because he just looked like he was unconscious. Or maybe it was because of what he had planned for me. Maybe I was in shock and simply couldn't process the situation. But whatever the reason, when I opened the door and shoved him out, the *thwump* of his giant body hitting the dirt hadn't upset me.

Honestly, it had given me a sick sense of accomplishment.

And, an idea.

I'd turned the fingerprint requirement off so that I wouldn't get locked out of his phone again, and instead of going home, I drove for two and a half hours with my hands and feet tied together—all the way to Kent Station.

My heart was in my throat as I pulled into the parking lot. There were dozens of cars scattered across the asphalt, but the moment my gaze landed on a little Ford Fiesta in the very back row, I pressed my bound palms together and said a silent thank you to any entity, angel, or lake spirit who happened to be listening.

"You have arrived at your destination."

I had locked the keys to the Fiesta in the trunk—along with my phone, purse, and the contents of John's suitcase—but with the windows broken out, I was able to get into the car, no problem. And not only did I find the keys right on top of the pile of stuff in the trunk, but I also found John's monogrammed fingernail clippers, which made short work of those cable ties.

I left Ronan's car parked at the train station, and twenty minutes later, I pulled the Fiesta onto the shoulder of a long, dark road, flanked by tall, thick trees.

I'd used GPS to find my way back to the docks and retraced my turns from there.

A right and three lefts.

That was the mistake that had caused us to go from heading north on this road with a pair of homicidal maniacs on our tail to heading south on this road and coming at them head-on.

I parked right where I remembered the shoot-out happening, but other than a fresh set of tire marks veering off the road, there was no sign of the BMW.

"You are so fucking stupid." A deep, familiar voice chuckled in my ear.

"Of course it's gone, dummy.

"That car crashed over forty-eight hours ago. Did you really think the wreckage would still be here?

"You saw the text message on that meathead's phone. Your little boyfriend is getting on a private plane bound for Russia at noon. So, what did you do? You wasted three hours of what little time he has left—"

"Shut up!" I screamed, covering my ears with both hands. "Shut the fuck up!"

John's voice went silent as I got out of the car and slammed the door. I paced back and forth between my headlights, my silhouette slashing angry black shadows across the scene of a crime that now only existed in my memory.

It wasn't John's voice telling me I was stupid anymore. It was my own.

What the hell had I been thinking?

A frustrated growl clawed its way out of my chest as I grabbed a rock and chucked it as hard as I could into the woods.

Thunk.

The sound of stone landing on metal stopped me dead in my tracks. Swiveling my head back to the source of the sound, I noticed a gap in the tree line that I hadn't before. A gaping black hole where the underbrush had been trampled.

A hole the size of a car.

My feet nearly slid out from under me as I skidded down the muddy embankment and plunged headfirst into that opening. I didn't care what kind of creatures I might find lurking in there. In fact, what I hoped to find was most people's worst nightmare.

Pulling Ronan's cell phone out of my pocket, I turned the flashlight on and swept it from left to—

Oh my God.

The white license plate glowed like a full moon on a clear night the second my light hit it. The surfaces around it were glossy and black. And just above it, igniting a spark of hope in my hollow chest, was a small, round BMW emblem.

I held my breath as I ran to the driver's door—twigs and branches lashing my face in the dark—and exhaled in shock and relief when my light revealed what was inside.

The body of a man, slumped over the steering wheel.

And thankfully, he wasn't nearly as big as Ronan.

When I'd asked Kellen if the guys who had shot at us were still out there, he'd refused to answer me. At the time, I thought it was because he didn't want me to worry that they were still alive. But after seeing his reaction when I found out what he did for a living, I knew.

Kellen hadn't answered me because he didn't want to admit that he'd killed someone.

At least, that was my hunch. It was a hunch that had been strong enough to bring me all the way back to Cork, and for once, my instincts were right.

Part of me wanted to weep with joy. The other part—the part that knew what I had to do next—already wanted to vomit.

With a deep breath and firmly fastened seat belt, I clutched the Fiesta's steering wheel with both hands and smashed the gas pedal. A shriek burst out of me as the car barreled down the hill and through the hole in the tree line, following the BMW's path. Right before I crashed into the back of it, I jerked the wheel to the left, shooting past the wreckage and careening into a tree a little deeper in the woods. I probably wasn't going more than thirty miles an hour, but the force of the airbag slamming into my face made it feel like I'd been going three hundred. My heart was racing, and my ears were ringing, and my nose felt like it had been punched by a prizefighter as I stumbled out of the car, but I forced myself to shake it off. I had to stay focused. I had so much left to do.

DEVIL OF DUBLIN

Walking back over to the BMW, I yanked the car door open without thinking ... and immediately puked on the ground.

The smell. Good God.

I hadn't considered the smell. Ronan's body hadn't smelled, but he'd been dead for all of two seconds. This guy had been dead for two whole *days*. My stomach lurched again as I scrambled back to the Fiesta.

When I returned, I was ready for battle. I had tied one of John's silk Tom Ford ties around my head so that the widest part of the fabric covered my busted nose. Then, I'd tightened it to the point that I couldn't even breathe. Smelling was out of the question.

Grabbing the guy under his armpits, I dug my heels into the ground and pulled as hard as I could. Wet twigs and leaves squished under my feet as his back began to slip down my chest, but I squeezed him tighter and just kept walking backward. I didn't stop when his feet tumbled out of the car and hit the ground. I didn't stop when my arms began to shake and my thighs began to burn. I didn't stop until I dragged him all the way to the Fiesta and sat him awkwardly in the driver's seat.

And then I wanted to barf all over again.

His head rolled toward me as his body slumped over, and from that angle, I could see that the side of his neck that hadn't been visible to me before was a bloody, crusty, mangled mess.

Kellen *had* shot him. Right through the freaking jugular.

"Ugh." I shook off my revulsion and walked around to the trunk. Lifting the lid, I propped Ronan's cell phone light up in the corner and went to work.

I left the guy's pants, shirt, socks, and underwear on—they were basic enough—but I swapped out his shoes and belt for John's. I swapped out the contents of his pockets for John's wallet and cell phone. And, as the cherry on top, I slid John's Emory University School of Law ring on the pinkie finger of his right hand.

None of it was a perfect fit, but it didn't need to be. Because after I dug my wallet and cell phone out of the trunk, I doused Mr. Stanislav Lipovsky—according to the Russian ID in his wallet—and the rest of the Fiesta with an entire bottle of Ralph Lauren cologne. Then, I sparked the lighter I'd found in his pocket and lit him up.

The woods were soaked from the recent rain, so I knew the trees wouldn't burn, but "John" would, and that was all that mattered. By the time the sun rose, the cops would need dental records to identify his body.

Or ... a positive ID from his fiancée.

I still had so much left to do, but what I didn't have was John's voice in my head telling me that I was a stupid, worthless piece of shit anymore. In fact, the only voice I could hear as I walked back to the train station was the soft British accent of Ronan's GPS.

"You have arrived at your destination."

Walking up to the main entrance, I dropped Stanislav's personal items into the same trash can that Kellen had shoved his blood-soaked T-shirt into two days before, and my heart constricted like a fist. It felt wrong to be there without him. It felt wrong to be anywhere without Kellen. But as I walked in his footsteps through the entrance and over to the ticket machines, I realized that, in a way, he *was* there, guiding my every step. Kellen's presence stood next to me as I bought a one-way ticket to Dublin, just like he'd shown me how to do. His memory held my hand as it led me to the same platform we'd waited on two days earlier. And when the café finally opened, it was Kellen's voice that I heard, whispering that we should buy one of everything.

But Stanislav hadn't had much cash on him, so I settled for the largest coffee they had to offer and a breakfast sandwich.

The older woman behind the counter eyed me up and down as she poured steaming hot salvation into a paper cup. "You all right, love?"

I knew I looked like I'd just crawled out from under a bridge with my riot of tangled hair, oversize jacket, mud-caked

Converse, and sagging, sleepless eyelids, so I allowed myself to be honest. Not just with her, but also with *me*.

I shook my head with a bitter laugh, but what started out as a giggle quickly devolved into a delirious, full-bodied, manic kind of cackle. I wrapped my arms around my body as tears streamed down my filthy face. Every inhalation was a shuddering gasp. Every exhalation a broken sob.

Without a word, the barista came around the counter and wrapped me up in a soft, warm, espresso-scented hug. Her body was too plump to be my mother's, but her embrace felt just as strong and sincere. Strong enough to hold me while I fell apart.

"Shh, child," the woman cooed, smoothing a hand over the shiny material of Kellen's jacket. "It's gonna be all right. You know how I know?"

I shook my head with a sniffle.

"Because yer covered in freckles. Everywhere ya have a freckle is where an angel kissed ya, you know? So, I can tell that yer thoroughly protected."

I laughed again and released her, wiping my eyes with a napkin from the counter. "My grandfather used to say that."

"Well, maybe he's sayin' it to ya now." She smiled, placing a freckled hand of her own on my shoulder. "Spirits work in mysterious ways."

I hugged her again and gave her all the cash in my pocket before taking my seat on the first train to Dublin.

I felt a little lighter, watching the sun rise over the rolling green fields. Warmer with a hot coffee between my palms. And even though my table for four had three empty seats, I didn't feel alone.

Because Grandpa, my mom, and Kellen were all there in spirit, cheering me on.

CHAPTER 33

KELLEN

The ride to the airport only took half an hour, but it felt like fucking five with the amount of tension in the car.

Séamus was in a shite mood. Sean was so nervous I thought he might blow the entire plan. And Ronan was conspicuously absent.

Because the fucker was dead.

Séamus seemed to be taking it pretty hard. I hadn't thought the son of a bitch had a heart, but his dark sunglasses, deep frown, and complete lack of smart-ass shite talk told me that losing his right-hand man and his top enforcer to the Bratva within twenty-four hours wasn't sitting too well with him.

Good. Fuck him.

"Have the guards sent Darby back home yet?" I asked, watching his reaction in the rearview mirror.

His already-clenched jaw flexed.

"Well, have they?"

"Yeah, sure," he deadpanned as Sean took the Dublin Airport exit.

Everybody in Ireland knows that *yeah, sure* means abso-fucking-lutely not.

My blood boiled as I thought about everything that could have possibly happened to Darby in the twelve hours since I'd seen her last. What would have happened if the Bratva hadn't interfered. What could be happening to her now that they had.

I knew what they did to pretty little girls. What other rich bastards would pay them to do to her if I failed. It was a fate worse than death.

One that I would die to spare her from.

"Where's Ronan?" I asked, twisting the knife.

Sean glared at me in the rearview mirror as he drove toward to the back of the airport, where the private planes take off.

Séamus shrugged weakly. "Prob'ly balls deep in that American cunt."

I raised an eyebrow but said nothing. Séamus wanted me to lash out at him, and I wasn't about to give him the satisfaction. At first, I couldn't understand why he'd been so quick to turn on me after the Bratva decided they wanted my head. I'd been like a son to him. I'd done everything he'd ever asked. I'd been the perfect fucking soldier. But I finally understood. Séamus didn't want to hand me over. He was doing it to avoid a war. He was doing it because he and the elders were fucking cowards. So, the only way he could make himself feel better about that was to behave as though I deserved it. By treating me like a piece of shite, he could pretend like he wasn't one.

But there is no honor among thieves. We were all pieces of shite.

And I was about to prove it.

Sean pulled to a stop in front of a small, unmarked private jet. The door had already been lowered, revealing stairs that I promised myself Darby's feet would never touch.

My eyes scanned the tarmac, but it appeared as though we were the first to arrive. The clock on the dashboard read 11:59. Séamus *must* have been scared of the Bratva. He was never on time for shite.

The second the clock struck noon, a black Mercedes with tinted windows rounded the corner, and it took every ounce of what little self-control I had left to keep from chewing through my restraints and running straight fucking toward it.

Alexi usually traveled with a deeper entourage than just one carload, but I had killed three of his men in the past three days, so his reinforcements were probably running a little low.

I expected Séamus to have some quip about my ride being there, but he didn't say a word as he got out of Sean's Volkswagen and opened the door for me.

My hands were tied behind my back, but they'd left my feet unbound. Probably because climbing the stairs to the jet would prove to be a little difficult with my ankles lashed together and also because the last thing they wanted was to draw attention. That part of the runway might have been secluded, but it was still a public place.

With his hand around my bicep and the muzzle of the loaded gun in his jacket pocket jammed into my side, Séamus walked me over to the Mercedes. Both of the front doors opened, and out stepped Alexi and his tracksuit-and-gold-chain-wearing driver. No one got out of the backseat, but that didn't mean Darby wasn't in there. The Bratva were dramatic as fuck. Knowing them, they probably wanted to save that little surprise for later.

Alexi snapped his fingers in the driver's direction, and the grunt immediately hustled to the back of the car and began unloading their luggage. Then, he shoved that hand in my direction, forming a finger gun.

"You." His voice boomed as he marched toward us. "First, you kill my uncle. Zen, you kill my men!"

Spit flew from his thin lips as he stopped directly in front of my face, grabbing my shirt in his fist. I was a few inches taller than him, so he had to look up to scream at me. He didn't fucking like that.

"I vas going to take you to my father," he snarled, his already-heavy unibrow creasing in the middle. "Let him kill you. Avenge his brother. But now?" His downturned mouth widened into a crooked yellow sneer. "You vill suffer. Greatly."

I knew exactly what that meant.

Darby.

It took everything I had not to look over his head at the black sedan parked behind him. I couldn't let him or Séamus know that I suspected anything, but it was almost impossible when I felt as if my own heart were in that backseat, bleeding outside of my body. I needed to see her. Needed to make sure that she was okay. I knew that she'd look at me with the same fear and disdain that everyone else wore when they saw me now. And I'd made peace with that. What she'd felt for me had been based on a lie, but what I felt for her would haunt me for the rest of my life.

All three minutes of it.

Just then, two white Garda cars came flying around the side of the airport building, sirens blaring and blue lights flashing. Alexi's head snapped in their direction. Then, his beady eyes narrowed and landed on Séamus, who looked more surprised than anyone.

"You stupid fuck!" he barked at Séamus. "You vill die for zis!"

"It wasn't me!" Séamus blubbered, casting a murderous glance over his shoulder at Sean.

Sean shrugged and shook his head in genuine shock as the guards pulled up directly in front of us, parking in the gap between Alexi's and Sean's cars.

When they opened their doors and pulled guns on us, I sighed in relief. These weren't just unarmed airport security guards. These were the big dogs. The Emergency Response Unit. I'd borrowed Sean's phone in exchange for his gun and made an anonymous tip, informing them that the Russian Bratva had the missing American girl and would be attempting to fly her out of the country at noon.

If the Russians didn't kill me for this, the UIB definitely would. There was an unspoken code in the underworld. Law enforcement was off-limits. Period. Even against your enemies. Rats were considered to be the lowest form of life, and the punishment was usually slow and sadistic.

DEVIL OF DUBLIN

"Hands on your heads!" the driver of the car on the right shouted.

"What seems to be the problem, fellas?" The metal barrel jammed against my side disappeared as Séamus lifted both hands and stepped in front of me.

Alexi did the same.

"We have reason to believe that a person of interest might be on board this aircraft."

"You there, in the middle," another one shouted, and I knew the situation was about to go arseways. *Fast.* "Hands on your head!"

Séamus and Alexi both glanced backward at me as time shifted into slow motion. I returned their furious stares with a glimmer of *fuck you* on my face, then turned my back to the guards, revealing my bound hands.

"Fuck," Séamus hissed, and before the word had even left his mouth, bullets started flying.

Alexi and Séamus both opened fire as they ran back to their cars, and panic gripped me as I realized that they were going to try to escape. That *Alexi* was going to try to escape.

With my girl.

I sprinted through the chaos over to the Mercedes where I frantically tried to open the back door with my hands tied behind my back.

Alexi was on the passenger side, using his open door as a shield while he blasted the guards and waited for his driver.

The grunt slammed the cargo door closed on the plane and ran back to the car just as two more Bratva soldiers appeared in the doorway of the plane with fully automatic AK-47s strapped to their chests.

When I finally pulled the door open and turned to look inside, the deafening sounds of six hundred bullets flying per minute, glass shattering, and guards screaming in pain all dulled to a muted roar as my eyes took in something I'd never expected to see in the back of that Mercedes.

Nothing.

The black leather seats sat completely empty.

She wasn't there.

She wasn't fucking there.

Alexi barked something in Russian from the passenger seat, and before I could react, his driver was shoving me inside.

I couldn't brace myself or push back with my hands still tied behind my back, so the second my upper body hit the leather upholstery, I turned and planted my boot in the grunt's chest, shoving him backward at least two meters.

Alexi attempted to hold my shoulders down while shouting something that I assumed meant, *Go, go, go!* because the tracksuit soldier dived behind the wheel and took off, leaving my door wide open and my legs sticking out at the knees.

"Where is she?" I shouted, planting my heels on the seat below my arse and pushing myself deeper into the car.

Alexi's fist connected with my face.

"Where the fuck is she?"

"You vil never. See her. Or anyvone. Ever. Again!" Alexi punctuated every few words with blows to my eye, nose, jaw, and cheek, but I barely felt his fists once I understood that wherever we were going, it wasn't where Darby was.

And that wasn't a fucking option.

I couldn't let them take me until I knew where she was. Until I knew she was safe.

Pulling my knees up to my chest, I kicked out and planted both feet on the side of the driver's head, smashing it into the window beside him. The glass cracked from the impact, and his body slumped forward, hitting the steering wheel and pulling it to the right.

The car began to spin in a tight circle as Alexi cursed in Russian and reached for the wheel, attempting to yank it back to the left. The distraction gave me just enough time to sit up and dive for the open door.

Or so I thought.

"Nyet!" Alexi bellowed as I threw myself out of the car, grabbing the back of my collar a split-second before my feet hit the ground.

DEVIL OF DUBLIN

I'd expected to tuck and roll the moment I hit the runway, but instead I felt my shirt catch around my throat. While my upper body was suspended above the ground by the strength of Alexi's grip and the sheer force of his hatred, my lower body was being dragged across the runway. My feet and legs were covered in thick leather and denim, but the sides of my hands, wrists, and forearms—which were tied behind my back and pinned under the weight of my hanging body—were being skinned alive. I thrashed and kicked and tried to roll onto my side, but the noose around my neck only tightened the more that I struggled.

While my lungs burned and my vision blurred, the pain grew like a funeral pyre until there wasn't a millimeter of my body that hadn't been engulfed. My mind scrambled, not to find a solution, but to find a corner where it could hide from the agony of dying.

And it succeeded.

The blaze consuming me shrank to the size of a crackling glow in a woodstove. The tarmac scraping the skin off my bones softened until it became a comforter on a living room floor. The scent of burning flesh and rubber melted into the earthy, smoky sweetness of cedar. And when the tunnel vision finally pulled me under, all I could see was a freckle-faced girl with full lips and green eyes, staring up at the moon next to me.

"She fought back at first," Darby had said, her story from that night tattooed on my soul. "But ... eventually, she learned how to die."

Her eyes flicked to mine then, and where I had originally seen fear, desperation, and shame swirling in their emerald depths, I now saw the fierce, unflinching power of conviction. Darby's pink mouth was set in a hard, determined line, but I still heard her voice, commanding me from beyond the pain.

Stop fighting.
And learn how to die.

That was it.

I stopped struggling. I pulled my legs up to my chest so that I couldn't use them to keep myself up any longer. And I let my body become dead weight.

The collar around my neck tightened to the point that I thought it might rip my head clean off, but then I was falling, rolling, tumbling, *breathing*. It felt like I'd been dropped into an ocean of hammers, but there was no time to process any additional injuries. Because when I slid to a stop and finally opened my eyes, I realized something.

The Mercedes had stopped too.

With my cheek pressed to the tarmac and what was left of my hands bound behind my back, I managed to pull myself into a kneeling position. I was just about to stand, to try to run toward the airport, when I felt the cold kiss of steel against the back of my head.

"You mother*fucker*." Alexi's panted words morphed into a growl as he pressed the barrel against my head even harder. "Zis ends *now*."

And he was right. I couldn't run. I was in no position to fight. It was over.

I closed my eyes and bowed my head and used my last few seconds on earth to send a silent plea to God, to Saoirse, to fucking Satan himself to do what I hadn't been able to. To find her. To save her. To give her a life far, far away from the hell that I'd dragged her into and to accept my tarnished, battered soul as payment.

I didn't know which one of them had accepted my offer—probably Satan—but I didn't care. Because the next sound I heard wasn't a bullet blasting through my skull.

It was sirens.

Lots of fucking sirens.

CHAPTER 34

KELLEN

A black Soviet handgun toppled to the ground beside me as at least five Garda vehicles surrounded us.

"That's him! That's the man they were trying to sell me to!"

Maybe God was the one who'd accepted my bargain after all because the voice I heard definitely belonged to an angel.

Turning my head, I squinted at the car closest to us and saw a halo of copper emerging from the passenger seat.

I struggled to focus on the angel's face as I clung to consciousness. Flashing blue lights enveloped her—enveloped *us*—as she ran toward me, but a round, balding guard caught her by the arm before she could reach me.

"Darby, stay back. It's too dangerous."

Darby.

A silent, shuddering laugh ripped through me.

Darby.

She was alive.

Darby.

She was safe.

"Darby," I whispered as I surrendered to the darkness at last.

"So, let me get this straight …"

Voices filtered in and out of my dreamless sleep, disjointed and unfamiliar.

"You and your fiancé were lookin' for a B&B near Cork Harbour when ya got lost and accidentally witnessed some kind of *transaction* happenin' near the docks."

"Yes, ma'am."

I fought to open my eyes, but the weight of my exhaustion was simply too heavy.

"And when these men realized that they'd been seen, they chased your car, shot at ya, and one of 'em ran ya off the road?"

"That's correct."

"Your fiancé, Mr. John David Oglethorpe, died in the crash, and you were taken by that man over there, Mr. Séamus Rooney …"

I finally won the battle against my eyelids, forcing one open, just a crack. The world was sideways. Darby stood a few meters away in between the round, beer-gutted guard she'd arrived with and a female guard clutching a clipboard.

She was *not* wearing my jacket. The rush of irrational bitterness that surged through me upon that realization gave me just enough strength to open my other eyelid.

"Then, your friend over here, Mr., em"—she flipped through her notes—"Kellen Donovan, traced your phone to Dublin, where you were bein' held by the United Irish Brotherhood with the intention of sellin' ya to the Bratva for human trafficking purposes. Mr. Donovan attempted to help ya escape—"

"He bleedin' succeeded," the guard on her left interrupted. "If it wasn't for him, my niece would be halfway to goddamn Russia by now."

"Yes, thank you, Detective O'Toole. So, Ms. Collins, during this rescue attempt, you escaped, but Mr. Donovan was injured by a shotgun blast and captured?"

DEVIL OF DUBLIN

The world spun as I pushed myself to a sitting position. The ground felt wrong under my hands. When I looked down, I discovered that not only was the ground actually a stretcher, but my hands had been covered in bandages. Ribbons of gauze spiraled from my knuckles to my elbows. The last two fingers on both hands were wrapped in tape. My shirt was gone. And I could feel additional bandages on my lower back, shoulders, and eyebrow.

But what commanded my attention wasn't my injuries or the fact that I'd been out so cold that I'd actually allowed someone other than Darby to touch me. It was what I noticed balled up on the end of the stretcher, where my head had just been.

I picked up the bundle of shiny black fabric, which wasn't easy with my fucking mummy hands, and buried my nose in it.

It smelled like rain and the woods and vanilla custard creams.

"Kellen!"

I lifted my head as a vision of divine perfection bounded toward me. The light attached to her coppery hair as if it were just as magnetized to her as I was. But I knew that feeling wouldn't be returned. Not now that Darby knew the truth about what I was. What I'd done. That my sins had almost cost her her life. I held my breath and braced for the impact of her rejection. I could take it, now that I knew she was okay. I would rip out my own heart and hand it to her on a silver platter if I knew she'd skip away with it to safety.

But the only impact I felt was Darby's body colliding with mine.

She threw her arms around my bandaged shoulders and buried her face in my neck with a sob. "Don't *ever* leave me like that again! I thought I was too late, Kellen. I was almost too late."

That wasn't the reaction I'd been expecting.

Placing my hands on her shoulders, I gently pushed her off of me until I could see the shimmering green well of honesty in her eyes. I needed to see her pink lips form the words, see the sincerity on her face as she said them before I could allow myself to believe what I was hearing.

"What did you just say?"

Darby swallowed and placed her hands on the sides of my face. A tear spilled over her freckled cheek, and I never got the chance to hand her my heart because the tortured, relieved, enraptured smile she gave me next reached in between my ribs and stole it from me.

"I said, no more leaving." Her chin buckled as more tears flooded her eyes. "Never again. Promise me."

Pulling her back against my chest, I held her shuddering body as I made a vow that I would spend the rest of my life earning the right to keep. "Never. I promise."

"Thanks for your help, lad, but next time, maybe just let us handle it."

I looked up at the uniformed bloke looming over us as Darby released me and turned to face the old man with a smile.

"Uncle Eamonn, this is my friend, Kellen."

Uncle Eamonn. Darby had told me all about that fucker. He hadn't lived in Glenshire since before I was born, but from what I'd heard, he was a real piece of shite.

"Another Glenshire man, I hear." Eamonn extended a hand, then pulled it back when he saw the state mine were in. "Shite. Sorry, lad. Prob'ly won't be shakin' hands for a while now, will ya?"

I stood and looked the bastard in his beady little eyes. I wanted to make sure the smug prick knew exactly who the fuck he'd be answering to if he ever spoke to Darby the way he had back in Glenshire.

"Ms. Collins, we have your statement. You and Mr. Donovan are free to go," the female guard announced, stepping up beside Darby's uncle. "I'll contact ya if we have any further questions. And Detective O'Toole, great work today. Your unit successfully brought down one of Ireland's most wanted criminals and led to the capture of Alexi Abramov. You should be very proud."

DEVIL OF DUBLIN

She clapped him on the shoulder, and the man blushed so hard he looked like he'd just polished off a fifth of whiskey.

"You know, we could use someone like you on the Emergency Response Unit. Have ya ever considered …"

I wrapped my jacket around Darby's shoulders and led her away as Eamonn stood there, getting his arse kissed for what I suspected had been *her* hard work. No wonder he was pretending to be Uncle of the Year all of a sudden.

Fucker.

The place was crawling with police activity. Every Garda vehicle had at least one arsehole in a tracksuit sitting in the back of it. Photographers took pictures of the dead guards on the ground. Ambulances arrived to haul off the bodies once they were done. Drug-sniffing dogs searched the plane and the pile of luggage outside. Machine guns were carried out of the jet two at a time. And over by the Volkswagen, Séamus and Sean stood with their hands cuffed behind their backs, watching as a detective searched their car.

I was surprised they hadn't sped away during the shoot-out, but then I realized that Sean's car was now several meters away from the plane and had at least three flat tires.

"Well, well, well … what do we have here?" The guard who'd been digging through the boot pulled out a massive black bag and set it on the ground. The moment he unzipped it, he let out a low whistle. "Hey, Brian. I got at least a dozen AR-15s here, and … holy shite …" Pulling a cloth out of his pocket, he carefully lifted a Russian-made pistol with a long silver silencer attached to the end. "Didn't you say the murder weapon used on those Bratva bastards at The Brazen Head last night was a 45 cal with a silencer?"

Séamus kicked Sean in the shin. "Fucking muppet!"

"What? Diabhal told me you wanted 'em back. We went and got 'em this morning before we picked you up."

Séamus let out a scream as I steered Darby away from that world.

Away from all of it.

Forever.

CHAPTER 35

DARBY

Kellen couldn't get off that tarmac fast enough. I struggled to keep up, clinging to two of his unbandaged fingers as he jogged around the side of the airport, up a handful of cement stairs, and into a vacant loading dock, where he kissed my panting mouth until I lost the ability to stand. Kellen commanded every ounce of my energy and attention, leaving nothing left for trivial things, like resisting gravity. So, I surrendered to it, sinking to the ground, where the two of us became a tangled mass of twisted limbs and salty tears and clutching hands and whispered apologies.

Breaking our kiss, Kellen finally spoke, tucking a lock of hair behind my ear. "How did you get away from Ronan?" he panted, his usually soft, velvety voice sounding raspy and rough. "I thought the Bratva must have taken you, but they didn't, did they?"

"No." I slid my hand along his stubbled jaw and down his neck, as if I could heal the injury I'd heard in his vocal cords.

Just thinking about what Ronan had planned on doing to me caused me to shudder, but the warmth of Kellen's shirtless body melted away my fear.

"I strangled him with a seat belt."

Kellen sat straight up, his wide eyes the exact same color as the wintry sky overhead. The gash above his eyebrow had been closed with a series of small butterfly bandages. The other eye had a puffy, purple lid. His nose was swollen, his cheekbone was scraped up, and his angular jaw was covered in three days' worth of beard stubble. But when Kellen grinned at me, the sight was breathtaking.

"You're bleedin' serious."

I nodded.

He threw his head back and laughed as he pulled me against his chest again. "How the *fuck* did you do that?"

I nuzzled into his embrace, overwhelmed with gratitude that once again, we'd found our way back to one another. "I don't know," I admitted. "I just ... did what I thought you would do. Every step of the way, Kellen. You kept me alive. You showed me what to do."

"You shouldn't have had to do it at all." His laughter died as he rested his cheek on the top of my head. "I'm so fuckin' sorry, Darby. For everything."

"I'm not." The words were a shock to us both, but I meant them. "Before I met you, I'd been convinced that I was weak. Worthless. Unworthy. I never fought for myself. I never thought I deserved better."

I pressed my lips to the side of Kellen's neck and felt his arms tighten around me in response.

"You opened my eyes. You showed me that power is something you take back, not something you wait to be given. You showed me a life I'd never even dreamed of."

"Yeah," Kellen huffed bitterly. "The life of a UIB hitman." He shook his head, causing mine to swivel back and forth along with it.

"No." I slid out from under his chin and met his self-deprecating gaze. "A life that was finally worth fighting for."

Those stormy eyes dropped to my lips a moment before he claimed them with his own.

"Wait," I breathed, forcing myself to pull away long enough to slip an envelope out of my back pocket. "I have something for you."

Kellen brushed my hand away and reached for my face, diving back in to pick up where we'd left off.

I laughed against his parted lips. "Open it."

With a sigh, he slid the plain white envelope from my hand, eyeing me skeptically as he broke the seal. Then, he glanced down and thumbed through the contents.

I grinned as Kellen's face morphed from amused to confused to utterly overwhelmed.

He shook his head as his fingers traced the letters on his new driver's license, his passport, his birth certificate. "Darby ..."

Kellen's eyes lifted to mine, and the gratitude I saw there made my chest ache. I knew what those documents meant to him. They were his ticket to freedom. His all-access pass to a real life. But it was the disbelief I saw under that appreciation that broke my heart.

It was as if he'd never been given a gift in his life.

Not unless you counted biscuits and pickle-flavored water.

"How ..." He shook his head, the words failing him as emotion welled in his exhausted eyes.

"Well, after I ... *got away* from Ronan—"

"Strangled," Kellen corrected, beaming with pride. "Ya fuckin' strangled him."

I shook my head with a smirk. "Well, after *that*, I drove back to Cork, got my wallet and phone out of the Fiesta, crashed it into the woods next to the BMW, dressed a dead guy up as John, put him in the driver's seat, lit him on fire, took the train back to Dublin, pawned John's vintage Rolex for fourteen thousand euros, used Ronan's phone to call The Butcher, had his driver meet me at the pawn shop with your papers, and then called Eamonn and told him you'd just helped me escape from the UIB and if he hurried he could catch a bunch of bad guys at the airport."

"Holy shite." A stunned laugh caught in his throat as Kellen stared at me, in awe.

"With all the text messages on Ronan's phone and the story I gave him about John, Eamonn was able to convince his department to come make the bust. And here I am."

"Here ya fuckin' are." Heat licked its way up my neck and flooded my cheeks as Kellen's eyes blazed with recognition. "*This* is the girl I fell in love with back in Glenshire."

He leaned forward, pressing his forehead against mine as his gaze dropped to my lips.

"Fearless." He said, sealing my parted lips with a reverent kiss. "Clever." Another kiss. "Badass." One more. "Beautiful."

A smile spread across my face at that last compliment, and Kellen took full advantage. Tilting his head to the side, he claimed my mouth, swirling his tongue around mine as his battered hands clutched me tighter. As his strong arms guided me to straddle him. As the rigid bulge I felt there throbbed in time with my own desperate need.

"There's more," I whispered, clinging to the sides of his fuzzy head as the world spun around me.

"More what?" he growled, nipping at my bottom lip.

"More in the envelope."

Dropping his forehead to my shoulder, Kellen caught his breath before opening the white envelope again. Thumbing to the final document, he pulled it out and unfolded it.

Then, he was quiet for a long, long time.

"It has today's date." I forced a smile, but on the inside, I was teetering on the edge of cardiac arrest.

Finally, Kellen lifted two guarded gray eyes, veiled by the shadow of his heavy, worried brow. "You still want this?" His gaze fell back down to the marriage certificate in his hands. "You still want *me* ... now that you know the truth?"

Oh my God.

Lifting Kellen's strong, clenched jaw, I forced him to look at me again.

"Of course I do. Kellen, I want you *because* I know the truth. The *truth* is that you are good, and brave, and strong, and smart, and humble, and sweet, and"—I let him watch my eyes slide down his exposed, chiseled, bloodied torso—"honestly, just ridiculously hot. I mean, look at you. Seriously."

Kellen grinned, and I could almost feel his self-hatred crack like a glacier and start to melt in my hands.

"The *truth* is that I've been yours since the moment we met. I thought you were magical then, and I still do. You are my past, you are my present, and according to a thousand-year-old lake spirit, you are my eternity. So, yeah, I still want—"

Kellen's mouth slammed against mine at the same moment that he stood, lifting me off the ground with his bandaged hands under my ass. He winced against my lips, and I immediately scrambled to get down, but Kellen only held on tighter.

"What are you doing? Your hands!"

"Ah, they're fine. They're only fucked up on the back … and the sides." He smirked against my lips as he carried me down the concrete stairs. "But we have to go."

Every step caused our bodies to rub together in a way that made me wish Kellen would press my back against the wall and show me what other parts of him were uninjured. "Why?" I managed to ask, the word breathy and desperate.

"Because if we stay here another second, I'm gonna fuck you in an airport loading dock."

I laughed. "And that's a problem because …"

"Because it's our wedding day, *angel*." Kellen kissed my nose, and a flood of familiar glittery tingles washed over my skin and cascaded down my spine.

"I'm taking you on a proper honeymoon. *Now*."

CHAPTER 36

DARBY

Kellen added another log to the fire while I added the final layer to the mountain of sleeping bags, blankets, and comforters I'd piled up in the middle of the cottage. The central layer was a pocket I'd made by zipping two individual sleeping bags together, and as soon as I stripped my clothes off and slipped inside, my muscles turned to putty. It was deliciously warm—the round stone walls radiating heat from the fire—while the missing roof and leafless branches above gave me an unobstructed view of the clear, starry winter sky beyond.

"I still can't believe you chose this place over Transylvania," Kellen mused, his angelic face looking positively sinister in the firelight.

I closed my eyes as a dull ache settled in my chest. "I just ... wanted to spend one last night out here, with you, before we leave."

Crouching beside me, Kellen brushed the hair away from my face, dragging his rough, warm thumb over my temple and cheekbone until I finally opened my eyes. When I did, a startled gasp caught in my throat. It felt like the same gasp I'd swallowed twelve years before, in that exact same spot, when a boy with silver eyes claimed my heart with a single glance.

"You don't want to go to New York?" he asked, his dark eyebrows creasing in the center.

I shook my head, something twisting inside of me at the admission. "I love it here, but I understand why we can't stay. I mean, you flipped on the UIB. They'll kill you if they find you."

"*If* they find me. But they won't. They don't even know my name." Kellen pulled the black T-shirt he was wearing off over his head.

We'd stopped by the house we'd borrowed in Dublin to shower and get our stuff before heading back to Glenshire. Well, I showered. Kellen stood there with his bandaged arms in the air while I scrubbed him down. *Thoroughly.* After changing into some clean clothes, we said good-bye to the house, and as we made our way out the back door, Kellen placed a stack of hundreds on the kitchen table.

Just when I didn't think I could love him more.

"The UIB knows *my* name though," I said, trying to stay focused on the conversation at hand while watching him undress. "My disappearance was all over the news. That's how they found me."

"We can take care of that." Kellen cast me a reassuring glance before leaning over to unlace his boots.

Luckily, Kellen's thumbs, index fingers, and middle fingers had been left unscathed, but I knew the road rash on the backs and sides of his hands and arms probably hurt. Not that he'd ever admit it.

"The Butcher can probably erase any public record of your name associated with this address. We'll figure something out."

"Would you really want to stay here though? In Glenshire? All those bad memories …" The rest of that thought evaporated in my mouth as I watched Kellen slide off his jeans and underwear and climb into the sleeping bag with me.

Just like our first night together, on the floor in front of a different fire, Kellen lay on his good side—the one without the bullet holes—facing me. But unlike that night, he wasn't guarded, panicking, or poised to push me away. He was simply Kellen. Calm. Intense. Captivating. I wanted to curl up against his body and bask in the miracle of that moment, but I was too ensnared by his gaze to move.

"Every good memory I have happened here too. Right here, Darby. With you."

Kellen ran a gauze-wrapped hand through my hair, and I had to close my eyes to keep the tears at bay.

"Hey …" he whispered, his voice soft and soothing. "Can I tell you a ghost story?"

I nodded, touched that he remembered my words from our first night together, and Kellen pulled me against his chest. The security of his strong arms around my body, the steady rhythm of his heart beneath my ear, the warmth of his skin pressed against mine—it only reminded me how close I'd come to losing him. I pictured him the way I'd found him earlier, down on his knees, blood dripping from his bound hands, gun pressed to the back of his bowed head, and I released the shuddering sob I'd been trying so hard to hold back.

Kellen smoothed a hand over my hair as he pressed his lips to the top of my head. "Legend has it, these woods are haunted."

I smiled, forcing what was haunting *me* to take a seat as I gave Kellen my full attention. I would have the rest of my life to process the trauma of almost losing him. I wasn't going to let it steal another second of my joy now that I finally had him back.

"Really?" I asked, wiping my eyes.

"Mmhmm." Kellen kissed the top of my head again as his hand roamed from my hair, to my shoulder, and down my arm, leaving a trail of tingles in its wake. "There was a boy who lived with a priest, just down the way. Strange lad. Never smiled. Never spoke."

Kellen's palm slid down my side and over the curve of my ass as his cock swelled and lengthened against my hip.

"People said he was the son of Satan. They spat on him and treated him like a monster, so he lurked in the woods near a cursed lough, where no one else dared to go. Then, one day, an

American girl who didn't know any better stumbled upon his hideout."

Kellen's fingers traveled lower, tracing the seam of me, spreading my legs like magic as they glided along my slick center.

"She was kind to him," he continued, "and pretty and playful and brave. She made him feel human. Made him want to smile. And talk. And ... *touch*."

Something in that single word vibrated with a deeper meaning. It hung in the air like the strike of a tuning fork, sending shivers down my spine. I glanced up at Kellen with a question in my eyes, and he answered it with a single dip of his chin.

Yes.

My stomach tensed and knotted as I slid my hand down the crests and valleys of his torso. I held his gaze as I let my fingertips graze the side of his rigid cock. And Kellen didn't flinch. His lips parted on a silent exhale, but it was one of wonder rather than panic. Again, I stroked the length of him, my touch featherlight and full of love, and again, Kellen exhaled, this time with the softest of moans.

My heart swelled with pride and honor and disbelief as I watched him hand me the last of his fears. I took it slow, waiting to fully wrap my hand around him until he was thrusting against my palm, and when I finally did, Kellen lunged for my mouth, kissing me deeply, reverently, as we massaged away every touch that had come before ours.

"What happened next?" I asked, my voice a breathy plea.

Kellen smiled against my lips. "He fell madly in love with her."

Tears stung my eyes as the overwhelming need to be joined with him began to build.

"The boy spent every wakin' moment in the woods after that, waitin' for her to return." Kellen's husky voice vibrated against my neck, my shoulder, as we worked each other over. "Months would go by between her visits, sometimes years, until the girl stopped comin' altogether. While she was gone, the boy grew bigger. Stronger. Meaner. Eventually, he became as evil as everyone had claimed him to be."

A soft moan rumbled in my chest as a callused finger filled me to the last, scarred knuckle.

"The boy killed the priest with his bare hands and burned his house to the ground, never to be seen again."

My breath hitched at the mention of what he'd done. I'd already known the truth, but hearing him claim it once and for all, hearing him own his power without being afraid that I would leave him for it, only made me want him more. Kellen was the most courageous, most resilient, most formidable person I'd ever met. He'd found the strength to destroy the men who'd hurt us, and if that made him the Devil, then I would gladly burn in hell by his side.

"The villagers think the boy died in that fire, too, and now, his spirit haunts these woods, still waitin' for his love to return."

Lifting my thigh up over Kellen's hip, I kept my hand on his shaft as he thrust against my slippery flesh.

"Is that really what they say about you?" I asked, my words a breathy plea as I captured his bottom lip between my teeth.

"Mmhmm," Kellen groaned, the pace of his hips quickening.

I beamed, releasing his lip with a pop. "Kellen, you're a legend."

"I won't be once folks see that I'm alive and well and married to Patrick O'Toole's granddaughter."

I laughed. I laughed, and I laughed until tears of joy streamed down my face.

Alive and well.
Married to Patrick O'Toole's granddaughter.

It was everything I'd ever wanted and never thought I'd ever have.

"So, we're doing this?" I asked. "We're staying here?"

"Darby"—Kellen cupped my ass as he positioned himself at my aching center—"I would love nothin' more than to haunt these woods with you for eternity."

The moonlight was silver, and the firelight was orange, but as Kellen and I made love in the very place where our story began, the only color I saw behind my tightly closed eyelids was lake-spirit blue.

EPILOGUE

DARBY
ONE YEAR LATER

"G'mornin', Darby!"

"Morning, Ms. Nora." I walked through the overgrown grass to the rickety fence separating our yards and propped my elbows on top of a post. "How are the lambs doing?"

"Oh, grand." Nora was in her late forties with a head full of mousy-brown hair that she wore in a braid down her back. She strolled through the sea of grazing sheep in her pasture and stopped next to a particularly heavy one closest to the fence. "We're introducin' them to the rest of the flock today."

Nora patted the ewe beside her on the top of her head. "I think this one's gonna pop any day now."

The pregnant sheep glared at me with sad, weary eyes that clashed with the cheerful yellow spot spray-painted on her hip.

"I hope so. Poor thing looks miserable."

Nora smiled. "She was one of Pat's. If you'd kept his flock, *you'd* be dealin' with all this lambing right now."

I laughed. "One is plenty for us. Speaking of, have you seen Vlad this morning?"

"Aye." Nora looked around her pasture. "He's, em ... oh, there he is." She pointed in the direction of the only black sheep in the flock. "He's got himself a wee crush on Miss Petunia, I believe."

"Well, send him home whenever she gets sick of him."

"Will do." Nora grinned. "And happy anniversary, by the way." There was a twinkle in her eye that made me wonder if she knew something that I didn't.

I skipped off toward Kellen's workshop, which wasn't easy to do with the length of our grass. The downside of only having one sheep to take care of was that now we had an entire pasture to mow—or evidently, not mow.

With the money we'd gotten for the sheep, Kellen had been able to convert Grandpa's old barn into a woodworking paradise. He had workbenches, table saws, lathes, hammers, chisels, sanders, and sawdust as far as the eye could see. I loved the way it smelled in there. Woodsy. Earthy. Masculine. Like him.

Some days—okay, every day—I took my laptop in there and did my schoolwork at a table he'd built for me in the corner. The white noise of power tools helped me focus, and being together helped both of us relax.

I'd been seeing a therapist in Killarney once a week. Kellen wasn't ready to talk about what he'd experienced with anyone other than me, but a lot of what I was learning helped him too. We both had complex post-traumatic stress disorder from the repeated traumas we'd endured, beginning in childhood and ending with the events that had taken place the year before. And it seemed to manifest in an extreme attachment to one another. We lived in constant fear that the other was going to be hurt or killed—which wasn't completely irrational, considering that the Brotherhood still wanted us dead—but our panic attacks were at least becoming fewer and farther between. Doing my schoolwork in his workshop helped, but challenging myself to go places without him for short periods of time did too. Kellen wasn't happy about that part, but he didn't fight me on it. And I'd made some really good friends at the yoga studio I'd joined near my therapist's office.

As soon as we'd decided to stay in Glenshire, I'd transferred to an online English literature program through Trinity College. With Kellen's encouragement, I also added a minor in creative writing and began writing a creepy children's book series about Irish legends and fairy tales. So far, I'd written *The Ghost of Glenshire*, *The Lady in the Lough*, *The Witch in the Woods*, and I was working on *The Fairies in the Forest*. I hadn't found a publisher for them yet, but I had managed to land a literary agent, which felt like a dream come true all by itself.

I rapped my knuckles on the open barn door, but Kellen didn't notice over the clinking of his chisel and hammer. He was leaning over one of his workbenches, adding the finishing touches to a piece he'd been working on all week, and I stared at him shamelessly. The safety goggles on top of his head held most of his wavy, cheekbone-length hair out of his face, but one errant black curl had tumbled forward and was just begging to be wrapped around my finger. His dark eyebrows were pulled together in concentration, his bottom lip disappeared between his teeth, and the veins and muscles bulged in his arms as he exerted complete control over the tools in his scarred, callused hands.

It was a miracle I got anything done with him looking like that all day.

I had always assumed that Kellen would grow up to make furniture because that's what he'd made as a kid, but it turned out that he was also incredible at wood carving, especially intricate Celtic knot designs. A local brewery had found his work online and commissioned him to make a huge sign featuring their logo—an Irish harp, surrounded by Celtic knots—and now, every pub in Dublin wanted one.

"Happy anniversary." I beamed, my cheeks flushing the moment Kellen's eyes lifted and locked on to mine.

The intensity of his gaze still made my stomach do backflips, especially now that I knew exactly what kinds of thoughts were going on behind that mysterious gray stare.

Kellen set down his tools and met me halfway in three strides, pulling me in for a kiss that made my head spin and my heart race. "Happy anniversary."

God, that voice.

"I got up early to finish this piece so we could spend the day together. Didn't want to wake ya."

"Thank you." I smiled, tucking that loose lock of hair behind his ear. "Can I see it?"

Kellen stepped aside. "It's the same as the others. Nothin' special."

"Hey, what did I tell you about saying that?" I let my fingers glide over the three-dimensional woven pattern as my lips parted in awe.

Kellen stood next to me. "I believe your exact words were, 'Kellen, the next time ya say that, I'm gonna slap you in the face.'"

Without looking at him, I lifted my hand and smacked him on the cheek. I felt his smile, but I didn't see it. I couldn't tear my eyes away from the masterpiece on the table.

"It's incredible, babe."

Brushing my hair over my shoulder, he dropped his lips to the side of my neck. "I made somethin' for you too."

"Can I open my eyes yet?"

"Not yet. Watch out for that tree root."

"I can't watch out for it. My eyes are closed."

"Well, look down then, just don't look up."

"Why didn't you just say that?"

Kellen's hands on my shoulders brought me to a halt. "Okay, we're here."

When I opened my eyes, it took me a minute to recognize where we were. We were standing a few yards back from the edge of the lake, next to the giant oak tree with the tattered remains of Kellen's old rope swing hanging from it, but the blackberry bushes had been trimmed so far back that the path now reached all the way to the water.

At first, I thought that was my gift—the nice, woodchip-covered path to the lake—but then I noticed what sat on the edge of the glittering water, in the middle of that new clearing, and my mouth fell open in wonder.

"Oh, Kellen."

A polished wooden bench the color of caramel gleamed in the late morning sun. Instead of slats, the entire back had been carved out of a single piece of wood to look like a rectangular Celtic knot. I'd never seen anything like it. Tears blurred my vision as I walked in circles around the sculpted seat, stared at the intricate designs on the armrests, marveled at the hand-turned legs. But it was what Kellen had carved into the solid center of the knot that caused the dam of emotion to finally break.

Darby + Kellen
June 14, 2012

. . .

"Our freckles." I laughed, tears sliding down my cheeks as I traced the three perfect dots with my finger. "Oh my God, Kellen, I ... I don't even know what to say. It's perfect. It's ... it's *us*."

Kellen lifted my left hand and kissed the mark we'd shared since we were kids. "I know today is our first *government* anniversary, but as far as Saoirse and I are concerned"—he tipped his head toward the bench—"you and I've been married for goin' on ten years now."

Throwing myself at Kellen's warm, solid body, I squeezed him tight, closed my eyes even tighter, and said a silent prayer of thanks to any deity, spirit, ghost, or witch who'd had a hand in bringing us back together. We'd gone through hell apart, but together, our life was nothing short of heaven.

And hopefully, just as eternal.

"I have something for you too," I said, my tone turning serious as my soaring heart sank under the weight of what I was about to deliver. I gestured toward the bench. "You might want to sit down for this."

DEVIL OF DUBLIN

My dearest Kellen,

There is so much I want to say to you. I'm sure I'm going to leave something out, but hopefully, there will be plenty of time for us to get to know one another going forward. If that's what you want, of course. If not, I completely understand.

Simply writing this letter is a dream come true. I'm overwhelmed with gratitude to your lovely wife for giving me the opportunity to speak to you again. My hands are shaking, so please forgive my awful handwriting.

The first thing I'd like to say is that I love you and have missed you more than you'll ever know. Not a day goes by that I don't picture your sweet, smiling face and wish that I had been stronger for you. It's a regret that will go with me to my grave.

The second thing I'd like to say is, happy birthday. You are twenty-four years old today. I'm so very sorry that you haven't known that until now. Truly. I can't imagine what that must have been like for you.

You were born on February 28, 1998. I was fifteen years old at the time. Fourteen when I became pregnant. For months, I didn't know what was wrong with me. Only that I'd been feeling sick and was gaining weight for no reason. We didn't learn how babies were made at school, and it was something that my family never discussed.

Something else we never discussed was my relationship with Father Henry.

I was twelve when he told my parents that he saw something evil in me. He said I needed to start volunteering at the church after school so that he could see to my spiritual development himself. At first, he had actual work for me to do—shelves to dust, prayers to recite—but within a few months, he said that the evil inside of me was growing. I was terrified. I felt like I'd been diagnosed with some kind of cancer. I would have done anything to get it out. Father Henry said that the only way to keep it from claiming my soul was for him to begin performing a series of secret, sacred rituals.

Rituals that I was forbidden to talk about.

His abuse, as I now know it to be, continued until my mother realized that I'd become pregnant. She beat me and called me horrible names that I didn't understand and packed all of my things in a bag. I didn't even get a chance to say good-bye to my brothers and sister. She then drove me to a

Mother and Baby Home run by nuns, where dozens of other unwed pregnant women and new mothers were treated like cattle. You couldn't leave. If you ran away, the guards would bring you back. I stayed there until I began having horrible pain in my stomach. I was taken to a room with nothing more than a metal table in the center and left to give birth on my own.

I'd made friends there who'd given birth before me. After a few days, sometimes weeks, they'd ask where their baby was, and the nuns would simply say, "He's gone." That was it. They've since found mass graves at these places, filled with hundreds of infant bodies. Some were sent away or adopted, but others died of disease and neglect.

I couldn't let that happen to you. The reason you don't have a birth certificate is because I ran away with you before they had a chance to write up the paperwork. I stowed away on a bread truck that had been there making a delivery, and when the driver discovered us, he took mercy on me. He and his wife took us in, but I wasn't able to stay there long. If they'd been found out, they would have been punished.

I did the best I could on my own. We didn't always have a place to live, but we had each other. You were such a blessing to me, Kellen. Always happy, even when our bellies were empty or we were shivering cold. But my guilt over not being able to care for you properly, the sins I had to commit for food and money, they ate away at me. I became so depressed, so dependent on drugs and alcohol, that I was no longer able to care for you at all.

In my last act of love for you, I took you to Father Henry, told him to put you up for adoption, and then I attempted to take my own life as soon as I left.

I don't remember much from that time. My parents had disowned me. I spent years going back and forth between mental institutions and jail. But when I was finally ready to get sober and get my life together, my little sister took me in. She'd seen the investigations into the Mother and Baby Homes on the news as well as the reports about abuse within the church, and she wanted to help me set things right. We began looking for you, but there were no records anywhere. When I told her that I'd asked Father Henry to put you up for adoption, she said that right around that time, a little boy began living with him. A boy that he said was so evil he was unadoptable, so Father Henry had been put in charge of his "spiritual development."

My parents moved to a different town soon after that, so my sister didn't know what had become of the boy, but when we went back to Glenshire to

DEVIL OF DUBLIN

investigate, they told us that Father Henry had died in a fire and the boy had most likely died as well.

The agony of that discovery, Kellen—there are no words to describe the pain. It was worse than when I'd given you up. At least then, I'd believed that I was doing the right thing. It never occurred to me that Father Henry would try to keep you. Priests aren't even allowed to have children. I just wanted him to take responsibility for what he'd done and find you a good home. But learning that not only had you been raised by that monster, but that you'd also died along with him, it destroyed me.

I went to a very dark place after that, but my sister, who I hope you'll meet one day, never gave up on me. Your auntie Cara got me into therapy and group meetings, where I learned how to cope with the pain, but it never completely went away.

Not until Darby rang me and asked if I was your mam.

I want you to know that even if you decide that you never wish to see me again, I am the happiest woman in the world right now, and it is all because of you. Because you were strong enough to do what I couldn't. You survived what I should have been there to protect you from. You overcame nightmares that I can only imagine. You found love even when no one was there to show you what that meant. You are an inspiration to me, Kellen. I couldn't be prouder of the man you've become.

Happy birthday, son. I'll love you always and forever.

Your mam,
Kate

The paper crumpled slightly in Kellen's fists as I held my breath and waited for his response. I already knew what was written inside. Kate had addressed it to me so that I could give it to him when the time was right.

Like the time would ever be right for *that*.

I sat next to him, leaving at least a foot between us on the bench, but I could still feel the heat radiating off his body as he stared out over the lake with eyes that were just as deep and watery.

I felt as though I'd made a horrible mistake. Kellen had made me this amazing gift, and all I'd given him in return was heartache.

I wanted to touch him, to comfort him, but everything about him seemed sharp and bristled. So, I placed a hand on my own knee and squeezed.

"It's a lot to process, I know."

"How did you find her?" Kellen asked abruptly, still staring straight ahead.

"Father Doherty," I replied, shocked that he'd even spoken. "He was so nice when my grandfather died that I thought maybe he could help me find out more about your mom. The church keeps all kinds of records, and sure enough, there was a Donovan family that used to live here. They had two daughters and three sons. I didn't think either of their daughters were old enough to be your mother, but I looked them up anyway. It turns out that they own a bakery together in Limerick, and when I called the number ... Kate answered on the first ring. It was like she'd been waiting for my call."

Kellen swallowed but said nothing, so I kept talking to fill the silence. Hoping that we wouldn't have to address the *other* part of Kate's letter. The elephant in the woods.

"She sounded so happy on the phone, Kellen. She'd thought you were dead, just like me. And she's doing really well now. She makes the most amazing cakes. I saw pictures on the bakery's website. That must be where you got your talent—"

"He said my father was the Devil," Kellen snapped, his voice rough from being forced past the jagged shard of emotion lodged in his throat.

I slumped back in the bench as if the sheer size of that statement took up all the space in my lap. Then, I thought about what he'd said and nodded in somber agreement. "He was right."

Kellen and I sat like that for a long, long time. Until his features softened and his posture thawed. Until his hand found mine, still clutching my own knee, and squeezed.

"You okay?" I turned and studied his handsome profile.

Kellen hesitated for a moment. Then, with a soul-deep sigh, he nodded. "I think I always knew, deep down. I just didn't want to believe it."

I squeezed his hand back, and we sat in silence for an eternity. Long enough for me to muster the courage to drop one last bombshell on my poor, unsuspecting husband.

"You know what might make you feel better?" I cringe-smiled.

Kellen turned toward me, arching one scarred, suspicious eyebrow.

"It *is* your birthday, and I just found this amazing bakery in Limerick, so ..." I swallowed as Kellen's face paled. "I kind of ... sort of ... asked one of the owners if she'd like to bring you a cake."

I braced myself for Kellen's anger, which would have been completely justified, but instead I watched as twenty-four years of tension and pain vanish from his features. His stormy eyes widened, his full lips parted, and a sudden laugh burst out of him that I'd never heard before. It wasn't flat or jaded. Sarcastic or cynical. It was excited, and nervous, and the sweetest, most adorable sound I'd ever heard.

"So ... you're not mad?" My eyebrows lifted in hope. "There's still time to cancel if you're not ready, but after I read that letter, I just thought ..."

Kellen's colorless eyes shimmered with unshed tears as he beamed at me in disbelief.

"Mad?" He blew out a shaky breath that ended with another incredulous chuckle. "Jesus Christ, Darby. There are only two things I've ever wanted in this life. You ... and *her*."

After we christened the new bench—and tossed a few roses into the lake as an apology to Saoirse for what she'd just witnessed—I spent the next few hours preparing for our little birthday party for three while Kellen paced and mumbled and chewed his fingernails down to the quick. I actually sent him back to his workshop because he was making me so anxious.

When I finally heard a car door shut, I almost tripped over my own feet as I jogged outside into the driveway.

"Kate! Hi!" I waved even though she couldn't see me with half of her body leaning in to get something out of the backseat. "I'm Darby. I'm so happy you could make it. You have no idea how much this means—"

The rest of my thoroughly rehearsed greeting tumbled from my gaping mouth as Kate closed the back door of her blue sedan, revealing a little girl in her arms no older than four.

She was a doll-like thing, blonde, with a thumb in her mouth and big, sleepy blue eyes.

Unlike Kate, who was as raven-haired and arresting as her son.

Kate smiled at me warmly, but the way she held the child, almost using her as a human shield, made me realize that Kellen wasn't the only one who was nervous about this little reunion.

"It's so nice to meet you, Darby. I have somebody else here who's excited to meet you too. This is my niece, Scarlet. Scarlet, can you say hi?"

The little girl waved at me with her thumb in her mouth, four splayed fingers wiggling above her nose.

"When she heard that her mam and I were making a cake for her cousin's birthday, she insisted that I bring her along. Willful little thing."

The girl's eyes went wider as she surveyed her surroundings. Then, she pulled the thumb from her mouth with a *pop*. "You have sheep?"

She wriggled to get free from Kate's hold.

"We live in the city," Kate explained, setting the girl on her feet. "Not many sheep in Limerick."

"I have one sheep." I laughed, kneeling in front of the child as her head swiveled in all directions. "His name is Vlad. But he's out visiting with his friends right now. He's very social, so he likes to sneak out and play with the other sheep when he gets bored."

"How do you find him?" She frowned.

"Well, if he were white, we'd paint a blue spot on him to match our house, but his wool is black, so it's easy to tell him apart."

"A black sheep!" Scarlet looked up at her aunt, but Kate wasn't listening.

Her eyes were trained on something behind me.

And they were glistening.

I didn't need to turn around to know what—or who—she was staring at, but I did anyway.

Kellen stood about ten feet away, his expression unreadable, eyes guarded as he stared at the missing half of himself. He'd been so excited to see her, but now that she was there ... the anguish I felt radiating off of him was unbearable. He was trying to shut off his emotions—I could see it. The same way he had when he'd surrendered to the UIB. When he'd told me goodbye. I wanted so badly to take that hurt away. That coldness. But I couldn't.

The best I could do was give Kate a glare that said, *Hurt him again, and I'll kill you*, and try to figure out what to do with the girl.

"Scarlet," I said, breaking the silence, "I want you to meet Kellen. Today is his birthday."

The child's blonde eyebrows furrowed in confusion before she returned her attention to Kate. "You said it was my cousin's birthday."

"It 'tis, love," Kate rasped, her voice on the verge of breaking. "That's him."

Scarlet frowned and turned back toward Kellen. "But he's so old."

Kellen and Kate laughed at the exact same time, the staccato of their chuckles a perfect match, and in that moment, I knew.

Everything was going to be okay.

Stepping up beside me, Kellen leaned over and extended his hand to his three-foot-tall cousin, as if he'd never met a child before in his entire adult life. "Nice to meet you, Scarlet."

She glanced back up at Kate, who nodded in approval, before turning around and giving his palm an enthusiastic slap. "High five!"

"Scarlet"—I beamed, trying not to laugh—"how would you like to come look for fairies with me?"

"Fairies?!"

"That's right." I locked eyes with Kate, making sure it was okay before extending my hand. Scarlet grabbed it without hesitation. "They live right back there in those woods, but they're very hard to find."

As we turned toward the house, Kellen's eyes softened as they swept over the two of us, and something inside of me bloomed.

"Be sure to stop inside and get some biscuits before ya go." Kellen's words were meant for Scarlet, but the completely inappropriate smolder in his gaze was all for me. "I hear custard creams are their favorite."

I gave Kellen a warning glance before steering the child away from the messy, painful world of adulthood and into the comforting arms of magic, just as my grandfather had done for me.

"Do you know how to be super quiet?" I asked, relishing the warm squish of her chubby little hand in mine. "Fairies have excellent hearing, and if they sense a human nearby, they'll disappear like *that*."

I snapped my fingers, and Scarlet jumped with a giggle.

"I can be quiet," she said, demonstrating her best tiptoe walk. "See?"

"Oh, wow. That *is* quiet." I opened the kitchen door and gestured for her to enter.

As Scarlet stepped under my outstretched arm, she asked, "Have *you* ever seen a fairy, Ms. Darby?"

My eyes drifted over her head to the man standing in my driveway. Kellen's posture was tall and strong as he stood, facing his oldest, deepest wound—his arms folded across his chest, his face hard as polished stone. It was a bulletproof exterior, but I knew that peeking out from behind were the teary eyes and split lip of the mute, motherless boy I'd met in the woods all those years ago.

"I have," I murmured, unable to look away.

"Really?" Scarlet gasped. "What did it look like?"

"Well, he had wild hair, like black flames, and eyes like smoke. And he was sad and scared ..."

And he wanted to run.

I could see it in the way Kellen's shoulders were bunched and his feet were planted—he wanted to run now, too. To hide. To keep himself safe. But when Kate pulled a white cake box out of the passenger seat and turned to face him, her face shattered and her hand muffling a broken sob, I watched that little boy bravely step forward.

And give his mom a hug.

I closed the door quietly to keep from disturbing them as I followed Scarlet into the house.

"But he's much happier now." I smiled, my heart as full as it had ever been.

"Because of the biscuits?" she asked, only half-listening as she stared out the kitchen window at the pasture and the woods and the purple mountain beyond.

"That's right." I laughed. "The good people *love* biscuits."

BB EASTON

Thank you so much for reading Devil of Dublin*!*
*If you'd like to know more about what inspired this story, please read the **Author's Note** and **Acknowledgements** sections on the following pages.*

And if you enjoyed this us-against-the-world romance, then read on for a sneak peek from my dystopian romance **Bad Boys Don't Die**. *It has all the suspense, steam, and emotional intensity of* Devil of Dublin, *but instead of trying to escape from the Mafia, Rain and Wes are trying to survive a mysterious apocalyptic event. Enjoy!*

AUTHOR'S NOTE

I hope you enjoyed *Devil of Dublin*. I know it was a heavy read, but with this book, I tried very hard to open myself up to the cosmos and become a conduit for whatever story wanted to come forth. I didn't plot. I didn't outline. Instead, I did a lot of walking and meditating and staring out my window, and that's how I discovered Glenshire—a beautiful, fictional village inspired by Moll's Gap in County Kerry, Ireland. I saw the candy-colored houses and spray-painted sheep dotting the hills. I saw my grandfather kneeling in the meadow with a twinkle in his eye. And I saw the mystical woods behind that meadow, leading all the way to the Purple Mountain in Killarney National Park. Other than Grandpa Pat's character, I never set out to include anything personal in this book, but once I began peeling back the layers of Glenshire, it was my own family's secrets that I found buried in that soil.

The real Grandpa Pat was a proud Irishman who raised his children in a tight-knit Irish Catholic neighborhood here in the United States. Their community maintained the same cultural norms and customs as those practiced back in Ireland at that time, which meant that their lives revolved around the church. My mother and her sisters went to an all-girls Catholic school, attended Sunday Mass every weekend unless they were on death's door, and were never taught about sex or reproduction. So, when my aunt Kate became pregnant at a very young age by a prominent member of their church, she was sent away to a Catholic maternity home run by nuns, similar to the Mother and Baby Homes in Ireland.

Kate was still a child herself—confused and terrified by what was happening to her body—but she was treated like a criminal. The pregnant, unmarried women—and young girls—at the home weren't allowed to leave, had no contact with the outside world, and were abused and forced into servitude. When Kate finally delivered her baby, the child was taken from her immediately. Kate was never allowed to know what had happened to her daughter or if she'd even survived.

The compounded traumas of that event changed Kate forever. Dimmed her light. Extinguished her once-bright future. No one ever spoke about what had happened to her, except in hushed voices behind closed doors—the way my mother had told me. I grew up knowing, in an abstract sense, that I had a cousin out there somewhere, whom I would never meet. That was, until my mother called me a few years ago and said the words that would change everything:

"I just got a call from some Catholic agency looking for Kate. They said her daughter is trying to find her. What do I do?"

It turns out that my cousin had been adopted by a wonderful, loving couple who'd named her Erin. She'd had a good childhood and was married with children of her own. But after learning about the circumstances surrounding her adoption,

DEVIL OF DUBLIN

Erin developed a deep sense of empathy for her birth mother. She found a Catholic agency that helped reunite mothers and children who'd been separated by these church-run maternity homes, and it was through them that she'd found us and then Kate.

Nothing will ever undo the profound damage that Kate suffered as a child, but getting to be a part of her daughter's and granddaughters' lives after all these years has given her a huge sense of closure. And I knew as I neared the end of this book that Kellen's happily ever after wouldn't be complete until he got that closure too.

Another happy ending that I'm excited to report is that although the last Mother and Baby Home didn't close its doors until 1998—right after Kellen would have been born—the Republic of Ireland has made tremendous strides in the area of women's rights since then. They have passed sweeping legislation protecting women's economic and bodily autonomy, elected two female presidents, and become one of the top ten most gender-equal countries in the world, according to the World Economic Forum.

The Catholic Church has also admitted to and apologized for their horrific treatment of unmarried mothers, as well as their history of child sexual abuse. They've set up agencies to help the victims, such as the one my cousin used to locate her birth mother, and established zero-tolerance policies, safety training programs, psychological testing requirements for priests, and background checks for all Church personnel who interact with children.

While there is still a lot of progress to be made and healing to be done, I take solace in the fact that if Kellen and Darby ever have a fictional daughter of their own, she will grow up in a very different world than the one that Kate knew. A world where she has basic human rights and freedoms, where she'll have access to reproductive education and health care, and where she can be anything she wants when she grows up, even president of Ireland.

But of course, she'll still have a magical forest in her backyard. It *is* Glenshire after all. ☘

ACKNOWLEDGMENTS

In addition to my aunt Kate, this book was also inspired by two very different, very significant men in my life. One being my sweet, charming, magic-loving, redheaded Irish grandfather and the other being ... Edward Scissorhands.

Edward Scissorhands was one of my very first crushes as a child, and I blame his creator, Tim Burton, for every mysteriously quiet, potentially homicidal, emotionally damaged, black-leather-wearing bad boy I've fallen in love with since. (In fact, you can read all about my hilarious, harrowing, steamy, bad-boy misadventures in my memoir *44 Chapters About 4 Men* and the 44 Chapters spin-off series.) Edward was as dangerous as a man could be—he literally had knives for hands!—but what no one in the town bothered to see was that he was also the kindest, sweetest, most selfless person among them.

When I was trying to come up with Kellen's character, I knew I didn't want another generic alpha asshole. Yes, he would be dangerous and intense and intimidating, but when I thought about Kellen's inner world, I kept coming back to Edward. His silent awareness. His childlike innocence. His untamed black hair and pale, scarred skin. His fear of touch. Even his skill with a blade.

So, thank you, Tim Burton. You might have ruined my dating life, but you inspired one hell of a romance hero.

And speaking of heroes, I have to thank my real-life book boyfriend, Ken, for helping me every step of the way with this story. Five thousand of them per morning, to be exact. Every day, after the kids got on the bus, he and I would walk around the neighborhood, discussing potential plotlines and plot holes, character arcs and character motivations, until I felt confident about which direction to take the story in that day. I tried really hard to let this book take shape organically instead of plotting it ahead of time, and Ken was a big help during that process. But don't tell him I said that. Now that he's inspired a Netflix character, it's getting harder and harder to keep him humble.

I'd also like to thank my Irish consultant, Adele Halpin, and my audiobook narrator, Eric Nolan, for helping me make this story and these characters as authentic and accurate as possible. I am eternally grateful for your time, your expertise, and of course, your accents. I could listen to you two talk all day. *Go raibh míle maith agat!* (I probably butchered that. Sorry!)

And, as always, thank you to my copy editor, Jovana Shirley; my content editor, Traci Finlay; my beta readers, Sammie Lynn and Jamie Shaw; and my proofreaders (in alphabetical order), Hanna Calloway, Shanna Chow-How Leclair, Michelle Beiger DePrima, Katie Hague, Rhonda Lind, and Jill Silva. Your timeliness, attention to detail, keen eyes, gentle honesty, and ingenious insights are rare and precious things. I hope you know how appreciated you are.

And finally, to my readers. Thank you for taking another wild, weird, genre-bending ride with me. I know my books don't fit into neat little boxes. I know there isn't a Dark Mafia Romance Inspired by Irish Folklore and Family Secrets category on

DEVIL OF DUBLIN

Amazon. (Or Pre-Apocalyptic New Adult Romance or Steamy Autobiographical Romantic Comedy ... this combining genres thing is an ongoing problem of mine.) If you read this book, or any of my books, it was because you were willing to take a chance on something different. Unfamiliar. Unpredictable. I don't know if you realize how rare that is. I don't even like ordering new things at restaurants. It's scary, gambling like that. So, the fact that you're here only proves that you are a bold, brave badass. I cherish your adventurous, curious, open-minded spirit. It is the reason I get to do what I love every day. Don't ever change.

PLAYLIST

Strap in for a moody, vibey, angsty ride through mystical forests, deep desire, and fable-worthy first loves in this collection of songs that stoked the flames of my burning heart while I wrote *Devil of Dublin*.

You can stream the playlist for free on Spotify. Just search "Devil of Dublin."

"Hold me in the Moonlight" by Goody Grace
"right where you left me" by Taylor Swift
"Trees" by Twenty One Pilots
"Daddy Issues" by The Neighbourhood
"Auburn" by Goody Grace
"evermore" by Taylor Swift and Bon Iver
"willow" by Taylor Swift
"notice me" by ROLE MODEL and BENEE
"White Lie" by The Lumineers
"Devil Like Me" by Rainbow Kitten Surprise

"Renegade" by Big Red Machine and Taylor Swift
"Buzzcut Season" by Lorde
"What A Time" by Julia Michaels and Niall Horan
"Valentine" by Snail Mail
"Ophelia" by The Lumineers
"It's Called: Freefall" by Rainbow Kitten Surprise
"&Run" by Sir Sly
"Falling Down" by Lil Peep and XXTENTACION
"400 Lux" by Lorde
"You're Somebody Else" by flora cash
"Bloom" by The Paper Kites
"seven" by Taylor Swift
"Sick in the Head" by The Lumineers
"Asking For It" by Hole
"twin flame" by Machine Gun Kelly
"Ghost" by Justin Bieber
"When Am I Gonna Lose You" by Local Natives
"Skin To Skin" by Movements
"cardigan" by Taylor Swift
"die for my bitch" by ROLE MODEL
"Ode to a Conversation Stuck in Your Head" by Del Water Gap
"Violet" by Hole
"Can You Feel My Heart" by Bring Me The Horizon
"Hold You in My Arms" by Ray LaMontagne
"Every Side Of You" by Vance Joy
"Daylily" by Movements

THE DEVIL HIMSELF

WALL STREET JOURNAL BESTSELLING AUTHOR
BB EASTON

CHAPTER 2

CLOVER
TWENTY-ONE YEARS LATER

Giving the bundle of knotted rope in my hands an exasperated shake, I let my head fall back with a groan.

I'd never be able to prove it, but I suspected that Da took great pleasure in tangling up his own fishing nets. He was probably spying on me at that very moment, laughing his arse off while I struggled to straighten them back out.

Arsehole.

I stared up at the overcast sky and prayed for an afternoon shower, one so heavy that I'd finally be allowed to come inside and take a break. But all I got was a single drop of rain—one perfectly timed *splat*, right between the eyes. It felt like the almighty himself had just spat in my face.

Which was fitting, considering that I was in my own personal hell. Actually, in my version of hell, I wouldn't be standing in front of a house that resembled a crusty white barnacle growing on top of a cliff overlooking the Irish Sea. I'd be standing in front of a mountain. One so tall that it broke through the swirling thunderclouds overhead. So wide that it wrapped around me on both sides, caging me in. But this monstrosity wouldn't be made of stone or ice or flows of lava. No, the mountain of *my* nightmares would be formed from something far more horrifying.

An endless hellscape of reeking, knotted fishing nets.

With a defeated sigh, I dropped my head, wiped my rain-splattered nose on my shoulder, and allowed my attention to drift toward the sea. I could only resist that view for so long, and the more monotonous my chores were, the more difficult it became.

The wind was relentless as I trudged over to the cliff's edge, dragging the heap of tangled rope behind me. I'd thrown on a pair of shorts that morning, thinking, surely, it would be warm enough for them in mid-June—a decision that I was now regretting. Goose bumps covered my exposed legs, and every strand of hair that hadn't made it into my messy bun lashed me in the face, but I was too distracted to notice.

Dropping the net, I pulled the hem of my jumper down with one hand and shielded my eyes with the other.

I'd lived on the Howth peninsula my entire life, but the sight of the sea and the grassy little island that sparkled just offshore never failed to take my breath away. Ireland's Eye, as the island was called, felt like an oasis that was always just beyond my reach—a tiny, tranquil, floating hill, abandoned by civilization. The only buildings on the Eye were two small stone ruins, and the only creatures that lived there were a few rats and rabbits and sea birds and a colony of plump gray seals who liked to sunbathe on the rocky beach.

As beautiful as it was, the island wasn't what drew my attention to the sea day after day. It was hope. Dumb, stupid, pointless hope.

I still remembered the exact moment when I'd learned what a selkie was. It was my first day back at school after Ma's accident, and I had no real concept of where she'd gone. I was only seven at the time, and no one had bothered to explain to me what had happened. I'd just woken up one morning to the

THE DEVIL HIMSELF

sound of Da breaking things. He was fall-down drunk, slurring about Ma being "gone" and "not coming back."

Then, for the next few days, he just sat slumped over in his armchair, staring blankly at the TV with drool in his beard and a bottle of Jameson in his fist. He couldn't even sober up long enough to go to the funeral. My aunt and uncle took me, but they didn't want to talk about what had happened either. Everybody had just cried a lot and hugged me a lot and said that they were sorry and that I'd see her again one day.

When?
When will I see her?
Where did she go?
Can I call her?
Can I visit?
Can I go live with her instead of Da?

He was so scary now that she wasn't around. And mean. He said he couldn't stand how much I looked like her. He told me to stay in my room so that he wouldn't have to see my face.

Why did she have to leave me with him?

There were so many questions that I'd been too afraid to ask. Not only because I was terrified of upsetting my father, but because I was even more terrified that someone might tell me the truth. That she really was gone. Forever.

"A selkie," Ms. Bell announced, pointing to an illustration on the screen in the front of the classroom, "is a mythological creature, believed to live in the waters of Scotland and Ireland. It looks like a seal, but when it removes its seal coat, it looks human."

The class gasped.

"Legend has it that fishermen will sometimes find these creatures in their human forms, and they'll fall so in love with them that they'll hide the selkie's seal coat so that it can't shift back. Then, they'll take them home, marry them, and sometimes even start a family with them. But a selkie's place is in the sea, so they never stop searching for their missing skin. And once they find it, they'll disappear into the water and never be seen or heard from again."

My eyes watered, and my throat burned as an explanation more palatable than the truth took root in the cracks of my broken heart.

"Clover?"

I hadn't realized that I'd raised my hand until every face in the room was pointed in my direction.

I hadn't spoken to a soul since the funeral, and I wasn't sure that I was ready to start, but when I looked into Ms. Bell's concerned brown eyes, the words just tumbled out of my mouth. "Ms. Bell, I think me Ma is a selkie."

Thirteen years later, the cruel laughter of two dozen seven-year-olds still echoed in my ears as I scanned the island for seals, hoping one of them would show a glimmer of recognition. Nod in my direction. Maybe even wave.

But the seals were gone, just like I knew they would be. Because right behind the island, anchored about a hundred yards offshore, was a cruise ship the size of Mount Brandon.

Nine months out of the year, Ireland's Eye was Howth's little secret, but every summer, the tourists descended upon it in swarms. You could practically watch the island sink under the weight of all those Nike-wearing, picture-taking, flower-crushing foreigners. But the worst part was that their boats scared away the seals.

And the fish.

Which turned my da into an even bigger arsehole than he already was.

Most of the fishermen gave up on fishing during the summer months, using their boats to give tours of the island instead, but Oliver Doyle was "no fucking tour guide."

He wasn't much of a father either.

As if he were conjured by that thought alone, the sound of a van door slamming shut yanked me from the past back into the present with a violent, terrifying jerk.

Still decked out in his oilskins and wellies, my father walked to the back of the van, his boots crunching in the gravel driveway next to the house, and he pulled out a bundle of ropes as big as a washing machine.

THE DEVIL HIMSELF

My heart slid into my stomach, but not because of the nets. It was his posture, the scowl beneath his wiry blond beard, the stoop of his hulking shoulders.

The catch hadn't been good. It never was in the summer.

And *I* was going to pay for it.

I walked as quickly and quietly as I could from the cliff's edge back to my spot behind our house, but when my father's gaze landed on me—tiptoeing through a patch of grass with a net that was very much still knotted in my arms—I felt like a deer that had been caught in the crosshairs.

"Where the fuck have you been?"

I could feel my pulse in my throat as Oliver stomped over to me with joyous wrath in his bloodshot eyes. He was looking for someone to take his frustrations out on, and by not having my chores done, I'd just served myself up to him on a silver platter.

I looked down at the net that I was frantically trying to untangle as he approached, too terrified to hold his stare.

"Nowhere, Da." I tilted my head in the direction of the cliff without looking up. "I was just watchin' the boats while I worked. This last net's givin' me trouble."

"Watchin' the boats, were ya?" He mimicked in a high-pitched voice before snapping, "Look at me when I'm talkin', girl!" Oliver's black wellies appeared in my line of sight just before his meaty, callous hand wrapped around the nape of my neck and jerked my head back.

I gripped the rope tighter and swallowed a whimper as he forced me to make eye contact with him.

"*I* was *on* one of those fuckin' boats, workin' me arse off all day, while you were up here, doin' what? *Lookin' fer selkies and merfolk?*"

I pulled my gaze away from his blazing blue eyes and glanced over at a stack of neatly folded fishing nets piled next to the shed. It was the least confrontational way I could think of to answer his question about what I'd been doing all day, but when his head followed my line of sight, the tightening of his grip on the back of my neck told me that I'd made a terrible mistake.

Oliver didn't want to see that I'd been working too. He wanted to be angry with me, and now, thanks to that simple glance, he was.

Oliver shoved me to the ground so fast and so hard that the wind was knocked out of me before I had the chance to scream. I landed on my side in the rocks, and the bone-crunching pain in my ribs immediately brought tears to my eyes.

Don't cry. Don't cry. Don't cry. Don't cry …

Straddling my body, Oliver pushed me onto my back and clutched my face with one hard, rough hand. The gray clouds seemed to gather overhead, watching the spectacle.

"Ya think yer too good fer this now, don't cha? 'Cause yer goin' to some fancy fuckin' college. Ya think yer better 'n' me?" He released me just long enough to pull that hand back, flatten his palm, and slap me across the face.

The worst part about being hit wasn't the sting, not for me; it was the sound. That smack would ring in my ears for hours, sometimes days—long after the swelling went down—reminding me that I was weak, humiliating me over and over again, from the inside out. The sharp clap of skin hitting skin was the soundtrack of my youth. The vibration of my soul. And the source of all my shame.

I barely heard the rest of his speech over the sound of it repeating like a broken record in my head.

"Ya won't be thinkin' yer better than me when I put yer arse out on the street, now will ya? The only reason yer still here is 'cause Sheila begged me to let ya stay until you could afford a place of yer own. But yer twenty goddamn years old now, darlin'. I can kick you out whenever the fuck I want. So, maybe think about that the next time ya feel like bein' smart with me."

My cheek throbbed, my eyes burned, and panic took hold once I realized what was happening. I couldn't cry. Crying only made him angrier. I had to hold it in. I had to.

Widening my eyes to keep from accidentally blinking out a tear, I stared straight ahead at Oliver's heaving whiskey barrel of a chest. A stray beam of sunlight had broken through the clouds,

THE DEVIL HIMSELF

making the side of his bushy blond beard glow like hay that was about to catch fire.

I wished that it would.

"Ollie?"

Da pulled me to my feet so fast that the world spun out from under me and went black. The heap of green rope tumbled out of my arms and onto the ground as I struggled to stay upright and conscious. I felt his arm wrap around my shoulders as Oliver's girlfriend, Sheila, stepped through the back door, bouncing their thrashing toddler on her hip.

I hadn't even known Oliver had been seeing anyone until Sheila showed up on our doorstep, pregnant with his baby and crying because her husband had just kicked her out. She'd been a permanent fixture at our house ever since, and honestly, she was the best thing that had ever happened to us. I tried to stay within earshot of her at all times because Da never raised a hand to me when he knew she was around.

The downside of Sheila's arrival was that she'd given Oliver a son, which only solidified his disdain for me. He had a new family now. A new child. One that could carry on the Doyle name and wasn't a walking, talking redheaded reminder of the woman who'd shattered his heart.

"Can I borrow Clo for a minute?" Sheila asked, grimacing as my half-brother whined and wriggled in her spindly arms. "Odie's fightin' his nap again, and I need her to work her magic."

Odie was short for Odin, the Norse god of war. That name was one hundred percent my father's doing. He prided himself on his Viking blood. Sometimes, when I saw him standing on the bow of his fishing boat, I could almost picture him leading the longship full of Norsemen who had raided Howth all those centuries ago.

He would have fit right in.

Da tightened his grip around me in a fake show of fatherly affection, squeezing my injured shoulder with his viselike hand. It was a warning. Oliver didn't like it when I got involved with anything related to his new family. As far as he was concerned,

Sheila belonged to him and Odie alone. She was *their* special mother figure, not mine. And the sooner I got out of his life, the sooner he could start pretending like my mother had never existed.

The feeling was mutual. After two years of working part-time at the Trinity College bookshop, had almost saved enough money to put a deposit down on an apartment and afford some basic furnishings. Honestly, I probably had enough already, but I couldn't leave Odie. Not yet. Not until he was old enough to tell me if Oliver ever tried to hurt him …

Or make him untangle those goddamn fishing nets.

"Ten minutes," Da said, giving my shoulder a shake that made my freshly bruised ribs scream in pain. "Then, this one has to go check the lobster traps."

I could almost hear his smug grin.

More chores.

Sheila gave me a sympathetic half-smile as Oliver steered me across the yard and into the house. I didn't know how much she'd seen or heard, but it didn't matter. She knew. She knew what went on, and she pitied me for it. But I pitied her even more. Because once I left, she'd most likely be taking my place as his punching bag. And unlike me, he'd never let her get away. Ma had tried to do it, and look where it had gotten her.

The back door led into the kitchen, where Oliver left his wellies on a rubber mat and hung his oilskin coveralls on a hook above them. Beside the hook was one of Sheila's coastal-chic additions to the house—a wooden anchor with the words *Life's a Beach* painted on it. Like living on a rocky cliff next to the freezing cold sea in rainy Ireland was the same as having a beach house in the Caribbean.

Sheila tried to hand me the wailing one-year-old, but Odie clung to her with a high-pitched shriek. It felt as if he were crying all the tears I was trying to hold back. My ribs and cheek throbbed, my eyes stung and my throat burned, but what hurt the most was the fact that I had to pretend as if nothing hurt at all.

THE DEVIL HIMSELF

"Shut him up, will ya?" Oliver grumbled as he shuffled into the sitting room, popping the tab on a can of Guinness.

"He's just overtired." Sheila winced, prying his chubby fist out of her limp brown hair. "Nothin' his big sister can't fix."

"Well, she'd better fix it fast if she's gonna check those traps before dinner," Oliver sneered, flopping into a blue recliner that was at least a decade older than me. The springs groaned and squeaked beneath him as he yanked on the lever, extending the footrest.

As soon as Sheila extracted the last of Odie's fingers from her hair, I whisked him into my arms. Turning his body sideways, I pressed his belly against mine and began twisting my torso back and forth while making a shushing sound. He went still immediately. It wasn't magic—I was simply the only one in the house who'd bothered to research how to get a baby to stop crying.

With Odie taken care of, Sheila plopped down on the couch, her small frame landing in a pile of seashell-shaped pillows—another one of her design touches.

Da turned on the TV, and while the two of them watched the glowing screen, I stood behind them, rocking and shushing and soothing *myself*. Lifting Odie's sleeping body to my chest, I clutched him like a teddy bear as one of the tears I'd been trying so hard to suppress finally slid down the swollen side of my face.

Stop it, I scolded myself, wiping my wet cheek on Odie's soft head. *If Oliver sees you crying, it's gonna be so much worse.*

"In breaking news," Mia Patel, a BBC newscaster, announced, "a report released by the Irish Directorate of Military Intelligence indicates that a Russian invasion of Ireland might be imminent."

"What?" Sheila sat up with a jolt.

"Bah." Oliver waved a dismissive hand at the TV. "Don't be an eejit. Nobody's invadin' shite."

"According to the minister of defense, Ireland's recent conflict with the United Kingdom and hostile annexation of Northern Ireland—spearheaded by Ireland's Taoiseach Séamus Rooney and members of his radical nationalist party, the United

Irish Brotherhood—has left the small island nation alienated from the rest of the world. By making an enemy of the United Kingdom and its vast network of powerful allies, the Republic of Ireland is now relatively defenseless against the iron fist of Russian President Alexi Abramov, who has declared a personal vendetta against the UIB."

"Listen to this gobshite, will ya?" Oliver gestured toward the newscast with his half-empty can. "We finally take back what's rightfully ours, and we're the fuckin' bad guys."

"Anyone living within twenty kilometers of Dublin, an international airport, or a major harbor are advised to evacuate until—"

"Da, we live near all of those—"

"Clo!" Oliver's sudden shout brought a fresh wave of startled tears to my eyes. Turning around in his chair, he glared at me as I widened my eyes to hold in the moisture. "For Christ's sake, go check the fuckin' traps already. Didn't ya hear?" He grinned like a madman through his wild blond beard as he thrust a hand in the direction of the TV. "The Russians are comin' for dinner!"

CHAPTER 3

DAMIEN

"Smer-nah!"

The deafening rabble of Russian voices, screaming drills, and clanging socket wrenches fell silent as a hundred crewmen darted out from behind the tanks they had been servicing and stood at perfect attention.

Facing me.

It was a show of respect that I hadn't earned and damn sure didn't deserve. And they all knew it.

"Topside. Now," I barked in Russian, reigniting the noise and activity in the belly of Russia's most prized warship.

The sound of tools crashing into bins and boots marching across the floor echoed off the metal bulkheads until the last man disappeared into the stairwell and the hatch slammed shut behind him.

And then the hold was silent again.

I was supposed to be in that stairwell with them, but I couldn't make myself move. There were no windows in the hold. No sights or sounds that might remind me of where I was. Down there, I could pretend like we were anchored somewhere else.

Literally anywhere else.

It had been five years since I'd stepped foot on Irish soil, but it felt like five lifetimes. Every day that I'd spent sparring with Bratva soldiers in the Siberian snow instead of playing football in Phoenix Park, every day that I heard the guttural grunts of Russian instead of the songlike cadence of Irish, every day that I ate shchi and kasha instead of soda bread and shepherd's pie, I felt another piece of the boy that I'd once been burn away. Now, all that remained was a single charred cinder—a brittle, unwanted reminder of who I used to be.

Of who I would never be again.

Remembering that they had cameras on every inch of that ship, I clasped my hands behind my back and began walking between the rows of tanks. My eyes swept over the machines as if I were inspecting them for fuck knew what, but all I could really see was a merciless onslaught of memories from my childhood in Dublin.

For five years, coming home to Ireland had been my only goal—my singular obsession, my sole reason for living—but now that I was finally back, I couldn't even bring myself to look at it.

"Lieutenant," a man shouted in Russian over the intercom, causing me to stand at attention and face the security camera on the bulkhead beside me.

"This is Senior Lieutenant Petrov."

Petrov. My superior. I pictured the brass buttons on his overly decorated jacket straining to contain his swollen beer gut.

"What the *fuck* are you doing down there? The captain wants you topside for his speech. *Now*."

I answered with nothing more than a salute. I knew he would see it—he was obviously watching me—but I also tried to limit all conversation as much as possible. I'd been taught to speak Russian without a detectable accent as part of my father's rigorous training, but I didn't want to press my luck. I'd been warned that no Russian—Bratva or military—would ever trust me if they found out where I was from.

And honestly, they probably shouldn't.

THE DEVIL HIMSELF

I wasn't one of them, and I never would be. I'd been taken against my will at the age of fifteen—the second my father found out he had a bastard son in Dublin—and thrown into an underground Bratva development program called the Kletka. It meant *cage*, and that was exactly what the fuck it was. A prison-like boot camp in the frozen tundra of Siberia, where the organization trained their potential new soldiers to fight, kill, and most importantly, obey. I was fed a steady diet of steroids and beatings until I was big enough to fight back. And then ... the real training began.

Because my father had no other sons, he saw me as his only chance at immortality—an angry, hateful lump of clay that he could mold into his own disgusting image. Initially, he'd been training me to take over the Bratva and carry on the family's gun running, drug muling, and human trafficking businesses, but when Russia began planning to invade Ireland, he enlisted me in the Navy and pulled enough strings to have me start as a lieutenant. He didn't want me engaged in actual combat—I was far too valuable for that. He'd just wanted to solidify my identity as a Russian by making me participate in the destruction of my own homeland.

It was a ten-story climb from the hold of the ship to the deck, but I wished that it were ten thousand. I stared down at my boots as I ascended the stairs, focused on their rhythmic stomping, but all too soon, the dull black leather began to glow gray. The moment I lifted my head and saw that overcast Irish sky through the porthole, my heart began to pound against my ribs like a prisoner thrashing against the bars of its cell. The final glowing cinder of my boyhood longed to see home, but the betrayed, burned-out husk of a man that I'd become knew better.

Seeing it would only make what I'd been sent there to do that much harder.

With a deep breath and an even deeper sense of dread, I opened the topside hatch and stepped out onto the deck. I knew I wouldn't be able to see that green coastline without wanting to scream, so I shut everything out, except for what was directly in front of me. I didn't feel the summer breeze on my skin, I didn't taste the salt of the Irish Sea in the air, and I refused to hear the cries of the gulls I'd once fed as a boy. Instead, I did what I'd been doing at the Kletka since the day I'd realized that there was no escape.

I accepted my situation, and I armored the fuck up.

By the time I reached the stage, my longing, my rage, my powerlessness and despair were all safely locked away behind the numb, bulletproof facade of a Bratva-trained killer.

Captain Orlov watched me take my place in line next to the other officers with an impatient scowl on his vodka-flushed face, but he didn't reprimand me. Either my mask was terrifying enough to make him think twice or he was too excited about starting a war to waste his time on me.

Senior Lieutenant Petrov, who'd barked at me over the intercom, stood to my left, back stiff and belly out, leaving nothing to my right but the one fucking place I couldn't afford to acknowledge.

So, I stared straight ahead at the two thousand troops gathered shoulder to shoulder on the deck. This was what they'd been waiting for, what they'd been promised when they were drafted. The pay was shite. The conditions were worse. But on that shore, they'd be given complete immunity to rape, steal, maim, or kill anything and everything that crossed their path. And judging by the gritted teeth and wild eyes of the men staring back at me, their patience was wearing thin.

"Comrades," Captain Orlov's voice boomed through the loudspeakers, and two thousand hands immediately shot up in salute.

Including mine.

Like a fucking puppet.

I could almost feel my father tugging on the invisible marionette strings above me, lifting my chin, squaring my shoulders.

"Today, we fight not for Russia, but for the honor of President Abramov himself!"

Every saluting hand sliced forward with a guttural, "Ura!"

THE DEVIL HIMSELF

I felt nothing.

"Over twenty years ago, the United Irish Brotherhood ordered the murder of President Abramov's uncle, Dmitry. But when Alexi came here to avenge his uncle's death, like a man of courage, of honor, the UIB behaved like cowards. They had him arrested—*framed*—for unspeakable, heinous crimes."

The troops booed and spat on the ground, as if their precious president hadn't done *exactly* what the fuck he was accused of. Human trafficking, murder, arms dealing—that was probably the least of it. Everyone knew that Alexi Abramov was a Bratva kingpin who'd hijacked last year's election and taken the Kremlin by force. We just weren't supposed to say it out loud.

"President Abramov spent two years locked in a prison cell because of these deceitful, lying bastards." Captain Orlov thrust a hand in the direction of the shore, and without thinking, my gaze followed.

The sight of the Irish coast hit me like a sucker punch, forcing the air from my lungs in a sudden, nauseating rush. Gray stone cliffs sloped down to the sea, blanketed with green grass and dripping with wildflowers. Waves crashed against the rocks hypnotically, like the rhythmic curl of a beckoning finger, calling me home. And behind them, gray clouds gathered where the cliffs met the sky. It looked like smoke.

Like the cliffs were on fire.

An onslaught of childhood memories played over a soundtrack of my own silent, self-hating screams, and for one torturous second, I felt everything. Every useless, agonizing emotion I'd refused to feel for the last five years flooded my body like boiling toxic waste, scalding my skin from the inside out before I finally pulled my mental armor back on and clung to the numbness.

That's exactly what he wants, I reminded myself. *To hurt me. To break me. To control me once and for all.*

"Since then, the UIB has branded itself a *political party*, and like a virus, it has infiltrated every level of the Irish government. They promised to reclaim Northern Ireland from the UK, but in delivering on that promise, they have made themselves weaker than ever. Their military is depleted. Their allies have vanished. They are isolated, defenseless, and ours for the taking!" Orlov roared as the troops shouted and thrust their fists in the air.

I hoped that if anyone noticed my distraction, they'd assume that I was scanning the coastline for threats because I was incapable of tearing my eyes away from that sight. I followed the cliffs as they sloped down to sea level, the rocky beach giving way to a pier that stretched out into the water, dotted with barnacle-crusted fishing boats and a lighthouse that hadn't functioned in years.

Howth Harbour. I'd been there as a lad. We took a school trip to Ireland's Eye to see the ruins of a monastery that the Vikings had raided. I'd never been on a boat before that day.

Now, I was back, on a very different boat, and this time, I was the one doing the raiding.

Bile seared the back of my throat, but I forced that down too.

"Like a Trojan horse, this converted cruise ship has already allowed us to breach their defenses. She is too big to take into Dublin Bay without drawing suspicion, so from here, we'll take Howth peninsula and push through to Dublin by land."

I scanned the boats, the docks, the paths, the beaches—searching for signs of life and praying that I wouldn't find any.

The boats were all docked. The pavements were empty. The windows of every house, shop, and restaurant were dark. And a seed of desperate, masochistic hope took root in my chest.

Howth was a ghost town. We weren't sneak-attacking them—the residents had already left.

"Crewmen, deploy the tanks and head straight to the harbor. Infantry and intelligence, follow in the rafts. Once the bombing has stopped, set up an encampment, establish roadblocks, and deploy the drones to look for survivors. Artillery troops, remain on deck and report to your assigned officer.

THE DEVIL HIMSELF

"Tonight, we show the UIB that a crime against President Abramov is a crime against Russia, and Russia … never … forgets!"

The cheering was deafening, but I didn't feel a fucking thing.

"Lieutenant," Petrov bellowed, clapping me on the shoulder as he steered me off the stage. "You are a lucky man. Your platoon has been assigned to short-range shelling." He swept his sausage-like fingers over the Howth coastline. "It is much more fun when you can see the shit that you are blowing up, no?" He laughed, giving my shoulder a series of shakes. "My men on the rocket launchers will be jealous."

I wanted to rip his hand off and stab him in the throat with the severed bone.

Instead, those marionette strings forced my own hand to lift in a salute and my legs to march over to the artillery guns, where my platoon was awaiting my instruction.

I couldn't change what was about to happen. Despite the authority implied by my officer's uniform and the patches on my chest, I had no power here. I was just as much a prisoner on this ship as I had been in the Kletka. The only thing I had control over was whether or not they broke me. And at that, I would never fail. I would bury my humanity so deep that even I couldn't find it. I would carve out my heart, snuff out my soul, if that was what it took to deny them the satisfaction of my pain.

And that was exactly what I did. I took solace in the fact that the town had been evacuated, I accepted the situation, and I armored the fuck up.

BOOKS BY BB EASTON

44 CHAPTERS ABOUT 4 MEN
Inspiration for the Netflix Original Series SEX/LIFE.

THE 44 CHAPTERS SPIN-OFF SERIES
Darkly funny. Deeply emotional. Shockingly sexy.
SKIN (Knight's backstory, Book 1)
SPEED (Harley's backstory, Book 2)
STAR (Hans's backstory, Book 3)
SUIT (Ken's backstory, Book 4)

BB EASTON

BAD BOYS DON'T DIE
Intense, immersive, end-of-the-world romance.
BAD BOYS DON'T DIE
BAD BOYS DON'T STAY
BAD BOYS DON'T FALL

GROUP THERAPY
Hilarious, heartwarming psychologist-client romcom.

DEVIL OF DUBLIN
A dark mafia romance steeped in Irish folklore.
DEVIL OF DUBLIN
THE DEVIL HIMSELF

FOR UPDATES ON NEW RELEASES, SALES, AND GIVEAWAYS, SIGN UP HERE: WWW.ARTBYEASTON.COM/SUBSCRIBE

AUDIO EROTICA
BY
BB EASTON

When I'm not writing novels that make your heart race, flutter, and ultimately, soar, the Irish voice actor behind the Devil of Dublin series and I are busy writing and recording short erotic audio stories that have the same effect on a very *different* part of your body.

Each week, Eric Nolan and I publish a new erotic audio under the name The Devil of Dublin, exclusively on Quinn.

Quinn is a platform where content creators from all over the world publish erotic audio stories that are designed to make you, the listener, feel as though you're the main character, fully immersed in all the sexy sound effects, growls, moans, and sweet nothings that come along with whatever spicy scenario we've dreamed up.

To hear some steamy samples from our most popular audios, visit artbyeaston.com/audioerotica or scan the QR code below.

Or, to access our full catalog for free, just head over to the Quinn app or tryquinn.com to begin your free trial.

Happy listening!

ABOUT THE AUTHOR

BB Easton is the *Wall Street Journal* bestselling author of *44 CHAPTERS ABOUT 4 MEN*, the hilarious, steamy, tell-all memoir that inspired the Netflix Original Series, *SEX/LIFE*. Within the first month, *SEX/LIFE* was viewed by 67 million households worldwide, making it the 3rd Most-Watched Netflix Original Series of all time.

BB was a stressed-out school psychologist and mother of two when the inspiration to write *44 CHAPTERS ABOUT 4 MEN* struck. Through that process, she rediscovered her passion for writing, became dangerously sleep-deprived, and finally mustered enough courage to quit her job and become a full-time author.

BB EASTON

BB went on to publish four more wickedly funny, shockingly steamy, and heartwarmingly autobiographical books in the 44 CHAPTERS series: *SKIN*, *SPEED*, *STAR*, and *SUIT*. Since then, she's been hard at work writing fictional stories that appeal to her love for us-against-the-world romance, including a dystopian trilogy (*BAD BOYS DON'T DIE*), a psychologist-client romantic comedy (*GROUP THERAPY*), and a dark mafia romance series (*DEVIL OF DUBLIN*).

You can find BB procrastinating in all of the following places:

>**Website:** authorbbeaston.com
>
>**Instagram:** instagram.com/author.bb.easton
>
>**TikTok:** vm.tiktok.com/ZMeEKRLyS/
>
>**Facebook:** facebook.com/bbeaston
>
>**#TeamBB Facebook Group:** facebook.com/groups/BBEaston
>
>**X:** twitter.com/bb_easton
>
>**Pinterest:** pinterest.com/artbyeaston
>
>**Goodreads:** goo.gl/4hiwiR
>
>**BookBub:** bookbub.com/authors/bb-easton
>
>**Spotify:** open.spotify.com/user/bbeaston

Selling signed books, mugs, and apparel on Etsy: etsy.com/shop/artbyeaston

Publishing audio erotica stories under the name "The Devil of Dublin" on Quinn: tryquinn.com

And giving away free e-books from her bestselling author friends every month in her newsletter: artbyeaston.com/subscribe

Printed in Great Britain
by Amazon